DISCARDED IMAGES

THELMA HANCOCK

2QT Limited (Publishing)

First Edition published 2014 by
2QT Limited (Publishing)
Lancaster LA2 8RE

Printed in Great Britain

Cover Design Hilary Pitt
Images supplied by istockphoto.com

A CIP catalogue record for this book is available
from the British Library
ISBN 978-1910077-13-9

To Josie with love

GLOSSARY OF IRISH WORDS
AND PHRASES

A chuisle – O Pulse (Darling)
Athair – Father
Athair mor – Grandfather (formal)
Beannachd De, a Mhuirnin – God's blessing, Sweetheart
Chara – Love.
A chumann – O Affection (Darling)
Ciamar a tha thu, piuthar, a run – How are you (informal) Sister, Darling?
Dadaí – Dad
Daideó – Granddad
A ghra – Dear
A ghra. Dia Duit! – Darling, God to you (Greetings (informal))
Garda – Police
Inion – Daughter
Maimeo – Granny
Mamai – Mother/Mum
Máthair mhór – Grandmother (Formal)
A mhuirnin – Sweetheart
Mórai – Grandmother (Formal)
Na dean sin – Stop it!
Slan go foill – Bye for now
Tapadh leibh, Beannachd Leibh – Thank you; God's blessing (good-bye (formal))
Teaghlach – Family
Thu gu math, Brathair – I am good, Brother.
Uncail – Uncle

JUNE 1987

COUNTY GALWAY

THE SUN STREAMED THROUGH the open casement and threw a golden path along the uncarpeted wooden floors of the upper storey. A zephyr found the opening and followed the sun inside to blow the tight red-gold curls of the little girl. She skipped and ran along the corridor with the confidence of a three-and-a-half-year-old, headed towards the one person she was certain loved her most in the world.

She hadn't really understood what *Maimeo* was talking about, but she would go to the bathroom and see if she could spot the 'little devil' that was inside her. She knew her *mamai* was in the bathroom but that was OK; *Mamai* could explain to her and hold her up to the big mirror so that she could look down her throat as she had when the little germs had made it all sore.

She had been neatly dressed but, between leaving her grandmother's hands a few minutes before and escaping to find her mother, her dungarees had become unclipped on one side; one shoelace trailed like a small caterpillar on a leaf and her green jumper was bunched out. Still, the smile she had on her face reflected her inner certainties. It was the last time – for a long time – that she would smile like that.

She pushed the door open with a small hand – sufficient to allow her delicate frame to enter – and poked her face around, the ready gapped-toothed smile beginning to emerge. Her mother was on the floor, leaning against the bath. '*Mamai*, did you fall?' She approached on tiptoe, stretching out a small hand. '*Mamai*, wake up.' Her hand came away, covered in red sticky stuff, and her mother just sat there.

Kate peered at the figure, lying like a discarded toy: '*Mamai*, *Mamai*, wake up.' She touched the still figure of her mother again, and Theresa Maria Jardin slithered further away from the bath and collapsed like a blow up doll that was seeping air.

Kate shook the shoulder. '*Mamai*!' It was a wail that rent the fragile air and splintered the sunny morning like a sudden hailstorm.

Maimeo – coming up the stairs – muttered, 'What does the little varmint want now? Always making a fuss about nothing.'

She bustled along the same bright, sunny corridor calling, 'Kate, leave your mam in peace, for heaven's sake!' She gave a brief knock on the bathroom door and then she too pushed the door to the bathroom open. 'Oh, God! Mother, Mary and Joseph. What have you done now, you wicked child?'

Kate's lip started to tremble and her eyes fill with great, fat tears that began to roll down her cheeks. *Maimeo* grabbed a small arm and began to tow the three-year-old away from her mother's body, shouting, 'Eoin, Micheál: come, quick.' She thrust the child outside the gleaming wood and stood impatiently, holding the small figure – who was wriggling like an eel in her efforts to return to her mother's still body.

Maeve's husband and son pushed back chairs with a scraping of wood on slate, leaving the table downstairs scattered with the toast they'd abandoned and with the cups rocking dangerously as they landed crookedly on the saucers, responding to the urgency of the voice without knowing the cause. Eoin climbed the stairs with his heart thumping with fear and energy. 'Micheál, get this child out of here. Eoin, call for the ambulance.' Maeve lifted Kate and pushed the sobbing child into her uncle's arms. She went back into the bathroom to see if her daughter had succeeded this time.

Micheál, trying to digest a mouthful of buttery bread and holding an armful of toddler with a runny nose and

blood-smeared hands – squinted first into the opening
bathroom door and then scowled at the child in his arms. His
father – after a glance of his own – clattered down the stairs
in front of man and child as they turned away, his hobnails
rattling against the wooden flooring as he jumped the final
three steps into the hallway and leapt at the black phone on
the small wicker table.

Micheál carried Kate down the stairs, looking anxiously
back over his shoulder, but his mother had shut the bathroom
door. He deposited Kate on a chair in the kitchen. 'What have
you done now, ye little varmint?' He went over to the sink and
picked up a cloth to wipe off the worst of the blood from his
shirt where she had smeared it.

Kate sobbed even harder. She didn't know what she'd
done to her *mamai*, but if *Maimeo* said she was a wicked
child it must have been her fault that *Mamai* had fallen. 'I
want *Mamai*. I'm sorry; I didn't mean to hurt her.' The words
hiccuped out and Micheál shook his head as he came back
across the room with an old towel, drying his hands.

'*Na dean sin*. Stop it! Crying doesn't help, and you can't
always have what you want, *a mhuirnin*.' He laid a gentle
hand on the curls for a minute. 'Now stay there and be good
until I see what's happening, *a chuisle*.'

She sat statue-like on the hard chair, her legs dangling
above the floor and her delicate little hands gripping the sides.
The hands were turning almost as white as her face with the
pressure she was exerting. She watched the stairway, too
frightened to move in case she did something else wrong,
waiting for *Mamai* to get up and tell her not to worry. *Maimeo*
was an old silly, and *Mamai* loved her.

She was still holding firmly to the chair when the
ambulance arrived. No one spoke to her. Big men in big boots
and heavy uniforms came. They went upstairs with long poles
and blankets; there were loud voices; she could hear *Maimeo*
shouting at her *athair mor*.

'This is the third time, Eoin. She'll have to go. I can't cope
any longer.'

Kate shivered, her small body covered in goosebumps. Where would she have to go? Was she going to be sent to bed with no lunch or supper again? *Maimeo* sometimes locked her in her bedroom when she'd been naughty. Ben would sit outside and sometimes he sneaked her a piece of his bread when he came to bed himself. He never got locked up.

There was a thump of heavy feet coming downstairs again. She saw *Maimeo*'s black skirt and the slipper with the hole in the end, where *Maimeo*'s poorly toe poked through. Kate slipped off the chair to hide underneath the table where the breakfast cloth still hung a little low on one side, the plates of half-eaten toast curled up and the cold cups of tea sitting as grey and scummy as an Irish beach.

Crouching with her little arms wrapped around her legs and her chin resting on her knees she tried to stop the big fat tears from rolling down her cheeks, wiping the wetness on the sleeve of her jumper. *Maimeo* would sometimes give Kate a slap and say that now she had something to cry for, but *Mamai* would kiss her and tell her it was OK. She wanted her *mamai* so much, and it was her fault Mam had fallen.

Kate shivered again. She could see lots of feet, now: *Maimeo*'s slippers and *daimió*'s hobnails and *Uncail*'s smelly rubber boots, and the big men with strange laced shoes. Where was *Mamai?* Where was Ben? Kate moved an edge of the cloth, peeping around the leg of the table with reddened eyes: her twin brother was hiding behind the corner of the coal bin, over near the blacklead stove. He smiled at her but he didn't move until the adults had all left the room, going out of the kitchen stable door and into the yard where the sun still poured out of a bright blue sky.

Ben made a quick dash across the room and the two children huddled under the table. Ben put his arms around his sister, patting her gently and whispering, 'Are you all right? What's wrong with *Mamai*? She was lying on the bed thing that the men carried.'

Kate shook her head. She didn't know what was happening. But *Maimeo* said it was her fault; she must really be a wicked

8

child and she'd have to go to bed early again.

Ben patted her some more. His sister was always getting into bother. He watched the tears rolling silently down and pulled a dirty handkerchief from his own blue dungarees. 'Don't cry, Kate. *Mamai* will make it better.'

Kate sobbed even harder, her little body shaking with her efforts to suppress the noise and tears.

Ben scowled. He hated it when Kate got into bother. It hurt him somewhere inside to see her crying. He put his arms around her and hugged. 'I've been at the pigsty; Betsy's had her little ones. I saw the big van come, Kate, so I came to see what it was but *Maimeo* looked cross … so I hid. Do you want to come and see the piglets?'

Kate shook her head. She wanted *Mamai*. Ben, his golden curls tickling her chin, huddled closer to his sister. They could feel the warmth of the stove and catch the yeasty smell of *Maimeo*'s bread as it rose in a big brown bowl set at the side of the grate. But *Maimeo* didn't come to put it on the table. Sometimes she let them play with a small piece of it, making their own baps for their lunch. But not today; nobody came.

They crouched under their makeshift hideaway, watching the open door to the yard, expecting someone to come back inside and shoo them into the bright sunshine. Kate watched the scrubbed cobbles outside. A brown hen pecked its way across the open doorway, poked its beak inside and then lurched away again. The old black and white sheepdog came and lay down next to the white step and panted, his pink tongue hanging out and leaving a small puddle on the stones. Still no one came.

The silence allowed Kate to hear the small wheeze of her brother's chest and the big clock in the hall with its one-legged tick. She said, 'Tick, tock,' and smiled sadly at Ben. *Mamai* sometimes played 'The Mouse Ran up the Clock' and tickled them, but she hadn't done it for a long time now.

Eventually they crept out from under the table and went outside. They could hear *Uncail* Micheál in the milking parlour. He was using the hose, the water making a splashy gurgling noise as it ran in the gutters and the shush-shush sound of the big broom as he swept out the cows' byre. The twins held hands as they crept away to look at the piglets. Kate's smile was a poor thing, but if the farm business was going on then everything must be all right. *Mamai* would come back and Kate could say she was sorry for hurting her and everything would be fine again.

Micheál didn't remember them until nearly midday, when he went in for a bite of bread and cheese. He looked around and saw the breakfast dishes still on the table and wondered where the children were. 'Oh, Lord. Mam will do for me if they're into something.' He found them asleep in the hay barn. Like a pair of spoons in a drawer Kate and Ben lay curled together: her thumb in her mouth, her face streaky with the dirt of tears and blood. Ben – who hadn't quite mastered his bladder – was damp, his arm curved protectively over his sister.

JUNE 1987

NEWCASTLE, ENGLAND

THE SIBLING OF BEN and Kate was undergoing his own baptism of fire.

'He looks all right: he's still conscious, but the adults are both dead.' The words washed over Anthony Grey, as he was known, as he hung half-suspended by the seat belt and booster seat in the upturned car. 'I think we'll have to take off the roof to get them out, but we need to get the kid out first.' Hands came in and held the child's dazed head still as another set moved, trying to release the fastenings.

'If I can get the seat out we won't need to worry so much about his neck. It is a he, isn't it?'

'Yeah; got the same T-shirt as my son.' The first paramedic managed to hold the child still. 'I reckon he's maybe four or five.'

'Bugger; cut myself. Stay still, will you?' (This addressed to the seat belt securing the child seat in place). 'Got ya. OK; ease it out and we'll check him over.'

The two green-clad paramedics eased the child, still in his seat, onto the grass verge of the main roadway. Newcastle's rush hour was not a good time to have an accident, and the smell of petrol and burning was creating a stench in the nostrils of the men working to free the injured.

Between rubberneckers nearly causing further accidents, a shocked crowd from a bus which had ploughed into the car – which had back-ended this one after it had already been sideswiped – there were a lot of people milling about, too.

'Let's get him into the ambulance, Colin; out of view, poor

little beggar.' The child, who until then had been quiet, began to grizzle as strangers took him out of sight of his mother.

He was yelling loudly enough to wake the dead – if that had been possible – by the time he was in the ambulance and being checked over. Unfortunately, some of the dead who didn't want to wake were his mother and the man he called 'Dad'.

Eventually they finished undressing and dressing him again and he was placed on the knee of a mature policewoman who hushed him and cuddled him and brushed back the mop of red hair, and dropped kisses soft as a butterfly's wing on his brow. He settled back, clutching the one-eared rabbit that had been found in the footwell at the back of the car.

For now, shock and tiredness had reduced his ability to cry. A constable came to the back of the ambulance and looked over at his female colleague. 'Some people get all the jammy jobs,' he said. But the smile didn't reach his eyes. He'd just had to help remove two very dead people from one car and listen to a drunk protesting his innocence while he sat in another.

The drunk would be lucky if they managed to save his leg, which was trapped under a dashboard concertinaed out of shape by the impact. At the moment he was anaesthetised from pain by alcohol, but that would wear off and the copper hoped it would hurt.

'Do we have a name?'

'Not yet. Parents are called Grey; Carol and Henry.'

'Social Services been called?'

'Yeah. They want him taken to A & E. Maybe ward him for the night, until a relative can be found.'

The female constable nodded, smiling as the little boy dozed off on her lap, a thumb sneaking into his mouth as he began to breathe more deeply.

'I hope they find someone quickly. My grandson's about this age and I'd hate him to be among strangers after something like this. This poor little mite's life is never going to be the same again.'

AUGUST 1987

NEWCASTLE, ENGLAND

SHE WAS HIDING BEHIND the settee in the sitting room, and she was rocking again. Scarlett watched unobserved from the doorway. Her stepdaughter had a riot of red-gold curls, deep pansy brown eyes and an oval face. She wasn't a pretty child, just an ordinary one. Her thumb was firmly fixed in her mouth, her rag doll was caught in a stranglehold between arm and sky blue jumper, and she rocked gently back and forward with the persistence of a small human metronome.

Scarlett went in, her voice low so that she wouldn't startle Kate. 'Hello, poppet. I wondered where you'd gone.'

Kate stopped rocking. The stillness, statue-like, had an artificial feel to it; an imposed holding of the little body as if she feared a blow or a harsh word. The thumb was hastily removed from the mouth and placed behind her back as she looked up, as one caught doing something that had earned reprimands before and feared more of the same now.

'Would you like to go out to the swings? The sun is shining, it's a beautiful afternoon.' Scarlett watched as Kate stood up. The child rarely opened her mouth, and when she did she could hardly speak for a stutter that made every other word a torment to listen to. What she did say didn't really make much sense to Scarlett.

The child was as submissive as a whipped cur. Scarlett tried to give her choices, but it was clear to Scarlett that choice had never yet played much of a part in the first few years of Kate's life.

13

'Put dolly in her cot and go and get your coat.' She pointed up the stairs and watched as Kate edged out of the room, giving Scarlett a wide berth like a small animal fearing a kick. Scarlett followed her up the shallow flight to the bedroom.

Kate had been living with her father and his wife, Scarlett, for two weeks and not once had Scarlett found the bedroom left untidy. The bed would have made a sergeant major proud. Scarlett had come in the first morning and found Kate struggling with the sheets, tugging them straight and putting the pillow carefully on top of the eiderdown.

She had praised the child. But Kate had looked at her blank-faced, not a glimmer of a smile touching her lips or eyes.

The toys they had bought her were still in their boxes, as if newly delivered from the shop. Only the rag doll and cot had been unwrapped and set up in the small box room. And the child's father had done that before he had gone to fetch Kate from Ireland.

Scarlett – watching from the doorway as the doll was set down in the cot and a small blanket laid tenderly over it – recalled the conversation.

'I'll not be able to bring many of her things back, Scarlett. I want her to be happy here. I'll get her some playthings.' He'd come home with the doll and cot, a child's tea set, crayons and paper, and a blackboard.

Scarlett had looked at the pile of toys and smiled at his childish excitement over the playthings. 'That should keep her going for a day or two.' She'd been wrong, she thought now. The toys would never be used if they didn't open them and set them up for Kate.

Scarlett opened the wardrobe and lifted Kate's coat out. It was dark brown and a little small. She would have to get a new one before Kate started school: something prettier, thought Scarlett. 'Play shoes, pet.' Scarlett pointed at the trainers sitting side by side under the end of the bed.

Kate lifted the big brown eyes to Scarlett, sat on a little chair and struggled with the buckles of her new red shoes.

Scarlett sighed under her breath. Why couldn't the child ask for help? She came across and bent over the small figure. She huffed out another breath as Kate stilled and drew back in the chair as if fearing a blow.

'It's all right. I only want to help.' What the devil had her mother's relatives done to the girl in that house? She was well fed and clothed – perfectly healthy, but totally remote.

Scarlett asked the same question that night of Philip Jardin, her husband of two years. He'd dropped the child off and then gone away 'on business', leaving wife and child to get acquainted as best they might. Now he was back. 'I don't understand, Phil. She never speaks; she doesn't cry. I'd be really happy if she had a temper tantrum at bedtime or left her toys all over the floor, but no. All she does is cuddle that doll and hide.'

It was easy to see the source of the red-gold hair. Jardin was a slight man. His very ordinary features were his biggest asset for his chosen profession of thief and conman. 'I don't know. I suppose she's missing her mother, Lettie.' His accent was almost stage Geordie; he'd read somewhere that it was the most trusted accent in the British Isles and he hoped to trade on it. 'I had that phone call from Theresa's brother in Ireland, saying that Theresa was in a hospital and they wouldn't be responsible for the child any more. They said they were going to put my daughter into a children's home, Lettie, unless I came and got her.' Phil shook his head as he looked up at the ceiling where Kate slept.

'Did they say what was wrong with Theresa?'

'No. I told you; they just said she was sick. They wouldn't even tell me where she was. They said to take Kate or else they wouldn't be responsible for the consequences. I couldn't let her go into a home. I was brought up in one of those, Lettie; I wasn't letting my child suffer that way.'

Scarlett frowned. 'What was the house like? Were they poor? Is that why they gave her to you?'

Philip Jardin scowled at her. 'No. It was a big, sprawling, white farmhouse opposite the Isle of Arran in Galway. Plenty of cash, so far as I could see. Tess's brother lives there, and her parents. They hardly spoke to me. I wasn't good enough for their daughter and nor, apparently, was Kate. I got to the door and they didn't even offer me a cuppa. I'd been travelling all day and half the night, and they kept me on the doorstep. Her brother stood there watching me, like a cat watches a mouse.' The bitterness held all the resentment and hurt of old rejections and wounds.

'Then Kate's grandmother brought her to the door and handed me that case and pushed the girl at me and then they shut the door in my face. The poor kid didn't know who I was. You wouldn't believe the looks I got on that ferry, and her crying fit to break your heart all the way, but not one word would she say to me. She cried on the train too – all the way up here to Newcastle – but she went stiff as a washboard if I tried to hold her so I stopped trying, aside from holding her hand.' He shrugged, hiding the pain from his wife. 'She still hasn't spoken to me. I don't know what to do with her, Lettie.' Philip Jardin was used to rejection, but that his own daughter should do so cut him to the quick.

Scarlett didn't know what to do, either. She wasn't a mother, would never physically be a mother, and wanted desperately to become a mother. Kate was her only chance: if only she could find a way through to the child. August was bleeding into September and other children ran riot on the streets, rejoicing in their freedom. Kate didn't seem to know that freedom existed, her mind locked away in some hidden place.

Scarlett had enrolled Kate into the local infants' school for the new term, but unless they got her talking the school would not be too happy with the child. Scarlett didn't even know if she'd been taught her letters. She shrugged. She would have to think of something, and soon. 'Do you want a cuppa?' She walked through to the kitchen and picked up the kettle.

AUGUST 1987

NEWCASTLE, ENGLAND

'HERE YOU GO, ANTONY. This is your bed and here's a new friend for you to play with.' The small boy looked at the teddy bear being held out and a half smile appeared on his small mouth, while the tracks of tears were still visible on his thin cheeks.

The sulky ten year old standing at the side of the carer scowled as he listened to the talk that passed over the child's head – and into his own receptive ears – between the two apron-clad women in the small room of the children's home.

'She was living with him: he's been registered with his name because we don't know what else to call him. Poor bugger. His mother's dead and it seems nobody wants to know.'

Antony wiped his nose on his sleeve at this stage and had a handkerchief swiped over the offending organ. 'Never mind, hinny; we'll look after you.' He had a kiss too, and a hug, before being set down again.

He sat on the floor, holding the teddy and looking at no one, while the carer turned her attention to the second child. 'Come along, Stan. Would you like the same room as you had last time?'

Stan shrugged.

The first carer smiled at him. 'Pick up your bag. I'll take him along, Delia; I suppose he'll be here for a while now his mother's passed away, too.'

Delia Cartwright nodded. 'Yes, until the father is in a fit

state to have him back or one of the other relatives comes forward.' She looked at Stan Hunt. 'It's nice to have you with us again, Stan, even if it's a sad reason.' She laid a gentle hand on his shoulder and had it shrugged off. She raised an eyebrow but said nothing; she had had a lot of damaged children through her hands and knew it took a while for them to settle in the children's home.

SEPTEMBER 1987

COUNTY GALWAY

THE KITCHEN OF THE farmhouse was warm and smelt of yeast and roasting meat. The small boy sat on the hearth next to the fire, making 'vroom, vroom' noises as he pushed a car along the carpet. He looked up, his face momentarily lighting up as his grandfather entered the room. Then the light went out again.

'Kate?'

His grandfather picked him up and sat down in a rocking chair next to the blacklead stove, settling the child on his brown corduroys. 'What you got there, then?' He spoke in old Irish Gaelic, and Ben Jardin replied in the same tongue.

'I've got a car, *Daideó*. It goes vroom.' He wriggled around and pulled out his granddad's hunter watch from the waistcoat pocket and held it up to his ear. 'Tick tock.' A smile crossed his face, lit his eyes, and then died as he looked towards the door. 'Kate?'

Eoin's eyes followed his wife as she came over and took the big brown bowl from the front of the stove. She walked over to the pine table in the centre of the room and upended the bread dough on to a circle of flour. She didn't look at him but he saw her lips firm into a thin line, on cheeks that were lined with age and weather, as she heard Ben speaking.

'We shouldn't have sent her away, Maeve. It's been nearly a month and he's still pining.'

Without looking at man or child Maeve spoke, 'I couldn't cope with her, Eoin. He's no bother: he goes out with Micheál

19

and helps with the animals, but she wanted her *mamai* all the time. I've got lambs to raise, you lot to feed, this house to keep. I hadn't got the time for her; it wasn't fair to either of us.' She began to knead the dough, the flour coating her arms up to the elbows and dusting her grey hair.

Eoin shook his head. 'He's missing her.'

'He'll soon forget.' Maeve stopped working the bread for a minute, looking across at her husband. 'Haven't I shame enough with an unmarried *inion* bearing the two of them? I've had the coping with them for nearly four years now, Eoin, and her too; sitting there silent and then trying to kill herself with my best carving knife. I can't cope any longer. And the child, she looked like that man.'

'Tess was married, Maeve.'

'She was not. A Proddy man and a register office. That's not a marriage. She never stood before the Father and said her vows. She wasn't married.'

'The babes bear his name. It was legal.'

'It wasn't godly, Eoin: I'll hear no more about it. She's paid for her sins, and the father is saying mass for her soul. I'll not pay for her in my own home, too.' She began to pound the dough, her hands working rhythmically over the table.

Eoin shook his head again. He didn't agree with her, but he knew better than to argue too much. He liked a peaceful existence, and getting the wrong side of his wife was guaranteed to lead to rows.

But he tried once more because he loved his daughter, too. 'Tess wasn't that bad, Maeve.' He let the little boy slide off his knee and stood up, crossing the room and standing next to his wife. 'She was troubled in her mind.'

'Aye; so troubled she had no thought to the little *chara* coming in and finding her dripping blood all over the washstand. Kate hasn't been the same after. I can't cope, Eoin. I'm sorry, but that's how it is. She'll be better elsewhere, away from the scene. I couldn't keep her out of that room. I was frightened for her. She didn't speak except to ask for her *mamai*.' Maeve briefly glanced at him before looking down at the dough again, where her hands squeezed and folded automatically.

'But are we right to keep the twins apart? Twins are funny things.'

''Tis too late now, Eoin. I'll hear no more. He'll take our name and be ours now.' She didn't look up again and Eoin O'Connor, reading the determination overriding the anger and grief in her face, closed his mouth on the words he wanted to say.

SEPTEMBER 1987

NEWCASTLE, ENGLAND

KATE NODDED AS SCARLETT picked up the chalk and pointed at the blackboard and set the white stick in the small hand. 'Now you do the letters, darling.'

Scarlett watched as the small hand gripped the chalk and began to trace the shapes of the alphabet she had drawn. The white dust coated the right finger and thumb and the little girl stood right next to the board looking from Scarlett to the shapes and back again as she completed each letter. 'Can you say the names for me?'

Kate nodded. Going back to the top of the board and the first letter she opened her mouth. The 'a' was clear enough but though the lips pursed for the 'b' no sound accompanied the shaping. Tears began to form in the corners of Kate's eyes as she struggled to speak.

Scarlett leaned near and rubbed the small back, watching the tears pool and run silently down the pale freckled cheeks. 'It doesn't matter, Kate. Say the ones you can. No one is angry with you.'

Kate stood, not so much accepting the caress as allowing it. Scarlett shook her head. School started next week. Kate had been with them for seven weeks now. She still refused to speak to her father. She hadn't appeared to understand him when he told her to do anything, standing looking at him – not with defiance, which might have earned her a slap – but with total incomprehension on her face.

Scarlett had suggested that they take her to the doctor.

'Maybe she's a bit deaf, Phil.'

Philip Jardin had shrugged, feigning indifference. 'You can if you want. Better get the poor mite checked out before she goes to school.'

So Scarlett had made an appointment. Doctor Hardy was a big man but the children normally responded to him well. 'So what's the problem, little lady?'

He looked from a silent Kate to Scarlett. Scarlett filled in the details. 'We've got the paperwork from her mother's family: she's had all her inoculations. She starts school next week. We, er … we just wanted to make sure everything was all right before she started. She's a bit wheezy sometimes in the morning and she doesn't seem to hear us always, but it's not naughtiness. She's a good girl.'

Doctor Hardy nodded. 'Nearly four, you say.' He pulled his stethoscope from a drawer. 'Just lift her top for me and I'll check out her chest.'

Kate stood quiescent while he placed the cup of the instrument to her chest and listened back and front. 'Maybe a bit of asthma. We'll keep an eye on it, but it isn't that bad.'

'Open your mouth for me, Kate.' He demonstrated by opening his own mouth wide and picked up a wooden spatula.

Kate looked at him, and then slowly opened her mouth. 'Not sore,' she whispered. Then tears gathered and slid down her cheeks but not a sound emerged.

'Hey, hey. No need to cry.' Hardy shook his head. 'If your throat isn't sore that's fine; I don't need to look, hinny. I'll just look in your ears. Is that all right?' He set down the light and spatula and picked up the auroscope.

Kate stood looking at him with a puzzled look on her face, the tears drying slowly on her cheeks.

Hardy looked from her to Scarlett. 'I'm just going to look into your ears like this, pet.' He nodded at Scarlett, who obligingly turned her head and allowed him to peer into her ear. 'No, Mummy. Your ears are fine,' he smiled at Scarlett. 'Now you, hinny.'

Kate peered closely at the instrument and then allowed

Hardy to put it into one ear and then the other. 'Seems fine.' He walked away to wash his hands at the sink and, with his back turned, said quietly, 'Go and get teddy for me please, Kate.'

Kate looked from the man to Scarlett. Scarlett nodded. She went over and picked up the teddy on the examination couch, taking it across to the doctor. He smiled down at her as he dried his hands. 'Thank you, Kate.' He took the bear and set him on a shelf where his little black eyes looked down on the child.

He came back and sat down opposite Scarlett. 'Nothing wrong with her ears. You say she's been living with her mother and that mother is ill. Perhaps she just needs more time to get used to you and her father again.'

Scarlett opened her mouth to explain that Kate had never met them before and then thought better of it. 'Thank you, Doctor … so long as it's nothing serious.'

Scarlett was thinking about that now as the child struggled to say her letters. It was clear that Kate enjoyed learning. Scarlett, aware of time rushing by, had taken her home and set up the blackboard straight away. She had begun to school Kate. At the end of another week Kate was obeying her father, even if she didn't answer him. Scarlett felt she would be all right at school.

CHRISTMAS 1989

COUNTY GALWAY

MAEVE O'CONNOR WAS RIGHT and wrong. Little Ben O'Connor – as he was now known – didn't forget straight away but, between the excitement of going to school and learning his letters, beginning to learn English instead of the Irish Gaelic his grandparents and uncle spoke and making friends, he pushed the longing for his other half into a deep dark corner and never allowed anyone to see how much the missing of his sister hurt him.

Kate refused to remember anything. She closed the door as the young and traumatised do at times, unable to cope with the painful memories. Being surrounded by English every day, she quickly began to understand what the strange woman said to her. The words were often accompanied by pointing, and Kate was a bright child. She didn't like the man, though. She couldn't understand him and he shouted at her and sometimes the words were accompanied by a cuff around the ear. So she kept out of his way.

She learnt to say the right words, but her tongue often tripped her up. So she learnt to keep quiet, too. She guarded her feelings and, as she grew older, she guarded her privacy too. If people didn't know what she was thinking they couldn't tease her. As the years progressed she forgot that other earlier life, with one exception: she knew she'd done something really bad. She couldn't remember what, but she knew she didn't deserve to love – or be loved – and it shaped her attitude to all around her.

She had been with Scarlett and Philip Jardin nearly eighteen months when he left. She had woken from sleep to hear them shouting at each other downstairs. It wasn't the first time she'd been woken by loud angry voices – but this time they were accompanied by the person she considered to be her mum, crying.

'You promised, Phil; you swore you would stop. No more thieving. When we married you said it was a whole new life. You said killing that man had changed you, made you see life differently. How could you?' The words came out through broken sobs.

Kate crept out of bed and pulled the door of her bedroom further open, inching along the floor runner at the top of the landing until she stood at the top of the stairs. A cold wind whistled around her bare toes and her short nightie blew about in the breeze so that her feet grew icy and her hands turned first white, then blue, as she eavesdropped on a conversation she was never intended to hear.

'I have changed, but I was trying to earn us a bit of extra cash. It will be Christmas soon. I wanted to get Kate something nice. I'm not used to providing for a kid.' Philip Jardin's voice had a whine in it as he tried to bluff his way out of the situation. 'And another thing: you promised never to mention ... well ... me killing that bloke. I didn't: it was manslaughter they charged me with, Lettie, and even that was wrong. It was an accident, I swear. I should never have done the time. You said you forgave me and now you throw it back in my face.' If he had hoped to change the subject, his wife wasn't falling for it.

Kate held tightly to the stair rail, peeping through the banisters. She could see the man as he walked back and forward, appearing and disappearing like the sun behind grey clouds, as his head of red hair passed the half-open sitting room door. She couldn't see her mum but she could hear her, noisy sobs blurring the words as she answered Philip Jardin.

'So now you're going to spend Christmas behind bars again. A fine Christmas that will be.'

'I'm sorry, Lettie.'

'So am I, Phil, because I can't live this way, wondering if the next knock at the door will be the police. I want a divorce.'

Kate could hear even more sobs and her own eyes filled in sympathy. Her dad was speaking now. 'You can't. They'll put Kate in a home. If we hadn't had Kate I wouldn't have been tempted this way.'

'So it's poor Kate's fault?'

'Of course not! Oh, hell. I love you, Lettie.'

'You have a funny way of showing it, Phil. No, don't try kissing me. I want a divorce. I can't live this way. I'll look after Kate for you while you're inside and while I wait for the divorce, but then you'll have to care for her yourself. Maybe that will make you see sense.'

'You can't mean it, Lettie.'

'I do. I'm leaving you, Phil, for good. I'm going to have a bath and then I'm going to bed. Alone, Phil. After all, it won't be the first time and I may as well get used to it.'

Kate heard the creak as her mum walked across the bit of wood next to the door and slithered backwards, before turning and pattering quietly towards her bedroom. She hadn't understood much of the conversation but the bit she had understood was terrifying: she didn't want to be left with her dad and she'd done something else wrong, but she didn't know what.

It was all her fault that her mum was leaving; she'd heard Dad say so. It was all her fault. The tears pooled and dripped off the little face as she stood shaking just inside her bedroom door. She slid down onto the carpet and wiped her hand across her face before wrapping both arms around her knees and absently started to rock in an effort at self-comfort.

The next morning she came downstairs on tiptoe, afraid that her mum would have gone away already and Dad would be in the kitchen waiting to shout at her. She'd tried to stay awake last night so that she could make sure Mum didn't go without her, but had woken up in her bed even though she couldn't remember getting into it again.

Scarlett was in the kitchen making toast. She gave Kate a smile. 'Do you want to put the cereal packet out?'

Kate looked all around the kitchen, checking to see if her dad had had his breakfast first and gone, or if he was still upstairs in bed. There were no plates and bowls on the table or in the sink; she looked at Scarlett and then went to the cupboard to get the bowls.

'We only need two bowls, Kate. Dad has to go and stay somewhere else for a while.'

Kate nodded, rather owlishly, looking at Scarlett with a trembling lip.

'Oh, hell.' Scarlett smiled at the little girl. 'It's OK, Kate. I'll look after you. We might have to move house, but you'll always be my little girl.' She came over and gave Kate a kiss on the pale cheek. 'Get your breakfast ready, love, or you'll be late for school.'

Kate didn't see her dad again for a long time, but as she grew up she was told a little. None of it was pleasant hearing.

SEPTEMBER 1991

COUNTY GALWAY

'BEN, COME ALONG! YOU need to get your wellingtons on. Stop dawdling, lad.'

Ben looked at his *uncail* Micheál and nodded his nearly seven-year-old head. He had become a quiet child. 'I won't be a moment. *Maimeo* wants me to fetch the eggs first, *Uncail*.'

'Fine, but don't be all day.' Micheál headed out to the milking parlour where the farm's dozen cows waited stoically. Ben finished putting on his footwear and went to get the basket. He had allotted tasks, as did everyone on the farm: tasks that had to be finished before school, church or other activities.

He loved the farm, spending hours tending to the stock: a little shadow of either Micheál or his beloved *daideó*. The outdoor life suited him, but he wasn't allowed to neglect his studies. *Maimeo* had listened to him reading his book already today and Micheál expected him to write down the figures for each cow's yield on the big blackboard in the shed.

He came rushing in at eight to a dish of porridge and a glass of milk. He set the spoon in the empty dish as his grandmother came in from feeding the hens. 'Have you finished, *a ghra*?'

'Yes, *Maimeo*.'

'Away and change then, for the priest will be waiting.'

Ben offered a milky smile as he left the table, and went up the stairs, pulling his old blue jumper over his head as he went. 'Don't forget to wash behind your ears.' The voice of his *mórai* followed him upwards.

He came down in his school uniform of grey trousers and jumper, his socks half-masted and his shirt already escaping the confines of his trousers. 'I've only my shoes to tie, *Maimeo*.'

Maeve didn't quite agree with that assessment, combing his blond curls with a ruthless hand that left him more than a little watery-eyed, before pushing and pulling his body around as she tucked and tidied. 'There. That's better. What would the priest say if you turned up all messed? You don't want to shame us.'

'No, *Maimeo*.'

'Good.' Maeve pulled her own black coat on and led him by the hand out of the door and into the waiting car. Church on Sunday was as inviolate for them as the Sabbath was for an orthodox Jew.

Ben had been singing in the choir for nearly a year now. He knew *Maimeo* was proud of him, no matter what she said. He also knew she wanted him to be an altar boy. He wasn't so sure about that. The Father was very strict with the altar boys. If they had sweeties in their pockets or were caught talking at Mass he wasn't above giving them a slap.

However there was no evading church. He had his first communion next month and had been struggling with the catechism. *Maimeo* said God loved him but he had to be good if he wanted God to keep loving him. She took him around to the back door and into the small room, helping him to fit his surplice over the little cassock before going away with a 'Be good.'

Ben stood waiting to process up to the choir at the start of the service next to his best friend, Padraic O'Leary. Padraic was red-headed and had nine brothers and sisters. Sometimes Ben would go and play at their house. He loved all the yelling and rushing about. Padraic had to share a room with his three brothers and Ben tried to imagine what it would be like not being able to choose when to put the light out or having to share toys and clothes. Padraic was always in trouble with the father too. *Maimeo* said he'd go to hell for sure.

Ben couldn't imagine what hell was like; the way *Maimeo* talked about it, though, he didn't want to go there. Padraic was grinning and Ben gave him a curious look before giving an upward lift of the eyes to the choirmaster and whispering, 'What you doing?'

'Nothing. Wait and see.' He shook his red mop at Ben.

Ben jiggled on one foot and they set off up the aisle, one of the older boys waving the thurible, with the candle and gospel bearers following behind them.

Ben could see Padraic's shoulders shaking with the giggles. He hoped the Father couldn't. He gave him a quick nudge but that only made his friend giggle even more. Just as they were genuflecting at the steps a dappled green frog leapt out of Padraic's pocket and gave a huge croak. Ben froze, one leg bent and one arm arrested in the act of crossing himself.

The frog, on wire legs, shot behind them; the thurifer bringing up the rear tried to stop himself standing on the frog; the nearest acolyte let his candle dip dangerously next to the hem of the other acolyte's cassock, and hell – on a par with Dante's imagination and *Maimeo's* predictions – broke out in the centre of the church.

Ben, looking at the antics of the adults and his friend bent double with laughter, felt the bubble rise in his own chest and started to giggle. The humour lasted a very short time but it was glorious while it did. Then his *maimeo* was shaking him like he was the kitchen rug, calling him a wicked boy; the priest was shaking with rage and half a dozen small O'Learys were running about trying to catch their brother's frog, which was hopping down the central aisle uttering fretful little croaks every time it managed to slip from a small child's grasp.

When the dust settled Ben stood next to his friend and in front of Father Kelly. 'Who brought a frog into Holy Mass? Come on, which of you did it?'

Both boys stood mute, Padraic because he didn't want the punishment he knew was due to him, Ben because he was loyal to his friend.

'Very well: if you won't answer then I can't allow you to

31

take first communion, for how will you say your confession without admitting your guilt?'

Ben and Padraic glanced at each other, then at the Father, then they looked at their feet. It was Ben's first real introduction to his *maimeo*'s God. A God who couldn't forgive high spirits and childish pranks, apparently, and took no account of loyalty to one's friends.

SEPTEMBER 1991

NEWCASTLE, ENGLAND

'ANTONY GREY, WHAT HAVE you done now?'

The young boy gave a very small shrug. A few loyal friends would have been very welcome but in a children's home of this size it was every man (or boy) for himself – though he did try to protect the little ones a bit when they arrived, bewildered and crying. He remembered what it had been like when he first arrived. He'd quietly help them find shoes and show them how to keep their few precious possessions safe from the other children.

He couldn't do much but when it was his turn to feed the babies or change the nappies or watch out for the toddlers he did his best, because he did remember a little of what family life had been like. And what it was like when it was gone for ever.

He looked at the square face, framed in brown lank hair which had been tied back into a ponytail at the beginning of the day, but which was now hanging in wisps about pale cheeks. He schooled his features to a blankness he'd perfected since he'd become aware of himself as an entity. He could rival the inscrutable Japanese. The brown eyes looked back at him with a mixture of impatience and sympathy.

'The hole in that window didn't just grow there.'

'No, Miss Cartwright.'

'So...'

He gave another infinitesimal shrug. He had been hiding in the shrubbery of the gardens, evading both the need to join in a game of football he had no taste for and the wrath of a carer who wanted him to 'mix'. He had been examining a piece of slate he'd found, wondering how to get the fossil out. He knew a little about fossils and his book said they could be found in slate. Now he slid the slate into the pocket of his grey short trousers and put his hands behind his back.

'What have you got there?'

'Nothing.' He brought out his empty hands, showing their grubby palms to Delia Cartwright.

'Hum! So if it wasn't you who threw this stone which I've just gathered from the staffroom carpet, who did throw it?'

'Don't know, Miss.' Antony looked at the piece of slate she held out. He could hear some soft sniggers off to the left and thought he did know. Stan Hunt never lost a chance to get him into trouble. They had arrived at the home on the same day nearly four years ago and been bitter rivals ever since. Antony wasn't quite sure why.

Miss Cartwright had good hearing, too. She looked at Antony, placed a finger on her lip with one hand, and stepped smartly to the side. Her arm reached out over a small bush and Stan emerged into view, ear firmly gripped by the long fingers of her other hand. He was yelling like an Indian on the warpath. He was given a shake, which pulled the ear a bit harder. He tried to surreptitiously drop the stones he had been throwing at Antony to annoy him before he'd accidentally caught the low window.

'You smell disgusting, Stan. What have you been doing with yourself? You' – the unoccupied hand pointed at Antony – 'go indoors and tell Cook you have been sent to peel potatoes as punishment for lying.' She transferred her gimlet eye to a grinning Stan. 'You – go to Matron. You can fold clothes until supper time.' She paused, wrinkling her nose. 'After you've had a good wash.'

The smile slunk away in embarrassment as a scowl streaked into view. While peeling potatoes was hard work for a nine-year-old, it carried the benefits of any titbits the cook cared to share with her helpers. Folding clothes was not only boring for a thirteen-year-old who'd rather be outside – but also Matron was strict enough to make a boy wash not just his hands first and his neck as well, and then redo the folding until she was satisfied.

'What's more, Stanley Hunt, you will lose your pocket money for the next month to pay some of the repairs.'

Both boys slouched away as if heading for the first day of school. Antony kept his eyes on the side door but he heard Stan's, 'I'll have your pocket money or else, Antony Grey.'

Antony kept walking, headed for the warm kitchen and a marathon session of potato peeling. The children's home was full of children like Stan – who managed to boost their self-esteem by bullying – and Antony, who protected themselves by taking refuge inside themselves. He generally managed to keep himself out of trouble by being in the presence of authority without actually acknowledging their presence, which is why he'd thought himself relatively safe outside the staffroom window.

He'd been in one children's home or another since he had turned five years old. The carers generally were kind but they couldn't show favouritism, even if they'd had time for such a thing. Antony accepted that he wasn't going to get kisses and hugs now and had hardened his small heart to the abuses. He evinced no curiosity any more: it hurt too much.

NOVEMBER 2010

SALISBURY, ENGLAND

'NEARLY DONE, LOVE.' PROFESSOR David Walker set the mug of tea in front of his wife Kate and sat down himself as he watched her carefully putting bills, letters and brown files into a box. He picked up a photo lying on the floor next to the box waiting to be packed, and looked at a very young Kate in school uniform of blazer and tie. It had been on the side table next to her mother's bed.

Kate Walker née Jardin had grown into a pretty woman but black was never going to suit her, David thought. He eyed the neat suit and hair which strained against the restraints of bands, but whose colour couldn't be diminished by such restrictions. The brown eyes now looked out at the world from behind glasses which not only aided sight but hid Kate's thoughts.

'Th … this is the l…last one, David.' Kate smiled tiredly, her voice bouncing back off the bare walls and uncarpeted floorboards of the room. The people from the Salvation Army had been earlier in the day and taken away most of the furniture, with thanks on both sides. David had arranged for a man to load up the rest – the few pieces she wanted to keep.

Scarlett Hamilton was dead. It had all happened so suddenly. One week she had rung to say she'd got the flu, the next a neighbour had rung to say, 'Could they come?' – Kate's mother was seriously ill in hospital. By the time they'd driven down from Cumbria it was too late. Kate was still reeling from the multiple punches of death, funeral and house clearance.

David watched his wife's face, seeing her tuck her emotions away. He wanted to shake her ... tell her to cry ... talk ... anything... For the two years he'd been married to Kate he'd struggled with her. He loved her so much, but he rarely got anywhere near the real Kate – the one she kept hidden from the world.

Kate looked up as the stillness and silence in the room touched her. 'I'm OK, D...avid.' And both of them knew she lied.

David nodded. 'Drink your tea. I'll put the boxes in the back of the car.' He gathered up the remnants of a life, sealed with Sellotape, and took it outside to the big black 4x4 Discovery.

Last week they had been dreaming about what Scarlett Hamilton might like for Christmas. It was to be the first one for their twins, too. The broken shards of that dream were packed into these boxes and David wondered if they could ever stick them together again. He went outside carrying the last of the boxes. He shoved it in the boot with a viciousness out of all proportion to the task. Giving vent to his feeling of frustration – the frustration of a man who didn't have the power of God – and who wanted that power to help someone he loved beyond life itself. It wasn't Kate's fault. He hated the fact that his wife was hurting. He wanted to shield her from all the nastiness that was in the world.

He slammed the tailgate shut and pulled the door down, shutting in the boxes and standing looking up at a sky filled with storm clouds. The rain fell on his hair and turned it as dark as his mood. Why did these things have to happen? He gave a half-grunt of laughter – which had as much humour as the funeral had contained – as he answered his own question. Because life was like that.

He would look at the contents of the boxes with Kate and sort out the paperwork when she was a little stronger. For now he wanted her away from here, back home where she could relax and not have to wear the society face she'd donned for the funeral and which looked as if it was becoming a fixture.

He wanted to put this whole event behind them. He glanced around. Not even a stray dog was stupid enough to be out in this downpour: evidently he was the only one who hadn't got the sense to come in out of the rain. He looked at his watch, coming to a decision. If they set off in the next hour, he thought, they might make it in time for the twins' bedtime.

The journey from Salisbury to Wisbech, to David's parents' home, had been silent. But he'd been right: Kate was better away from a house that only held sad memories now. He watched as she held her young son in her arms, sniffing at his unique baby smell. 'Hello, darling. I'm s...sorry we had to leave you be...hind. I bet you've had a lovely t...time with P...Pops, th...ough.' She looked at her father-in-law and offered him a weary smile. David nodded in agreement with himself, even while he hugged his daughter, Rose.

'Oh, indeed. We've been to the river, haven't we?' Paul Walker answered his daughter-in-law's query as to the behaviour of her offspring: he grinned as Paul junior placed a wet kiss on his mother's eyebrow. 'We took a jam jar and tried to catch tiddlers.' Paul Walker looked on as the rapturous reception continued between mother and children.

David grinned affectionately at his father. 'I remember that walk. I never caught anything and you always seemed to find at least one fish.'

'What, in November?' His father raised a grey eyebrow above his glasses, like a caterpillar scanning for birds. 'But we did get them some new wellingtons. Paul junior insisted on having ones with faces on.'

'Oh, yeah. They aren't even one yet, Pops! And all my son can say is dada and din din; I think it was you who took a shine to them.' Rose Walker pulled her father's ear. 'Yes, Topsy; I am paying attention.' He planted a kiss on her pink cheek then blew a raspberry into her neck before looking across at Kate. 'I think we'll give these two their tea and bath before we talk about the last three days. OK, Pops?'

His father grinned. 'Fine ... er ...there is the small matter of the flotilla in the bathroom; I feel I should mention this before you do.'

David shook his head at his parent. His mother, coming into the sitting room and bringing with her a faint aroma of chocolate cake, smiled and took Rosie from him. 'Come along, young lady. Let's get you into your chair and then you can have something to eat.' She walked off into the kitchen, carrying her granddaughter in her arms.

She was strapping Rose efficiently into a highchair when Kate came through with baby Paul. She looked up at Kate. 'He would buy them things, Kate. I hope you're not cross.'

Kate shook her head. 'Why sh...ould I be cross?'

Her mother-in-law smiled. 'They are barely walking yet. But Paul junior was so taken with the wellies that Pops just couldn't resist. Come along, young man; sit next to your sister and we'll get you some tea.'

The two children were fed, bathed and settled in their cots before David and Kate ate the evening meal and then adjourned to the sitting room.

THE ROOM WAS COMFORTABLE, smelling of lavender polish, the early Christmas hyacinths on the coffee table and just a hint of the fine roast beef they had enjoyed for their supper: it hung on the air like a friendly wraith. The peaceful sound of a grandfather clock was sounding off the minutes in a leisurely manner as the four adults finally relaxed.

The furniture was old, but of that durable kind that comes with quality. Kate was sitting holding a china cup and saucer and leaning back in the easy recliner with her eyes closed. David went and sat on the broad arm of her chair and pulled her near so that she rested against him. 'All right, darling?'

'I'm just t...tired, David. It's b...been a long w...week, s...somehow.' The words were spoken with effort and David found himself kneading her shoulder as she struggled to speak.

His father looked across at him, offering a faint smile. 'You can stay here as long as you need to, Kate. We love looking after the children. I know David has to get back to the site, but we can drive you home when you're ready.'

Kate nodded and smiled. 'That's kind of you, b...but I'd r...rather go home and get b...back into the routine of th...ings. It will s...soon be Christmas. The children's f...first. I want it to be s...special for th...em.' Her eyes behind the glasses filled with tears.

David nodded at his father. 'Yes, Pops; very kind.' He looked down at his wife's red-gold curls and smoothed them. 'I'd rather Kate was at home. But I'm selfish, darling.' He looked down at her and watched his hands threading through the curls, disguising his eyes and emotions from everyone in the room as he watched her struggle to maintain her calm.

Kate looked up at him and gently shook her head. 'Home, please.' She looked across at her father-in-law. 'I'm not un...grateful, Pops, but...'

'That's OK, my dear.'

'We'll be off early tomorrow, then.' David stood and went over to the small coffee table, picking up the teapot from the tray and pouring his mother a cup of Earl Grey as she came into the room. 'Mum.' He handed her the tea and saw her seated before going back to Kate's side.

'Have you sorted everything out, David?'

David nodded. 'Most of it. The removal man will bring the van up at the weekend with the pieces of furniture Kate wanted. We've got the paperwork in the boot. We'll sort it out later. The neighbour has promised to see to the utilities for us.'

He rubbed gently at Kate's shoulder again. 'We'll go back down and do anything else later, when things are less raw.' Even now, when his wife was distressed, he couldn't keep his hands off her. He smiled grimly to himself.

Paul Walker watched his son watching his Kate. David was fifty-three. His once auburn hair was now sprinkled with white except for his beard, which still had more red than anything else. His green eyes usually twinkled but today they were sober and serious; dull as agates, as they looked at Kate. At twenty-five she was a long way his junior; the hair was the same colour as his had once been, but glasses disguised her deep brown eyes to a certain extent and made her face seem plainer than it actually was.

'What are you excavating at the moment?' Paul Walker turned the conversation into more mundane channels and David took his lead and talked about the archaeological dig for which he was preparing the desk work.

Both men studiously ignored the fact that Kate hardly spoke for the rest of the evening. Later that night David made love to her with a restrained tenderness that night that made her weep. 'I love you, my Kate.'

Kate smiled through her tears in the darkness. A poignant smile. 'I know you do.'

MAY 2011

COUNTY GALWAY

THE KITCHEN WAS QUIET. The two men looked at the elderly woman – and then at each other – in stunned silence. Eoin touched the cool hand of the woman again and then abruptly sat on the floor next to the stove, still holding onto the rough, limp hand.

'She's dead?'

'Yes. I thought I'd best be fetching you in, before I rang for the doctor and such.'

'But, but … she's set the bread.'

Micheál nodded. He pulled over one of the hard kitchen chairs and pulled his father up and onto it. He looked anxiously at the older man, who was cheese yellow with shock, before he moved away and into the hall. His eyes rested on the earthen pot of pussy willow stems and early narcissi his mother had set there that morning, as he waited for the doctor to answer his call.

Eoin was dimly conscious of his son speaking on the phone. He kept his eyes fixed on his late wife. He heard her voice echoing in his head. 'I'll be away to confession after I've cleared the table, darlin'. The priest said the service would be at nine, so the bread will have risen nicely by the time I get back.' He looked again at the bowl containing the bread, its striped tea towel nicely domed as the dough pushed up against it. He could smell the yeast and the faint lavender talc his wife always wore. 'She set the bread: why would she die?'

Micheál, coming back into the kitchen, looked curiously at his father. 'The doctor is on his way and he says he'll inform the *Garda* for us. We've not to touch the body, *Dadaí*.' He pulled the kettle to the front of the blacklead stove and frowned. 'My Bridget will be over in just a minute.'

Eoin looked up. 'Why would we be wanting the *Garda*?'

Micheál shrugged. 'I don't know. Was she sick, *Dadaí*?'

'No, no. My Maeve was never ill, not a day. She said she was too busy to be ill.' He shook his head and continued to hold the old hand of his wife, as he had done so many times before. He gave it a soft squeeze, almost expecting he was dreaming and that she would squeeze back.

The two men sat. Bridget, coming in from the cottage she shared with her husband and three teenage children, looked first at her husband then at the corpse. They exchanged a silent look. Bridget moved quietly about, making the tea and pouring it into mugs. Aside from a quiet 'thanks' from her husband the room was silent, waiting for the doctor and police to arrive. When they did they had to get Bridget to take her father-in-law away. Eoin seemed totally confused by the events unfolding in front of him.

The doctor was a young man called O'Neil. He came from Dublin way and didn't speak Gaelic at all – but he'd been in the district for over a year now and Micheál knew him by sight, if nothing else.

'I came in for a cuppa, about half eleven, expecting Mam to have the kettle on and she was asleep – seemingly – in the chair. So I tiptoed out again.' Micheál shook his head. 'I thought she was sleeping. She's been complaining she was tired. I niver thought no more than that she was having a nap while she waited for the bread to rise.'

Doctor O'Neil nodded while he examined the corpse, checking the pupils and feeling the limbs. He looked at the policeman standing quietly, taking notes. 'She's been gone about three hours, I should say, by the stiffening. Rigor mortis is just beginning to set in.' He looked across to Micheál. 'If you'd give me a hand we'll set her on a bed 'til the van comes.'

The men shifted their grisly burden to the spare back room and Bridget, Micheál's wife – coming back down from settling her father-in-law – brought a clean sheet to lay over the corpse. The men left and went back to the kitchen, where the air seemed lighter now that the body was no longer dominating the room.

The policeman looked from Micheál to the doctor, waiting for them to settle on chairs before he started asking questions.

'You came in at eleven-thirty you say? And she was sleeping then, yes?'

Micheál nodded.

The policeman glanced at the doctor as he cleared his throat. 'She was probably already dead then, Micheál.'

Micheál nodded again.

'I've been treating her for several months now, for angina. I admit I didn't think she was as ill as this, but I shouldn't think this is suspicious, Officer. We'll know better after the PM.'

'PM?' Micheál shook his head. 'Angina? Mam wasn't ill.'

The doctor shook his head. 'She came to me complaining of chest pain last autumn. I thought it was a chest infection at first, but then – when I had the blood work back – it was obviously her heart. She wouldn't go to the main hospital for tests. So I did what I could with spray and tablets.'

'She niver said anything to us. Not a word.'

The doctor frowned. 'She didn't say a lot to me. I tried to get her to go for more tests. We might have been able to fit a stent and give her several more years. She refused: said she wanted to go to God in his time, not a doctor's. She was worried about what she called her "big sin".' The doctor looked quizzically at Micheál. 'I tried to tell her God forgave, and that nothing was too big for him. But she was obviously fretting about something.'

Micheál nodded, the tears finally beginning to pool and run down his cheeks. 'Aye, well. She'd been to confession this morning so she should be shrived.' He thought he knew what that big sin was.

Paul O'Neil looked on with compassion. 'I haven't seen her for a month so there has to be a PM, Micheál: it's an unattended death. It's just routine. OK?'

Micheál sniffed and wiped his face with the back of his hand. 'Do you need to speak to my *athair* about it?'

'No, we can sort it out. Shouldn't take too long; you can arrange the funeral.' He glanced across at the *Garda* standing, pen poised, listening to them. The policeman gave a quick bob of acknowledgement.

'Aye; start to make arrangements, Micheál.' He had been to school with Micheál, had been in awe of his mother, but he would do his duty by the family regardless of his familiarity with them all.

The ambulance arrived then and they took his mam away. Micheál went about in a daze, ringing relatives and answering their questions. He put off until the evening the most important phone call of all, that of calling the seminary where Ben was currently finishing his training.

'Monseigneur, Ben's grandmother has died. Will you inform him? The funeral should be in about five or six days.' He paused, listening. 'Yes, it was sudden. We didn't realise she was even ill. But it seems she has been under the doctor for months now.' He nodded at the telephone and the voice answering him.

'Yes, she'd been to service. She always made a big thing of special services.' He nodded again. 'Yes, that would be good, Father. She'd want a mass said. Thank you.' He put the phone down, half relieved that he hadn't had to speak to his nephew and break the news, half ashamed that he'd allowed someone else to do the job for him. Ben was going to be devastated.

He looked across at his silent father, sitting slumped in the rocking chair near the stove. 'The father will tell Ben for us.'

'And then we'll have to speak to him, Micheál.'

Micheál nodded. 'Do you think…?'

'We have to speak.'

Micheál nodded again and sat in the other chair, saying nothing. For there was nothing left to say.

MAY 2011

WHITBY, ENGLAND

HIS EYES SETTLED ON The young man in academic robes in the photograph tacked to the wall. The lettering underneath said: Anthony Grey BA (Hons.) DD. 'I worked so bloody hard for that, and look where I am now.'

He stood up and paced to the window, looking out onto the untidy patch of grass three floors below. He leaned a tired head against the pane of glass and watched Stan Hunt, his old adversary – wearing a hoody and pushing a bike – leave the area through a gate swinging off its hinges. 'How did I come to this?' He gave a harsh, choked laugh. 'What did I expect? No better than Stan down there. Out of work, on the dole, and wondering what the point of it all is.'

He turned and looked around the small, cramped room. The flat was more than dingy; it resembled a combination of second-hand furniture and book shop – one that no one had visited for a long time. It smelt of must and unwashed clothes.

He walked over to the sink in the corner of the bedsit and filled a kettle, putting it back on a slightly rusty tray depicting the royal wedding of Princess Diana. He pushed his hand through his red hair and slumped back into the wooden chair next to the desk as he waited for the water to boil.

He got up wearily as the kettle signalled, by sputtering water onto the tray, the fact that it had reached boiling point. He made the tea absently, looking at the pile of books stacked near the desk and wondering if the answer was in one of those. He returned to the desk and set the mug down, the tea bag tag dangling over the side and the spoon sticking up from the clear depths.

The paper fluttered on the desk in the breeze from the window. Antony Grey was just twenty-eight but appeared ten years older, partly through the start of male pattern baldness but mainly because he was worried and undernourished. He looked at the badly stacked file and sighed. He pushed back the chair and rubbed both ink-stained hands over hair that was on the retreat. 'It's there. I know it's there. I just can't find it.' The empty room absorbed his words, sponge-like, and returned no answer.

'Now, let's take this logically, Antony.' He lifted the first book from the pile and started to work a finger down the index. The tea grew cold and scummy and the afternoon drew into evening before he looked up again, and then it was only because he couldn't see what he was doing any more.

He straightened and stretched his limbs, throwing down his pen, before picking up the mug and pulling a face at the contents. 'Time for a walk, I think.' He stood up, picking up an envelope addressed to Professor David Walker, before going over to the only door in the room. He lifted a grey coat from a hook on the back of it, stuffing the letter into the inside pocket before putting it on. The coat had seen better days, but then so had the wearer.

The lift down smelt of urine and cabbage and Antony wrinkled his nose but shrugged. What could he say, after all? The sun was setting over the council estate where he lived, masking the dirt and decay in a warm red glow and making the wrapping from a late Easter egg glitter like gold underfoot. Antony sighed softly as he made his way to the local pub, posting his letter on the way.

'Hello, love. Do you want the usual?'

'Yes, please, Amy.'

Amy smiled and pointed at the seat in the corner near the window with her chin while holding tightly to the five pint mugs in her hand. 'I'll be with you in a minute, then.' She set down the pints in front of one of a group of young men and walked briskly back behind the bar, through the swing doors and into a kitchen reflecting the controlled chaos at the start of a week terminating in the May bank holiday weekend of 2011. 'My chap's in, Vinny. Nice big plate for him, poor bugger.'

Vinny the chef grinned. 'I think you'd marry him if he asked you.'

Amy grinned. 'At least he's interesting to talk to, not like you lot with yer cars and football and sex.'

'Nothing wrong with sex.' Vinny leered at her suggestively.

'In yer dreams, Vinny.'

'At least I'd have you in my bed, then.' He grinned at her splutter of laughter as he deftly plated up the house special: tonight it was sausage and mash with onion gravy. He handed it over and Amy nodded her thanks.

'I'll take my break in fifteen and have a cuppa with him. OK?'

'Yeah, fine.'

Amy delivered the meal and stood back. 'I'll bring you a cuppa in a minute or two. You can tell me what progress you've made.' She smiled nicely at him.

Antony Grey nodded both his thanks for the meal and in agreement. He liked Amy. He'd been coming to this pub for the last nine months, since he moved into the flat on the housing estate. The house special was always good and since it was his one meal of the day he thought it was a reasonable price to pay for the company.

Amy was always cheerful. He knew about her little girl, Joy, and that her mother looked after her at night while Amy worked, her ambition to get a degree one day. She'd talked – though not in detail – about her ex, who had beaten her up and had a restraining order placed on him, and he recognised her thirst for knowledge.

'So what have you been doing today, then?' Amy appeared at his side as he cleared the plate and set down his knife and fork. She set two mugs of tea on the small round table and sat down opposite him. Their twin images reflected incongruously in the small panes of the window so that ten Amys talked to ten Antonys.

Antony hadn't been sure of her at first; she wore the conventional white blouse and black skirt of a waitress, both rather tight and showing off her assets. But over the months he'd come to recognise her genuine interest in the project he was engaged in.

'I think I might have tracked down a subscript relating to a letter from Darwin to Strata Smith.' He smiled, looking at the rapt young face. 'It probably won't come to anything; I need the letter itself to prove that the two men not only knew each other but discussed the theory of descent with modification. They were contemporaneous, but only just. Smith kept his ideas pretty close as well, as I was telling you yesterday.'

'So ... if Darwin knew him ... would he have shared?'

Antony shook his head. 'Doubtful. They were both fighting the establishment in their own way. If they did correspond it would have been in a very guarded fashion.'

'So tell me where this subscript was and what it said.' Amy pushed his mug closer and picked up her own, her blue eyes twinkling as she sensed his enthusiasm was about to cause yet another beverage to go to waste. She had learnt to 'manage' him a bit.

At about ten Antony got up to go. Amy had chatted to him for the half-hour of her break and then come over every so often with a fresh mug and a quick word. But ten was when he went home, regular as clockwork. He had the habits of an old man.

Not only Amy knew that. Someone else did, too. Tonight he was waiting. He watched as Antony walked slowly out of the car park and started down the street. He revved the engine of the souped-up and borrowed car and, as Antony started to cross the street, head down as he thought about the latest piece of research, the driver pressed the accelerator and aimed for Anthony with murderous intent in his heart.

MAY 2011

CUMBRIA, ENGLAND

David Walker raised his head from the paperwork he'd been absorbed in a few minutes ago and glanced up at the ceiling. What on earth was his wife doing now? He cocked his head on one side, listening to the giggles floating down from the room above like dust motes in sunbeams: they lifted his heart up and filled him with pleasure. She had the children with her; he could hear them all pattering about.

There was a sudden large thump and he threw his glasses carelessly down on the paper-littered, mahogany desk in front of him, and pushed back the chair with his legs, preparing to go and join in the fun. Then he sat still, his hands resting on the sides of the chair, stunned by the sound filtering downwards. Kate was laughing. He grinned: it was an almost forgotten sound.

Kate hadn't been truly happy for months. The last time had been when they were celebrating their second wedding anniversary last November. They had been so delighted with each other. Then her mother had died. His mind drifted backwards as his body settled back into the seat, recalling the events of the day her happiness had been stolen away, and wishing he could blot them out.

He came back to the present to find his wife standing at the study door, looking at him with a raised eyebrow and a half smile on her face. 'Wh…at on earth are you th…inking about, love?' Kate leaned casually against the doorjamb holding a very dusty, miniature carbon copy of herself. 'Rosie h…here wanted Dad to h…help us,' she grinned. 'And so do I.'

David smiled at the picture she made. Jeans hugged her legs and the collar of her shirt was half in and half out of her sloppy green jumper. Her hair was coming out of the band she'd imprisoned it in and she had a streak of dust on her cheek. He stood, scooping his son up from his position next to his knee and tucked him under his arm in the manner of a rugby player heading for the touchline as he strolled across the room.

'I was thinking I would come and join the fun upstairs but you came to find me instead.'

'Yeah?' Kate shook her head at him. 'Very s…serious decision that, if your expression is anything to g…o by.'

'Huh! Playing with you three is a serious decision. I've got proper work to do.' David came over to her and dropped a kiss on the lips he still couldn't resist. She tasted of honey and dust. 'So what were you doing?'

'We were getting the r…room r…ready for Mum and Pops. These two were,' she sniffed, 'h…helping me. At least, that's w…what I understood them to say.'

'I would have come up, Kate. I don't want you lugging things about.'

'I'm not made of Dresden china, love. Besides I w… wanted to sh…ift those boxes out into the attic.'

David frowned slightly. He had been thinking about 'those boxes', and it explained why his wife's stutter was so much in evidence today. He glanced down at his giggling son. 'Have you finished helping Mum? You're certainly dirty enough.'

His son laughed up at his father from his position under his left arm. 'Dad, Dad. Din din. Soup.'

Rosie leaned over and patted her father on the cheek then grasped a handful of beard hairs. 'Dad … help.' And David grinned, shifting the hand before it tugged any harder. 'You've come unwashed, the three of you. I think we'd better go to the bathroom before lunch.'

Lunch was filled with giggles as the children learned the art of feeding and their parents learned patience. Putting the children down for a nap was accompanied by lots of laughter, but when David and Kate came back downstairs for a post-lunch coffee, Kate's face was serious again.

'W...what were you th...inking about w...when we came in earlier, David? You looked very st...ern. Is there a p... problem with the desk s...survey?'

David held out a hand and led her over to the squashy seats in the window embrasure. He ignored the coffee tray that Thea, his housekeeper, had set on the table between the chairs and sat, pulling Kate down and enjoying the weight and warmth of her on his knee.

'Nothing that can't be fixed with a bit more research, love. I need to go back out to the other site. I was just wondering if you wanted to come with me tomorrow, or if you wanted to stay and finish getting things ready for our visitors.'

Kate leaned back against him, relaxing while she thought about the tasks needing to be done before his parents arrived in two days' time.

'I think I'd b...better s...stay here and s...sort things out, love. The children have nursery for two hours in the m... morning. I can get the b...beds made up while they're out of the w...way, and d...do the ironing.'

'I employ a housekeeper to keep the house in order, Kate: you don't have to do things.'

'Thea is nearly s...seventy-five, David. I know, I know; she loves h...helping with the children and she would be h... heartbroken if we s...suggested she retired, but I can't let h... er do too much.'

'All right, darling, it's your home. Just,' David pulled her closer, 'just don't go wearing yourself out. My parents don't care about a bit of dust. They've come to see us, not examine the tops of the doors and under the beds.'

'Yes, David.' Kate grinned at her husband and rubbed her cheek against his beard as she inhaled the scent of his aftershave. 'I like th...is one much b...better than "Old Mice", David.'

'Why, thank you, I think.' He sniffed. 'You taste of sugar

and spice and all things nice but you aren't going to distract me.' He promptly proved the statement a lie by indulging in a kiss, but when they both came up for air said, 'Don't work too hard.'

Kate grinned. David was a casual housekeeper at the best of times. 'I hear you.'

David noted the twinkle in her eyes and whipped off her glasses to better enjoy kissing her some more.

Two days later Kate sat on the floor in the guest bedroom with an open box before her. The room was silent. More than an absence of noise, it was the silence of someone afraid of what they are going to find next.

She had been sorting the bundles into neat piles about the floor so that it looked like an exposed Roman hypocaust. One pile for the shredder in David's office, which had mainly paid bills and circulars in it; a second pile containing old policies, rent books and receipts from shops. A third pile had some of Kate's certificates from school: one for a reading prize when she was seven; a small bundle for swimming and one for the egg and spoon race. She had smiled and sniffed through a haze of tears. It looked like her mum had kept every award she had ever won. There were even some of her early drawings.

It was when she had come to the bottom of the box, and the final bundle, that she had been stunned beyond sentimental tears. It was a much smaller group of papers and it had birth and death certificates. Her father's birth certificate, registered in Newcastle upon Tyne by a Helen Nyman. Who was she? Kate scanned the paper. For the first time she discovered her father had been placed in a council-run foster home at birth, with parents unknown. Kate frowned at the piece of paper. How could you not know your own mother?

Fastened to these by a paperclip was the death certificate. She read the details: death caused by broken neck. She said the words and gave a faint shiver. Her father had been pushed into a deep pit on the archaeological site she and David had been working on. The young woman who'd pushed him had been sent to prison for seven years for his murder. It had been the best of times and the worst of times, she thought, for she had finally found out how much David loved her.

She laid the papers down and picked up the next set of paper-clipped certificates: her mother's birth certificate; more death certificates for Scarlett's parents. Both Scarlett's mother's and father's death had been registered by a Samuel Hamilton (son) down in Southampton: these appeared to be copies. Kate stared at the papers. Did she have an uncle out there whom she didn't know? No. He must be dead. Kate's lip twitched and twisted upwards as she recalled her mum saying, 'It's just you and me, Pumpkin. You're the last of the line.'

The next piece of paper was a lawyer's letter, dated when Kate was about six. Reading it, Kate frowned even more. The letter said there was a will enclosed. They hadn't found one at the time of the funeral, but Scarlett had told Kate she had no living relatives. She read on, trying to follow the spidery handwriting. *'A bigamous marriage is void: it is the same as if no marriage had taken place.'*

Why was her mum enquiring about bigamy? The sentence was obviously in answer to some question her mother had posed, but it didn't give a reason. Had she been married before, to someone who had still been married? It was giving Kate a headache trying to make sense of it all.

Kate reread the letter again, trying to take in all the facts. Scarlett had tried to get Kate's name officially changed to Hamilton.

'You can change her name to Hamilton. In fact, providing there is no intent to defraud, you can call yourself whatever you want. However, the child must use the name Jardin for all official documents for them to be legal.'

Kate mouthed the words and nodded. Jardin wasn't a good name to carry when your father had been convicted of murder and then been murdered in his turn. She frowned. He hadn't committed that crime when she was six, though. Still … he had been in and out of prison. *'You cannot adopt without permission. However, having…'* She shook her head over the paper, which ended mid-sentence, turning it over and looking at the blank back of the page in frustration. Perhaps her mother was trying to protect her from recognition, but who was she trying to adopt? If it wasn't Kate she didn't know who it would be. And if it was Kate, why? How much more legal did you have to be than giving birth to a child?

There was a certificate of marriage between her father and Scarlett Hamilton. The date made her raise an eyebrow. Ah, well; accidents happened sometimes. Kate laid the paper aside and looked off into a far corner of the room, only vaguely aware of the noises of the old house, while her active brain worked out what she'd just read.

She turned back to the box, searching through the remaining papers. She wanted the second page of the letter and the will that this solicitor said was enclosed. She tipped the box out and pulled up the bottom flaps to make sure nothing had slipped under them, then turned to the other papers strewing the floor – knocking over a pile and scattering others – but she knew she wasn't mistaken. This was the last box and she had brought all the paperwork from her mother's house after the funeral, even the till receipts and scraps of paper.

The solicitor's letter was full of the party of the first and second parts, clauses and sub clauses. Kate turned it over and the second page was still missing. She reread the page then sat staring at the print in her lap in a totally unfocused way, absently biting her bottom lip and frowning at nothing. She was struggling to understand the legalese but it was more than that which was troubling her. She could think of only one reason for her mother to try to adopt her own daughter. Scarlett hadn't been her mother.

Thea came into the spare room as Kate reached this horrifying conclusion. 'Kate, what are you doing? Master David's parents will be here in half an hour.' She smoothed down a tabard covered in swirls of paisley and looked about the cluttered floor.

Kate looked up, 'S…sorry, Thea. I'll c…clear a…way and c…come and give you a h…hand.' She looked at the grey hair surrounding a round face as wrinkled as a russet and tried to smile.

'Now, now, don't you go getting upset: it's only Paul and Ruth.' Thea bustled into the room. 'Leave all those papers for now and go and have a wash and comb your hair, and by the time you're ready I'll have cleared them up and have a nice pot of tea brewed.' Thea bent to gather up the first pile of papers from the floor.

'No.' Kate spoke sharply and when Thea looked at her with her mouth forming a round 'O' said, 'Sorry, Th...ea. I'll c...clear away the m...mess; I'm d...dirty already. I'll be d...own in a few m...minutes. You're r...right – they'll be h...here soon. Go and put the k...kettle on.' She softened her order with a smile.

Thea gave her a doubtful look and nodded. 'All right, but see you are only a few minutes. You didn't get a cuppa at eleven.' She left after another frowning look at Kate. She had been David's nanny and she saw no reason why she shouldn't look after his young wife and his children, too.

Kate stood waiting for the sound of Thea reaching the bottom step of the stairs, which always creaked like a clipper rounding the Cape. She began to put the paperwork back into the box when she was sure Thea was headed to the kitchen. The boxes were stowed in the bottom of the wardrobe and then Kate gathered up the rubbish to take down to the study.

She didn't know what she was going to do about this problem. But she was sure she didn't want to talk to David about it just yet. Not until she figured out just what the problem was, anyway.

MAY 2011

COUNTY GALWAY

'YOUR UNCLE SAYS "WILL you come for the funeral, Ben?"' The man who had spoken adjusted his cassock slightly over his knees and placed his hands on the desk in front of him. It was a small room given an air of lightness by the white plaster on three of the four walls. The fourth wall had a small glassed bookcase and a prie-dieu facing a crucifix that was hanging from a hook embedded in the paintwork.

The atmosphere was the comfortable sort found where men don't fear to keep silent. Beineon Aiden O'Connor was sitting in the Monseigneur's room looking at his mentor. The small, blond-haired twin brother of Kate had turned into a sturdy young man. The golden curls still remained but the matching brown eyes had a careful shuttered look to them these days, and the ready smile of the three-year-old Ben was rarely seen.

He had been summoned from silent prayer time to be told the news.

'I'm sorry, Ben. She died peacefully. She'd been to confession and taken communion and when she got home she said she was tired and she'd just have a little nap.' Father Joseph watched him carefully: here was a man who never showed much emotion. It would make him a good priest when it came to hearing the confessions, but Father Joseph wasn't sure it was going to make Ben a good human.

'Aye; well then, she will be with God.' Ben crossed himself and closed his eyes. Father Joseph nodded and closed his own eyes. The two men prayed for the soul of Ben's grandmother for a few minutes.

Father Joseph stirred and Ben opened his eyes.

Ben nodded. 'I'll go and pack.'

Four hours later he was standing in the kitchen of the only home he could ever remember, facing the two male relatives who were there. There was his *maimeo*'s chair and the big scrubbed table where she'd made bread and rolled out pastry and where everyone had dined. The blacklead stove was kicking out welcome heat after the hundred-mile journey. Ben felt his fingers tingle and his nose begin to run slightly after the chilly drive through the early spring morning.

He fished in a pocket and pulled out a square of cotton to wipe his nose as he looked around, finding it strange not to see his grandmother's bread rising, or her bustling about waiting for the kettle to boil. '*Uncail* Micheál, how are you?' He looked from uncle to grandfather as he tucked the cloth away again.

Micheál gave a smile with effort. 'We're managing, Ben.' He too looked around the room, ''Tis odd, her not being here. She ruled us all for so long that I hear her voice echoing in my head when I come in fouled from the dairy or the stable.' The smile went a bit crooked.

Ben nodded. 'Aye. Will we wake her?'

''Tis arranged. My Bridget has been baking and buying to do her proud before the funeral on Thursday next.'

Ben looked at his grandfather. Eoin seemed to have shrunk. He still wore his working cords and hobnails but they appeared too big for his frame. 'Daideó.' He went over and sat on the little stool that he'd used as a child. It was still near his grandfather's rocking chair, as if just waiting for his small former self to come and hear a story before bed. Ben took the rough hands in one of his. 'Can I do anything for you?'

'No. I must speak with you, Ben, now she's gone. I promised I wouldn't speak before, but now I must speak.'

'*Athair*.' Micheál shook his head, speaking a trifle sharply. 'It'll wait.'

'No. He needs to know before my Maeve is buried. He needs to seek her forgiveness, Micheál.' Eoin turned slightly in the old chair making it creak, and taking the other hand of his grandson and holding both tight. 'We need your forgiveness, too.'

Ben waited, returning the pressure from the old hands. Micheál shrugged and pulled out a hard chair from the side of the table, watching his father as he settled on the seat. The brown eyes of Micheál – so like Ben's – remained fixed on Eoin, while the sun-spotted hands of the older man clasped together and came to rest on his knees.

'Do you remember your *mamai*, Ben?' Ben looked from his uncle back to his grandfather as Eoin spoke.

Ben frowned. 'Not really. A scent of roses and gentle kisses. But the face, the voice? No, *Daideó*. *Maimeo* said she died when I was little and she took over the care of me. She wouldn't talk about Mam. I thought maybe 'twas too painful to have lost her daughter so young.'

Eoin nodded. Ben watched his grandfather brace himself. 'She wouldn't have us talk, either, for your *mamai* killed herself.' His grandfather reached out and gripped Ben's hands tightly, as he would have pulled away. 'Wait, now.' He watched the struggle, felt the denial and the need to find physical and mental distance.

'No, no. That can't be right, for isn't she buried in the graveyard and haven't I taken flowers every Easter and birthday?'

He might be old, but Eoin held on with a strength born of desperation until he saw the bunched muscles relax and the face of his grandson smooth out. He nodded. Ben had hidden his thoughts for many years; today would be no different.

'Micheál, put the kettle on.' Eoin looked at his son and waited for him to stand before he started to speak again. 'I loved your *máthair mhór* very much, Ben. But she was a hard woman. She had to be. We had a farm to run and, at first, both your great-grandparents to support and care for. We only had Micheál and Theresa. It was always a sadness to her that she had only given me two, but we would have struggled to cope with more.

'I loved your *mamai*. She was bright and beautiful and she wanted to see something of the world, so when she grew up we sent her to my relations in Liverpool to see would she like it in England. We thought she'd be safe there.'

Eoin nodded, as Micheál came and sat down again, waiting for the tea to brew. 'She met a man; she wrote and told us she loved him and that they wanted to marry.' He smiled. 'What could we say? She was old enough. But he was Protestant and they married in the register office. Your *mórai* never accepted it; said she wasn't wed to her face and would have cut her off.' He watched his grandson's face. It was stern and closed.

'Tess was pregnant and near her time when the man abandoned her. She didn't know what to do so she begged: would we take her in? For she had no money and nowhere to go. Your uncle and I went over to Liverpool and brought you all back.'

Eoin watched the word 'all' shape itself on the firm lips, but Ben didn't speak out loud.

'Theresa had you and your sister, Kate.' He licked his lips as Ben stood, shaking off the old hands, took two paces towards the door and then went over to the window … standing looking out onto the scrubbed yard but seeing nothing.

'I am sorry, Ben.' Eoin spoke to the rigid frame presented to him.

Ben swung back. 'I have a sister. Yes … I do remember.' He swung back to the window. 'I remember.' He spoke quietly, so that the two men almost strained to hear the words. He looked out on the familiar scene, hiding from his grandfather and uncle the pain swimming in the brown eyes. He saw in his mind's eye the two little children holding hands and giggling as they escaped the adults, scampering across the yard and running towards the hayloft for forbidden delights. Yes. He remembered. It was like someone digging out a splinter, long buried under a fingernail. The agony ripped through him.

Eoin looked at the stiff back, at the slightly over-long

blond hair curling at the nape of his neck against the clerical collar, and at the clenched fists.

Micheál stood and poured the tea and set the mug next to his father, then looked at Ben. 'We brought you back, Dad and I. You were good babies, but Tess couldn't cope. First she couldn't feed you both and then Mam was forever telling her how she'd brought shame to the house because she wasn't married.' He glanced at his father as he started to speak. 'No, *Athair*. If you want him to know, you must tell all of it. Come and sit down, Ben.' Micheál waited for his nephew to move. 'Come. No good will be served by standing there.'

Ben spun round. 'You knew. All these years and not once did you speak.' He looked from one face to the other. 'Not even a photo to show she existed. You hid her as if shamed by her very existence.'

'What purpose would it have served? You were happy.'

'Happy in my ignorance!' The bitterness could be tasted by the two older men.

'We did what we thought right, Ben. 'Tis no good you shouting at us. 'Tis too late to change things now.'

'Where is she now, my sister?'

Micheál shrugged. 'We don't know.'

'You ... don't ... know?' Ben spaced out the words and looked – aghast –from father to son, as if he didn't recognise them.

Micheál sighed. 'Let us finish the tale and then you might be able to understand and forgive us all.'

'Forgive?' Ben looked at his hands, at the bands of his clerical shirt, as one unsure of their meaning any more.

'Aye. Forgive. It's what you've spent four years learning about. What you want others to do. We're human, Ben: we make mistakes.' Micheál shook his head, growing impatient and angry himself.

'Your *máthair* married against Mam's wishes. She came home with the two of you and Mam had the looking out for you. Tess was never the same; it was what they call post-natal depression. But none of us understood it back then. She tried to take her life three times in this house; the last time she succeeded. Your sister Kate found her in the bathroom, half dead. My sister died within the week.' He watched as the colour leached from the cheeks of his nephew, leaving them ashen as he recited the bare facts.

'Kate was distraught by the event. We none of us could help her. She cried for her *mamai* and haunted the bathroom and Tess's room. Mam couldn't cope. We found an address for your *athair* among Tess's papers so we rang and asked him to come and take her; we thought it was for the best. To remove her from where it happened.'

Micheál pushed the mug towards his silent father. 'Your *daideó* didn't want to do it, but Mam had a way with her. Kate went and life went on. Dad phoned and Kate was all right. Your *athair* had a woman he lived with, and she was caring for the little one. She had started infant school up in Newcastle. But then we heard as how your *athair* was in prison … Lancashire way.'

Micheál picked up the mug and wrapped his hands around it to draw what comfort he could from its warmth, as Ben continued to stare stony-faced at him. 'We phoned to ask what had happened to Kate as soon as we heard the news, but the phone number belonged to someone else and no one knew where they had gone. I took time and went over and asked at the address, and the neighbours. But all we could find was that your *athair* was in prison.'

Ben still stood, but now he leaned back against the window, his arms and legs crossed. 'And what did you do then? To find my sister, my Kate?'

'What could we do? She had gone.'

'Fine. Then I'll go too.' Ben stood up and walked towards the door while the two men watched.

'Ben!' Micheál followed him to the door.

Ben kept walking; he walked to his car and climbed in, started the engine and left the cattle yard and the two men to grieve for a woman who had died and a boy who had grown

to a man before them that day.

MAY 2011

WHITBY, ENGLAND

THE YOUNG NUN WAS sitting at the side of the bed. She was specialling, as is the practice with all head cases at the hospice. Her patient hadn't been agitated even while unconscious but now she noted that he appeared to have dropped into a normal deep sleep. She checked his pulse and nodded her head. Without moving from her seat she pushed the call bell.

'He's moved into natural sleep. Will you inform the consultant, Sister?'

The sister who answered nodded and rustled away. She returned with a consultant. He was young and tired looking, his blue eyes serious as he nodded at the seated nun. He spoke quietly. 'How long?'

'About an hour ago now, sir.'

'Good; very good.' He waited for her to stand up and move to the side before gently holding the wrist and checking the pulse for himself. 'Yes, I think he's coming out of it. It's a shame we don't know who he is, Sister. Has there been any response from the police?'

'No, but it's only been a week. I think they were hoping for someone to come and claim him before they did any more. But he might be able to tell us himself now.'

'Let's hope so, Sister.' He stood looking at the rise and fall of the chest, monitoring the respirations. 'Let me know immediately of any changes. If he is stable we'll move him out to the nursing home for a few days. I think it's been exhaustion and malnourishment that's held him under for so long but we'll run a few more tests, just to be on the safe side.'

Antony Grey surfaced three hours later and looked at the nun sitting at the side of his bed in some astonishment.

'Hello.' She spoke quietly, even as her hand was reaching for the buzzer. 'Would you like a drink of water?'

Antony opened his mouth, which resembled the bottom of a parrot's cage, and was astonished at the rusty 'Yes' which came out.

She poured some ice cold water into a glass, with a pleasant chink as the ice landed, then offered him a straw to sip. 'Can you tell me your name?'

Antony looked at her, 'Antony.'

'Good. And your second name?'

He frowned, looking at the pretty face surrounded by a veil, and revealing a cluster of brown curls on her forehead. 'Grey.'

'Mr Grey, I'm Sister Patricia. You had an argument with a car and you've been sleeping for seven days now. Can you remember it happening?'

Antony shook his head. 'No, can't remember that.'

'Doesn't matter. Is there someone we can inform? We haven't known who you are, so…'

'I don't have anyone to inform, Sister.'

'That's all right. You can go to sleep again now.' Sister Patricia nodded as he obediently closed his eyes and instantly fell back into the arms of Morpheus.

The consultant – when he arrived a couple of hours later – listened to her comments carefully, while keeping a quiet eye on the sleeping Mr Grey. 'I'll inform the police. It gives them a place to start at least, Sister. Bloods and another scan, and if it's all clear he can go over this evening.'

'Very well, sir.'

Antony Grey was taken to the nursing home late that afternoon. He was settled into a private room, spartan as a monk's cell, and feeling as old as a centenarian. He lay back in his bed and promptly went back to sleep before the nuns could serve him supper.

The police came the next day, in the form of a Constable Britten. He had been born in this area of Whitby and had returned after completing his training. He was on the chunky side with a shaven head, one eyebrow covering both brown eyes and a friendly Geordie accent.

'Good morning, Mr Grey. I'm Constable Britten.' Antony had been arranged by one of the nursing sisters on a chair, in hospital issue pyjamas and dressing gown. They were a little on the large side and made him look as if he was wearing his big brother's clothes. 'Sister tells me you don't remember the accident, but we would like a few details – if you feel well enough to supply them.'

Antony nodded. 'I'll help if I can, Constable. Have a seat.' He waited for the young man to seat himself and pull out his notebook. 'How did I end up here?'

'You were admitted to the infirmary after a hit and run. This nursing order is a hospice-cum-convalescent home on the outskirts of Whitby town. You had no obvious injuries, so it was suggested that you might finish your convalescence here rather than blocking a critical bed.' He smiled nicely. 'You had your accident in Whitby so, since this is where we found you, we thought maybe...' He shrugged.

'The theory being that someone might come looking for me in a more local area.'

'Precisely, sir.' Constable Britten smiled.

'Unfortunately there isn't anyone to look, Constable.' The tone defied the constable to pity him.

Constable Britten nodded. What he felt stayed hidden behind his blank professional face. 'Be that as it may, sir, someone deliberately tried to run you down.'

'Me?' Antony couldn't have looked more startled if the young man had poked him with a stick. 'I'm an out-of-work academic; I don't see that many people. I certainly don't think I've offended anyone that grievously, Constable. I live a very solitary life.'

'Nevertheless, sir, I need a few details.'

Antony shrugged, supplying his address and occupation.

'I'm doing some independent research of my own; however, I do a little freelance work for other academics to supplement my dole money.'

'Can you give me a few names, sir?'

'I don't think they would want to run me down for inaccurate information, Constable.' He looked at the young man who sat, emulating The Thinker, as he waited for the information he'd requested.

Antony hesitated before saying, 'Professor Downey, Richard; he's at Cambridge. Professor Rawsthome, Joseph; he's over in Dublin at the university there. Professor Walker, David; he lives outside Carlisle. I can give you telephone numbers, emails or addresses. Which would you prefer?'

Constable Britten raised an eyebrow at the slight testiness. 'All three. Please.'

Antony shrugged again. 'Very well.' He reeled off the details.

'And what exactly were you doing for these gentlemen?'

'Mainly looking for references in obscure books to assist them in their research projects. Professor Walker is doing a desk survey for an archaeological site outside Whitby in the very near future. He was given my name because I've lived here for most of my life and might be presumed to have local knowledge. I haven't met the man myself. But I sincerely hope he will give me some work in the near future. The other two I know from college days. They found me some teaching work in the final year of my degree.'

'And who else do you see day to day, sir?'

Antony shook his head. 'The local shops, the post office … most nights I eat at the Five Bells. Amy, one of the waitresses, generally serves me and has a chat. That's the height of my social life, Constable.'

Constable Britten nodded, busily taking down the details. 'And you say you have no one who might have missed you?'

'My parents died at Gateshead one night, near midsummer, when I was still a preschooler. I can't even remember them. I've knocked around from one foster home to another until I went to uni. I got a scholarship.'

'Right, sir. And this Amy?'

'Amy is a pretty twenty-year-old who has taken pity on me, Constable. She definitely doesn't want to kill me off.'

A few more questions later, Antony's head felt as if the axe man had been practising on it, and Constable Britten was preparing to go. 'We'll be in touch, sir. If I might have your keys?'

Antony nodded again. 'They'll be in the wardrobe, in my jacket pocket.' He pointed in the general direction of the tall narrow cupboard set in one wall of the room.

Constable Britten stepped over and opened the door. The suit swung gently on a hanger, a pair of shoes underneath on the floor. He felt in the pocket and pulled out a leather key fob with two keys attached.

'And we have your permission to check around your premises?'

'I've said so. I don't think it will help you in your investigations but you're welcome to look.' A smile that was a wicked as sin suddenly flashed over his face, making Britten realise that Antony Grey was about the same age as him. 'You could check for my mail and get someone to bring it in. It's that thin key there.' He nodded at the keys in the constable's hand.

'I'll arrange it personally, sir.' He offered a grin back, 'We're here to serve the public.'

'Oh, yeah,' Antony sniffed.

'I shall call back tomorrow, sir.'

Antony watched the door shut and closed his eyes. Constable Britten set off along the corridor. He was going to follow up the information he had just gleaned. Forensics and witnesses both said that a car deliberately aimed at Antony Grey, knocking him down and speeding away. So, regardless of the young man's opinion, someone disliked him enough to – as Grey had said – try to kill him, and Constable Britten's superiors wanted to know who that was and to get them off the street.

The top floor flat, when he arrived at it, was cold and uninviting. He stood at the open door of the one-room apartment and looked over the scene carefully. He hadn't needed to use the key, for the door lock had obviously been forced. Unless Mr Grey was very absent-minded and had broken down his own door, someone had been in before him.

Britten's first thought – that it might have been trashed – was revised as he realised it was just the chaos of a man with lots of books and too little space to keep them in. But the place had been, to his experienced eye, turned over as well.

He went in and shut the door on what was obviously a shared landing and on the smell of the neighbours' boiling cabbage. Advancing to the desk, he pulled a face at the mug. It looked – and smelt – as if a mouse had died in the bottom of it. The table was strewn with open books and an A4 pad covered in scrawled handwriting. Britten bent and tried to read a few lines; he absently raised a hand and scratched his head as he scanned them.

He shrugged and looked around. There were a few spare clean clothes behind a curtain in the corner. A settee that obviously doubled as a bed; an unmade bed at that. A chest of drawers with the drawers pulled out to reveal tumbled undies and socks. A stainless steel sink with several teaspoons and three dirty mugs in the bottom and a shelf above it with tinned soup and beans.

Antony Grey was on the poverty line. A drawer in the table revealed a couple of bank statements that agreed. He was only just in the black. The electric was on a debit system; the social appeared to be paying his rent. BT was supplying him with broadband. Britten looked but could see nothing that might receive such a luxury.

Britten – after a final look around – went out, carefully locking the door behind him.

In the hall Stan Hunt, bête noire of Antony's council-run children's home, stood leaning against a doorway. He hadn't aged as well as Anthony, running to a paunch and a bald patch. He was unshaven and unashamed: the room behind him looked as chaotic as the room Britten had just left. It smelt slightly worse.

'Hi, Copper. What ya doin' here?' Stan Hunt shifted gum from one side of his mouth to the other and looked at Sergeant Britten.

'Do you live in these flats?'

'Yeah.'

'Know Mr Grey?'

'Yeah. Me 'n Tone go way back.'

'And your name?'

'Stanley Hunt.'

'When did you last see Mr Grey?'

Stan shrugged, 'I ain't his keeper.' He absorbed the stolid stare that would outwait a snake. 'Maybe last week sometime.'

'And didn't it occur to you that he might be in trouble, since he wasn't in his flat?'

'Nah. Tone does his own thing; thought maybe he was shacked up with that barmaid.'

'And you didn't see his picture in the paper as being injured?'

'Which paper? I only read the racing news.'

Sergeant Britten frowned. 'He has been injured and is in hospital.'

'I'll send flowers. Triffids.' And Stan Hunt stepped back into his room and slammed the door.

Well, there was one man who didn't like Antony Grey. Sergeant Britten noted the flat number and name before opening Antony's box. The postbox in the hall yielded up a handful of circulars, a bill for a book with book included and some obviously private letters.

He locked the box and pocketed the key and contents. Now for young Amy. Women didn't pity men of Antony's age and their interest was never platonic, in Britten's opinion. He wanted to see what was in it for her.

The pub gave him the address and his knock on the door was answered by, as Grey had said, a twenty-year-old. She also had a toddler on her hip.

'Nothing to worry about, Miss Watt. We're just making a few enquiries about a Mr Grey. We understand you are a friend of his.'

Amy nodded. 'I don't know where he is; he stopped coming for his evening meal a week ago.' She jiggled the toddler and looked at Britten suspiciously.

'Might I step in for a moment?'

Amy took a step back, nodding and holding the door open a bit more. She turned and led the way into a cluttered sitting room with toys scattered over the floor and an airer of washing in the bay window. 'Off you go, Joy.' She set the toddler down and then sat herself, looking at policeman curiously. 'Is Antony in trouble?'

'Not to say trouble, no. He was knocked down last week and sustained a serious concussion. He is improving now.'

'Oh! The poor man. Where is he?'

'Up at the hospice.' Britten smiled. 'Perhaps you can help him, and us. Mr Grey was knocked over deliberately. Did he talk to you about any arguments – or enemies – he might have?'

'What, Antony?' Amy shook her head, a smile slowly replacing the frown of concern. 'He's the softest thing. Half the time he doesn't know what day of the week it is. Always got his head in a book. He doesn't make enemies, or friends for that matter.' She shook her blonde locks again. 'Are you sure?'

'Very sure.' He watched as the smile vanished and she scowled at the washing while she thought about his words.

'Sometimes one or two of the locals get a bit annoyed with him, usually when they've had a drink or two. You know, trying to jerk his chain. He doesn't always know they're talking to him; never mind what they're talking about.' She looked back at the policeman with a half smile.

'Names?'

'Oh, but...' She scowled some more, absently picking up the toddler as Joy came over and scrambled onto her knee. 'I don't think they'd want to really hurt him but ... OK. Only you won't say I told you, will you? Or I'll get the sack.'

'We'll be very discreet.'

Amy nodded, giving the names of one or two troublemakers already known to Britten, before saying, 'Can I go and visit him?'

'I don't see why not,' Britten nodded his agreement. 'I wouldn't let anyone else know for the time being, though.'

'Oh, no, of course not.'

Britten left the house and walked down the garden path, reflecting that for someone who thought he had no enemies, Britten was beginning to acquire quite a long list of Antony's.

MAY 2011

CUMBRIA

DAVID CAME INTO THE kitchen of his home and nodded to his mother, who was washing mugs at the sink. He slipped an arm around his wife's waist as she stood stirring something deliciously aromatic at the stove. He stole a kiss from the nearest cheek and sniffed appreciatively. 'Hello, love. Had a good morning?'

'You sound like a starving wolf, David.' His mother half turned to look at him, offering a smile.

'P...Pops is in the s...study with P...Paul, David.' Kate accepted the kiss on her cheek but kept her eyes firmly fixed on her cooking.

David nodded. 'Yeah, I heard.' He kept the arm in place even while his wife wriggled slightly. 'All right, darling?' The question was asked so that only Kate heard.

She nodded. 'F...fine, but I n...need to get lunch r...ready. Can you s...set the t...table?' She half turned to him then looked back at the contents she was stirring without making eye contact.

David frowned, gave her waist another gentle squeeze and said, 'Sure.' But he knew something was going on. He glanced at his mum, who was busy at the sink again, then left to set the table with the dubious assistance of his sixteen-month-old daughter.

Lunch was a noisy affair. The twins weren't exactly expert with a spoon, and food tended to have aerodynamic properties when they attempted to feed themselves. The adults took turns to help and ducked to avoid flying peas and carrots. David did his share of assisting, but he was covertly watching his wife too.

Kate was aware of the scrutiny but did her best to ignore it. 'H...how was the journey, P...Pops?'

Paul Walker grinned, popped a spoonful of mush into the nearest open mouth and looked at his daughter-in-law. 'Well, given that it's the Friday of the May bank holiday, and that Ruth drives like a maniac, not too bad.'

His spouse of fifty-odd years gave him a gentle thump on the arm. 'My driving is fine, it's all the other mad people on the road, Paul.' She smiled across at Kate. 'Talk about back-seat drivers. I shall be glad when he gets his licence back. We're just waiting for the DVLA to send it.'

'How is the eye, Pops?'

Paul shrugged. 'It was a stupid accident, David. One minute I'm going for a brisk walk, the next I'm flat on my back and can't see a thing. And boy, did it hurt!'

His wife nodded. 'I felt such a fool filling in the insurance form: "hit by flying tree". But they paid up for the broken glasses, no bother, and the surgeon said there would be no lasting damage.'

David nodded, watching as Kate took over from his mother and carefully spooned puréed apple into his daughter's mouth. 'I don't like plastic lenses, they scratch too easily. But I'm almost tempted to get some given your accident, Pops.'

Paul took off his new glasses and looked at the lenses, before putting them back on. 'Yeah, I know what you mean. I don't have to wear them all the time now, thank God.' He looked at Kate busy wiping a pair of sticky hands. 'I thought you were going to try contacts, Kate? You were saying it might be easier when you were on site.'

Kate looked up from her task and smiled. 'I tried th...em. B...but they aren't w...worth the headaches, P...Pops.'

'Oh, shame! And you have such beautiful eyes, too.' Paul Walker grinned as Kate blushed, then winked at his son's scowling face.

David grunted, then gave a half laugh. What the hell was he thinking about if he could be jealous of his own father?

The children had been settled for their afternoon nap and the dishes stowed in the dishwasher before conversation of any import could be renewed. Paul started the conversation as he nursed his mug of coffee. 'So ... tell us about the work, David.'

David, lounging back on the settee with an arm around his wife, looked across to his father. 'It's an Anglo-Saxon site. Probably seventh century. We've got a partial skeleton, which young Grace is excavating for me. Not many finds to help the dating, though.' He took a sip of coffee and pulled Kate slightly nearer, his arm sitting snugly around her waist. 'Kate's done some beautiful drawings to go with the plans.' He sipped again and set the mug down. His hand moved to her shoulder and absently played with a curl.

'It's nice being married to someone in the same line of work. She understands when I trail mud into the house, or get so caught up chasing a clue I forget what time of day it is.' He smoothed down the red curl and rubbed his cheek against the soft hair.

'How much longer will you be working there?'

David wrinkled his nose. 'Tomorrow, and then the gang get a long weekend. Back on Tuesday, and we should close the site down next Friday. It's not a large area. Of course digging it up is only the start. I've got all the site diagrams and reports to write up.' He shrugged. 'But Kate has promised to help me with that, haven't you, darling?'

Kate nodded.

'So where are you going next, love?' Ruth Walker leaned back in her chair, and put her feet on a small stool, 'Oh ... that's nice.' She dropped her slip-on shoes off her feet and wiggled her toes, and then looked over her mug, waiting for David to reply.

'I have to fly to Germany to oversee a site; probably take about a month or six weeks collaborating with my German colleagues but the next big job is the one I've already started, unofficially.' He looked at Kate. 'It's that desk search for the area over near Whitby.'

'Oh, yeah. You p...promised me a trip to the s...sea...s... side. I m...might have guessed it would be w...work-c... connected.' Kate fought to say the words smoothly, without noticeable success. The hand that had been smoothing her hair started to gently knead her shoulder. 'I haven't b...been to the n...new s...site.' She looked across at her father-in-law. 'I've b...been to Newcastle, to see the Transporter B... bridge, of course. And during my p...post grad year I did that b...bit of excavation next to the b...bridge with you, David.'

David frowned, his hand continuing to soothe as he tried to remember, 'The Transporter Bridge. No, there aren't any Roman remains... Oh, Pons Aelius: the Swing Bridge.'

Kate nodded.

'They built the modern swing bridge over the old one, and that was built on the Roman site, Pops.' David nodded over at his father.

'I remember them changing the Swing Bridge.' His father nodded. 'The hydraulics are fascinating. It's just a shame they've switched from steam to electric.'

David agreed.

Ruth Walker set down her empty cup and bent to put on her shoes. 'You're a pair of Luddites. Kate, come and see the cardigans I made for the children. We'll leave these men to talk engineering.' Ruth smiled at Kate and watched as she stood up and came across the room.

David smiled at his mother as their eyes met. He gave her a slight nod. Something was troubling his wife. He'd find out, but if she needed a bit of space then she could have it. For now. His mother thought there was something wrong, too; he could tell. Perhaps Kate would confide in her. If not, then he would winkle it out of her. He loved Kate very much; he wished she could learn to trust him. It was hard being kept at a distance when you loved this much.

He pushed his worries to the side as he continued the discussion with his father. 'I'm only organising the watching brief in Germany. But I am worried about Kate. Something is troubling her, Pops.'

'We can go if it would be better for you, David.'

'No.' David exhaled softly. 'We both appreciate you being here. Maybe Mum can get to the bottom of things.'

'If we can do something you only have to say, David. We're very fond of your Kate.'

'Thanks. I love her to bits.' David grinned. 'I shall use you both shamelessly to get time with my wife.'

'Good.' His father offered an identical grin. 'Now what are you doing over in Whitby?'

MAY 2011

COUNTY GALWAY

BEN O'CONNOR HAD NEVER had a girlfriend; the only kisses he knew were those of his *maimeo* and his uncle's wife. He had gone from school to university to seminary. He had had it dinned into his ears for years that he must be pure. He was far from a saint. What he lacked was opportunity; what he had was a conscience. He eyed the girls at college but couldn't quite reconcile their flirting with his *maimeo*'s teaching, so kept his head down and avoided involvement.

He needed someone to share his pain and he looked around and found himself bereft of those he could share with, for they too were in silent agony.

He drove away from the border of Galway and Clare at a speed that might have seen him causing a serious accident anywhere else on the British Isles. But his grandparents lived in an area so remote that the narrow winding roads were frequented by nothing but leprechauns and the ghosts of the Celts. The soft Irish rain was soaking into the ground and turning the dark evening darker by the time he hit a road that saw the occasional car.

He was driving without thought; his mind filled with images of his childhood. It was only when the *Garda* pulled him over that he dragged his mind from the past to the present.

Ben pulled up the handbrake and wound down the window as the policeman approached; the rain soaked his face as he waited. The man was stocky and dark; he was frowning, but when he caught sight of the dog collar he lifted an eyebrow.

'I'm sorry, Officer. Was I speeding?'

'No, no, but 'tis dusk, near dark, Father. Would you be putting on your lights, please?'

Ben looked out at the scenery, the tree branches whipped about in the wind, mere charcoal etchings of themselves, and gave a half smile. 'I am sorry. I was deep in thought.'

'That's all right, Father. But save the praying for the church, not the road.'

'I'm inclined to think driving requires prayer too, Officer.'

'Perhaps you're right at that, Father.' The officer watched as Ben flicked the switch and the road in front of him sparkled in the headlights.

'Take it as a warning, Father.' He touched his cap and Ben nodded.

'*Tapadh leibh, Beannachd Leibh*, Officer.' He watched as the man walked back to his squad car and pulled out into the traffic, before winding up the window and pulling onto the highway again. He needed to get off the road for the night and find somewhere to think and sleep.

He found a bed and breakfast on the outskirts of a small town. The woman was thrilled to be putting up a priest and Ben's lips twisted wryly at her effusive reception of his request for a bed.

The room was modern and comfortable. Ben walked across it and opened a French door on to a little balcony overlooking a field of horses. He could see them moving, silent as grey ghosts against the foreshortened horizon. He heard the musical gurgle of a river and caught the occasional glint of water in the starlight. He left the window open to feel the fresh breeze and hear the patter of the rain on the railing outside.

He unpacked his night things and looked at the single divan. Its cosy covering had him considering the thought of just climbing into bed and burying his head under the covers, but that wasn't going to solve his problems.

He was just unpacking his toiletries and heading for the en suite when there was a knock at his door and his hostess popped her head around, without waiting for his reply.

'Will you take a bite, Father? Or I've hot chocolate or Horlicks?'

'No, thank you. It's been a long day and I just want an early night.'

'Breakfast at eight-thirty then, Father.'

'Thank you. Goodnight.' Ben stood waiting, looking at the closed door and listening. He heard her shoes as she walked heavily downstairs. He turned the key in the lock quietly and sat down in the one easy chair, its chintz cover a riot of huge roses all running together. Thoughts of a wash slipped away as easily as the water would have gone down the plughole.

He closed his eyes and folded his hands in his lap, sitting perfectly still but far from relaxed, inhaling the smell of rain, polish and fresh bed linen.

'What the hell am I going to do?' He spoke out loud and was almost shocked at the harshness of his own voice. He took a deep breath and started to speak softly. 'Lord, there is no forgiveness in me for them. All I feel is hurt and anger, bitterness and guilt.' He opened his eyes and looked at the black sky outside through the open door; it felt as if he was looking inside himself.

'Kate, I'm so sorry that I forgot about you. I'm sorry you were sent away, I'm sorry you missed out, I'm sorry we didn't search for you ... that they treated you like a shameful secret. But I will find you, Kate.' It was a vow.

He leaned back in the chair, remembering. Remembering the little girl with the golden curls and the deep brown eyes which had sparkled at him. He tried to bring her face into focus but it kept slipping away and merging with other small children he had known.

What had Kate's life been like ... her father in prison ... her mother dead ... and some woman looking after her? Would the woman have put her in a home when her meal ticket was imprisoned?

His father was a jailbird. What had he done to be sent to prison? Was it a white-collar crime – fraud or tax evasion?

Was it violent? Theft? Murder? Ben shuddered. That blood ran in his veins: son of a criminal and a woman who had killed herself.

He looked at his hands resting in his lap, imagining them giving a blessing, a blessing tainted by his heritage. He shuddered again and buried his face in them. How could he offer others absolution when he couldn't absolve himself of the taint that marred his own life?

He sat on through the small hours, thinking about his youth. For the most part it had been good. He was the spoilt darling of his *daideó*. The only child in an adult world for a good few years, he had enjoyed many liberties. There had been toys and time for him. He was praised when he succeeded at school, whether in the classroom or on the football pitch.

But it had come at a price. Instant and utmost obedience. Yes, he had received the odd clout from the males in the family for a misdemeanour, but worse than that was the sorrowful looks and the lectures from *Mórai*.

Guilt was his constant companion, guilt for thoughts, commissions and omissions. As he grew he realised that far more was expected and demanded of him than of his cousins. He hadn't known why until now. Now he thought he had the key.

No wonder his *mórai* had insisted on his attendance at church. He had heard her speaking about men and women who defied their God and sinned. She had seemed hard and unforgiving at times, but no wonder. She probably thought he was her punishment for sinning. She was trying to cleanse him from sin by sending him to church.

He had gone from choirboy to altar boy, always trying to please her. And he had; he knew he had. By the time he was ten he knew that his *mórai*'s dearest wish was for him to take Holy Orders. He hadn't really questioned it. He was comfortable with the rhythms of the church year; he accepted unquestioningly the God of his *mórai* – a God who loved him – but expected only the best from him; a God who punished mistakes.

He was due to start as a deacon in a few weeks' time. He shook his head. He thought he had his life mapped out and now... Now he wasn't even sure if he believed in his *mórai*'s God, a God he was supposed to be serving. If his *mórai* could lie and conceal the truth for years, ignore a grandchild, drive her daughter to suicide, then what kind of God had she served and did he want anything to do with Him?

But to ignore God ... that made a mockery of the last twenty years. He was truly cast adrift. He looked around the quiet room and wondered again what he should do.

WHITSUN 2011

CUMBRIA

'You need time to talk to each other, don't you? We won't interfere but we want you to be happy, so let us care for the children and you can take some time for yourselves.' Ruth Walker looked from her son to her daughter-in-law and back. David had returned from the dig at lunchtime on Friday to find his parents settled in and his wife somewhat *distraite*.

As his mother spoke for both parents, David looked startled and Kate horrified. 'I'm s...sorry if we've m...made you uncomf...ortable.'

'You haven't, Kate. We've just become aware that something is troubling you both, and it isn't easy getting time for each other when you have to work and the children are so small.'

David looked from his parents to his wife and went to sit on the side of her chair, putting an arm around her and holding her close before speaking. 'You're right, Mum. We could do with a little time to ourselves, much as we love the babies.' He looked down at Kate. 'Kate won't admit it, but they wear her to a frazzle at times.'

He shook his head at his wife's stifled, 'No, they d...don't.'

'Yes, they do, love.' He looked across at his father, watching him. 'We'll leave them with you this afternoon and go for a drive, discuss our options. It's good of you to offer and we accept. Don't we, Kate?'

Kate looked at her husband. His lips smiled but the emerald green eyes were deadly serious and they were not about to

82

brook any arguments. She sighed gently. It seemed her time was up, ready or not. She stood up and followed him out of the room after murmuring her thanks.

A SHORT TIME LATER David and Kate were to be found walking up some stone steps. They led up the side of a stone keep towards some battlements; he was holding tightly to Kate's hand and swinging it gently.

'It's quiet h...ere, isn't it, David?'

David smiled. 'Oh, it can get busy in the summer; but this early in the year we can have the place pretty much to ourselves.' He reached the top of the flight and stepped forward towards the parapet overlooking the old gun emplacements. They had come to Carlisle Castle because David knew his Kate; she would argue and avoid and try to blind him with words. He recognised the tactics; he used them himself. But he didn't want her to feel trapped, either. Here in the open air she might feel free enough to open up to him.

He smiled down at the curls tossing in the light breeze and suddenly picked her up and swung her onto the greensward – grass that helped to maintain the stability of the crumbling mortar – on the inner curtain walls of the castle. He hoped he could maintain her inner stability, too. But he was also determined to find out what was wrong.

'Oh!' From her seated position Kate was on an eye level with her husband. 'It's a good j...job I've got j...jeans on.'

'And very nicely you fill them too, my love.' David smiled wickedly at her.

'You c...can see right over the c...city from here.' Kate held back a few errant curls and twisted around to look off into the distance, ignoring her husband's eye. She didn't think he had brought her here to flirt, and anyway she really wasn't in the mood.

'Yeah, it's a great view. You can imagine the poor sods on sentry duty, marching along here and seeing their attackers advancing from miles away. They got plenty of warning.'

'You m...mean like you're doing with m...me, love?' Kate turned her back on the scene and faced her husband.

David took the hands in front of him. 'I love you, Kate.' He twisted the gold band around on her wedding finger before looking up. 'I love you, wildly and passionately ... and you're hurting, love, and that hurts me. Can't you tell me what's troubling you? I thought it was just grief from your mum. But it's not that, is it? Is it the new job?'

Kate bit her lip, looking back over the panorama of the city before turning back to her husband. 'It's true; I am a b... bit worried about this new d...dig. I'm going to miss you d... dreadfully and so will the b...babies, but it's no w...worse than other w...women have to face. If you were in the s... services, I'd have to f...face s...separation a lot more often.'

She paused and took a deep breath, trying to overcome the damn stutter that was giving her away every time she opened her mouth. 'And it's not as if you c...can't c...come home at the w...weekends. Germany isn't that far away. I c...could get a p...passport, and then I can even c...come over and visit you. It's only six w...weeks at the most.' She gave him a smile that barely lifted her lips. 'I'll b...e all right.'

'Very true, my Kate.' David raised the hands he still held and kissed the ring. 'So if you've got as far as working that out, then it can't be what is troubling you so much.' The emerald eyes glinted at her. 'So I think you'd better "'fess up", love, or I will be imagining all sorts of other things.'

Kate opened her mouth to deny his deductions, but David only smiled and shook his head. She pulled one of her hands away and smoothed down the beard then ran a finger over his lips. 'It's j...just ... I don't quite know w...what to do.'

David turned his head slightly and kissed the soft palm. He waited for her to come to the point.

'You know that I s...started to go through m...my M... Mum's papers earlier in the w...week.'

'Yeah. I said I'd go through them with you, love. You don't talk much about the past, Kate, but if there's a problem...' He paused. 'Had she got some debts, Kate? We can pay them off, love. Don't fret.'

'No, it's not th...at. Actually there's a p...policy I th...
ink will cover what w...we p...paid for her f...funeral.' Kate
sniffed, and David could see the tears gathering.

'Come on, love, out with it.'

'I don't know wh...ere to st...art. Th...ere's several th...
ings, David.' Kate paused, scowling through her glasses at her
husband. David waited. He had looked through some of the
papers already when they had gone to register the death and
thought he knew what was coming.

'I c...couldn't f...find a w...will.' Kate sniffed back more
tears, 'I f...found a letter from a s...solicitor. It said there was
a c...copy of her w...will enclosed. So th...ere is one s...
somewhere, David.'

David frowned. That hadn't been what he was expecting.
'You're her only living relative, Kate. A will isn't that much
of an issue.' He smiled a bit crookedly. 'She had less than five
thousand in the bank, love.'

Kate nodded; they had enquired about probate but at less
than five thousand pounds no probate was required. She took
a deep breath. 'I found her m...marriage licence to my f...
father as well; they didn't get m...married until 1986.'

David gave a light shrug, mentally bracing himself; he'd
known about that – seen the certificate by accident and been
aware his Kate would figure out the meaning eventually –
but he hadn't said anything, hadn't wanted to. It didn't affect
his love for Kate. 'These things happen in the best-regulated
families. I don't care if they were a bit late tying the knot and
nor should you, darling.'

'No; you d...don't understand, D...avid. She wasn't m...
my m...mother. She was my s...stepmother. At least I th...
ink she was.'

David raised an eyebrow. 'Think?' he felt slightly winded.

'He m...married Scarlett H...Hamilton in '86. I was b...
born in '84. I think she was tr...ying to adopt me.'

'Oh.' David paused. 'Oh, I see.' He paused again. 'At least
I think I do. Why couldn't they just have been a bit late with

the ceremony, love?' He paused, looking at the serious eyes watching him.

'I don't know, b...but she was trying to adopt s...someone and I th...ink it was me because the s...solicitor's letter said I had to be called Jardin for all legal p...purposes. And that you c...couldn't be adopted without c...consent. I thought she was just t...rying to p...protect me by giving me her m...maiden name, but if I wasn't hers... she w...would have to adopt.' Kate took a deep breath, 'B...but the real question is...' Kate scowled fiercely to hide her emotions 'w...why did m...my real m...mother leave my father and me?' She turned away and looked out over the city again.

David frowned, trying to make sense of what she'd told him. 'Scarlett loved you, Kate, whether she was your real mother or not. She took care of you, and she had custody of you while your father was in prison. I met her; she loved you, and she was proud of you.

'We've only talked about your childhood a little bit, but I thought that was because you were ashamed of your father. I don't care about that; you know I love you. We got to know each other when he was murdered, Kate, and if I'd wanted to avoid you then would have been the time.' He tried to see Kate's face but she was hiding away from him again. 'You shall show me this letter when we get home, but maybe Scarlett was just trying to protect you from gossip, love.'

'There's worse.' She looked back at David, 'I don't know wh...ich of them it was, but Scarlett was enquiring about bi...gamy too. I think maybe my f...father was m...married before he m...met her. I'm not sure; it could have b...been someone Scarlett tried to m...marry, or was still m...married to. It's all a bit confusing.'

She looked out over the vista of hills towards Scotland, then brought her gaze back to her frowning husband. 'There are no divorce p...papers. I ch...ecked on the n...et. You c...couldn't get div...orced that q...quickly in the eighties. No "qu...ickie" divorces b...back then. The s...solicitor's letter s...stops half way through a s...sentence.' Kate by this time was struggling to get her own sentences out coherently, too.

David rubbed his nose to hide the smile. He wasn't quite quick enough.

'D...avid, it isn't f...funny.' The tears glittered on her eyelashes.

'I know it isn't, Kate. But your father certainly knew how to muddy the waters, didn't he, love?'

Kate sighed and offered a small smile. 'I suppose b...bigamy's not that b...big a deal, when c...compared to the theft and m...manslaughter he did time for.'

'So, what do you want to do, Kate?' David smiled a bit wryly. 'Do you want to find out if Scarlett was your mother? Do you need to know why she left him, because I should think that was obvious?'

'It's not wh...y Scarlett left my f...father, David. But if she wasn't my m...mother, why did my m...mother leave me? New b...babies are nearly always given into the c...custody of the m...mother. Wh...y didn't she w...want me?'

David lifted her down off the wall and pulled her into his arms. He used his thumbs to brush away the tears swimming in her eyes and beginning to trickle down her cheeks. 'I don't know, love, but if she exists she must have had a good reason ... but let's not torture ourselves until we're sure. OK? Hush, Kate.' He pulled a handkerchief out of his pocket and mopped efficiently. 'You are the best thing to have happened in my life, Kate. If you need to know, we'll set things in motion.' He held her away slightly. 'You might not like the answers, Kate.' He wiped away a stray tear from her nose with a long forefinger. 'Whatever we find out isn't going to affect how much I love you. You know that, don't you?'

'Yes, but w...what if our c...children...? What if Scarlett...? What if my real m...mother was as b...bad as my f...father?'

'What are you imagining, that little Paul will turn into the mad axe killer because of a few stray genes?' David grinned. 'I'll have to tell you a bit more about my infamous youth, love.' He tucked her hand through his arm and began a gentle stroll around the battlements. 'Let us make plans, Kate. We can talk to my parents – not the details, if you don't want them to know – just ask them to babysit, and we'll go down to Salisbury. It's where you lived with Scarlett, so it's the best place to start. We'll ask around … see if we can't chase a few leads. OK?'

'Yes, David.' Kate rubbed a finger under her nose like a small child. 'I love you, too.'

'Good.' He gave a quiet sigh of satisfaction. She didn't tell him that anywhere near often enough. He noted the stutter had receded. Action, he thought: that was the best thing, to stop his Kate worrying herself silly.

They were walking towards the car park and away from Carlisle Castle when Kate suddenly stopped in her tracks. 'David, if I'm not her d…daughter, I sh…ouldn't have taken her th…ings.'

David looked down at her; she was biting her lip and scowling at the railway line in the distance.

'My darling girl, who else would have them?'

'But the m…money.'

'If we find a stray relative they can have the money. But she was the only mother you had and she would want you to have the things you both grew up with.'

David tucked her hand through his arm, linked her fingers, then began to walk towards their car. 'You shall show me this letter. If there was a copy of a will, then there should be the genuine article somewhere. The chances are the solicitor has it. OK?' He looked down on the curls blowing in the breeze and gave the fingers a squeeze.

'OK.' But it was clear Kate was still worrying. 'Are we m…married, David?'

David gave a chuckle, 'Very much so, my love.'

'No, I m…mean, if I gave the w…wrong name at the c… ceremony are we m…married?'

'But you didn't, Kate. You proclaimed yourself. Katherine Róis Jardin. That was your legal name.'

Kate sighed. 'OK. Can we just ch…eck? I want to be m…

married to you.'

'Whether we have the bit of paper or not, Kate, you are my wife. I have taken you in the sight of God and the congregation.' David swung her around as they arrived at the passenger door of the big Land Rover Discovery. He wrapped both arms around her waist and held her close for a minute, just breathing in her unique scent and feeling her warmth seeping across the barrier of their clothes. 'You're mine. And don't let anyone tell you different.' He bent his head and kissed her deeply, regardless of the public venue, then opened the car door and waited for her to get in.

Kate sat down and looked at him holding the door for her. This was her David. He would sort things out. She sighed quietly and smiled at him; it quivered a bit on her lips, but it was a smile.

They talked on the journey home, and decided that his parents would be more help if they knew what was going on. After that things moved rapidly. David rang around and found a hotel. Kate voiced worries about how much it must be costing him to find a hotel on May bank holiday at such short notice. But David said you couldn't put a price on peace of mind and swept on with his plans as unstoppably as an express train.

JUNE 2011

WHITBY

SHE'D BROUGHT GRAPES AND a sleeping toddler in a pushchair. Antony Grey watched as Amy Watt advanced in the manner of a small invading horde. He looked in astonishment and a certain degree of confusion as she came to a halt in front of him. He struggled to stand up from the deckchair, his rise so rapid that he nearly overbalanced and rapped his shins hard against the chair leg.

'Amy.'

'Hello, Antony.' Amy put the buggy's brake on and placed the grapes in the hand outstretched to shake hers. Having arrived she felt, all of a sudden, shy. She looked around to avoid his eyes, 'It's nice out here, isn't it?' She subsided cross-legged on the grass, looking at him as he all but fell onto his seat again, clutching rather desperately at the grapes and suddenly very aware of the borrowed stripped pyjamas and dressing gown the nuns had loaned him. He muttered something inarticulate about the bees and then felt a total fool as Amy said, 'Eh!'

'Doesn't matter. Why have you come, Amy?'

Amy grinned, showing a nice dimple and crooked top teeth. 'What a question; it's what friends do. You're in hospital, I visit.'

'Are we friends?'

Amy sobered. 'I thought so.' She began to push herself upright.

'I'm sorry; that was a stupid thing to say. Don't go.'

She sat down again slowly and began to pluck blades of grass from the nuns' lawn. The silence grew uncomfortable before she said, 'The police came. I didn't know you'd been knocked over. They said it was a hit and run, only deliberate.'

Antony heard the question but shook his head. 'I can't believe anyone would want to mow me down. I think it was just an accident, or a drunk, or maybe one of these hoodies. I'm not the sort that gets anyone worked up enough about to want to kill me.'

Amy shrugged. 'They seemed very sure. They said I could come and visit, but only after they'd talked to my boss and everyone at the pub.'

'I seem to be causing a deal of bother for you.'

''Tain't no bother. I like you, Antony. You treat me like a human being. I get fed up of being treated like something beneath their notice by these self-righteous sods, just because I've got Joy.' She glanced at him and then at her sleeping daughter. 'You don't touch, either. Just because I have her it doesn't mean I'm an easy lay.'

Antony shifted uncomfortably in his seat. He looked at her sitting on the grass. She didn't look old enough to have a two-year-old daughter. 'I don't want to offend you – and I know it's not politically correct – but actually I admire you for keeping her and I never thought you were a "lay", easy or otherwise.'

She grinned, the freckles on her cheekbones beginning to hide among the slight redness. 'No, you don't; you hardly notice I'm a woman, but that's all right. It's kinda nice.'

The silence this time was restful. The scent of a few tulips in a nearby bed was wafted to the pair and the sun was quite warm on their bodies. When the conversation started again it was about his research. 'I'm a bit worried that Professor Walker won't employ me if I'm not available. I wrote to him the day I got knocked over.' He gave a wry grin. 'He's supposed to be my ticket to a better flat. One with two rooms.'

'It's horrible having to scrimp and save, ain't it? I'm lucky my mum will look after Joy for me, night times. She's been really good; my dad nearly had a fit when I got pregnant at seventeen. But she said it wasn't just my baby, but their grandchild, and they would support me.' She looked him full in the face. 'I was stupid; I got drunk at a party and then found I was pregnant. I dunno who the father was.'

'We're all stupid at seventeen. It's part of growing up. Girls bear the consequences though; boys can walk away scot-free.' He glanced at the chubby child. 'I don't know much about babies, but she seems a nice wee thing.'

'She's beautiful and I love her to bits. I'm not sorry I kept her. But it is hard sometimes.' She watched as he looked over her daughter in the manner of a horse-coper sighting a pretty filly. 'I could go and get your post if you want me to; see if this professor's written to you. You could write and tell him you got hurt and that you're getting better.'

He thought about his one room, and the mess he'd left it in, and squirmed a bit more. He was saved from answering, however, by the stately entrance of Constable Britten, who strode across the neatly trimmed lawn towards them.

'Mr Grey, your post.' Several envelopes and a book from Amazon were laid gently in Antony's lap, along with the keys.

Antony looked up into a face all shadows and darkness, with the sun forming a halo behind, and thought incongruously of saints. 'Thank you very much, Constable. I appreciate it.'

'I understand you are expected to be here for four more days, sir. Is there anywhere you can go when you are discharged?'

Antony looked at him, surprise rippling over the surface of his cheeks. 'Well ... home, I suppose.'

'I wouldn't advise that, sir.'

'Well ... advised or not ... I haven't a lot of choice, Constable.'

Britten looked from Amy, sitting on the grass, to the man in the deckchair. 'Shall I go away?' She prepared to rise.

'No, it's all right, Amy. What's wrong with me going home? Have the council chucked me out or something?'

'No, sir. But someone had been in your room, we think.

92

Nothing was taken, as far as I could tell, but the drawers had been rifled and left open.' Britten gave a soft cough. 'Unless, that is, you left them that way.'

Antony frowned. 'Untidy, yes, but ... what do you mean, rifled?'

'Well, pulled out and the clothes tumbled. Stacks of books on the floor and not on the shelves. I don't know if you kept valuables but there weren't any electrical goods about. It just had the look of being turned over, sir. You get a – a feeling for these things.'

'Bugger. No computer?'

Britten shook his head.

Grey folded his lips on the next curse that wanted to escape, and looked down at his clenched hands before looking back up at the looming constable. 'I had a very ancient computer. It isn't worth much. The software is so out of date it isn't compatible with most of the things I'm trying to look up, but it was better than nothing at all.'

'Anything else?'

'A small radio; didn't work ... it wasn't digital. A toaster and a two-ring hob. There wasn't any money; what I've got is in my pocket.'

'Then I'd say you'd been turned over for sure, sir. I'll alert the CSE to run fingerprints. It might just be opportunism.' Britten nodded at Amy. 'Have you been to Mr Grey's room?'

'No. He's just a friend. I told you.'

Britten felt his cheeks warm a bit at the indignation in her voice. 'I meant no offence, Miss Watt; it was only so that we could eliminate your fingerprints if necessary.'

'There shouldn't be any fingerprints but my own, Constable Britten.'

'Fine, sir. We'll get on to it.' He backed away with a final sketchy salute and the pair watched him walking rapidly back across the lawn and disappear through a side door.

The silence he left behind was as fragile as angel cake. Both parties were digesting various thoughts and ideas. Amy was realising that this man she'd befriended was so solitary that no other fingerprints would be found in his room. She thought it was really sad and she was glad she'd come to visit, even if he was as prickly as a hedgehog.

Antony Grey was wondering how he'd manage to replace any of his meagre equipment but especially the computer, which was his lifeline to work. He stared at a weeping willow just coming into bud and scowled.

The reverie was broken by Joy waking up with a small squawk. 'I'll have to take her home. She gets cranky if she doesn't get her lunch on time.'

Antony, returning to the present, watched as she stood and got to his own feet. 'Thank you for coming, Amy. I do appreciate it.' It was very formal and Amy pulled a face as she glanced at her daughter, then she nodded to herself.

'I'll come again if you want.' She leaned over and gave him a gentle peck on his cheek. 'It's what friends do.'

He smiled and nodded, standing to watch her go through the same door as the constable had left by. Then his hand crept up and rubbed softly against his cheek where the kiss, light as thistledown, had landed. He sat down and looked at the letters in his hand.

The large white envelope was addressed to him in a scrawled hand. He thumbed open the flap and extracted a letter from David Walker. He still had a job. How the hell he was going to do it was another matter. A second letter had his name and address printed in black felt tip; it contained lined paper from the makers of Basildon Bond. The print owed its origins to *The Sun* newspaper: GET OUT OF TOWN OR NEXT TIME YOU WON'T JUST HAVE A HEADACHE. He stared at the paper for several minutes before rising and walking unsteadily towards his room. He just didn't get it. Who could want to harm him? He didn't know enough people to offend anyone.

JUNE 2011

COUNTY GALWAY

Ben was seated yet again in the quiet study of his father confessor. 'I walked out on them, Father Joseph. I know well I should have stayed, but my mind was set all on end by the news.'

No one had questioned his whereabouts or his actions. He had been welcomed and his request for an interview granted straight away. He had sat, hands dangling between his legs and head looking at the hands, while he'd poured out his troubles uninterrupted.

'Well, now, and that's understandable, Ben.' Father Joseph looked compassionately at the young man before him. Ben needed a shave and he didn't look as if he'd eaten anything, or slept, since he had left the comforts of the seminary three days before.

He had arrived back this morning just before lunch time. Father Joseph lifted his chin to the mug of coffee before Ben. 'Have something to drink, then close your eyes for a moment while I pray about this.'

Ben's lips twisted wryly, 'I daren't. For I'll fall asleep if I do, and I've been dogged by the nightmares since I spoke with my *teaghlach*. Have they ... have they been in contact with you?'

'Well, your family were concerned for you, lad.'

Ben opened his mouth, then closed it again on the harsh words that wanted to escape. Father Joseph watched the internal struggle with pity and sympathy.

'Sit quiet, then, while I think and pray a bit.'

Ben sat, his hands wrapped around the mug, taking some of the warmth into himself. It had rained for the last three days and he didn't think he'd ever be warm again. His eyes were fixed on the crucifix on the wall, but he couldn't pray. He'd tried. Words started to rattle around in his head like the echo chamber of St Paul's as soon as he stopped concentrating on physical tasks.

Five slow minutes passed. The Father's brown and wrinkled hands rested gently against his black cassock. He too was looking at the crucifix. Eventually he withdrew his gaze and looked at the young man in front of him, whose hands were now twitching restlessly on his own cassock-clad knees.

'You've never been in the desert before, have you, lad? Your faith was the faith you were taught, not the one you worked out for yourself. 'Tis a lonely place, the desert, both by its nature and its vastness. You need time to come to terms with it. Our Lord struggled there, so he knows what you're experiencing.' He held up a hand as he saw the lips part for a word. 'I know you're due to start your retreat – before you take up your place as a deacon – but I think you need a sabbatical, not a retreat.' He reached out and laid one of his gentle hands on the restless ones, stilling them.

'Now this is what I'm going to recommend. You should go to England and search out your sister. You'll never be easy in your mind until you know she's safe and happy.' He smiled, and his brown eyes twinkled a bit. 'I might as well send you as have you go without my blessing.

'You can go in mufti or with the collar; it's up to you. Perhaps you need to take it off and see how it feels to be "normal".' Father Joseph put 'normal' in inverted commas with his fingers. 'And while you're finding your sister, maybe you can find yourself and the Lord again. He hasn't gone away, Ben. He's just giving you a chance to feel what it's like without him. You never value a thing until you haven't got it any more, lad.'

Ben nodded. 'I want to go, but I'm a bit afraid of what I'll find.'

'You'll find peace – whatever else you find – if you give God a chance. Now, to practical matters. Have you enough funds?'

Ben half smiled. 'Aye, I've more than enough in the bank for my needs.'

'Where will you start this adventure?'

'We were born in Liverpool, according to my birth certificate. I'll see can I find the electoral rolls and a neighbour who might know more. My uncle said my father was in prison in Lancashire. I'll go to the *Garda* over there and see if they can tell me which prison and what for. They might be able to tell me where he's living now. I'm told they keep track of jailbirds.' Father Joseph felt the bitterness spewing with the words.

'You are not your *athair*. You know right from wrong, Ben.' It was a softly spoken warning. Father Joseph saw the bitterness as well now, as it crept onto the young face. 'Whatever your *athair* did, he's paid for his crime. Forgiveness, son: that will be your first lesson. Forgive him and forgive yourself, for you didn't send your sister away.' He watched as Ben lifted sorrowful eyes to him. 'I'll give you a note for the convent near Liverpool; you can stay in the guest house there if you want, while you carry out your investigations.' Father Joseph was a pragmatic pastor and used this role to help the many young men who had passed through his hands.

Ben nodded.

'Go and pack and then have something to eat and I'll see you on your way. You can get the ferry across from Dublin to Birkenhead tomorrow.'

Ben bent as Father Joseph laid a hand on his head and offered a prayer for a safe journey.

He travelled away from the seminary as the rain eased, and found himself lodgings near the ferry terminal. He'd managed to book the car on the 7 30am sailing, so went to his bedroom as soon as he'd eaten a couple of sandwiches.

He settled in yet another chair of the overstuffed variety

found in bed and breakfasts and pulled out a notepad. He began to make notes of the facts he had so far.

He and his sister were born in Liverpool. That's where they had been collected from by his grandfather and uncle. He could speak to his relatives there. He had met some of them at weddings and funerals; they were scattered broadside over the city. He paused, wondering how many knew about his twin sister and hadn't said anything about it. He scowled. Hadn't they known, or had his grandmother forbidden them to speak? There were a couple of old aunts who might remember events. He'd only met them once; he would trade on the collar for those interviews and hope that guilt might work now that Maeve O'Connor was dead.

Kate had been living in Newcastle with their father before he went to prison. Maybe the police would know where. He could ask when he tried to find his father's prison records. She might still be in the area if 'the woman' with whom he was living had dumped her in a home when his father went to prison. He would ask around for children's homes in the area to see if they could supply him with details. Ben nodded to himself. He was beginning to get a plan together.

He looked at his Bible. His grandmother had given the black leather book to him when he entered the seminary. He had lifted it from the case automatically when he unpacked. He shook his head. Tomorrow he would buy a new one – one with no taint of memories – until he could look those memories in the face again.

JUNE 2011

SALISBURY, ENGLAND

'WELL, THAT'S THE ADDRESS, Kate. Shall we go and knock on the door?'

Kate nodded. She could only dimly remember the house now that she was standing at its gate.

'They might not remember. People move more often these days.'

'I kn...ow, David. But it's the only lead w...we have at the m...moment.'

'Come on, then. Courage, my Kate.' They got out of the car and crossed the street, knocking on the door of the address listed on the solicitor's letter.

The young woman who answered was clutching a tea towel in one hand and had a small toddler wrapped around her hip. 'Yes.' She blew her fringe off her forehead and looked at them as if they were unwanted beetles in her bathtub.

Kate opened her mouth and closed it again; she could physically feel the blockage that would prevent her speaking. David glanced at her and then took her hand firmly in his. 'My wife lived in this house as a child. We wondered if you had any knowledge of her parents, or the previous tenants.'

Even before he'd finished the sentence the woman was shaking an untidy thatch of blonde-streaked hair, apparently cut with kitchen scissors and without the aid of a mirror. She sniffed. 'I've only lived here a few months. The council got me the place. I don't know who lived here before. The old woman next door – she's lived here forever. She might be able to help.' She was closing the door on them before she'd finished speaking. The word 'help' seemed to whisper through the woodwork.

David shrugged. 'OK. So shall we go next door?' Kate nodded as he brought her hand through his arm and walked her along to the next gate and slipped the latch up. The elderly lady who answered the door this time had a head of curlers wrapped in a scarf so that only the front two poked through, as if she'd stuck a small pair of binoculars on her head and tied them in place. 'Hello.' She held firmly to the half-opened door, ready to slam it shut at the least sign of danger.

David took the initiative. 'Do you happen to remember the Jardin family who lived next door?'

The elderly woman looked David over carefully. She took in the neat blue suiting and heavy black topcoat of wool, and then turned her attention to Kate. 'Philip Jardin was a bad lot.' She looked at Kate again, taking in the good quality royal blue duffel coat and black leather shoulder bag that matched the half-inch heels. 'You've got the look of him.'

'My f...father wasn't a good m...man. But...' Kate floundered to a stop and looked at David helplessly.

'My wife has just discovered some private papers and is trying to trace a relative of hers, both her parents being now dead. We don't know quite where to start, but this seemed to be the best place.' David offered his charming smile along with the explanation. 'We would really appreciate it if you could spare us a little of your time.' He watched as he was sized up again.

'My name's Mary Swann.' She released the door to hold out a hand and had it gently shaken. 'What do you want to know?'

'Scarlett Jardin?'

'Well she called herself Hamilton, but your father visited once. I remember his hair – red like yours. Scarlett said she'd divorced him; she told me he'd gone to prison.'

'Can you remember Kate here, as a baby?' David nodded at his silent wife.

'No; you were a little thing, infant school age, when they moved here. Philip Jardin was inside, six months I think Scarlett said he'd got, and when he got out he came calling but she sent him away.'

'Did Scarlett say where they moved from?' David smiled nicely and took his wife's hand.

Mary Swann frowned. 'I think it was up Newcastle way. But I don't know just where up there.'

'When did Philip Jardin visit?'

She looked at David again as he asked the question.

'He came once, as I said. Scarlett had been living here about eighteen months. He turned up on the doorstep out of the blue.' Mary Swann paused. 'Scarlett cried after he'd gone; said he was going to sue for custody of you.' She frowned. 'You moved about three weeks later. I don't know where you went but it was somewhere in the area, for I saw her in the town once.'

David looked down at Kate, then back at the woman. 'Thank you for all your help.'

'That's all right, love. He was a bad lot, but she was nice. Always had a pleasant word; used to hold them Tupperware parties to make a bit extra. Kept her place nice, but she hadn't got much. I hope you find what you want.' But she sounded like doubting Thomas talking to a couple of new disciples.

David held out his hand and had it shaken again, but the woman was shaking her head. 'Good luck.' She shut the door and they turned away. They had reached the gate when she popped her head back out again. 'It was Benwell Dene. Does that sound right?'

David swung back and nodded. 'Thank you again.'

''S all right, love.' The door shut with a snap and David looked at Kate.

'Where now, Kate? Back home?'

Kate nodded. 'I c...can just about r...remember my f... father, when I was small, David. I th...ink I r...remember the m...move, too.' She looked up at the familiar and beloved face of her husband. 'Or I m...might just be b...building a p...picture from what Mrs Swann has j...just told us.' She sighed.

'He wanted you, Kate.'

'Th...ank God he didn't g...get me, David.'

'Yes, love. She might have hidden things from you but she loved you, Kate.'

'She would never talk about him, said what I didn't know couldn't hurt me.' Kate sighed. 'I'm w...working on understanding, David. I'm trying to imagine wh...at it w... would be like to give up P...Paul or Rosie.'

'She was obviously hiding from him. And maybe your mother, too, Kate. She didn't want to part with you.' David held the door as his wife got into the car. He shut it and walked around the car, climbing in and fastening his seat belt.

'No.' Kate pulled a face, thinking about Scarlett. There had never been much money but Scarlett had tried to give her every little treat she could. 'She s...stole me, David.'

Kate had realised when she was about eleven that if she wanted something and said so, her stepmother would go without to give it to her. She'd been horrified to discover that Scarlett was going without meals to buy her extra drawing lessons. That had been the first day they'd really argued. 'But she w...was de...sperate to have me, wasn't she?'

'Yes, love. She might have deprived you of your roots, but she loved and wanted you.' David spoke as he swung the big car onto the main road towards home. 'I wonder what the solicitor will have to say.'

Kate nodded. She wondered, too.

JUNE 2011

WHITBY

To his astonishment, Antony Grey was collected, after four days in the hospice, by a man who could only have been Amy's father: the same blond hair and blue eyes, but set in a masculine mould.

'Our Amy says you need a place to stay. We've got four bedrooms in our house.' The man was tall, built like a stevedore and dressed like a builder. He stood inside the doorway, looking across the room at the frail specimen to whom his daughter had taken a shine.

'But...'

'She says you're as proud as Lucifer, so you'll pay rent by helping me on the allotment. I need the help. So don't think I'm finding work for you.'

'I can't just come and stay with you.'

'Why not? Too good for us, are you? She says you've got a degree and summat else; a PhD or summat. Still need a helping hand, don't ya?'

Antony stood looking at the older man; it seemed to him that he wasn't the only one with a problem with pride. 'It doesn't matter about what I've got or not, I can't just move in to your home.'

'Give us a good reason then, man. Or I'll just get your bag and shovel you into the car; you look as though the wind'd blow you away, so I shouldn't have that much bother with ya.' He watched the struggle, suppressing the inward pity. 'Look, man, I don't aim to go without ya. Our Amy will gang up with my wife and I can't be doing with the rowing. Not again.'

Antony stood swaying from foot to foot until Jack Watt came further into the room and picked up his brown paper bag with the few clothes Amy had brought from his room. 'Come on, man, I ain't got all day. I've got a roof to repair ower Durham way. Get a rattle on.' He swept out, taking Antony's possessions, so that if Antony wanted to see his best trousers again he was forced to follow.

He offered quiet thanks to the sister who was on duty at the desk and went out into the morning sunshine. Jack Watt was standing at the open door of a very dirty long wheelbase Land Rover. The back appeared to be full of wheelbarrows and spades. 'In ya get. Amy said she'd be back from shopping, time I got home. She can talk to you. I ain't got time.'

Antony got in. What choice did he have? He could go back to the dingy bedsit where he'd have to shop and wash and sort himself out or he could go with this man and be looked after. Being looked after wasn't an experience he'd had much of: it was both humbling and novel and, in his slightly battered condition, he would opt for it.

The journey was a short one. Jack Watt whistled under his breath for most of it and ignored his passenger. He parked on the outskirts of a council estate, more or less ejected his passenger, pointed to the door, handed Antony his brown paper bag and roared away.

Antony looked at the door with some trepidation. He had been in this position before, when he had moved from one foster home to the next. It stirred up in him all the fears and feelings of rejection he had suffered over the years.

Before he could either turn and go, or knock, it was opened by Amy herself. 'Dad gone? I thought I heard the Land Rover. He's in a bit of a rush today.' She pulled him in and shut the front door, blocking his line of escape. 'I didn't think you'd come if I asked you.' She stood in the dark hall, looking at him. 'Mum says you can have the back room. It's up here.' She found herself gabbling a bit, afraid he'd say something nasty or go away again.

If she had but known it Antony couldn't have got a word past the lump in his throat. He followed her up the stairs to a spacious back bedroom with a single divan bed and a small desk set under the window. There was a computer set squarely in the middle of it.

'Dad says someone was chucking it in his skip, but it works OK. I tried it out. It isn't new. And he says he's arranged the broadband but you'll have to pay for that yourself.' She stood next to the door, looking as if she expected to be shouted at any minute.

Antony sank onto the bed. 'I am overwhelmed and I don't know how to thank you, Amy.'

She grinned. 'Oh, we'll all use you shamelessly. I've got a paper for the OU that I need some help with, and Dad's got his allotment, and Mum needs someone to help her with the shopping and such. You won't have time to do your own work.' She pushed back her blonde fringe. 'I'll see you downstairs in a mo. Mum's just putting the kettle on.'

She whisked out of the room and closed the door on him, enclosing him in polish and lavender-scented silence. He stood up and walked over to look out of the window onto a back lawn and a sandpit. Joy, the toddler, appeared to be busy constructing Hadrian's Wall in miniature. He could hear Amy's voice murmuring, and a different female voice answering. He gave one more look around the room and then left his clothes bag on the bed and made his way downstairs.

Amy nodded to a seat at the kitchen table and came over with a mug of tea. 'I've bin around to your room, like you asked. There were another couple of letters for you.' She pointed to the one white and one brown envelope lying on the table. Antony looked at them. He recognised Professor Walker's handwriting; he also thought he recognised the other writing too.

He hadn't told Amy about the poison pen letter. Now he wondered if he was wise to come here; he didn't want to bring trouble to these kind people. The police had taken the first letter away for forensic evidence and almost grilled him about his activities until he had a mammoth-sized headache.

He carefully ignored that envelope and picked up the other. 'Will it be about the job?'

'I hope so, Amy. I sent and told him I'd been in an accident but I still wanted the work.' He slit the envelope and pulled out the sheet of paper, quickly reading the few lines. He looked up at Amy. 'He says he will be coming through to Whitby next week and will talk to me then about what research he needs me to do.' He grinned. 'Phew. I've still got a job. I'd better let him know where I'm living now.' He picked up the other letter and looked at the writing. He was almost sure it was another nasty letter. He stuffed it in his pocket without reading it. 'I'll read that later. I'd better let the coppers know where I'm staying. They said I should keep in touch with them.'

Amy's mother walked in on the words, 'I'm Joyce.' She came over and offered a hand.

'Mrs Watt.'

'Don't be formal, lad. Call me Joyce or Mam if you want; I'll answer to either. Get yourself settled in and then we can sort out meal times and such and what you eat.'

'I eat pretty much anything.'

'OK. Well you can peel the spuds later. Amy, Joy needs to have a sleep before she gets whiny. And I've got the ironing to do. Go and have a rest, Antony, while the bairn sleeps.' She swept them before her, and Antony found himself lying on a bed with his eyes closed, thinking about this strange turn of events.

Being in a strange house wasn't a novelty. Nor living with strangers, listening to a family that wasn't his own going about their business. The first foster home had been when he was four, only a few weeks after the accident that made him an orphan. The house had smelt of wet nappies and always seemed to have a baby crying in one of the bedrooms.

He had been handed over with a change of clothes in a black bin bag. The 'mother' had huge breasts and smelt of bleach. He didn't like her; she kept hugging him and saying he was 'a poor lost soul' to anyone who came to the house. He could still recall the humiliation of being looked at when he went to school and she told his class teacher he had been unwanted until she took him from the state-run home.

She hadn't wanted him, either. By the time he was six she had handed him back, claiming he was too much bother – always asking questions. He'd returned with a slightly bigger bin bag which made his clothes smell for weeks. He hadn't been allowed to take any toys away with him, not even the teddy he'd 'adopted' from the toy box.

The next foster home hadn't been so bad; he was just beginning to feel safe when the man had died and he'd been returned – like an unwanted parcel – yet again. He began to grow a shell about then, never feeling totally part of any family, hardly daring to unpack and waiting to be sent away again, which had happened all too frequently.

By the time he was twelve, eight families had fostered him for varying lengths of time and he was no longer fostering material. He could remember Saturday afternoons, when the sun would be shining outside and he would have to sit in the front room of the foster home – in clothes which weren't guaranteed to be his – with the others who hadn't been fostered, while couples came and looked him over as if buying a second-hand car or washing machine.

Some were nice, talking to him and asking him questions about himself; others would talk over his head, as if he was deaf. 'Oh, he's got red hair; I couldn't look after a red-head.' 'He's not very tall.' 'The boys wouldn't like him if he couldn't play football with them.' 'I wonder why he's still here. Must be difficult to look after if he's got to this age.'

Afterwards the other boys would tease him unmercifully about the things that had been said, especially Stan Hunt. So that, eventually, he refused to be put on display. He had stayed in the home until he got his A levels. His head teacher had helped him find a scholarship to university, and at eighteen the state didn't want to know of his existence any more.

He didn't talk about his past to anyone, so why had he told

Amy? He lay looking at the ceiling, listening to the sounds filtering up the stairs. Perhaps he was just feeling extra lonely at the moment, with threatening letters and thumps on the head. He frowned a frown that smoothed out as he drifted into a doze, unaware that he'd relaxed in these strange surroundings.

After lunch he went for a walk with Amy, the toddler fastened safely into a pushchair.

'I need to call into the police station.'

'That's all right. We can go the short way and you can meet me down the harbour, if you want. Joy likes to see the boats and the people.' She grinned. 'So do I. Wouldn't it be wonderful to sail away to Australia, like Captain Cook did?'

'Not really. Those boats were small and cramped and half the passengers got scurvy and dysentery before they arrived Down Under.'

'Pooh. Don't be such a killjoy. I think it would be an adventure. Me and Joy, we're going to see the world one day: the Louvre and Florence and Versailles. You wait; when I get my degree I'm gonna go places and she's coming with me, aren't you poppet?'

Joy was understood to say she'd rather see the duckies just at present. Antony walked beside the pushchair and felt happy for the first time in a long time. He watched as Amy pointed things out to the toddler, seeing how much she cared for the child. When they arrived outside the police station he was sad to see them walk away with a casual, 'See ya.'

He entered the slightly gloomy precincts with as much enthusiasm as a man going for a filling *sans* anaesthetic. 'Sergeant. My name is Anthony Grey.'

'Ah, yes, sir. Sister Patricia said you'd been discharged.'

'I'm staying with Miss Amy Watt's family for a few days until I'm feeling more capable. I came to give you the address and, er, I think you might want this.' Antony held out the brown envelope, which he'd opened before lunch in the privacy of his own room.

The sergeant raised an eyebrow and took the letter in a

hand decorated with hair along the top of the knuckles. 'Another interesting missive, is it?'

'They might be literate but they aren't polite.' Antony offered a smile that tipped up one corner of his mouth but left his eyes sober.

The sergeant pulled on a pair of vinyl gloves before extracting the paper. Badly-cut letters spelt out the words: GO, BEFORE YOU DIE. 'Well that's clear enough. It's more than menaces now, sir. This is a death threat.'

'I know. The question is: am I endangering the Watt family?'

'Can't say "no", can't say "yes". You need to speak with the detective; I'll just give him a ring. Take a seat for a minute, sir.'

Antony shrugged and went to sit on a hard, green, leather-covered bench within sight of the reception area.

Five long minutes later, a man doubling for Kojak came through a pair of swing doors, looked at the desk and then walked over to Antony. 'Mr Grey?'

'Yeah.' He breathed out heavily as he stood up.

'Detective Sergeant Tierney. We'll just pop into an interview room for a minute, if you don't mind.'

Once they were seated in the featureless room, the detective nodded at the letter, now sealed in an evidence bag. 'Who else has handled it?'

'Only Miss Watt when she went to pick up my mail, and presumably the postman.'

'OK. Have you thought of anyone who might want to get rid of you this badly?'

'No.' Antony sighed. 'No,' he said again, more quietly. 'I've got very little money but I'm not in debt to the moneylenders, I have a limited social life and I haven't offended anyone. I can't think of a single thing I've seen or heard that might make anyone want me to go away.' He looked at the steady brown eyes watching him. 'I'm frankly scared, Detective Tierney, and not just for myself. The Watt family have offered me accommodation, but I think maybe I ought to go somewhere else.'

The detective was shaking his head. 'No. Not a good idea. We'll put extra patrols round their house. But if you go away … one, the bugger's succeeded in intimidating you and will think he or she can do it again and two, we'll never catch them.'

'Believe me, Detective Tierney, I am intimidated. I'm shit-scared if you want the truth.'

'Yes, sir. I can well believe it: I would be in your situation. We are watching your flat. We are tracking the letters back, and we are investigating. Unfortunately there were no unaccounted-for fingerprints. It's a common adhesive, typical newsprint and generic writing paper. But don't give up, because we haven't.'

'I don't want anyone hurt on my account.'

'No, sir, nor do we. With your permission, I'll go and have a word with Jack Watt. We can keep you safe so long as you cooperate with us. We need to know your movements, who you are meeting and who you are corresponding with – snail mail and email. That way we can protect everyone and track the culprit down. They all make mistakes eventually.'

Antony sat staring at the detective, trying to decide if he was doing the right thing. He didn't want to uproot and go somewhere else; he didn't want Amy hurt, either. Detective Tierney wasn't waiting for his compliance, though. He stood up. 'Keep in touch, sir. I really mean that.' He went over to the door and stood with the knob in his hand, obviously waiting for Antony to leave.

Antony made his way down to the harbour with a scowl on his face. He spied the toddler and her mother from a distance. Both were eating ice cream: Joy from the comfort of her pushchair, Amy perched on a black bollard. He grinned despite his worry; what a pair of urchins they looked, sitting by the side of the water.

'Hi. Are you both enjoying yourselves?'

JUNE 2011

LIVERPOOL

BEN DROVE OFF THE ferry and away from the Irish Sea into the mid-morning traffic of Birkenhead. He hadn't driven on the mainland before. Driving on the left hadn't presented any problems; that was normal. Miles per hour instead of kilometres fooled him, though; he slowed his 30km speed down and signalled to change lanes at the lights and waited for the Go signal. An irate truckie shouted things at him from his cab as he too waited for the green light. 'Oi, mate. Get yerself a dodgem and go play at the fairground!'

Ben glanced at the unshaven face glaring at him across the gap between the lanes. He frowned. He was lost in a one-way nightmare. 'I want the Kingsway,' he shouted back.

The trucker scowled, having just caught sight of the clerical collar. 'Wrong lane, wrong way; yer need to turn back there.' He jerked his head, then at a hoot from behind, put his foot down and revved his engine, leaving Ben in a haze of blue-grey exhaust and a cacophony of noisy car horns.

He pulled over in a relatively quiet back street and had another look at the map, trying to work out how to get to the Kingsway, and then across the Mersey to Liverpool itself, without some other scouser beating him senseless. He refolded the map and sighed. He wished he could treat this as a big adventure, but he felt too saddened by the last week's events to enjoy things now.

Having taken in the sights of the same small shopping centre twice he finally managed to find his way into Liverpool proper – deciding that the town council really didn't want anyone staying in their fair town, just passing through. He pulled up at the small convent on the outskirts and sighed with relief.

'Hello, Father. Father Joseph said you wanted a bed for a night or two while you visited relatives.' The nun was old and small. She barely came up to Ben's shoulder. Her face was so wrinkled her eyes seemed to peer out like currants buried in a suet pudding. She had a tuft of grey hair poking out from under her short veil and a small mole with a single matching grey hair on her chin. But the eyes twinkled and the smile was beautiful.

Ben relaxed slightly. 'Sister?'

'Sister Carmel.' She smiled. 'Won't you come in? I'll make you a cup of tea. Most of the sisters are at the school, but a few of us are here. We run a holiday school for the mothers who have to work.' She bustled along the dark corridor, talking as she went.

'They have to work on bank holidays?'

'Sales – and the tourism, of course.' She looked over her shoulder at him before pushing open a door and leading the way into a large kitchen.

'I'll just put the kettle on then I'll show you to your room, Father.'

Ben nodded, watching as she flitted about filling the kettle and setting out mugs on a tray. She looked up and smiled again. 'Won't be a minute.'

'Take your time, Sister. I'm just glad to be out of the traffic.'

'Yes, it's a busy place. Come along; bring your bag, Father.' She set off again up a wide staircase. 'We only have the one other guest – Father Jan Gorski. His English accent is a bit thick.' She grinned, glancing back over her shoulder at him as she climbed rapidly. 'I can't understand him and he can't understand me, but we manage in the Lord.'

Ben, listening to the Irish accent, could well believe her. 'Have you lived here long, Sister?'

'Fifty-seven years at the last count, Father. I don't go out much now; it was hard enough when they took away my habit.' She stood with her hand on the doorknob of a room and turned to face him. 'I hadn't seen my legs in years.' She gave a chuckle of laughter. 'I'd no desire to show them to the world.' She opened the door. 'Here you are, Father. Home for as long as you need it. Can you find your way back or will I wait for you?'

Ben shook his head. 'I'll just settle my things, Sister, and then I'll be down.'

She nodded and left, closing the door quietly behind her. Ben sank onto the single bed. It was a nice interior-sprung divan; the blue-covered duvet modern and easy-care. He looked around: a small chest of drawers against one wall, a wardrobe against another, a partitioned area that stood open to reveal a shower and toilet. It was similar to his room at the seminary.

He stood and went into the small en suite, using the facilities and washing his hands. He was wondering what it would be like to live in a convent for fifty-seven years. Back in the fifties if you joined a convent you didn't see your family again, not for a long time. You had to be really sure of your calling. Sister Carmel obviously was sure, to have lasted this long. What must it be like to leave your family? What must that be like? His sister Kate would know. He thought, a week ago, that he knew what God was calling him to do. Now he didn't know any more, about his calling or his family.

The sisters were helpful, supplying him with a map and a copy of the bus timetables, along with the cup of tea. Now Ben made his way into the centre of the town and then onwards to the other side, seeking out the address of his Auntie Lara.

'Ben, *a ghra*, how are you? In you come.' His great-aunt Lara was very like his grandmother. She hugged him and drew him into a house that smelt of baking and polish, talking nineteen to the dozen as she asked about his uncle and his grandfather.

'We didn't expect to see you here. I was coming over for

the wake, but my asthma has been that bad I didn't make it. 'Tis sad the way Maeve died so suddenly.' Her eyes filled with tears as she led the way into the kitchen. 'Is Eoin all right?' Alarm flitted across the old face as she suddenly wondered why her great-nephew was on the doorstep.

'Grandfather is coping. I have business in Liverpool and thought I'd see you. I have some questions, Auntie.'

'Oh.' She turned and switched on the kettle and pulled out a chair at the table. 'Oh.' Her eyes slid sideways away from him and focused on a photograph on the wall before she sat down with a little sigh.

Ben pulled out another chair. 'The question is: will you answer them, Auntie Lara?'

His aunt looked across the table at him. 'I suppose Eoin feels he can speak now.' She jumped up as the kettle began to whistle and switched off the gas.

'I don't really want tea, Auntie. I want answers.'

Lara nodded and sat down again, the old kitchen chair making a faint protesting squeak as she settled. 'Has Eoin agreed to tell you? For I'll not go against Maeve's word, Ben.'

Ben nodded. 'He would have told me everything, but I was too angry to listen. Will you speak for him?' He held her eyes as he asked the question

'I don't know much, Ben.'

'Tell me what you know.' He took a deep breath. 'Please. I need to know about my mother … and my sister.'

Lara nodded. 'It was all a long time ago. And I never held with it. But Maeve … well, you know your gran. She thought it was for the best.' She stopped again and looked at the young man in front of her.

'Tell me about my mother.'

Lara smiled. 'Oh, she was a pretty one. She'd hardly been here five minutes and the lads were queuing up at the door. Hair like a newly opened chestnut, it was. You've her eyes and her nose.' Lara smiled; 'She got a job down the local Woolworths and she went out and about with her cousins here, exploring the town. She had a lovely time and then she met Jardin in the pub one night.' Lara shook her grey curls. 'I never did see what she saw in him. There were plenty of fine Irish boys hanging about, but no: she wanted a weedy red-headed Englishman.'

Lara looked up and then gave a half smile at the look on Ben's face. 'I'm sorry, Ben. He was your father, but I couldn't see the attraction. But Tess, she idolised him; couldn't marry him fast enough. She loved him, if it's any consolation.'

Ben nodded, the picture of his parents building in his mind. '*Daideo* said he went to prison. Do you know anything about that?'

'No,' Lara shook her head again. 'They married in the register office here and went to Newcastle somewhere within a few days. The next time we saw her she was big as a house and he was nowhere in sight and not a word could we get out of her as to what happened. Your uncle and granddad came over when she gave birth to you and Kate and took you all home to Ireland.'

Lara looked him in the eyes. 'Then she died, by her own hand.' She made the sign of the cross and her eyes followed Ben's hands as they too moved up and down in a practised manner. She realised for the first time that he was wearing a dog collar. 'Heavens. You're priested. Maeve would have been so proud.' She started to sniff and tears sprang into her eyes.

Ben's lips twisted wryly. 'I haven't taken my final vows yet, Auntie, but yes: she was proud of me.' He pulled out a hanky and offered it across the table, watching as his aunt mopped her face.

'What more do you want to know, Ben?'

'Do you know where Kate is?'

'No.' She looked startled, 'Don't you?'

Ben slowly shook his head.

'But ... but, Maeve, Eoin ... I thought you'd come to take her back to Ireland. I thought you knew where she was.'

'They "lost" her, Auntie Lara.' Ben could feel his teeth trying to grit and the anger simmering below the surface trying to erupt. He swallowed, hard. 'They lost her and they don't know where she is.'

'Oh, dear God.' Lara held out a hand and took the two lying clenched on the old table top. 'No wonder you're angry, Ben. I thought 'twas just how Tess had died that was needing to be told you. Maeve was so ashamed of that. She said you mustn't know. I thought it was just the...' – she bit her lip before whispering – 'suicide.'

'No, 'tis not the suicide. That I can understand *Maimeo* hiding. It's Kate, Auntie Lara. How could they "lose" her?' His hands flexed and closed under his aunt's as they lay in front of him. 'Why this conspiracy of silence? Who else knew about it?'

Lara squeezed one of the clenched fists on the table. 'Maeve was a hard woman. She was my big sister and life wasn't easy for us growing up, Ben. She looked after us while Mam and Dad worked: missed out on her own schooling to make sure we had ours. But she was ambitious for us and blamed herself when we didn't have careers and make happy marriages.

'When your granddad came along and married her it was as if she'd won the lottery. And when Micheál and Theresa grew so big and beautiful she was so proud of them. But she still thought she was being punished because she only had the two of them. She lost four babies. Did you know?'

'No. I thought there were just Mam and Uncle.' Ben shook his head, not wanting to allow pity for his grandmother to push out the anger he was nurturing.

'If was as if she thought it was her fault that things didn't go perfectly. Then Tess married against her wishes and had you babies. Maeve was ashamed – not of you – but that she hadn't kept you all safe. Tess dying just confirmed her in the belief that she was a terrible sinner, Ben.'

'But Mam was sick, so Uncle said.'

Lara nodded. 'Maeve couldn't see that. She took it personally. She sent Kate away because she couldn't cope with her. She thought the little one would be better gone. She thought that it was her fault and the constant reminder of how she'd failed Tess that was tearing Kate apart.'

'But ... to "lose" her.'

'Yes.' The sigh was long. 'Maeve tried to find Kate: she paid Tom to look. My poor husband was a feckless sort, but he did search. When it seemed hopeless she told all the cousins who knew about you both to never mention Kate again. She said you were too distressed. She cared about you, boy, and she never forgave herself.'

JUNE 2011

CUMBRIA

KATE AND DAVID SAT on the side of an excavation and drank coffee from pottery mugs. The dig was winding to a close this Wednesday afternoon and they had nearly finished backfilling a grave. 'It's a shame we can't say for definite just who this poor man was.' David prodded the topsoil with a dirty boot and sniffed. The air this morning was decidedly chilly. He glanced around the site, seeing his team relaxing on various patches of grass. It would soon be time to go home.

He was deep in thought, though, as he and Kate prepared to go home for their lunch. Kate had been silent for most of the morning. She'd been far too quiet since the previous weekend's phone call to the solicitor.

David climbed into their 4x4 and started the engine. 'C... ould we go for a little d...drive before we go h...home, David? I need to get m...myself in h...hand before I see your p...parents.'

David nodded 'What's troubling you, love?'

'Aside from wh...o I am, wh...ere I come from, wh...at kind of people my real parents are?' Kate muttered the words – sounding half angry, half desperate – and shrugged.

David glanced over and nodded. Yes, it was time they talked. He hadn't wanted to push, but now he wondered if he'd left her to her thinking for too long.

He scanned the road and half smiled as he caught sight of the lay-by he was looking for. Pulling in, he set the handbrake and opened the door. 'Out you get, Kate. Let's look at the view while I tell you what I've been thinking, and you can give me some of your thoughts.'

His wife grimaced, but obediently undid her seat belt and stepped down onto the roadside.

David took a hand and led her over to a gate which overlooked the river Liddell, running like a grey ribbon in the valley below them. He stood watching her as she watched a few ducks coming in to land with a splash, and leaving a silver trail on the water, then took her other hand to gain her attention. 'When you first came on one of my digs as a young student I watched you secretly, Kate. I loved your enthusiasm, your thirst for knowledge. I was so much older than you and – in my youth – I'd been accused of getting one young woman pregnant, so I wasn't going to risk going down that path again.' He swung the hand up and kissed her knuckles, while his green eyes watched her face.

'When your father was murdered, Kate, I discovered that I could hide the truth from everyone else – but not myself – and eventually not you, love. If we keep chasing this it will hurt. We've been through a very public washing of our linen at the trial of his murderer: I didn't care for me, but I do care for you, Kate. So...'

He took a deep breath. 'What do you want to do now, Kate? We have to wait for the solicitor to get back to us, but...' Kate focused on her husband's face, reading the love there. 'We can take this as far as you want or abandon it here, Kate. But I don't think you'll be really happy not knowing the who and what and why and where, will you, love?'

'She t...took me away; she knew who my m...mother was, but she d...didn't tell me. She d...didn't give me a chance to find my m...mother, David. I'm not s...sure I c...can forgive her for that.'

'Perhaps they didn't know how to tell you.'

Kate looked at her husband. 'I c...could believe that w... when I was little, but not n...now, David. She kn...ew. Even after my father d...died, she d...didn't say anything. She just let me b...believe she was all the f...family I had left. All my life I've b...believed one th...ing and it wasn't t...rue. They both lied to me.'

'Yes, love, I'm afraid they did.' David pressed another kiss onto Kate's hand and stood holding it as he watched her face. He felt impotent and angry and desperately sad as he watched his wife coming to terms with the idea that her parents, the people she should have been able to trust implicitly, had lied to her. 'I love you, Kate,' he paused before adding softly, 'so much.'

'My father was a m...murderer, David. My mother ab...andoned me to him, and then he ab...andoned me to a w...woman who had no claim on me and whom I don't th...ink I ever really kn...ew.' Kate pushed her hair off her face and looked at her husband. 'He h...haunts us, David. You don't kn...ow how grateful I am th...at you t...took me on, w...warts and all, love. You're the b...best t...thing that ever happened to me, David.'

David swung her round, holding her firmly by her shoulders as he looked into her face. 'Don't you ever say that again, Kate. You never have to be grateful to me. I wanted you. I still want you: I need you. If anyone is going to be grateful around here, it's me.' David was so angry even his hair seemed to bristle. 'I don't give a fuck about your relatives. I never have. It's you that counts: you. Don't you get it yet?' He pulled her close, burying his face in her hair.

Kate stood slightly bemused as her husband shook her slightly. The part of her that she kept separate, hidden and safe in its frozen box, began to crack under the heat of his gaze as he stepped back. 'Let's go and find out what other skeletons are in your closet, Kate, but' – he held up a finger – 'only because then you will have peace, love. I really don't give a stuff.'

Kate nodded; she was trying to 'get it'. But this latest revelation on top of twenty years of school bullying and the insecurity of a father in the nick, before she met David, couldn't be overcome that easily. She had held part of herself in and away from scrutiny for too long. It was safer that way, even if it wasn't honest.

THE LETTER WAS WAITING for them when they arrived home. The house on the Solway that David had called home for the past twenty years was quiet. His parents had taken the twins down the road to see a herd of cows while he dealt with his wife. He was worried after their conversation in the lay-by: she had gone too quiet again.

David opened the solicitor's letter and shook out the contents; a smaller white envelope slithered into view along with crisp headed notepaper. He began to read out loud to them both: '*Further to your phone call on Saturday afternoon I enclose the Last Will and Testament of Scarlett Jane Hamilton. There was also a letter from Philip Jardin, which she lodged with us. This I have also enclosed.*

Further to our conversation I have spoken to my father, who dealt with Ms Hamilton before I took over the briefs. She did indeed enquire about the adoption of Katherine Róis Jardin but, as she had no legal status and Mr Jardin refused to give permission, she remained in loco parentis only.' David could almost taste the dry and dusty legal jargon; either that or it was fear clogging his throat. 'No legal status' meant she couldn't have been married to Jardin. He was sure of that now. How soon would Kate realise? He held the letters out to his wife.

Kate was sitting absolutely still in the chair opposite him at the big mahogany desk. She made no move to take the envelopes from his hand. 'I don't want to read anything he might have written to me, David.'

David frowned, removing his glasses the better to focus on her. 'It might answer some of your questions, love.' He spoke gently. 'Do you want me to open it?'

Kate shrugged. 'I think I hate him. B...before I didn't; I don't know what I f...felt, but it wasn't hate. B...but now, now I hate him, David. I've n...never hated anyone b...before.'

David nodded, laying the papers down. 'Do you want to

read the will?'

Kate shrugged again. She felt numb, had felt that way since she started going through her foster-mother's papers; it was a strangely familiar and comforting sensation which she almost hugged to herself in the manner of a child with a comforter. 'You read it.'

David picked up his glasses, perching them on his nose before he slit the envelope open with his thumb. He pulled out the thick cream parchment and scanned the print, turning over the page and looking at the signature before looking back at his wife. She wasn't showing any curiosity at all about its contents and David could feel himself getting even more worried and just a little angry with her.

'It's a standard all for mother will, Kate. She gives and bequeaths all she dies possessed of to you, Katherine Róis Jardin, her beloved daughter. It's witnessed by the solicitor and his clerks.'

Kate raised expressionless eyes to her husband. 'But I w... wasn't, was I?'

'Not physically, Kate, no. In every other sense yes, love. You can't dismiss the care and love of twenty years, darling.'

Kate gave a quick bobbing nod of the head. 'I'm t...rying to accept that, David. B...but I'm f...finding it hard to set it against the h...huge lie she lived. I don't kn...ow who she really was ... if she had r...relatives still alive. Wh...at about her b...brother in Southampton? Did she cut herself off f... from him so that she might keep me as her s...secret? Was she ashamed of me, r...really? Was I just a d...duty she accepted after my f...father left me with her? I just don't k...now any more.'

David opened his mouth to refute the comments and then closed it again; he couldn't answer. He hadn't known Scarlett Hamilton that well. She'd just been a very pleasant woman he'd accepted as his new mother-in-law, and he'd thanked God she wasn't the interfering kind. She hadn't told him very much about Kate's formative years because they hadn't met very often and, worse, because he hadn't asked. And now it was way too late. Kate wasn't the only person to be left with unanswered questions.

JUNE 2011

LIVERPOOL

THE RESTAURANT WAS FAIRLY full on the Thursday following the May bank holiday but David nudged Kate towards a table in the window and handed her his heavy black coat. 'I'll get it. Sit.' He smiled to take the sting out of the order and Kate obediently sat, hitching her chair nearer to the table and the plate glass window. The atmosphere was warm and tended to fog her glasses up a bit. She pulled them off and rubbed them on her jumper as she waited.

It had been rather a fruitless journey. David was taking advantage of the fact that they had built-in babysitters at present. Not that he or his parents thought in those terms. They were delighted to look after the children and said so.

Kate, therefore, found herself sitting in the rather pleasant surroundings of the Liverpool Metropolitan Cathedral's pizzeria waiting to see what her husband would bring her for lunch.

'I ordered baked potatoes with tuna. They won't be a moment.' David spoke as he came to a halt behind her. 'They're just zapping them. OK?'

His wife gave him a rather bleary look from unfocused eyes before putting the glasses back on. 'Sounds fine.'

'I nipped over to ask if you wanted some of their cheesecake? It's passion fruit.'

Kate gave a half smile and nodded, only to see her husband stride back across the dining area.

He came back within minutes with a loaded tray and began

to distribute mugs and plates. 'This is a rather nice place. I'm glad Mum thought of it.'

Kate looked around as he sat opposite and set out his knife and fork. She picked up the teapot and poured the brew into their mugs while her husband grinned at her.

'I think I deserve a kiss; I resisted the temptation of chips and bought the healthy option. Aren't I good?'

Kate eyed the hefty slice of gateau he was setting in front of his own plate and felt her lips twitch. 'Yes, darling; very g...good.'

'It's a pity this morning was a wild goose chase, Kate. But we haven't exhausted all the angles yet.'

'I don't kn...ow wh...at else to do, David.'

'We know your birth was registered here.'

'Yes, b...but the house has been p...pulled down and none of the neighbours were in.'

'Doesn't matter. We can go to the local churches, see if you were baptised, check the electoral role for the district. It might be online. If you were registered here then chances are you were born here; we can enquire of the hospitals. Don't give up hope, Kate.' He smiled at her and indicated her food with his knife. 'Eat.'

'Yes, David.'

Both took the edge off their appetites before speaking again. 'Would you like to look around "Paddy's Wigwam" before we go any further?'

'"P...Paddy's Wigwam"? Really, David.'

'Yes, really.' David grinned, setting his knife down for a minute to take a sip of tea. 'It's not polite, but it is descriptive, and very typical of the Liverpudlians who love their nice new Cathedral. It was built by Gibberd and opened in '67.'

'I th...ought it was Lutyens who b...built it.'

David raised a mobile eyebrow and popped in the last morsel of potato. 'Did you, my love? You never fail to surprise me.'

'Well I kn...ow Lutyens comes into it s...somewhere.' Kate frowned.

'True. His design was the greatest building never built. But how do you know about it?'

'Cenotaphs.'

'Ah.' David nodded, picking up his mug and emptying it. 'Of course.' His wife collected cenotaphs in the same way some people collected stamps. He himself found it a weird obsession but, since he had a number of his own, he obliged by finding odd cenotaphs for her to look at.

'Lutyens w...as responsible for the Cenotaph in Wh... itehall and Ontario, Quebec and the one at Th...iepval.' Kate's face glowed for a moment. 'I w...would love to go and see them all one d...day.'

'One of the best excuses to travel I've heard yet.' David's lips twitched, then broke into a grin as his wife gave him a proper smile.

'Th...ere's one in India, too.'

'Hmm. So do you want to look around the cathedral?'

Kate nodded, picking up a fork to start on her cheesecake. 'And after that?'

'We'll go back and check out the local post office and church.'

Twenty minutes later Kate was standing in the entrance to the Catholic cathedral, gazing at the ceiling. 'Wow!'

'Impressive, isn't it? See how the lights change?'

Kate brought her eyes, which had developed a tendency to stand out on stalks, back to her husband. 'It's so airy.'

David linked her arm and they began a slow wander around the perimeter, talking quietly about the murals, before descending to the Lutyens Crypt – the only part of his original design left.

Kate was so busy gazing at the 'rolling stone door' that she walked into a young priest just exiting.

The blond-haired, brown-eyed man set her back on her feet and smiled, apologising. 'I'm so sorry. I was miles away.' His Irish accent was as strong as Guinness, and as soft.

Kate nodded. 'It's so b...beautiful.' She gave a shiver as if someone had walked over her grave – or maybe she'd walked over someone else's grave, she thought.

She looked back over her shoulder as David came up and put an arm around her waist, nodding.

'Father.'

Ben O'Connor smiled at both, and walked soft-footed along the corridor.

'I'm so pleased he's a priest.'

Kate looked at David with a frankly puzzled face. 'Eh?'

'I could get very jealous of all these young men, my Kate. And he did give you a very unpriestly look.'

'Nonsense. Anyway, why?' She took a breath and swung around into his arms, standing facing him. 'I love you, David.'

David gave her a brief hug. 'Pity we're in a church; I can't kiss you here, love.'

Kate leaned forward and dropped a quick butterfly kiss on his mouth before swinging around and going to look at the grave of a bishop.

Ben, who had reached a corner and glanced back at the couple, sighed as he saw the kiss. Had he really heard the call? What must it be like to have a girlfriend, a wife, to share with and touch? He missed human touch sometimes, and that young woman had definitely given him a frisson of something.

He walked up the steps and into the great circular nave, where a party of school children were approaching the high altar. He stepped nimbly out of their path, nodding to the young nun in charge of the group. He was lonelier than he'd ever been in his life and he didn't know what to do about it.

He sat down in one of the side pews and watched the activity around him. People came in as tourists to admire the architecture. They came as penitents to talk to God where they thought they might find him; they came to learn about the history of the place. But what was he doing here in this cathedral? Looking for answers, he supposed, but he wasn't finding any. Just more questions.

He looked up to find a small girl had broken away from the group and was standing in front of him, her school uniform slightly on the big side. Her braids were so tight they stuck out like an old Dutch cap and her deep brown eyes regarded him hopefully.

'*Beannachd De, a mhuirnin.*' He spoke to the child while his mind posed other questions. What would Kate have looked like at this age? What did she look like now?

'Hello, Father. Sister says this was a workhouse.' The child ignored the strange greeting, totally focused on finding answers. 'She says if you don't know you should ask someone who will. What's a workhouse, and what did they work at please?' She held a sheet of paper in her hand – obviously a questionnaire upon which the class was working.

Ben smiled. 'A workhouse was a place that poor people went to if they couldn't look after themselves: they were given food and a place to sleep. Sometimes whole families had to live there.' He smiled at the advancing nun. 'The mums and dads did different jobs, like washing or shoe mending. The children went to school in the morning and in the afternoon they helped with chores so that everyone got fed on time and had their beds made. They sometimes worked in the gardens growing vegetables.' He stood up. 'Sister.'

The sister was young; she smiled nicely at him, but spoke to her charge. 'Have you the answers then?'

'Yes, Sister.'

'Good. Go and tell your group; see if they have other answers for you.'

'Yes, Sister. Thank you, Father.' The child skipped away to a small group of girls in the central aisle.

'Sorry, Father. I meant them to ask the ushers and guides.'

'Not to worry. She was very polite.'

The sister grinned, a flash of teeth lighting up her young face. 'She's a bold one. Thank you again, Father.'

Ben nodded, watching her retreat and gather her charges around her like a mother duck with several broods in her care. He sat down again while he thought about that brief conversation. Had Kate been put in a modern-day workhouse? He knew that foster homes were much better now but the thought that his sister should have been forced to live among

128

strangers, be separated from all she knew and loved, filled him with a bitter sadness.

He stood up abruptly and went out through the main entrance and down into the café, getting a mug of coffee and sitting in a corner to watch the passing parade. After the third woman had smiled shyly at him and asked him to bless her new rosary, he gave up. He would go and see if some of his second cousins had returned from work and see if they had any more ideas about the whereabouts of Kate. What had the child said? 'If you don't know you should ask someone who will.' Tomorrow he was going to go to Newcastle.

He pushed back his chair and made his way to the lifts. The young woman he'd met in the crypt was just getting in as he arrived. She was holding tightly to her husband's hand. He smiled at both but didn't speak. Kate was too shy and David too busy working out where they should go next. The journey was completed in the kind of stilted quiet only the English can manage when obliged to share a small space with a complete stranger.

ONE WEEK LATER

LIVERPOOL

KATE AND DAVID WERE talking to another complete stranger the following Saturday morning. David had felt that a second visit might pay dividends, so they had returned to Liverpool. Well, David was talking; Kate was, as usual, tongue-tied by nerves. The parish priest of the Anglican church was shaking his head. 'I'm very sorry, Professor Walker, but we only keep the records for twenty-five years. After that they go to the diocesan offices.'

'Thank you for your time anyway, Mr Malone.'

'Have you tried at the Catholic church? They keep theirs a bit longer.'

David shook his head. 'Jardin was brought up an Anglican, I believe.'

'Oh. Well, it was just a thought. You have got an Irish second name and they tend to be Roman Catholics around here.' He smiled nicely at Kate. 'I hope you find your relations, my dear. We get a lot of people trying to track down their roots these days. They go on the net, and the Mormon site. I'm told both are helpful. And of course there's the probate office too.'

'Thank you, Mr Malone. That's helpful. It gives us other places to look, doesn't it, Kate?'

'Yes, th...ank you for your t...time.' Kate stretched out a hand and had it firmly pressed before they turned and left the church, heading for the car and a map.

David opened the driver's door and pulled a city directory out of the glove compartment while Kate stood next to him,

130

patiently watching as he ran a finger down the page. 'Ah, here we go, Kate. It's two streets over. The Church of the Blessed Sacrament. We'll have a word with the Father if he's around.'

'Well, that was enlightening, Kate.' David was walking his wife back towards the car. 'The Father couldn't have been more pleasant, could he? It will be great if he can find records for you. We know you were born around here.' He looked at the rows of houses, their front doors opening onto the pavements. 'You've probably got relatives lurking behind one of these doors, if we only knew which bell to ring.' His mouth twisted a bit wryly as his wife uttered what could only be described as a grunt.

'I wish!'

'So do I, my Kate.' But David spoke under his breath. Part of him was scared for his wife and what she might find out about her relatives. His next comment was apparently addressed to the nearest lamppost. 'I hadn't thought of the probate offices.'

'B...but she didn't leave enough for th...em to be involved.'

'Not Scarlett, no. But her parents might have. We don't know your mother's name, but Scarlett might have told them something. Her mother had died after she fostered you but we don't know how much she might have told them before they died.' David watched the wince cross his wife's face, but he didn't know how else to describe his wife's relationship with Scarlett without prodding at the open wound.

'The death certificate was issued to her son so he must have been alive, too. We can try to find out if he knows anything, Kate.'

'OK. But I don't want other p...people hurt, David. He m...might not have known about me.' She looked up at him. 'And h...ow do we f...find him, anyway?'

'I don't know yet, love. We'll go carefully, Kate. I think for today we'll go back home, unless you want to go somewhere else?'

Kate shook her head and David walked her briskly towards

the blue Citroën which she normally drove. He opened the passenger door for her and saw her comfortably seated.

They had been driving for a good ten minutes before either spoke. 'I knew Róis meant Rose. Th...at's why I w...anted to call our girl th...at name. I hadn't realised it w...was Irish.'

David glanced across the space between them before looking back at the traffic. 'No, I don't think I wondered at its origins either; I just thought it suited you,' he smiled across again. 'It's a pretty name, and you can be very like a rose, love.'

'Flattery w...will get you anything you w...want, sir.' Kate offered a smile of her own and David sighed under his breath, thanking God that she didn't seem too stressed by the day's events.

That evening they sat down to relate their finds, or lack of them, to David's parents.

'So far, Pops, we've discovered very little. I've arranged with the register office to send a copy of Kate's full birth certificate. I've asked the local Father of the Catholic church if he could go through his records too; possibly send a photocopy of the page, too, if it's there. We drew a blank at the Anglican one. I don't know if it will help but I'm willing to give it a try. I'll write to the probate offices; see if that leads anywhere.' David glanced across at his silent wife. She offered a half smile. 'I know it's important to Kate, but I have to admit I'm fascinated by the hunt now.'

'Trust you, darling.' Kate sniffed. 'I'm b...becoming a b...it more enthusiastic myself. I was th...inking on the way home. I might have been a Roman Catholic, Pops, according to the p...parish p...priest in the neighbourhood. I don't really understand m...much about it. Religion didn't l...loom that large in our s...school.'

'If you were Irish, love – as the man suggested – it would depend on which part of Ireland you came from.' David nodded at her and then looked across at his father. 'Remember I was talking about the research at Whitby, Pops? A possible hermitage, seventh century. They weren't Roman Catholic then. That's what the schism with St Hilda was about.'

'Ah. Yes, I remember you saying, David.' His father looked from one face to the other. 'Tell me, how far have you got with the research now? When are you going over there? We can stay a bit longer if you need babysitters.'

David grinned. 'Any excuse to play with the babies. I'll let you know; for now, let's just enjoy the weekend.'

JUNE 2011

WHITBY

THE WEEKEND PROMISED TO be fine and bright for others, too. Antony was carrying the pushchair up the 199 steps to the ruins of Whitby Abbey. Amy had Joy's wriggling body in her arms. About halfway up the couple stopped and looked at each other.

'I must be mad, and so must you.' Antony paused to draw much-needed oxygen into his lungs.

Amy nodded, too out of breath to speak. When she'd taken several deep lungsful she said, 'I'm sorry, Antony. I'd forgotten what a climb it was, and you just out of hospital.'

'Hospital be damned.' Antony gulped in a breath. 'I'm just unfit.' He glanced around. 'I'm blowed if I'm going give up now though, Amy.' He looked at her hot face. 'OK?'

'Yeah, OK.' She adjusted the toddler and Antony said. 'Will I take her?'

'Nah.' She grinned and began to climb again, her pace now slower. 'I keep saying...' she paused to pant, 'I'll have a break when I've got to that clump of grass...' she breathed out, 'or when I get...' she breathed again, 'to that yellow flower.' She grinned again as she looked at Antony's reddened face.

'Yeah; know what you mean.' He transferred the pushchair to his other hand and put his arm around her waist. If Amy was surprised she didn't say anything. They kept climbing. Mountain goats they weren't ... possibly ancient ponies. They certainly sounded winded enough for the knacker's yard.

When they reached the top the view proved more than

worth the effort. They drew in deep lungsful of salt-laden sea air. Amy set the toddler down; Joy promptly sat on the grass and chuckled up at the adults. She hadn't had to climb the steps and she was cool and comfortable.

Amy looked at Antony; he grinned back and sat down on the grass himself. Amy fished in the little bag attached to the handle of the pram and pulled out first a child's bottle with a capped spout, then two bottles of energy drinks.

'No wonder it was so heavy.' Antony took the drink and unscrewed it while Amy fished in her jacket pocket and handed Joy a biscuit.

'I'll let you carry her down; the pushchair will be lighter then.'

'Thanks.' He wrinkled a nice straight nose at her, but the brown eyes were laughing as he looked up at the impish smile she was giving him. 'I think!'

Amy sat herself down, then slowly collapsed onto her back. 'Phew. Just why did we come up here, again?' She looked up at the powder-blue sky scattered with rows of cirrus clouds and closed her eyes for a minute.

'Your homework?'

'Oh, yeah. Homework. You know, I never did my homework when I was at school. I couldn't wait to leave. I so regret that.' She opened her eyes and looked at the young man sitting holding her daughter and looking out at the sea. 'I bet you always did yours.'

He swung his head round and looked at her. 'Mostly. It kept me out of mischief.' He grinned down at her. 'Actually, I rather like study.' He said it as one confessing to a social solecism on a par with burping in public.

Amy sat up and uncapped her own drink, taking a long drink of virulent blue liquid. 'Well I do, sometimes. I'll put it off and put it off but then once I sit down to the books it catches me, and I don't want to stop. It's really odd; it never happened like that at school.'

'You probably never studied anything you were really interested in.' He paused to sip and then said, 'Now, the latest question for the OU was, "What were the two main reasons for the synod of Whitby". Yes?'

Amy nodded. 'I can answer 'em in two sentences but I kinda think my tutor is gonna want a bit more.'

'One...' He paused, waiting.

'Haircuts.'

'Two...'

'Easter.'

'So tell me about haircuts.' He smiled. 'And listen to yourself. You'll be amazed how much you really know. Remember it and the essay will be brilliant.'

'Haircuts or tonsures were worn by men who were monks...'

'Why...'

'Why?'

'Yes. Why did they wear tonsures?'

'Er...'

Antony drew information out of her as the sun rose in the sky. Joy had fallen asleep in his lap as they talked. Now he said, 'So put part one together for me.'

'Tonsures were a sign of slavery to Christ. In the Celtic church they shaved the front part off and in the Roman church they shaved off the patch at the back, like the nobility. The Celts thought the Roman faction was deserting God. The Romans: they thought the Celts were still pagan underneath.'

'And part two...'

'Easter. Easter was at different times for different groups. Sometimes the King – Oswiu – was celebrating Easter Roman style when his wife was still in Lent, Celtic time.' Amy grinned. 'Bet that caused a few arguments.'

'Still is causing a few.' Antony grinned back. 'It goes like this... The Angles said there must have been indigenous Christians long before the Roman Christians arrived, so they weren't in need of saving – thanks – and being so old they must have got it right because Columbanus, their saint, was very well established already.

'The Roman Christians said, "Ah, but you gave in. So you

must have realised that St Peter and Rome had the right of it".'
He grinned again, 'Basically, our old bones are better than
your old bones.'

'Can I quote you?'

'Yeah; all nicely referenced, if you want to.' Joy stirred
in his lap and he looked down. 'I think it's time she had a
run around and I showed you these 'ere ruins that 'oused this
famous argument.'

Amy nodded, standing up and brushing the grass off her
jeans. She watched as Joy came around and climbed into the
pushchair and then they began to walk across the headland
towards the crumbling pile. 'I really do appreciate the help,
Antony.'

'I really do appreciate the help too, Amy. So shall we call
it quits?' He nodded at the building they were approaching
and avoided her eyes. He didn't want hero worship on his
conscience as well as endangering this young woman's life.
'Which paper are you going to do after this one?' He steered
the conversation away onto neutral ground.

Anthony was right to be worried, for his attacker was
observing them. But this was a very public and, during the
school holiday season, busy place. So observation was all that
he could do. He glowered and kept his distance.

JUNE 2011

LIVERPOOL

BEN WAS BACK IN his aunt Lara's kitchen this sunny Saturday morning. It wasn't a peaceful place to be, however. Apparently a nursery school had escaped and encamped on the floor. Second cousins, wives, children, teenagers: Aunt Lara had rounded up as many of the tribe as she could and the whole house seethed and bulged at the seams with family.

One small child, indistinguishable as to sex, came crawling over and tugged at his trouser clad leg and Ben bent and scooped up the infant. It settled on his knee, placed a thumb in its mouth, and stared at him with the large pansy brown eyes that seemed to run like a benediction through the family.

'Hello, *a chumann*. Who are you, then?'

A smiling brunette came over. 'Her name is Einin and I'm your second cousin, Siobhan. Will I take her?'

Ben shook his head, 'No. It's fine.' He became aware that the children were being swept up and taken into another room and the remaining adults were finding seats and nursing mugs of tea or coffee.

Lara came over and sat at the table and silence of a sort fell. Ben could hear the children next door and the occasional voice of an adult.

'Ben ... you've met everyone?'

Ben looked up from his contemplation of the wispy curls of the child on his lap. 'Well, met; yes. Remember who you all are? I'm sorry; no.' He grinned at the assembled group and got a few grins in return.

Lara shrugged. 'No matter, it'll all fall into place, Ben.' She looked around the group. 'Ben has lost track of Kate, his sister. We've got enough in this family who can help you find her, Ben. And would have done, if we'd known of the need.' She looked him in the face, noting the slightly clenched jaw. 'Maeve, bless her, was a good woman. She did what she thought was right. Now we'll do what we think right, too.' She nodded at a tall man leaning against the door jamb. 'Robert?'

Robert half smiled, a gentle lifting of the lips. 'I can start looking into the prison records for you, Ben. It shouldn't be too difficult. I am a copper.' He was Liverpudlian: if he died his heart would have Mersey carved into it.

Ben nodded. Another man, Thomas, spoke up. 'I might be able to help with the tracing of this woman who was looking after her. Aunt Lara still has the few details your gran gave her. I have a friend works in the education department up Newcastle way: he might be able to find Kate's name on the school rolls.'

Lara smiled. 'We'll find her, Ben. It may take a bit of time, but we will find her for you.'

Ben smiled; his hand was automatically patting the small back of the child on his knee. 'I'm grateful.' He grinned. 'And somewhat overwhelmed by you all. I thought there was only a few of us.'

'What? And us good Catholics.' Robert nodded at the child. 'Mind, you've got the third – and last – of mine, on your lap.' He grinned at his wife, who grinned impishly back.

Ben smiled. 'She's beautiful.'

'Why, thank you, cousin.' Siobhan smiled at him.

'I've got some photos for you, Ben. Everyone's had a rummage around and we've got a few of your mother and one of her husband. There was a couple of the wedding, and ... well, see for yourself, boy.'

Lara passed a small collection of prints across the table. She had spent a busy week ringing around the relatives, most of whom lived in the area, to arrange this meeting. She hadn't been sure how Ben would feel about it, but he seemed to be accepting the help offered.

Siobhan came and took the now-dozing child from him, and Lara started telling him who and where the photos had been taken.

'That's your mammy, Ben, when she first came over to stay. Oh, but she was bonny. The boys were after her almost before she got off the ferry. It's a black and white so you can't see how dark her hair was.' Lara passed him the snap and picked up another. 'Who's she with here, Paul?'

'It was her friend from work.' He frowned. 'Pamela, I think her name was. She married one of the Magee boys and they went back to Ireland.' He looked at the picture, 'I know Tom Magee: he'll know where his brother is, and Pamela. But I don't think that would help you, Ben, would it?'

Ben shook his head. 'No, probably not.' He looked at the two young women with their arms wrapped around each other's waists and big smiles on their faces. 'Unless she would know where Mam went, up in Newcastle.'

'I'll give Tom a ring – see will he give me the address – and maybe we can ask Pamela. It can't hurt.'

They continued to look at the snapshots, some of them in colour, so that Ben was forming a picture of the happy laughing woman who had been his mother, and the group of people of both sexes who had been her friends. The final picture showed her with a red-headed man. 'That's your father, Ben.' Lara laid the snapshot down in front of him. 'It's the only one we could find among us. He was a bit camera shy.'

Ben nodded. The face was in profile and even then the man was half turned away so that Ben couldn't really see what he looked like.

Ben's face blanked and Lara wondered if she had been wise to arrange this get-together after all. He looked at her then, and Lara shivered. The last thing she'd expected to see in a priest's eyes was implacable hatred.

Robert, not seeing the look, was speaking cheerfully. 'You say he was in prison, Ben. Do you know what for?'

Ben looked across the room, offering a rather grim smile.

'No idea.'

'Ah, well. Lot of good Irishmen were sent to prison. I'll
check him out for you, but for now I think we'd better let the
children back in before my sister murders them.'

Ben nodded and glanced at the worried look on his great-
aunt's face. 'Thank you for all this, Aunt.'

His aunt shook her grey curls. ''Twill be fine, Ben, you'll
see.' But in her heart she was worried.

The children had swarmed back in then, and between
feeding them and family talk it was nearly four o'clock before
Ben had managed to get back to the sanctuary of the convent.
Sister Carmel answered his knock on the door with her usual
calm face.

'Hello, Father. It's a beautiful afternoon. The sisters have
put the tea table on the lawn; Father Gorski is out there, poor
lamb, all on his own. Would you like to join him and I'll bring
you a cuppa?'

Ben looked at the cheerful, wrinkled and hopeful face and
sighed under his breath. In truth he wanted to go to his room
and shut out the world. He offered a tired smile and nodded.

Ben followed her through corridors darkened by contrast
to the sun and lack of windows and emerged onto a pocket-
handkerchief-sized lawn. The Polish father was sitting on
an upright kitchen chair set under a weeping willow, a small
folding table to one side of him. He didn't look lonely to
Ben's eyes, only tired.

'Father.'

Jan Gorski opened his bright blue eyes and looked, from
a face that had seen more than its share of suffering, at the
young man standing next to his chair.

'Hello, Beineon, my son. Sit down and rest.'

Ben sat on another kitchen chair and leaned back.

'It was not good, this meeting with your family?'

Ben's lips tipped up in a half smile. 'They welcomed me,
Father. There were a great many of them, though.'

'It's good. We need our families.'

Ben said nothing.

'I miss my family. Much. "To seek a solitude in a pathless sea…" Was not that what your Columba did? I wonder how he managed. Or your Patrick, when he was ripped from his family and sent into slavery. Family is our support in troublous times, no? But sometimes we are denied that comfort for reasons that God reveals to us only many years later. And sometimes we can never go home.'

'When did you last see your family, Father?' Ben spoke curiously, for the longing had been unmistakable.

Jan Gorski smiled softly. 'Twenty-three years ago. I was dissident. It's safer for my family I stay here.'

'But surely things have changed?'

Jan shrugged, 'Some things, yes; but still it would not be wise to go into Russia.'

'I thought you were Polish.'

'I have family in Georgia as well.'

Ben waited for more, but Jan shook his head. 'And you, Beineon: you said you were visiting family you had never met, so you have family here as well as Ireland. Where will your parish be?'

'I don't know, Father.'

Jan Gorski regarded him quietly, perhaps catching the hint of desperation that said he didn't know if there would be a parish. 'As God wills then for you, too, my son.' He smiled and stood up as Sister Carmel arrived with a tray of tea and some scones.

'How good of you, Sister; we would have come in.'

'It's no trouble, Father. We're lucky to have such a fine day. Dinner will be at seven, Fathers.' She set the tray on the table and left them.

Jan Gorski watched her walk away before speaking. 'She tells me she is a penitential exile from her home in Ireland, rather than here to evangelise the heathen English.' He grinned at the younger man as he quoted the old nun, waiting to see if it would lift Ben's spirits.

Ben burst out laughing, the misery of the last few hours dispersing for a while. 'Possibly, Father, but it's hardly polite to say so.'

'No.' Father Gorski picked up one of the buttered scones and bit in. 'But I thank God for her choice. These are delicious.'

JUNE 2011

WHITBY

IT WASN'T FORGETTING TO rain. David was of the stated opinion that there were small, spiteful creatures up in the clouds, who were tipping buckets of the stuff down on the town of Whitby with such ferocity that there was a very real danger of drowning on the High Street this Friday morning without going anywhere near the sea.

Antony Grey hurried through the swing doors of the hotel entrance for his meeting with the Walkers and shook the water from his hair; he used a wet hand to unsuccessfully wipe more water off his face.

David and Kate had arrived for their meeting about ten minutes earlier and Kate had immediately ordered a pot of tea and some hot buttered toast, before they had made their way to a small table and four chairs set near a window overlooking the harbour.

David was looking around for his new researcher and Kate was looking just as anxiously for her tea, when Antony shot through the door. He'd put his best trousers and jacket on, but covering them with the ancient coat rather spoiled the effect he was trying to project.

David noted the dripping human who had just arrived clutching a very battered specimen of the briefcase family, nodded to himself and stood up. 'I think that's our man over there, Kate.' He walked over as Antony looked around with a slightly desperate air. He was wondering if he had time to go to the loos and try to tidy himself a bit before the meeting.

David strolled over, 'Would you be Dr Anthony Grey?'

Antony nodded.

'I'm David Walker. Come and take your coat off and sit down. It's filthy out there.' He led the way over to where Kate was sitting distributing a large silver teapot and three cups around the small table, along with a covered plate of toast.

Kate stood up and smiled, holding out her hand. 'Hello, Dr Grey. Kate Walker, I'm j…just along for the t…trip. Sit down; th…ere's tea but we can easily o…order coffee if you'd p… prefer it?'

Antony shook hands and both men waited while she subsided on to the comfortable chair. Antony took off his coat and slung it over the fourth chair before the men sat down. 'Tea would be very welcome, Mrs Walker.'

'Oh, Kate, please.' She offered a smile and poured out tea while the two men settled and took a good look at each other.

Kate, looking at them, was put forcibly in mind of two dogs squaring off, and cocked her head on one side slightly, looking at her husband. David wasn't usually as territorial. She glanced across at Antony Grey, but couldn't see quite what it was that had caused her husband's hackles to rise.

She set a mug in front of her erring spouse and gave him a gentle nudge. He looked at her and offered a very faint smile before turning his attention back to Antony.

Kate set another mug before Antony, 'Are you f…fully re…covered, Dr Grey?' Kate smiled nicely at the young man across the table. He was absently wiping rain, which was still dripping from his hair.

Antony nodded. 'It's all a bit of a mystery. The police seem to think I've incurred someone's wrath.' He shrugged. 'All I know is they've done me a huge favour. I've discovered I've got some friends who are prepared to extend a helping hand, and I'm grateful.'

Antony hadn't intended to tell this professor anything personal. Now he found he was pouring out the whole story of the accident and its consequences to the man's wife.

David raised an eyebrow and sipped his tea, giving the

odd look at his wife. It wasn't like his Kate to engage a stranger in conversation. It required too much effort and she got embarrassed when she knew how impatient they could become with her stutter.

Eventually Antony wound down and David set his mug on the table and pulled his briefcase from the side of his chair. 'So, shall we have a look at the work I want you to research? It chiefly involves ploughing through Bede, Paulinus and the Anglo-Saxon Chronicles and maybe Caedmon. But I understand, from Professor Downey, that you've lived in the area for most of your life?'

Antony nodded. 'I was born in Newcastle, I believe, but I was educated in Whitby and – aside from university – I've always lived here.'

David raised an eyebrow. 'You believe?'

Antony swallowed tea and embarrassment in equal parts. 'Er ... my parents died when I was only a few years old. I spent most of my childhood under the care of the state.'

'Richard Downey sang your praises; he assures me you are more than capable of doing my research for me, Antony.' David answered the unspoken worries obliquely before he picked up his glasses, settled them on his nose, and began to pull thin buff files out of his briefcase. 'Now this is the area where the proposed building site is to be placed. As you can see there is some query about the extent of the hermitage that existed in 630.' He spread a map over the table and Kate rescued her cooling toast.

She sat back with her mug and the plate on her lap, watching as the two men became absorbed in the desk-top survey requirements ... looking at Antony and wondering why she felt so comfortable with this young man. Normally she took a lot longer to trust – and then talk – to strangers, but there was something about him that drew her.

Finally both men sat back with sighs. 'We'll go out to the site another day.' David cast another disgusted glance out of the window. 'No purpose would be served in getting ourselves wringing wet.'

'I can go out any fine day. I'm sure of the ground now, David. Is there going to be a GPR survey soon?'

'Next week, if the weather is as the man predicted.'

'I could go out at the same time and look over the ground. But essentially you just want me to do the spade work on these documents.'

David nodded. 'Yeah. Email me if you run into problems, or give me a ring. You may need access to one or two of these books.' He pushed the list across the table. 'And bill me.' David offered a half smile. 'It can be expensive with travelling and postage.' He sat back. 'I don't know about you, but I want my lunch. You will join us?'

Antony opened his mouth to say 'No, thank you'. However Kate added her plea. 'Do p...please stay, Antony.'

He smiled but shook his head. 'My friend is meeting me.' He looked out of the window. 'In fact there she is now.' Amy had just brought the pushchair to a halt outside the window and was looking at the revolving door with a mixture of impatience and awe.

'Bring her in, man. She can join us, too.'

David had gone from serious and businesslike to very cheerful, and Kate looked at him with astonishment.

Antony shook his head again, standing up. 'No, thank you. She's got little Joy with her, and Joy gets cranky when she's ready for her nap.'

Kate grinned. 'We've got t...two like th...at.'

David nodded. 'Yeah, cranky babies are part of our lives, too. Go and bring her in; I'll organise the meal.' He stood up and walked over to the reception desk, leaving Antony dithering beside Kate.

'F...fetch her in; I'd like to m...meet your f...friend, Antony.'

Antony hesitated a moment longer, then walked off and through the doors. Kate saw him speak to the blonde outside. She saw her rocking the pushchair as Antony spoke to her and then the blonde shake her head. He took her arm and nodded at the building. Then Amy started to walk beside him.

'Has he persuaded her?'

'I th...ink so, David.'

'Good.' David looked at his seated wife. He couldn't for the life of him explain the surge of jealousy that had attacked him when Antony Grey had walked over. But it had slammed into him with the viciousness of an uppercut and he'd wrestled his feelings back with great difficulty, so that he could concentrate on the job in hand.

Antony came over with Amy following behind. Joy was asleep in the pushchair, her blonde wisps of hair just visible under a red hat and a dummy in her mouth.

'This is Amy,' he nodded at the pram, 'and Joy.'

Kate stood up. 'T...take off your c...coat, and have a seat. Antony says you're d...doing OU. It can't be easy, with a little one, th...ey're so d...demanding at this age.' Kate smiled and David pulled out a chair for Amy as she set the brake on the pram. She smiled a bit shyly up at him and then looked at Kate.

'Thank you for inviting us. But are you sure? Joy's been at nursery this morning and she's worn out.'

David grinned. 'She might sleep, then, and we'll get our meal in peace. But don't worry; I've asked them to get some of those little pot things.' He glanced at Kate. 'Like you feed Rosie and Paul.' His expression was verging on smug and Kate gave him a wifely look before turning to their guests.

'Not th...at he kn...ows how old Joy is or wh...at she eats. Men!' She grinned at Amy, who relaxed and grinned back.

'I need to telephone my mum, but OK. Thank you again.'

They settled down to quiet conversation and when the waiter came over they all went into the adjoining dining room for a very pleasant meal.

David and Kate watched them leaving a couple of hours later. 'That was very nice, my Kate. That young man should go far. He just needs a few introductions.'

'You h...haven't seen his w...work yet.'

'Don't need to. He asks the right questions, Kate. He'll get me my information.' David frowned. 'He reminds me of someone.'

'A y...younger David Walker. It's that air of t...total absorption in the t...topic.'

David grinned at her and swung an arm around her waist. 'Are you feeling neglected, my love?'

Kate smiled back up at him then raised her pert little nose. 'I don't n...need you to entertain me, sir.'

'Oh, what a shame; and I was going to offer to take you to the Screaming Tunnel.'

Kate looked at him in astonishment. 'Screaming...'

'You can go and lose all your inhibitions there.'

'I have no in...hibitions with you.' She grinned, but David didn't smile back.

Suddenly the conversation had taken a serious turn. He pulled her closer. 'You do, my Kate, but now isn't the time to talk about them.' He dropped a light kiss on her nose and turned her around, walking her to the reception area. 'Could you bring our coats, please? And I'd like to settle the bill.'

'Certainly, sir.' The receptionist was a very efficient young man. He pressed a bell and sent a porter scurrying for the coats, while he bent to the paperwork.

Kate was still wondering what had got into her husband today. His mood was as variable as the weather, which was now showing signs of being a gloriously sunny spring afternoon. She had to wait to find out.

ANTONY WALKED BACK THROUGH the town, pushing the pushchair and listening to Amy. 'Weren't they nice? I thought he'd be a bit too posh for me, him being a professor and all. But he'd played with Joy and didn't say a word when she spat out that last mouthful.'

Antony's lips twitched a bit. He forbore to mention that he had the same qualifications as David Walker.

Amy grinned suddenly. 'So tell me about this project you're going to do for him. What does a researcher do exactly?'

Antony glanced down at the young face next to him.

'Well, actually … I've already started it all, unbeknownst.' He watched her lips shape the final word and grinned. 'You can take a cut of the pay cheque because some of the information you've already pulled down for your OU course. So I won't have to search for them.'

'What? Is he researching tonsures?'

'Not exactly. Your dad might be able to help too.'

'Dad?' The word was all but yelped.

'Wait 'til we get home, and after supper I'll talk to you both.'

THE COUPLE THEY'D LEFT behind were also discussing the research project. 'Trust the weather to improve now I've sent the young man on his way. Never mind, love; it gives us a chance to explore a bit of Whitby Abbey on our own. How do you feel about a climb up a few steps?' David helped his wife on with her thick duffel coat and watched her flick the hair from under the collar.

'You won't c…catch me out th…at way, David Walker. I know all about th…ose s…steps.' Kate slung her bag over her shoulder and watched as he picked up his briefcase. 'But I'll c…limb them b…because I've w…wanted to ever since I read Bram Stoker's *Dracula*.' She stuck her tongue out at him and allowed him to take a hand as they walked out of the hotel.

'OK. First we put the trusty – and much abused – briefcase in the boot and then we'll go and look at the view.' David tried to sound resigned, without much success. 'I don't know; some people never work, always sloping off on holiday.'

Kate grinned at him, allowing him to gently swing their clasped hands as she said, 'Who's on h…holiday? I'm h… helping you with your research.'

'My research is five miles outside the town.'

'Well, we'll be able to s…see it from the Abbey m… mount!'

'An irrefutable argument, my love.'

Having disposed of the briefcase, they found the steps and began to climb. At the top Kate stopped for a breather. David paused beside her; he wasn't even out of breath. 'I don't know h...how you do it, David. I st...ick to my diet and exercise like mad, and you eat all th...e wrong st...uff and st...ay fit. It's not f...fair.'

David assumed a false air of virtue. 'It's because I have a young wife to support.'

Kate nodded, breathing out. 'Oh, yeah.' She put her hand on her chest as she drew in another couple of breaths. 'So why did you eye th...at poor man like he was st...ealing your only b...bone? I am *your* wife.'

'Ah!' Kate watched the colour steal into David's cheeks. He took both her hands, drawing her closer. 'You aren't usually so relaxed with people, love; I guess I just got a bit jealous.'

Kate shook her head. 'No, love. You were m...making sure he kn...ew that I was your pr...operty before he'd opened his m...mouth, poor man.'

David shook his head in puzzlement. 'I don't know, Kate.' He pulled her even further into his arms and stole a kiss. 'I love you. I don't want to lose you.'

'Not likely any time this c...century.' Kate offered her lips for another kiss before moving back. 'We've come th...is f... far; let's see the view.'

They stood on the headland, following with their eyes the line of the harbour and outlet to the sea via the river Esk. 'It used to be crammed with whaling ships and fishing vessels and now you're lucky if you catch a glimpse of one on the horizon.'

'I s...suppose its EU quotas and the p...price of f...fuel, David.'

David nodded. 'Imagine the Vikings stealing up the river for a raid on this crumbling pile. I think they razed it twice and stole the silver and books. And that was before the Dissolution.'

'Is that why th...ere was this other h...hermitage?'

David nodded. 'Perhaps it was part of it. There was a schism. To do with the way you calculate Easter. By the seventh century we'd lost a lot of books and knowledge. The Irish were collecting books and writing them but it really was the Dark Ages, love – for most of Europe, anyway. The visible image had assumed a far greater reality than invisible thought by then. They weren't arguing about how many angels sat on a pin any more.'

Kate smiled as David frowned off into the distance. 'I don't get religion, Kate. I can't be bothered with all this killing over who's got the greatest God. If there is such a being then he ought to make sure we don't go around killing each other and allowing suffering to happen to good people.'

He brought his frowning gaze back to his young wife, who was looking at him with a frown of her own. 'Wh...at's wrong, David?'

'I don't know, Kate. Perhaps I've become aware of my mortality.' His lips twisted a bit. 'Maybe it's all this trouble with your mum. I don't want you hurt again, my Kate.' He scowled, before kissing the tip of her nose, 'And I feel so bloody useless.'

'I love you, David, and you are f...far f...from useless.' Kate swallowed unexpected tears. She smiled at him a bit mistily and, hugging his arm, said, 'Sh...ow me this s...site and tell me how f...far you've got with the de...sk report.'

THE KITCHEN TABLE HAD been cleared and the dishes were in the sink. The family sat around with mugs of tea in front of them. Joy was being rocked to sleep on her mother's knee, her eyes slowly closing.

'My Amy says I can help with your research, lad.' Jack Watt settled back on the kitchen chair, which gave a faint creak as he rocked onto the back legs slightly.

Antony glanced from the impish face of Amy to the interested one of her father. He set the mug back on the table and smiled. 'I've been asked to do some background work on a building site.'

'Oh, that'll be the PPR.'

Antony hid his surprise and nodded. 'You being in the building trade, I thought you might know a bit about the proposed site. It's overlooking Robin Hood's Bay, this side of Ravenscar, where they were going to build the village back at the turn of the century. The one that was going to rival Scarborough as a Victorian seaside resort.'

Jack nodded, giving a half cough of laughter as his eyes met Antony's. 'Are you talking about the village itself? For I have to tell you, there's nay chance of owt being built out there. Though you can pick up the odd kerbstone or drain lid.'

'No, about a mile away, I think, back from Ness Point.' Antony stood up and brought his briefcase over. Pulling out a map he smoothed it out on the table and held the corners down with a pepper pot and his mug, before sitting down and saying, 'This area here.'

'Oh right, the old 'ermitage. I did hear tell as how someone was thinking of building on that.'

'You know it was a hermitage?'

''Course.' Jack raised an eyebrow and sipped tea. 'From 617 to about 800 the Danes sacked and burnt it. Wasn't rebuilt, not with the abbey so near. I thought it had been some sort of daughter house. There're some lovely corbels on the ground around there. There are some window arches too. It's good land.' He grinned at the astonishment on Antony's face. 'I like good masonry, lad, even if I'm just a jobbing builder.'

JUNE 2011

LIVERPOOL

THE CONVERSATION WAS BEING conducted in Irish Gaelic. However, Lara – sitting at the kitchen table – had no trouble following, even though she hadn't used the tongue since she was a teenager fifty years before.

'I am sorry, *Daideó*. I spoke without thinking and caused you hurt.' Ben held the white receiver to his ear and shook his head, even as the question reached him via the satellite.

'Will you come home?'

'Not yet; I haven't found Kate.' Ben still couldn't quite keep the bitterness out of his voice but he tried, for the sake of the elderly man on the other end of the line and the woman watching him.

'I am sorry too, Beineon, for we have all hurt each other by keeping this secret.'

'Yes, *Daideó*.' Ben nodded. 'The time for secrets is over. I will bring Kate to meet you, if she'll come.'

'She may not want to come here, Beineon.' The note of caution rattled against the spoken vow like hail on a window. Ben ignored it. He needed his sister; he felt incomplete without her. She would come home and he would make it up to her.

A few more words and Ben said, '*Slan go foill*,' and replaced the receiver on the phone before looking at his aunt.

'Your grandfather is right, Ben. She may have a life of her own now. She may not have forgiveness in her, Ben.' She watched as Ben slowly nodded.

'I have to find her, Aunt Lara.'

'Yes, Ben. But you have to be prepared for her not wanting to be found.'

'I can't.'

'You must, boy.'

He sat quietly at the table. It was Friday night and a select few relatives were due to arrive to pass on the news they'd managed to collect over the past week. He had spent that week kicking his heels in Liverpool. He had made the acquaintance of several members of his family. But the bulk of his time had been spent at the convent, his mind a blank – as blank as the wall that surrounded the small garden.

Lara stood up and put the kettle to boil, then went to open the door for the first of her visitors. Robert the policeman nodded as he came in, bringing the smell of rain with him.

'Ben. Cousin. I have good news and bad news.' He swung his raincoat round the back of a kitchen chair and sat down, nodding thanks as Lara set a mug of tea in front of him.

'Wait now 'til Thomas and Paul arrive, Robert.'

Robert nodded again as a thump at the door heralded more visitors. He glanced across at Ben and offered a smile.

Thomas, coming in behind Lara, brushed drops of rain from his hair and grinned. 'I haven't got Kate, but...'

'Wait.' Lara spoke quickly to stem the flow of words. 'That'll be Paul at the door; I don't want to miss anything.' She grinned and went to answer the door a third time.

When they were all seated round the table she looked at Thomas. 'You first, then Tom. You haven't got Kate, but...'

Tom grinned across the table. 'I haven't got Kate, but I have got the woman who cared for her.'

'Where?'

'Wait, now. I haven't got her now: I've got her twenty-three years ago.' He watched the eagerness fade from Ben's face and smiled a bit wryly. 'She was a teacher in Newcastle. The school's closed now, so my colleague up there tells me. It was called the Royal Victoria School for the Blind, at Benwell Dene.'

'School for the Blind?'

155

'Yes. She was a teacher there.'

'Then surely she was a good person, Ben?'

Ben nodded his head slowly at his aunt. 'My grandfather said Jardin was living with "some woman". I thought she might be ... I don't know...' Ben waved a hand – endangering his mug – 'a sort of scarlet woman.'

'Well, she was called Scarlett: Scarlett Hamilton.' Tom grinned, 'But from what my friend could find out she was a very respectable young woman.'

'So where is she?'

Tom shrugged. 'I'm afraid that trail is cold, Ben. The Victoria closed in '85 and the teachers scattered to the four winds. But...' He held up a finger as one pulling a rabbit from a hat. 'Kate went to school in Newcastle for nearly a year. West Jesmond Primary, from 1988 to '89. Jesmond Dene is just down the road from Benwell Dene. I suggest you go up there and look in the electoral roll archives at the library.'

'It's a start, Ben. Maybe if you can't track this Scarlett down you might find a neighbour who knew her, or where she went.' Lara smiled and picked up her neglected mug.

Ben smiled faintly, his lips hardly moving: twenty-two years was a long time to remember a neighbour. He looked at Robert, one eyebrow raised above a brown eye that reflected his sadness for all the news he was receiving.

'The good news or the bad news first, Cousin?'

Ben shook his head, 'Either will do.'

'He's dead, is Jardin. He's your father, Ben, so I don't know how you class it.' Robert sniffed. 'He was murdered.' He followed Ben's hand as the young man automatically made the sign of the cross.

'When?' Ben paused. 'And how?'

'Three or four years ago.' Robert looked uncomfortable. 'He was a thief, Ben. And it was a falling-out among thieves.' Robert took a sip of tea, moistening his throat. 'He was a murderer too, or as good as: they tried him for manslaughter. I'm sorry, Ben.'

Ben read the genuine sorrow in the older man's face and

nodded. 'I'm sorry too. What else did you find out?'

'I brought you the newspaper of the trial of his murderer. She was just a youngster ... nineteen. They charged her with manslaughter, but the police up in Cumbria were of the opinion that it had been deliberate.'

'Oh, God.' Ben heard the softly spoken words of his aunt and they echoed in his own mind as he listened to his cousin relating the cause of the murder and the trial. He almost missed the most vital part of the story.

'Your sister was at the trial, Ben. She was working on the archaeological site where the murder happened.'

'What? But that was only just under four years ago. She might be still up there.'

'Well, Cumbria's a big county; she was living there then. But her address is listed as being somewhere down in Wiltshire.' Rob watched the excitement fade out like the sun going down and leaving Ben's face a dull grey.

'It's worth going up there. I can give you an intro to one of the coppers who worked the murder: he might be able to give you a bit more info. I've just been searching the past crimes and criminals on the police computer. It's all public domain stuff.'

Ben smiled. 'I am grateful, Rob. It's just not easy coming to terms with the fact that your father was a criminal.'

'No, I don't suppose it is, Ben.'

Rob reached into his pocket and pulled out a few sheets of A4. 'This is all the information I could come up with about Philip Jardin.' He pushed the papers across the table.

Paul coughed into the silence. 'What I've got seems a bit...' he shrugged, 'well, a bit useless, really. My mate over in Ireland – Tom Magee – his wife, Pamela, she couldn't remember the address but she says it was Jesmond Dene that Philip Jardin came from and took Theresa to. So at least you know you're in the right area, Ben.'

'No,' Rob grinned, 'it's better than useless, Paul; it's good. He can look up Philip and Theresa on the electoral roll, too. Maybe find their address up there.' He looked at Ben. 'If you find the address you might be able to track him for the year of their marriage.'

'I don't see how that helps me find Kate now.'

'If Kate was living in Jesmond Dene with your father – and this Scarlett Hamilton was in Benwell Dene at the same time – it gives you two places to start your search, Ben.'

'I'd rather go straight to the Cumbria police.'

'Fine. But they might not be able to tell you where Kate went after the trial. She's not a criminal, Ben. You need all the clues you can get, boy. They might not be able to tell you legally.' Lara shook her grey locks and looked from one face to the other, settling on Robert's face with the question.

'True. They aren't obliged to give you any details, except those recorded on the court records and already in the public domain.'

Ben sat silent, thinking about all he'd learnt. His sister might have been living with her father but she had someone who – on the surface – appeared to have been kind living with her as well. 'Thank you for all your efforts.' He looked around at the four faces. 'I'll pray about it and decide what I'm going to do next.'

'See that you let us know, Ben.' Rob grinned. 'And when you find Kate, bring her to meet us first.' The other two men nodded agreement.

Ben looked across at his aunt Lara. 'I think I'll go back to the convent now. I've got a lot to think about. I'll give you a ring in the morning, Aunt. Let you know what I'm doing.'

'And where you're going, Ben. We don't want to lose track of you, too.' Lara stood up and walked with him to the door. She stood on tiptoe and dropped a kiss onto his cheek. 'Don't be a stranger, Ben.'

JUNE 2011

WHITBY

ANTONY HAD GONE UP to his room after supper, ostensibly to sort out his notes from the morning's meeting but in reality to deal with his post. Another letter had arrived; he was beginning to recognise the handwriting now and could guess at the contents. It was just as bad as he'd thought it would be, in fact worse: WHAT WILL SHE SAY WHEN SHE FINDS OUT YOU'RE A BASTARD?

Antony shook his head over the message, puzzled as much by the content as the virulence. He knew he was no saint, but he didn't think he was that bad. He'd used protective gloves to open the letter, as Detective Tierney had instructed him. He would take it to the police station tomorrow morning and hand it over. This one had come to his new lodgings and that meant whoever was sending them knew where he was living, and that was a very real concern to him.

The police had told him they were keeping an eye out and he had to believe them, but he was more than a little worried. If this madman knew where he lived, was he watching where he went, and did that mean he knew about his meeting with Professor Walker? Should he tell him about this latest development? He had told Kate Walker a little of his trouble. He didn't wish harm to come to such a nice woman. Would the police tell Walker if he didn't?

Antony stared blankly at the wallpaper before he became aware that there was a gentle tapping at his bedroom door and Amy was calling his name through the woodwork. 'Antony?'

Antony slid the paper and envelope into his briefcase before standing up and going over to the door. He opened it and smiled at the sight that met his eye. Amy was indeed relaxed with him. Her hair was wrapped in a blue towel and the old sweat pants and T-shirt were not calculated to set him lusting after the nice figure inside them.

'Hello. What's up?'

'Mam says Dad's going down the pub and do you want to go, too?'

Antony raised an eyebrow, but shook his head.

'Only I've got to go to work soon.'

Antony nodded, 'I only went to the pub to eat. I'm not that keen on the pub scene, really.' He frowned at the face in front of him. 'I could babysit if your mum wants a night out, too.'

Amy giggled. 'Mum?'

'Why not? She might like a night out with your dad.'

Her mother, appearing at the top of the stairs with the suddenness of a jack-in-the-box, looked with some surprise from her giggling daughter to the grave-faced man who was her lodger.

'He says, "Do you want to go to the pub with Dad?" He says he'll babysit.' Amy turned a glowing face to her mother.

Joyce looked at Antony. 'That's really kind of you, Antony.' She nodded her head at some inner thought. 'That would be nice; it's ages since we went out together.' She spun on her heel and went down stairs again, calling, 'Jack.'

Amy looked first astonished and then guilty. 'I forget.'

'Eh?'

'I forget how much she's given up so that I can keep our Joy. She used to go out with Dad when I was younger. But, babysitting for me, she can't any more.' Amy pulled the towel off her head, allowing the blonde locks to fall anyhow about her face and, still dangling the towel, followed her mother down the stairs.

Antony went back to the bed and shut his briefcase, clicking the lock before placing it next to the table under the window. He glanced around the room. The window was closed and the curtains drawn against the cool spring evening. The place smelt fresh and airy and clean. Babysitting was small payment for this level of comfort.

He went downstairs to find Amy being hugged by her mother, both smiling. But both with tears on their cheeks. He shook his head in mystification; he didn't understand women. 'Anything special the little toerag needs while you're out?'

Amy shook her head, 'She's had a lovely afternoon in the fresh air; she should sleep until morning.'

'OK. I'll just make a cuppa and take it up to my room; if I leave my door open I'll hear her if she stirs.'

'What if she needs her nappy...?'

'I know how to deal with a nappy and a bottle, Amy; don't worry. Go and enjoy yourself, Mrs Watt.' He turned to the sink, filling the kettle and putting it on the gas. The two women exchanged a glance and shrugged before parting to get ready for their nights in the pub, one to work and the other to play.

JUNE 2011

CUMBRIA

DAVID WAS WORKING OR, rather, trying to work. His offspring were intent on playing with their father. He glanced up, looking rather helplessly at Kate as she came into the study. 'I'm sorry, David. They escaped.'

'Dadda.' The red tousled curls of his daughter brushed his knee as she tried to scramble up, little toes digging in through her all-in-one pyjamas. He gave her a helping hand and set her comfortably on his lap.

'Story.' It was a demand, not a request, as his son thrust a battered book at him and also tried to get onto the lap. David held his daughter firmly with one hand while lifting his son with the other. Both toddlers leaned back against him and pushed thumbs into their mouths.

Kate shrugged. 'I can...'

David shook his head. 'So what story is it to be tonight, as if I didn't know? The adventures of an alien?' He flipped open the book as his children giggled around their thumbs. 'No, it's just a talking dog.'

He began to read the simple words, lingering long enough over the pages for each child to point out something. Kate leaned against the doorjamb, watching them. Her family. She hadn't thought she'd have a family. From something Scarlett had said when she was a teenager, she had been Scarlett's miracle. At least that's what she thought Scarlett had meant. She had thought that conception was going to be difficult. She had been almost as stunned as David when she had conceived within a few months of marriage.

David glanced up as if becoming aware of her scrutiny, raising an eyebrow at her. She offered him a half smile and he turned his attention back to his children. He finished the story and hoisted a child onto each hip. 'Bedtime. Mummy needs a few minutes peace from you horrible lot and so do I.' He came towards, her carrying both children. Paul was transferred to his mother and both parents took them up to their cots and settled them to sleep.

As David walked downstairs holding Kate's hand, he looked at his silent wife. 'What were you thinking about, love?'

'When?'

'Just now. You looked really happy and then really sad.'

'I'm tr...ying to understand Scarlett.' David nodded encouragingly as they went towards the kitchen to make a drink before he returned to the study. 'I s...sort of understand why she k...kept me, David. If I was her one ch...ance of having a ch...ild, and she was desperate enough, then...'

'Yeah. It's a bit different for men, but I suppose there was always a bit of me that regretted I didn't have a son or daughter to pass on all those genes to. But women. Mostly you have this instinct to procreate; it's part of being female, I suppose.'

'That's a very ch...chauvinist thing to say, love, but I know wh...at you mean. Most women w...want children.' She sat down with a sigh, as David went over to the Aga and pulled the kettle forward to set it boiling. 'I'd b...been asking about why I couldn't have a brother or s...sister like the other children and she t...told me I was her one ch...ance.'

'She did love you, Kate.' David came over, pulling out a chair and sitting down while he waited for the tea to brew.

'I know, David. On th...ose grounds alone I'm tr...ying to f...forgive her. But I feel so cut adrift, s...somehow. I don't know wh...o I am any more. You were t...talking about your genes. I don't have m...much idea about m...mine, now.'

David waited patiently while she fiddled with a spoon on

the table, watching the restless hands.

'If Scarlett w...wasn't my m...other, then I don't know wh...at illnesses I m...might be a c...carrier of and p...pass on to the ch...ildren.'

David reached out a hand. 'Don't get worked up. There's nothing wrong with Rosie and Paul.'

He looked at her downbent head. 'Kate, I love you. The babies will be fine.'

'I know.' Kate looked up. 'But I'm pr...egnant.'

David opened his mouth and then shut it to allow the grin to spread. He stood up, coming around the table and hauling his wife into his arms. 'I really do love you, you clever girl.'

'But, David...'

'Don't you want...?' He leaned back looking worried, his joy dimming.

'Of c...course I do. But, David, I gave lots of in...formation for the last pr...egnancy based on Scarlett. I can't do that th...is t...time. And I'm so s...scared.'

'I'm here, my Kate, I'm not going to let anything happen to you.' He held her close for a hug before saying, 'How far...'

'Only a...bout eight weeks, maybe nine. I did one of th...ose over-the-counter th...ings. It was an accident; I think I missed a p...pill. I didn't mean to get pr...egnant; I was th...inking of coming back to work full time s...soon. Now I can't work...'

David nodded, still holding her tight. 'We'll get an appointment with the doc first thing Monday morning. As for work ... you shall work if you want, love, but if you want to be a full time mum then that's fine by me; we can afford it, thank God.'

'I'm s...'

'If you're going to say you're sorry, don't.' He grinned. 'It takes two to make a baby.'

'Yes, but I was su...pposed to take care of, of co...ntraception; I said I w...would...'

David offered another impish smile and shrugged. 'Do I look as though I care, Kate? So long as you don't mind having this baby I'm delighted.' He swung her round, lifting her feet off the floor suddenly and then kissing her breathless. 'Just wait until I tell Mum and Pops.' He set her down and turned to pour out the tea, swinging back to say, 'No more lifting the babies, Kate, or digging on site, or running after Thea. It's cotton wool for you, my girl.' He set her mug in front of her and sat down himself.

'You really are p...pleased. The tw...ins will only be tw...o when this one makes an app...earance.'

'I'm over the moon, darling.'

JUNE 2011

LIVERPOOL

If David Walker was over the moon at finding he was going to be a father and couldn't wait to share his life and his genes with his new child, Ben Jardin was appalled at the disclosures he'd discovered about his father, and had no wish to have anything to do with the man. However, there was no escaping the genetic tie.

He pulled the easy chair forward to the window and looked down on the garden of the convent, as he had a dozen times over the past week. The shadows were creeping stealthily over the grass, turning the small enclosed world sepia. Ben watched the grass disappear behind the curtain of the night before he switched on the side light and pulled out the papers that his cousin Rob had pulled down off the police computer.

There was a photo. It really was a mug shot and Ben frowned over it. His father hadn't been handsome. His hair hadn't just receded; it had totally ebbed away in the centre. He needed a shave and he looked at the camera with more resignation than anything else on his face.

Ben set it to one side and picked up the first printout. It was a list of what Ben understood were called previous crimes. He ran an eye down the list. His father had advanced from petty theft, shoplifting and opportunistic burglary as a teenager, to a more specialised branch of 'theft to order' as he got older, but not necessarily wiser. Archaeological artefacts. Ben raised a blond eyebrow.

He glanced away and picked up the next few pages. They

were a shorthand form of the charges against his father for the murder of a young man – again at an archaeological dig – the incident happening in Carlisle in the late nineties.

Ben read through the words three times before he realised he wasn't taking in the understanding along with them. He tried again, clenching his teeth. So it was accidental death; but if his father hadn't been stealing he wouldn't have caused the young man's death. Ben sighed and laid the papers down.

He stirred restlessly and flipped the page and read more. Apparently his father had been involved in a crime when he met his end, stealing from a dig to supply a dealer down London way. Ben laid the paper down and glanced out of the window. All he saw was a young man in black, his priest's collar a circle of white in the gloom.

He stood up before walking over to the window and pushing it open. He bent his head and began to read the final chapter in his father's life. A soft damp mist settled on his hair and turned the blond curls butterscotch as he stood breathing in the night air.

Philip Jardin had met his death when he was pushed into a large hole which was the site of a Roman well under excavation. The fall hadn't killed him, however: it had been the blow to his head – from an object wielded by a young woman of nineteen – which had done that. Ben looked out onto the dark night then walked back to his seat and sat down again, gathering up the remaining two flimsy pages to finish what he had started.

They turned out to be background information on Philip Jardin. For the first time he discovered that his father had been born in Newcastle and abandoned in the hospital after the birth. His mother had simply walked out and not come back. He used the name she had given him, but whether it was her real name was doubtful.

He had been placed in the care of social services who had subsequently tried, unsuccessfully, to have him adopted. He was brought up in one of the state children's homes in Newcastle. He left when he was sixteen and worked in a variety of jobs, which never lasted long. It had been a wasted life, really. Ben's eye skipped forward as much as the police record did. Here was another record of crime and imprisonment. Ben's eye and his heart stopped for seconds as he took in the import of what he was reading. His father had been married to a Caroline Bathurst. She was listed as next of kin in March 1984.

Ben's heart began to beat slowly and heavily. 'No, that can't be right. He was married to my mother in '84. I was born in '85; he can't have been married to anyone called Bathurst. Who the hell is she?' He was shocked to hear his own voice as he reread the words.

JUNE 2011

WHITBY

ANOTHER MAN WHO WAS shocked to hear his own voice was Antony. He had been head down, butt up, in research papers when the small wail from the next room broke into his concentration. He pushed back the chair and left the cursor blinking on the computer screen as he walked out of his bedroom and into the next. A dim night light showed him the cot set to the side of Amy's bed. He bent to pick up the distressed infant – who snuggled into his shoulder as he popped her dummy back into her mouth – and patted her back.

The quiet 'hell!' which echoed his disbelief at his thoughts – and which had shocked him – wasn't because he had been interrupted at an important point in his research, nor yet because the child was demanding his attention. No: what had shocked him was the impact of being in Amy's room. He had thought himself immune to the young woman. He hadn't reacted to her standing at his door earlier in tatty sweats and wet hair, except to think of her in terms of a kid sister. But standing with her indefinable scent in his nostrils and looking at the neatly made bed had his mind thinking thoughts that were more than inappropriate. They were strictly on the forbidden list.

He rocked little Joy and was rewarded by a small snore. Evidently it was just the missing dummy that had disturbed her. He gently set her back in the cot and pulled up the covers; a small sigh and she was contentedly sucking, her eyes shut tight. He backed out as if walking on eggshells.

Back in his own room he was surprised to find he had a light film of sweat on his brow. He stood irresolute, looking at the computer, then spun on his heel and walked down the stairs to make coffee. He would have preferred a stiff drink for once, but aside from the fact that he didn't have any alcohol around he wouldn't have drunk it while looking after the baby.

He stood watching the kettle, thinking of this new problem. Amy had said she liked him because he 'didn't touch' and treated her like a person, not a sex object. And the first time he got the opportunity to see her bedroom his mind was between the sheets. He sighed. 'No; I can deal with this. It's just a blip. I've been without a woman too long.' He picked up the box of tea bags and took one out, dangling it over the side of a mug. 'You can do this, Antony.'

'Talking to yourself is the first sign of madness, lad.'

Antony spun around as Jack Watt came through the door shaking raindrops off his head, followed by Joyce who smiled at their new lodger. 'Little Joy all right?'

'Yeah, no problems. She lost her dummy, but settled as soon as I gave it back to her.'

'Good. It was really nice to go out. Even if Jack had to curb his enthusiasm for shouting at the big screen.'

'I don't know what you mean, pet. Me, shout?' Jack grinned and went over to the oven, spinning the dial and clicking the pilot switch.

'We've brought a pizza back, Antony. Would you like some?'

Antony shook his head. 'No, I'm good, thanks. I'll make a proper pot of tea, though.'

'You're going to make some woman a great husband some day.' Joyce took her jacket off and ran a hand through her hair before sitting at the kitchen table, watching critically as her husband found a flat tray and took a pizza out of a box. He set it on the tray and put both into the oven.

Antony swung back as the kettle gave a piercing whistle and successfully hid the expression on his face. He wasn't thinking in terms of marriage; in fact, he guiltily thought, he'd been thinking of something else entirely just before Amy's parents had walked through the door

'Jack, get the plates out, love. Amy will be home in ten minutes.'

Antony, busy pouring tea, kept his back to the other couple before picking up his own mug and turning around. 'I have a bit of work to finish, so if you'll excuse me...' He smiled at Joyce and walked quickly out of the room, as if the Watt family had contracted some sort of plague. He had no desire to meet Amy just at the moment.

The next morning, when he awoke, he was considerably calmer. 'See, just a blip. Now I have to go to the library this morning so I can call into the police station on the way, and since it's tipping it down out there she won't want to get the baby wet. Best play it safe.' Thus he spoke to himself as he got out of bed and went into the bathroom. Unfortunately Amy had been there before him.

He could hear her talking to Joy in her bedroom and he closed the door smartly on both the noise and his thoughts. He took his shower cold.

Downstairs he decided he would skip breakfast and get out while the getting was good. 'Mrs Watt ... Joyce,' he offered a half smile at her look of reproach, 'I've got to arrange for some research books down at the library so I'm getting there before the school children arrive to change theirs. I'll see you later.' He shrugged into his old coat and shot out of the door before she could utter the protest he could see hovering on her lips.

Walking down the street he allowed the cold rain to fall unheeded on his head. He hadn't lied, but he could have waited for Amy. 'Better not, Antony. Not until you can get your hormones under control.' He was frankly puzzled. He wasn't exactly sweet sixteen and nor was he a virgin, but sex hadn't been much of an issue before last night. He swung into the police station and asked for Detective Sergeant Tierney.

The detective sergeant arrived promptly and Antony handed over the latest missive. 'It's the same hand on the envelope, and I should say the same brand of newspaper that it's been cut from.'

Detective Tierney, handling the paper through his gloves, nodded as he looked at it. 'Yeah, I'd agree with you there.' He offered a half smile. 'The good news is we have got a bit of DNA off the envelope flap; we'll check to see if this matches. The bad news is we might have the DNA, but we need a person to match it with.'

He continued to look at the paper for a further minute and then opened a file that he'd brought in with him. 'These are copies of the other letters.'

Antony looked down at the photocopies and then up at the frowning officer. 'This would seem to imply they know something about you, sir. Are you a bastard?' He held up a hand. 'I mean in the technical sense of your parents not being married.'

Antony shook his head. 'My parents were in a crash when I was about four years old. I escaped with a few bruises; my mother was driving and my father was in the passenger seat. A car hit the passenger side and he was apparently unrecognisable, but they were married.' He offered a half grin. 'Wedding rings, and they found paperwork on him to say his name was Grey.'

Sergeant Tierney nodded. 'And in the other sense?' He offered a half smile of his own.

'Only on a par with most other men, Sergeant.'

'I think we need to have a bit more of your history then, Mr Grey. You've got the wrong side of someone somewhere.'

'What do you want to know, Sergeant?'

'Start at the beginning. I'll stop you if I want more detail.'

'Crash.'

'How did they identify you?'

'Paperwork in the pockets, and the corporation house where they lived. They tried to trace relatives without success.'

'So...'

'Foster homes ad infinitum until I was sixteen.'

Tierney was making shorthand notes as Antony talked.

'Can you supply me with names and addresses?'

Antony shrugged, 'Some. You'd have to go to the home for the bulk of them. It's only up the road here.' He supplied the address and watched as it was neatly transcribed. 'I haven't been back for years; it doesn't exactly hold happy memories, Sergeant.'

The detective sergeant nodded again. 'Did you have friends there? Or enemies?'

'That was over twenty years ago.'

'Yep. We have to start somewhere.'

Antony scratched an ear, 'I can remember a few names but they came and went, Sarge, same as I did. Fostering doesn't exactly encourage one to make close and intimate relationships. They're apt to be snatched away from you without apparent rhyme or reason.'

'Yes, sir...'

Antony shrugged. 'There was Arthur Pool. I think he's still around the town. We nod if we see each other in passing. Mike,' he frowned, clicked his fingers and said, 'Pitts. Haven't seen him since I went to uni. Er ... Stan Hunt; he's around. Shares the same block of flats. He had relatives who took him in for short periods.' Antony frowned, shrugged. 'Better if you access the files.'

'Uni, sir?'

'I kept pretty much to myself. I had to pay my own way, despite my scholarship. I worked at the McDonald's the first year; I did some gardening the second year and the third year I found work tutoring. I suppose you want those names and addresses too.'

''Fraid so.'

'I shall have no reputation left, Sarge.' He offered another shrug; he really thought the whole thing was a wild goose chase. He looked at the serious face opposite. 'You really think this is someone from my past come to bite me?'

'We've asked around. We have to check out your story, sir. You didn't go anywhere much or do anything much for the last six months. Your tutor at uni speaks highly of you. You visited the pub for evening meals, but otherwise rarely went out or spoke to people. Your neighbours hardly know what you look like. Amy Watt and her family are respectable and law-abiding. So we have to find a connection further back.'

Antony sighed deeply. 'OK, Sarge; ask away.'

JUNE 2011

CUMBRIA

'ASK US WHAT THE news is, Mum.' David was talking on the phone to his parents while he watched his wife pottering about the study. It was only just ten o'clock in the morning but he couldn't wait any longer to tell them. He was like a kid at Christmas, Kate thought.

Kate grinned at him and sat down in one of the old leather chairs that lived in the bay window of his study. The view over the Solway today was lovely; she could see the tide coming in over the sands, white horses of spume dancing on the tops of the waves and some fluffy clouds hurrying up the estuary towards Gretna as if heading for an elopement.

'You're going to be grandparents again.' The grin on his face was threatening to reach his ears. 'Of course we're pleased; over the moon, dancing on air.' He looked across to Kate. 'Mum says she's getting out the knitting needles and she can't wait to see the newest addition.' He turned back to the phone. 'It might be a long wait, Mum. We haven't got an official date, but we think November time.'

He held the phone out. 'Mum wants a word.' Kate came over and he stood up and nudged her into his seat before handing over the receiver. He was just going to sit down when he heard the click of the letter box. 'I'll get the post.'

Kate was still speaking when he returned a few minutes later. 'Do you w…want another w…word?'

He shook his head. 'I'll talk to them tomorrow at our usual time.'

Kate relayed the message. 'Bye, Mum.' She set the phone down and smiled up at David. 'H...have we got anything interest...ing?'

'Post from the Register Office.' He held a certificate out. 'And the page from the Register book that the catholic priest in Liverpool promised us.'

She took the certificate but looked at her husband. 'Wh...at does it say? Does it h...help?'

Kate watched as David scanned down the written words of the accompanying letter. 'Oh, Lord! Here, give me my glasses: this script is terrible.' Kate obediently handed over a pair of glasses lying on the desk and waited impatiently for him to finish reading.

'Kate.' David came over and pulled her up into his arms, the paper held behind her back, the certificate dropping unheeded from her hand to the desk.

'Wh...at's wr...ong?' He heard the alarm in her voice.

'You have a brother.' There was no easy way of telling her. David decided bluntness and getting it over with had a lot to recommend it, but he held her tight nevertheless.

'B...b...br...brother?'

David walked her over to the easy chair and pushed her gently down before sinking onto the arm and wrapping his arm around her shoulders. He could feel himself shivering and it melded into the fine tremble going over his wife. They sat in silence, absorbing the news. David recovered first, assessing the colour of his wife's face which had turned the colour of skimmed milk. The pink was creeping back, but he didn't think it was recovery from shock that was putting it there.

'How c...could th...ey?' It was a sibilant whisper.

David grimaced, waiting for her to put the rest of the puzzle together.

'Hang on.' Ah! He hadn't thought it would take long. 'S...ame page. Twins?'

'I should think so. It certainly explains Rosie and Paul. I thought I was just lucky, but it seems I'm luckier than I thought.'

'H…how could I f…forget my t…twin?'

David's brain had been busy even as he watched his wife, 'I'm sorry, love, but … maybe he died. We could try to find his death certificate over the Net.'

Kate gave a half nod but it was obvious she was still dealing with the news.

'The births were registered by Theresa Jardin, nee O'Connor; she gives the father as Philip Jardin and Liverpool as the place of birth.'

'Wh…en?'

'Five days after the birth.'

Kate took a breath. 'What's my brother's name?'

'Beineon Aiden.'

'Ben,' Kate shook her head, 'I don't remember. I don't remember.'

David looked at her closely. He suspected that the stutter was part of the trauma of her upbringing. Kate always had a slight hesitation in her speech, but the last sentence or two had come out perfectly clearly. He put his head on one side, regarding his wife critically. 'Don't try too hard, darling. Let it seep back.'

'She m…might have st…olen me, David, but she loved me. Wh…at about h…him? If she w…wanted a baby, wh…y not two?' She shook her curls, sitting a bit more upright in the chair 'And what about my f…father? He really w…as a b… bastard, wasn't he, David?'

David raised a mobile eyebrow; his wife didn't swear, ever. The green eyes echoed the slight smile on his face. 'If you say so, love.' He'd rather have anger than the apathy of last week. He gave her a reassuring hug before he moved over to the desk where a computer lurked, like a bad deed in a good world.

He sat and began to look for the sites he'd been grappling with all week. He looked up as Kate came over and sat on the other side of the desk. 'I can't find a death, Kate. I've given it a margin of five years.'

'OK. Wh...at else does the certificate s...ay?'

'It hasn't got much more than your small one. It names both parents; your father's occupation.' David gave a grunt of laughter. 'Researcher. Oh, yeah. Into what, I wonder? And the fact that you were born in Liverpool Maternity.' He poked the certificate over the table and looked back at the screen, half his mind on the search for a death.

'B...beineon Aiden is Irish, David, like Róis.' He nodded absently. 'Maybe you should l...look on the Irish s...sites.' David looked up sharply. Then she watched his two fingers moving over the keys.

Five minutes passed as slowly as a traffic jam. 'No.' He sighed.

'Now I'm l...looking for a b...brother too, David. Do you th...ink they split us and t...took one each? Maybe that's why I don't r....remember him.'

'I don't know, Kate. It was cruel, though; imagine trying to split up Rosie and Paul.' As if on the words Thea came into the room with a tray of drinks – followed by the two toddlers – who made a beeline for their parent's knees, scrambling up like pirates on the Spanish Main.

'Coffee time, Master David. The babies have had their drink, so don't go throwing them about.' She watched as David stopped playing 'Ride a Cock Horse' with his son and looked at her a bit guiltily.

Kate grinned; Thea was one of the few who wasn't scared of telling him off. She moved the papers to the side and allowed Thea to set the tray down out of reach of small hands.

'Thea, we have some news.'

'Another baby, I'll be bound; you've been looking peaky for weeks.' Thea nodded at her.

David grinned, bouncing his son more gently, and Kate gaped at her. 'I only s...suspected it last w...week.'

'Well it's to be hoped it's not another pair like these two.'

David gave a quiet groan and looked at his wife who'd gone pale again. 'Oh, Lord! I hadn't thought of that.'

JUNE 2011

NEWCASTLE, ENGLAND

THE OLD SCHOOL STILL sat in the grounds, its red brick glowing in the afternoon sunshine. Ben placed a hand each on two of the metal poles that formed part of the large iron gates and peered through them. He wasn't quite sure what purpose could be served by finding the site where Scarlett Hamilton had been employed, but he felt he had to come and look.

'It's a listed building, lad.'

Ben turned at the words to see a middle-aged woman apparently watching him, at her heels a Labrador with a yellow jacket and harness. He offered a smile. 'What was it like?'

'When? It's been there a long time.'

'When it was a school.'

She gave a quiet smile. 'It's been that a long time, too. I used to dance on the lawns; it was amazing, all synchronised and not one with more than a tiny bit of sight.'

'Did you know any of the teachers?' Ben looked at her face, registering the thick lenses on the glasses she wore.

She looked down, pulling the dog closer, before she looked up and spoke to him. 'I knew the Head. He and his wife were lovely people; they worked so hard with us kids. Made us feel human and acceptable. Loved. It's not easy to do that.'

'Did you know any of the other teachers? I'm trying to trace one of them. I know she was working here in '84, but after that I lose track of her.'

She shook her head. 'I only knew my own. Some of them

lived in the school; acted as house parents to the children as well. But we didn't really see them; we really only knew those who taught us and I only went there for one year.' She offered a smile, 'You could try the post office along the road. Alice is a permanent fixture there.'

'Thank you. You've been helpful.'

'I haven't told you much, lad.'

'You've told me the place she worked at was filled with love. I shouldn't think a teacher there would last long who wasn't loving, too.'

'No, lad.' She walked away, the dog snuffling at the kerb as she walked along.

Ben watched her. She was a confident woman. It wasn't obvious she was partially sighted but she had attended the school, and she had a guide dog, so she must be. He nodded to himself. Scarlett was coming out as a caring woman, not the hussy his grandmother had described to her relatives.

He set off in the direction of the post office he could see in the distance. It had been a shock to discover that his own mother hadn't been married to Jardin. Or rather that her marriage had been bigamous. That made him illegitimate, he supposed, and his grandmother right all along. He walked quickly, his feet reflecting his inward agitation, kicking at stray pebbles as he thought again of that revelation.

He needed to find a computer network and go on the web. Start checking out the births, deaths and marriage sites. He didn't fancy any more exposés in front of other people, so an internet café wasn't on his list of places to visit today. He would wait until he could get to a library.

He stopped as he reached the post office, looking through the glass door, checking that his enquiries could be conducted in relative privacy. It seemed to be a paper shop, wool shop and general store inside.

The bell tinkled as he opened the door and he was assailed by the smell of newspaper and – he sniffed – possibly pipe tobacco. Someone who looked as though she'd had several birthday cards from the Queen came through from a narrow door in the corner, which was standing ajar.

'Hello. How can I help you?' The voice was thin and sweet like honey. There was a hint of tartness, too. The lapel badge had the name Alice Coote.

'Hello. My name is Father O'Connor. I was told you might be able to give me some information about one of the teachers from the Victoria School for the Blind?'

'Which teacher would that be, young man?'

'Miss Scarlett Hamilton.'

'And what would you like to know about Miss Hamilton?'

Ben frowned. He didn't actually know what he wanted to know. 'Was she kind?'

The old woman looked up at him, pushing a wrinkled hand through hair like a Brillo Pad. 'Kind?' she frowned at him.

'Good with the children?'

'Scarlett was a lovely young woman. She'd bring the little ones in, teaching them how to buy stamps and sweets and cards. She had the patience of a saint.'

Ben smiled at the shrewd blue eyes watching him. 'Did she live in?'

'When she first started there.'

'Where did she go when the school shut? Do you know?'

The old head shook but she avoided his eyes. 'They all moved away. It was good and bad, closing the school. Integration they called it. Putting the little ones into the mainstream. It worked for some. For some it was a terrible ordeal. They couldn't cope and the schools weren't set up for them.' She shook her head. 'The teachers had to find new jobs. Scarlett moved to Jesmond Dene, but that was years ago. I don't know where she is now.'

'Thank you.'

He was about to turn and go when a hand like a claw caught at his sleeve. 'Scarlett was a good woman. Don't let anyone tell you different.'

Ben looked at the old face. 'What aren't you telling me?'

'Nothing. Just you remember, she was good and kind.' She let go of his hand and stepped back behind her counter as a customer came through the door. He stood, hesitating, but it was obvious she was going to be occupied for some time. The talk was of the merits of angora wool against acrylic and merino. He nodded at her and fled, confounded by women's talk.

That had been a peculiar conversation. He reran it as he walked back to his car. It was obvious Alice knew more than she was telling and it was equally obvious she wasn't going to tell. He mulled over what he'd learnt. Scarlett had been a kind, conscientious teacher. She had lived with the children, which argued that she either didn't have a home in the area or was really dedicated to the children. She had been out of a job and a home when the school closed.

Ben set his seat belt and then pulled out a street map. He would find the nearest library to Jesmond Dene and see if he couldn't track down Miss Hamilton through the electoral rolls. A trawl through the newspaper stacks of the area might be helpful too. He had plenty of time. He wasn't going anywhere until he'd found his sister, Kate.

JUNE 2011

CUMBRIA

His sister Kate was also looking at newspapers. 'I didn't know you c...could look at all th...is l...lot on line, David.'

'Incredible, isn't it, love? Someone somewhere deserves a medal for putting all this lot on the net.' He scrolled down a page of information and clicked onto a likely source. 'However, I think I need to refine my search a bit. This is not about the Roman site in Germany at all. In fact it's pornography.'

'Eh?' Kate came round the table and looked over his shoulder. Both of them cocked their heads one way and then the other. 'Is th...at p...possible?'

David grinned at the screen. 'Well, they look normal.' He clicked the cursor. 'I was looking up the anthropology of borderlands; I don't quite know how that appeared on the screen.'

Kate looked at the list of sites on the search engine. 'I th... ink it's something to do with th...at author there; he seems to c...cross more than ethnic and c...cultural b...borders.'

David nodded, swinging round slightly in his chair to look at his wife. 'How are you getting on?'

'My f...father seems to have appeared in the police c... courts and then b...been reported in the p...paper a great many t...times, David.'

'Nothing new there, then.'

'No.' She heaved a sigh.

'Give up for now, Kate. Go and play with the babies;

they'll be up from their nap in a few minutes.'

'Part of the t…trouble is I don't know wh…at I want to know, love.'

'We could always ask Bob or Sandy to look into that for us.'

'I don't think the p…police – no matter how f…friendly – are allowed to give out that sort of in…formation, David.'

David nodded. He rather liked the pair of detectives he'd met a few times now. They had investigated Philip Jardin's murder on one of his archaeological sites and their paths had crossed a time or two since. But Kate was probably right about how much information they could give. He shrugged. 'I'll ask Bob the next time I see him.' He nodded as he heard a small wail coming from the room upstairs. 'Rosie. She always wakes with a wail.'

'I'll go and s…see to them. I'll t…ake th…em in the double b…buggy for a w…walk while you get on with your w…ork, love. We s…seem to be interrupting it a lot, j…just now.' Kate offered a half smile as David stood up and came around the desk.

'A walk in the fresh air sounds much better than stuffy files. I'll come with you.'

Kate gave him a wifely look. 'I am p…pregnant, not ill.'

David looked guilty for a fleeting second before he thought of the perfect excuse. 'Darling, you're always telling me I need to exercise; I'm just obeying you.'

'Oh, yeah.' His wife, heading out the door, poked her tongue out at him over her shoulder and continued to head towards her children in the room upstairs.

Ten minutes later, as David and Kate watched, the children – released from the confinement of the stroller – fossicked about on a patch of sand on the edge of the Solway Firth.

David stood holding Kate's hand, his eyes never straying from his son and daughter as he began to speak. 'I think we need to refine our search with your quest too, Kate. We started out trying to find your mother, love – and now we need to find your brother, too. We've muddied the waters going off at a tangent looking at your father's criminal record and trying to trace Scarlett's relatives. Yes?'

'Yes.'

'Let's look at what we've got, then. Theresa O'Connor: it's a good Irish name if ever I heard one, and Ben's and your names are also Irish. So I think we can assume that you are part Irish, love.' He glanced down at Kate standing so silently next to him. 'Nothing wrong with the Irish. We know you were born in Liverpool, so that would be one community to start searching among.'

'It's a huge c...community, David.'

'True, my Kate. But we've searched for harder things when we've researched a site. Now, as to your father. We know he came from Newcastle upon Tyne.'

'Are we sure a...bout th...at?'

David nodded, never removing his eyes from his son, who seemed intent on shifting a stone as big as his head for some reason unknown to his father. 'He'll trap his fingers in a minute and then perhaps he'll stop doing it.'

Kate nodded. It wasn't that his parents didn't love him – far from it – but baby Paul didn't take kindly to restraint, so they had agreed on a policy of allowing the toddler to do things his way and finding his own reasons why some activities were banned. Not that they would allow harm to come to him but getting mucky and testing themselves was part of childhood, in David's opinion.

The stone finally rolled several inches and came to rest away from Paul, who began to poke about in the freshly revealed sand. David nodded again. 'Yes, I remember his accent; Geordie through and through, Kate. But why are we looking at him? We know he is dead.'

'Because, I w...want to know wh...en and wh...ere he met Scarlett. She looked after m...me for a long t...time, David. I can't re...member anything before her. B...but there must have been s...something.'

'OK. Scarlett was a teacher, Kate. Perhaps we can find out where she worked. When you were little she would have passed her exams and be in employment, surely.'

'I r...remember her working in S...Salisbury. Part-time. She was a sp...ecial disabilities teacher.'

'That narrows the field a bit, love. Any specific kind of disability?'

'B...blind and deaf.'

David looked down at his wife who had her eyes fixed on her children. 'Ah!'

She glanced up. 'Ah?'

'There's a school up near the Roman fort at Benwell Dene. Or there was when I was an archaeology student. I wonder if that might be a good place to start, Kate.'

Kate nodded, looking at him. 'OK.' They grinned at each other and then David felt a tug at his trouser leg. 'Fishy.'

He looked down at his son's slimy, seaweed-bedaubed hand. 'Well ... not exactly, Paul, but close.' He hoisted his son up regardless of the sand and grime and walked the few yards to the hole so industriously dug by the child, crouching down and examining the small pool of water that had seeped into it from the nearby estuary. Kate watched as Rosie joined in the conversation and all three poked about in the sand, enjoying themselves after the fashion of children in mud.

JUNE 2011

WHITBY

ANTONY WAS STIRRING THE mud of his own past and he wasn't enjoying it at all. For the first time in nearly a decade he had gone to the children's home where he had spent many of his pre-teen years. He had had to take several deep breaths before he could bring himself to walk down the very ordinary garden path.

Nothing much had changed. It was true that where he had played cowboys and Indians among the shrubbery small children appeared to be playing with an assortment of strange-looking cars in the dirt. Cars that changed into spacemen, apparently. He tried not to look too hard as he waited for his ring at the doorbell to be answered. He remembered what it was like to be stared at.

The young woman who answered was neat and had a pleasant smile on her face. 'Can I help you?' She looked him over carefully in the manner of one not sure if she wanted to speak or not.

'I used to live here. My name is Antony Grey.' He offered a half smile. 'I know it's a bit of a long shot but I wondered if Ms Delia Cartwright was still working here.'

'Ms Cartwright retired several years ago.'

'Oh.'

'I don't suppose you could give me her address?'

The shake of the head was fairly emphatic, even if the smile stayed in place.

'No, I didn't think you would.' He shrugged. 'Can you tell

me who else is still working here?'

'No.'

Well, that was clear enough. He offered another half smile and shrug. 'Thank you for your time, anyway.' He turned away, half disappointed and half relieved, to come face to face with Stan Hunt.

'Good grief. What are you doing here?'

Stan Hunt smirked, looking over Antony's shoulder at the young woman who was still standing at the door. 'I'm here to see my girl. I don't suppose you've got one of those, or would know what to do with one if you had.'

He was still as obnoxious as ever under that veneer of charm, thought Antony. 'Whatever you say, Stan. Good afternoon, Miss.' He turned aside and continued to walk down the path.

Stan watched him go before smiling at the young woman. 'Are you ready, Kelsey?'

'Yeah. I was just getting my jacket when he knocked on the door.' She swung back inside and emerged with a blue jacket on her arm.

'What did he want?'

'Said he used to live here. Wanted to contact one of the old houseparents, he said.'

'You want to watch him; he likes little kids.'

Kelsey looked startled. 'Does he, then?' She said no more. Stan smirked, he hoped he had planted a malicious seed that would bear strange fruit for Antony in the very near future.

Antony, however, wasn't thinking about his encounter – except to think that life held some strange coincidences. He was walking back to his current lodgings, thinking about his research and planning a letter he wanted to write to a colleague whom he thought might have some information about the hermitage site.

Amy met him at her gate with Joy in her pushchair. 'Hello, Antony; we're just going to the shops for a loaf and some nappies. Want to come?'

Antony obligingly turned around in preparation for

walking along the street with her. 'Have you had a good day?'

'It's Saturday – no nursery – so she's been a right misery.' Amy looked at her child with some exasperation. Antony looked at Joy; she was riding in the pram like Boadicea on a mission, her little feet pushing against the step in an attempt to stand up. She looked cross and hot and it was obvious she didn't want to be in sitting in the pram at all.

'If you want to get her out she can hold our hands. Leave the pram in the garden. I can carry her if she gets tired.'

Amy looked at him in surprise. 'Are you sure? She's heavy.'

'She's fine.' Antony knelt down and unfastened the reins, freeing the little girl from the pushchair and swinging her onto the ground. 'There you go, pet.' He kept a firm hand on her while Amy turned around and set the pram back inside the garden, before coming to join him.

'Come on then, grumble-bum.' She took one hand and Antony took the other, the small child gyrating like a pendulum between them, giggling as they walked along the street and swung her gently.

'So where did you get to this morning?' Amy asked the question, then immediately said, 'Sorry, Antony; that's none of my business.'

Antony shook his head gently. He was relieved to realise that the urges he'd had last night and this morning appeared to have disappeared; Amy was once again the young woman he talked to in the pub. 'I had to go to the library to sort out some research books. And I wanted to go through the newspaper stacks as well.'

'Did you find what you wanted?'

Antony nodded. He had found some of the information he sought about the site. What he didn't tell her was that after his conversation with Detective Sergeant Tierney, he'd been stirred to look up the circumstances of his parent's accident, something he'd never wanted to do before. It wasn't just lack of curiosity; it was a putting behind him of something miserable. What could looking them up have told him, except that he was alone and no one wanted him? And if no one wanted him he wasn't going to go looking. At least, that had been his previous thought. Looking into his past had been as nasty as he'd suspected it would be.

He discovered for the first time that his father Edward Grey wasn't in fact married to his mother. They had been living together, but not married. Grey had been married to someone else entirely. His wife and her family didn't want anything to do with 'the other woman's' child. That had been in the local papers. Grey's relatives didn't know who Antony's mother was, but claimed the name of Carol Brown was obviously a false one.

So it appeared he was a bastard, after all. He didn't know how he felt about that. He pinned a smile on his face and walked along the street with Amy. Pushing his thoughts to the back of his mind, he listened to her talking about her morning. When they arrived at the shops Joy decided she didn't want to go shopping. A tantrum was threatening to drown out all conversation.

'I'll take her to the swings over there, Amy; you can come and get us.'

'We shouldn't give in to her.' Amy looked at her daughter's red face and gave a half smile, 'But ... OK. But you won't always get your own way, young lady.' She grinned at Antony, 'See ya in a mo.'

She went into the Spar and Antony swung the little girl up and crossed the road with her, going into the small park on the other side and sliding Joy into a swing seat, fastening her in place before going around her and giving her a gentle push.

He was enjoying the moment when the policeman loomed in his face. 'Are you Mr Antony Grey?'

Antony stilled the swing and looked at the blue uniform and stern face. 'Yeah.'

'We have received a complaint about you bothering children. I must ask you to accompany me to the station.'

'What?'

'Whose child is this?'

Antony, his mouth half open, shook his head in mystification. This couldn't be happening to him. He watched as the constable spoke into his radio, a creeping horror overtaking him.

'I'm arranging for social services to look after this child until we ascertain where you got her from, sir.'

'But...' He let out a huge sigh of relief when he saw Amy hurrying across the road towards them. 'Amy.' His voice came out as a croak as she stopped beside them.

'Is this your child, madam?'

Amy nodded. 'Is she all right?'

'As far as we are aware, madam. However, we have reason to believe this man might have taken her unlawfully. Is that correct?'

Amy looked in a bewildered fashion at the policeman and then at Antony. Then she said, 'No, of course he hasn't. He was minding her for me while I did the shopping. What is this? What are you talking about?'

'We have received a report that this man might be a risk to children.'

Amy looked from one male face to the other in total incomprehension. 'Antony's our lodger.' She looked at Antony for enlightenment.

He shook his head, part shock and part anger in his gaze. 'I have no idea what the man is talking about.'

'I am cautioning you, sir, and you need to accompany me down the station, sir.'

'Well, I'm coming too. I never heard such rubbish in my life.' Amy plucked a protesting Joy from the swing and turned to face the officer of the law.

'I can't stop you, miss, but is it wise?'

'I'm coming.' She walked off towards a squad car that she saw parked at the curb and stood waiting, her groceries at her feet.

JUNE 2011

CUMBRIA

DAVID SNIFFED THE AIR as he walked through the door, bringing with him his own peculiar aromas. Peculiar to the archaeological profession, anyway; a compound of fresh air and earth. 'Kate, where are you?' He headed for the kitchen, as her default place when at home. He could smell hot linen and Kate usually ironed downstairs.

Pushing the door open caused warmth to reached out and caress his cheeks and the aroma of cake to waft towards him from the Aga cooker; but no Kate. He closed it and went back along the corridor and up the stairs, two steps at a time, sniffing like a bloodhound on the scent of a cannabis trail.

A quick glance in the babies' room found two humps in cots illuminated by a light in the shape of a rabbit. He beat a retreat and headed for his own bedroom. His wife was stretched out on the bed, sound asleep under a light cashmere blanket. He was about to advance and steal a kiss when Thea touched his arm.

'Leave her be, Master David. She's fair worn out.' Her old voice whispered the words. She took an arm and led him into the spare bedroom, source of the smell of ironing.

'Is she all right, Thea?' he whispered back, and anxiety creased his face.

Thea pushed the door to and turned, nodding towards the bedside chair and going to stand behind the ironing board. 'Don't fret, Master David. She's not as strong as she pretends to be and she's worriting about her twin brother. I found her crying all over your shirts and settled her for a nap.' Thea carefully arranged one of those shirts on a hanger and stretched out a wrinkled hand for another.

David sat watching for a minute. Just so had he been watched when he was a small boy and she'd come up to the nursery to mind him while his parents were busy. 'I love you very much, Thea.'

Thea took on a glow; it could have been the energy she was putting into the ironing. 'Well, and that's nice to know, Master David.'

He smiled across the room, the smell of lavender and ironing bringing with it happy memories. 'I had a lovely childhood; if Mum and Pops were busy, you always had time for me. In fact I was spoilt rotten.'

'You're too nice natured to be spoilt, Davie boy, though I admit it wasn't for want of trying at times.' Thea set the iron down and twitched the collar of the shirt just so, before looking at him. 'She wasn't though, was she? You haven't told me much, and nor has she, but she's frightened of love. Of loving.' Thea, the shirt arranged to her satisfaction, licked her fingers and touched the iron, before thumping it down onto the material and running it across the collar with a fierceness totally out of proportion to the task in hand. She looked at him again. 'She's passionate about the babies and yet terrified that anyone should know. As if she feared we'd take them away if we knew she cared about them too much.'

David offered a lopsided smile. 'Yeah, that's about right. She hides from me.'

'She loves you too, Master David.'

David smiled; it was a compound of joy and superior male. 'I know, Thea, and you're right. She does show me, and then she retreats. I want to find her brother to make her happy, but I'm as scared as she is that he'll reject her.'

'She's a lovely woman, Master David. She was saying that she'd abandoned her twin, worrying that he might have ended in a home while she had it easy. Easy?' Thea hissed the word and spun round from where she was hanging the shirt on the airer. She shook a finger at him, her voice rising. 'I try not to listen but I've heard things. Easy, with the bullying and teasing, and that man making her life a misery by dragging her name through the courts?'

David saw the tears and came over, edging behind the ironing board and putting an arm around her shoulders. The familiar scent of violets surrounded him. 'Hush, Thea. We'll fix it.'

'Wh...at will you f...ix, love?' Kate came into the room, pushing back her hair from sleepy eyes and looking at them in a puzzled way.

'Thea thinks the iron is on the blink, and we've only had it a little while. I'm telling her it's the built-in obsolescence factor, not her fault.' He hoped she didn't notice the flush on his cheeks; David hated telling lies, especially to his beloved wife.

'Oh.' Kate looked at the iron gently hissing at them. 'Maybe it j...ust needs some more w...ater in the steam c... compartment, Thea.'

Thea looked down. 'You could be right, Kate. I must be getting old.'

'Not you, Thea.' David gave her another hug. 'Leave the ironing; it's time you were going home. That animal of yours will be crossing his legs at the door.'

Thea looked up at the green eyes and smiled. 'No; my Charlie is far too well trained, but it is time I went. You rest more, Kate; don't go getting in a frazzle over the housework.' Thea looked across the room at the young woman, then transferred her attention to the iron, switching it off and setting it carefully on the cooling stand. 'I'll do the rest tomorrow. You leave it be, you hear?'

'I hear.' Kate smiled as Thea came towards her.

'Goodnight, child.' She dropped a kiss quickly on Kate's cheek and headed out the door.

David came across the room, smiling at the tousled look of his wife as she held a hand to her cheek and half turned to watch Thea walk down the stairs. 'Hello, sleepyhead. Thea said you were tired.' There was just a hint of a question as he gave her a hug.

Kate smiled up at him. 'I'm f...fine, oh Lord and M... aster. Don't fuss.'

'OK, I won't fuss, but I do want to know what the doc said this morning.' He swung her round and they walked down the stairs arm in arm. Thea smiled at the pair of them as she pulled her jacket on and let herself out with a half wave, shutting the solid wooden door behind her.

Kate glanced up at him, but didn't speak until they had reached the sanctuary of the kitchen. 'I'm a little an...aemic, as usual; I'm b...booked for a s...scan in two w...weeks' time and...' She went over to the kitchen sink, picking up the kettle on the way and beginning to fill it.

'And?' David followed her across the room, coming up behind her and taking the kettle from her hand and imprisoning her against the sink and looking down into her face.

Kate took a deep breath, 'And it could be tw...ins; he can't be p...positive yet but he, "hasna much d...doubt, ma dearie, that there could be two of th...em in th...ere".' Kate frowned at her husband as she tried to mimic the doctor's Cumbrian accent.

David's grin gleamed through his beard. 'How do you feel about it?'

'I'm not s...sure whether to be h...horrified and b...book you for the s...snip now, or ... I have this little b...bubble of joy in me, David; it keeps rising and g...gurgling in me like I'd swallowed a b...bottle of f...fizzy too f...fast...' She grinned a bit mistily up at him.

David set the kettle down in order to kiss his wife, who had placed a hand on his chest to hold him off.

'David, if he's r...right, we'll have four ch...ildren under th...ree.'

'Yeah. And we'll cope fine. Now, can I have the kiss I've been dreaming about all day?' Kate nodded.

JUNE 2011

WHITBY

Antony Grey had no expectation of kisses. Amy had gone with him to the police station on Saturday and had only gone away when Joy began to fret too much. She'd sent her dad in her place. That had been Saturday. It was now Monday and he was still trying to decide what to do.

The police had been polite. So polite it hurt. They had released him 'pending further enquires'. Jack Watt had ushered him out to the old truck and waited patiently for him to fasten his seat belt before he spoke.

He set the vehicle in motion, then said, 'You'd better tell me what's going on. Our Amy said they were accusing you of being a paedophile and if you're one of those you can wait in the cab and I'll get your stuff. You aren't welcome in my house.'

Antony had shaken his head angrily. 'I wouldn't hurt Joy. But I think you'd better give me my stuff and I'll get out of your sight.' His stomach had clenched; he'd been questioned for nearly five hours. They wouldn't tell him who had accused him, or what information had been given against him.

'Nay; we'll go home.' Jack had swung his head and looked at the pale and angry man next to him. 'Amy will want answers, too.'

'I don't particularly care. If you all think I'm capable of that, then…'

'Shut up, will you?' Jack had put his foot down, then driven through the evening traffic with a grim look on his face.

The evening had been miserable. Antony just wanted to hide away from the accusing eyes of Jack Watt and the looks of pity that Joyce and Amy kept giving him. Aside from saying that he wasn't a paedophile and didn't know why the police had been questioning him, he'd refused to say anything.

Now it was Monday. He'd spent yesterday and today walking the streets, only returning when he could barely put one foot in front of the other. He didn't know whether to move his stuff back to the bedsit or not. Amy had said she believed him and called the police a number of names which might have seen her with a public order offence if any policeman had been within earshot.

Her parents were a different matter. They had reserved judgement, but the chilly silence that greeted him when he walked into the kitchen on Sunday morning had been enough to make him decide to move out there and then. Amy had come up to his bedroom and watched him hauling clothes out of the drawers and then told him in no uncertain terms what she thought of people who ran away.

'I'm an unmarried mum; do you think I didn't get filthy looks and sniggers behind people's hands? It might be common, but it still isn't respectable. Mum and Dad, they care about me and Joy. They just want us to be safe.'

'So I'll get out, then you will be.'

'No, you won't. If you're telling the truth, and I believe you are, then running away will just make you look bad. I thought you had more guts than that.'

She had turned and slammed the door and Antony had just stood staring at the white painted wood for five long minutes before getting his coat and going out to tramp the streets. Today had been no better. He didn't know what to do and he was so tried from the sleepless nights his eyes felt sore and gritty.

As he approached the house he saw the squad car in front of the house and almost turned around and fled, his feet slowing to a crawl. Where could he go? The police were watching him, anyway; that's how they'd found him so easily on Saturday. They were supposed to be keeping an eye out for his attacker, but it had worked against him instead.

'Officer.' He nodded as he walked into the kitchen, noting the uniform on the door and the plain clothes sitting at the table. 'I assume you're looking for me.' He kept his face impassive as he waited for the next blow to fall. Amy and her parents were also sitting at the table, with mugs of tea in front of them. All appeared to find the insides of the mugs mesmerising.

'Ah, Mr Grey. We just need to have another word with you.'

Antony sighed quietly, turning to go out again.

'Sir. Where are you going?'

Antony glanced back over his shoulder. 'To the police station.'

'Er ... that won't be necessary, sir. If I could just have a word in private.' He glanced at Jack Watt.

'Front room. Down the hall.' Jack scraped back his chair and stood up, going over to the sink and pouring away his mug of tea, keeping his back to both police and Antony.

Antony shrugged and went back out into the hall and into the sitting room, turning as the detective came in and shut the door.

'Come to arrest me, have you?'

'No, sir. We've looked into the claims made against you on Saturday and find no foundation for them. The informant who first gave us the information was repeating a piece of hearsay. But we do have to investigate – and quickly – when children are involved, as I'm sure you understand.'

Antony nodded. 'And do you understand that my name is mud in this house? How many others has your informant passed this titbit onto? Did you check your informant's credentials, too? Will you be issuing a public apology? I doubt it.'

'Now, sir, I have apologised and – yes – we have cautioned the person responsible about passing on unfounded gossip.'

'Unfounded gossip.' Antony was white with anger. 'Just

where did this "gossip" come from in the first place? Have you checked that out, officer?' He spun on his heel then spun back. 'Thank you for coming. Perhaps you could let my landlord know I'm not a paedophile before you go.' He turned his back again and stared out of the window at the gathering dusk. He heard the door shut and his shoulders slumped.

A small cold hand was pushed into his. 'I'm sorry about my parents, Antony. They were just trying to protect me.'

Antony released his hand, turning to look stonily at the pretty blonde. 'I do understand, Amy. But I can't stay here. If they could believe me capable of that then I don't want to be around them.' His voice was filled with bitterness.

'They feel guilty enough, Antony, and if you move out where will you go?'

Antony swung back and looked out on the quiet street again. 'I'll go back to my bedsit. That way I won't make anyone feel guilty. It's probably safer for you if I go, anyway.'

Amy frowned at the back presented to her. 'What do you mean, safer?'

'He means that the person writing the poison pen letters won't bother us!' Jack Watt stood in the doorway, looking across the room at the young couple.

Antony swung round. 'You want to protect her and then you go opening your trap and tell her that!' He scowled at Jack.

Amy was opening and shutting her mouth, looking from one scowling and angry male face to the other. 'What letters?'

Joyce walked in, gently pushing her husband further into the room and closing the door behind her before leaning against the wood and effectively blocking Antony's escape. 'Please sit down, Antony. We wish to talk to you.'

Antony shook his head. 'I need to leave you in peace. You've been very kind letting me stay here, but it's time I went home.'

'We haven't been kind at all, you stiff-necked bugger. It suited us all in our own way to have you.' Jack Watt moved further into the room and came to a halt next to his daughter.

'The police say it was all gossip. I should know better than to listen to it, but when it comes to our Amy and Joy, common sense goes out the window.' He looked up from contemplation of his daughter's face to the stern one next to him. 'There was gossip and more when she had our Joy; nasty stuff. I couldn't bear to see her suffer that way again. I'm sorry, lad.'

Antony shook his head. 'I couldn't hurt Joy or Amy. Amy's the first real friend I've had.' He frowned. 'But I can't stay. I should have gone before, when the first letter arrived.' He looked from father to daughter. 'In fact I shouldn't have come.' He moved over towards the door but found his way hindered by Joyce.

'Now you listen here, Antony Grey. I've always wanted a son; we didn't have any more after Amy, and when you came I felt like I'd finally got my wish. Someone Jack could talk man things to, someone I could tease and spoil a bit, and someone to be a big brother to our Amy.' She held out two soft hands and took Antony's. 'Stay, please!'

Antony shook his head, 'I don't exactly feel like a big brother.' The words escaped before he'd thought them through and the red flowed over his cheeks as if he'd been scalded. He tried to release his hands, only to find that Joyce was beaming at him and Amy was right behind him.

Jack looked at his wife, 'I think we'll go and put the kettle on again, love.' He followed his wife out of the room and shut the door firmly behind him. The couple left standing in the sitting room resembled a pair of beetroots.

'Perhaps you could tell me how you do think of me, Antony?'

JUNE 2011

CUMBRIA

BEN WAS WONDERING WHAT his sister would think of him when he finally found her. He had no doubts about if, only when. While he'd been cosseted and the pet of the household she'd been living with a thief and a woman who hadn't even been married to her father. He pressed the pause button on his thoughts as he remembered that his father hadn't married their mother, either. 'Oh, dear God! I'm not exactly going to bring her good news, am I?' He spoke to the windscreen as he drove into the small backyard of the hotel and parked his car.

If he had but known it the little bed and breakfast was barely twenty miles from the house his sister lived in. He glanced around the yard as he hauled his leather grip from the boot of the car, along with a briefcase. The yard was barely big enough to accommodate four cars; there was a white painted iron staircase running up the outside of the hotel, and an uncompromising steel door underneath the staircase and set into an otherwise brick wall. Steam issued from a heating pipe next to a row of windows, and a neat set of industrial-sized bins ranged along the fence next to the gate he'd just driven through.

'Father O'Connor? The boss said you were parking around the back. I'll just shut the gate.' The pimply youth loped across the small yard and swung the gates to. 'We've no other guests expected tonight. Better safe than sorry, eh, Father.' He pushed a bolt across the gates and came back and stood holding the door open. 'I'll show you to your room.'

'Thank you.' He followed in some bemusement as he was led along a dark panelled corridor smelling of bleach and cabbage and emerged in the light of the front hall.

Mine host, Gregory Rogers, was a dumpy little man, 'Ah, found your way, then. Thanks, Paul.' He nodded dismissal to the pimply youth and smiled at Ben. 'We're quiet here, but folks like to keep their cars safe. I'll take you up to your room. Do you want an evening meal? We don't normally serve them but you're welcome to have what we're having, since there's only you.' Talking all the time, telling him about the area and asking about his journey, Rogers led him up carpeted shallow steps to the next floor and into a small single bedroom.

Ben shook his head. 'That's kind of you, but I've eaten already.'

'That's all right, Father. Anything else we can get you?'

'No thanks. Breakfast?'

'Whenever suits.'

'Eight.'

'Fine.'

Rogers left and Ben sank onto the bed, sighing with tiredness and relief that he'd stopped travelling. He looked about him, noting the en suite and a tea tray with kettle and mugs.

He stood and took the kettle into the bathroom, filling the little jug and then setting it back on its stand to boil. While he waited for it he pulled the briefcase onto the bed and began to disinter the contents, spreading out the printouts and copies he'd obtained from various places that day.

He had got to the stage of stacking the photocopies of various newspapers into one pile and the information gleaned from electoral rolls into another, when his mobile and the kettle both whistled at him. He flicked the phone open and held it to his ear as he walked across the small room and switched off the kettle.

'Hello. Father O'Connor.'

'Ben? It's *Uncail* Micheál; *Athair* is sick. Will you come home, Ben *a chara?* He's asking for you.'

Ben glanced at his watch; seven in the evening. 'I'm in Cumbria; I'll need to arrange a ferry.'

No hesitation, just information. Micheál sighed softly and thankfully, 'Aye, lad.' He glanced at his father, whose face was blending into the white sheets. 'Don't be long, Ben.'

'What ails him?'

'His heart.' And Micheál spoke the exact truth.

'I'll pray for us all; but I have to get to Liverpool, then across. 'Twill take time. All right?'

'Aye. No, wait!' Micheál shook his head. 'Let me think a minute.'

Ben stirred from one foot to the other as the line crackled and hummed at him.

'Listen, Ben; if you drive up through Galloway and across to Stranraer you could get the midnight ferry to Belfast and drive down into Eire. It might be quicker.'

'I'll see what I can do.'

'Take care, Ben.'

Ben flicked the phone shut and scooped the papers back into his briefcase. He glanced at the comfortable room but felt no regret as he walked towards the door, going to see if his host could find him a telephone directory.

Half an hour later he was in his car, his bag in the boot and a packed meal on the seat next to him. He glanced again at the map he'd been given by the helpful Mr Rogers and then set off to drive through the deepening dusk and empty roads of Scotland's south west, to the coast and a ferry to Belfast. It looked like being a long and anxious night.

'SUCCESS, KATE. WELL, OF a sort.' David swung around in his chair and looked at his wife as she came in, drying her hands on a towel; she'd heard his yelp and come to check that everything was all right in the study.

'I th...ought you'd h...hurt yourself.'

David grinned, swinging back towards his computer. 'No; I think I've found Scarlett's brother on this list of people.'

'What, Sa...muel Hamilton? I'd almost f...forgotten about him.' Kate came over to the screen and looked at the eponymous list. 'How do you kn...now that's him and not any of the oth...thers?' She frowned at the cursor blinking against one of the names.

'Age, area; there's a telephone number, Kate. What do you think?'

'I th...ink you've gone m...mad. You're s...supposed to be w...working on the s...site research, my lord.' She smiled at him.

'I was, I am, only...' David reached for a hand. 'I was just having a break for a minute.'

'Oh, yeah?'

'So, shall I phone?'

'Wh...at have we got to lose? But wh...at do you w...ant to ask him?'

David reached for the phone with one hand while pulling his wife onto his knee with the other. Kate settled an arm around his neck and leaned back, waiting and watching while he punched in the numbers on the landline and held the receiver between them so that she could listen in to the conversation.

'Mr Samuel Hamilton? My name is Professor David Walker. My wife, Kate, is trying to track down some relatives; she was fostered by a Miss Scarlett Hamilton. Were you a relation of hers?'

Kate heard a gravelly voice cough before answering. 'Scarlett is my sister; we lost touch many years ago. Do you know where Lettie is?'

David's eyes met Kate's over the phone; in his pleasure at finding the name he hadn't thought through this part. 'I'm sorry to have to tell you that Scarlett died last November, Mr Hamilton.' David paused waiting. 'I really am sorry to have to give you such sad news.'

Samuel Hamilton sighed down the phone. 'It's no more than I expected. How can I help you, Professor Walker?'

David exchanged another look with Kate; 'Kate needs to

know a little more about Scarlett, Mr Hamilton. She didn't know that Scarlett wasn't her birth mother until after Scarlett died.'

Samuel nodded at the phone; he gave another cough. 'Is there anything particular you were wanting to know?'

'Well,' David frowned. 'We understand that Scarlett was a teacher. Could you tell us what school she taught at? We know it was in the north east.'

'Royal Victoria School for the Blind, at Benwell Dene. The last address I have for her was the post office there.'

David gave a soft grunt. 'Thank you. How? When? I'm sorry, Mr Hamilton; I don't mean to be rude but why did the pair of you lose touch? Can you tell me?'

Another cough and then Samuel Hamilton spoke again. 'I've never known. She wrote fairly regularly, then nothing. We thought the police would be in touch if something had happened to her. The school didn't know what had happened, either.' He coughed again.

'I know she left the Blind School when it closed down. She wrote fairly regularly. She was job hunting in a difficult climate. The letters were cheerful but they didn't tell us much, really.' He paused to cough. 'She had an awkward relationship with her mother. They loved each other; they just couldn't live together. Scarlett was a constant reminder of her dad's car accident. They never forgave themselves.' He paused to take a breath.

'She didn't tell us about Kate. It would have pleased my mum to know she'd finally got a child to care for; Scarlett was made for mothering ... always playing with dolls when she was little.' Hamilton coughed again. 'Cancer of the lungs.' He offered the comment by way of explanation for the cough, before carrying on. 'I was older than Lettie; I remember the accident. She didn't understand; she was in hospital for a long time. When she finally did understand she withdrew from us for a bit. But she never held it against us. Mum didn't understand that. Lettie loved us; she would never allow anything to hurt her family.' He sighed. 'I'm pleased it wasn't something we did to upset her. We always wondered – Mum and Dad and I – if she just couldn't face us any more. We should have known better.'

David looked at Kate. 'You've been very helpful, sir. Thank you so much.'

A couple of minutes later he put the phone down and looked at Kate. 'Fancy a trip?'

Kate grinned a bit feebly. 'Why, how k...kind of you.'

'I'm for a cuppa. Tomorrow I think we'll go and view the site at Whitby with a side order of Roman ruins. The children would like a trip to the seaside and it would do you good, too.' David allowed Kate to slither off his lap and stand up. 'I shall buy them a bucket and spade each.'

'David.'

'Darling Kate, don't argue.' He dropped a kiss on her nose and, taking her hand, headed for the kitchen and the cake his wife had cooked earlier in the day.

JUNE 2011

GALWAY

BEN ONLY JUST MADE the ferry. What his uncle hadn't known was that the ferry port had moved up the coast to Cairnryan and the midnight ferry was now at half eleven with a thirty minute check-in time. He hadn't dared to stop in case he missed it.

He dozed on the boat; he was bone weary and felt as though he had been travelling around the kingdom for weeks. He had committed his grandfather and uncle into the care of God and now he closed his eyes and wished for the journey to be at an end.

He surfaced with a desire for the loo and glanced up at the big clock to see he'd barely managed an hour's sleep. He rubbed at the five o'clock shadow and brushed his hair from his eyes, looking around. There were very few people on board this Monday night; most of them looked like reps, with nice suiting and leather briefcases.

He stood up and left the lounge, idly speculating on what could possibly cause a rep to lose a good night's sleep. An early start in the morning, he supposed. He found a small counter catering to the needs of tea lovers and coffee addicts and got a cup of coffee with the profound hope that it might keep him awake until he could find somewhere to have a rest. No purpose would be served by crashing the car on the way home.

The top deck allowed him to feel the wind and see an inky sky, the moon appearing in coy glimpses through the heavy cloud cover. That was how he felt, he thought; he kept getting little bursts of illumination, then the clouds – his and his sister's pasts – would crowd in and obscure his way again.

He breathed in deeply, wondering what had triggered his grandfather's heart attack and praying it hadn't been his attitude. He seemed to have quite enough on his conscience as it was.

He stayed on the deck until the port came into sight, shivering in the cold night air and worrying fruitlessly about each of his relatives in turn. The journey home, however, proved uneventful. He arrived as the cattle were being released from their milking stalls, the familiar sight a reassurance in itself.

'*Uncail;* how is he?'

Micheál stopped in his tracks, his white boots and overall as milky-white as his face. He stepped forward to embrace his nephew then halted, looking at the younger man, not sure of his reception. The parting three weeks ago had been bitter.

Ben lightly touched him on the arm and they fell into step together, going towards the kitchen door and speaking in Irish Gaelic. 'He's not well, Ben.' He looked up, then directed his eyes towards the opening. 'I'm not blaming you, lad, but the strain of the last few weeks and losing *Mamai* has been a lot for him to bear. I don't think any of us realised how strong the tie was.'

Ben nodded, 'Aye, I'm sorry; I was shocked. To tell the truth, *Uncail,* I'm still a little in shock.'

'Have you found the little colleen?'

'No.' Ben shook his head. 'I'll tell you all I've found when I've seen *Athair mor.*' He rubbed a hand over his face. 'And maybe had a bite.'

'Aye; you've made better time than I looked for. I'll set the kettle and make something for you to eat. Your auntie Bridget is sitting with *Athair.*'

Ben walked through the familiar kitchen and up the stairs, going along the landing to his grandparent's room and gently pushing open the door. Bridget was sitting with a book on her knees, but she was looking at the door. She offered a half smile to Ben, as unsure of her welcome as her husband had been. Before either could speak, however, the figure in the bed stirred and opened his eyes.

'Ben, *a chara*, I wanted to make my peace with you before I go.'

Ben walked softly over the carpet and dropped into the hard chair next to the bed. He took one of the old hands and smiled at his grandfather. 'Where were you planning on going, *Daideó*? For I have to tell you, you don't look so flash for running about just the now,' Ben gently teased as the old hand gripped his with surprising tightness. He was conscious of Bridget getting up and going out of the room but kept his eyes on his grandfather's face, examining the familiar and seeing the changes wrought by grief over the past few weeks.

JUNE 2011

WHITBY

'No, Paul, don't tip the water on your sister.' David rescued his daughter from the very real danger of drowning and frowned at his son. Paul's bottom lip trembled and Rose wriggled to get out of her father's arms.

'Building, Dadda.'

'Yes, b...but do it gently, Paul.' Kate, sitting on the sand, her skirts spread over a car rug, drew her son back a bit and watched as Rose patted her brother and smiled at him, before looking at her father reproachfully.

David shrugged. 'I give up; he's nearly buried her and half drowned her and when I tell him off she defends him!' He leaned back a bit and helped himself to an apple from a basket behind him. He took a good bite, crunching down, and looked at his wife's grinning face.

'Maybe it's a twin thing.'

'Maybe.' She'd just managed that sentence without hesitation. He filed it away with other pieces of information he had about his wife for future reference, as he swallowed apple.

'I s...still can't remember him, David.'

'It will come when we find the right trigger, love.' He watched his children playing, wondering if his wife had had that sort of relationship with her sibling, and how he would deal with it if she had. He looked out to sea, hiding his eyes from his wife. He felt very possessive about Kate. Always had. Not in the sense of preventing her from mixing or having other friends, but she was his, and he'd never imagined she would have him as a husband. Twins, though: everything he'd heard and read said they had a special bond and he didn't want to share. He finished the apple and threw the core onto the tideline before he risked looking at her again.

They let the children play for a further hour before Kate declared it was time to pack up the picnic basket and go back to the car. 'It's b...been a lovely morning, David.'

'Sun, sea and a beautiful woman; what more can a man want?' David, busy stowing things in the back of the Discovery, grinned as his wife went pink. The twins were safely strapped into their seats and already beginning to nod, the fresh sea air and play taking its toll on their young bodies and minds. 'How long do you think we've got?' He climbed into the driving seat and glanced back at the two angelic faces in the back seat before looking at his wife.

'P...probably about two hours. Th...ey didn't have a nap th...is morning.'

'Good. Time to go to Benwell Dene, I think.'

Kate nodded, 'I th...ought we were coming here to do a b...bit of research.'

'Why? I've employed a very nice young man to do my research in the library here; I'm taking a half holiday.' David swung the big car onto the dual carriageway and glanced across at his wife, who was opening her mouth – he had no doubt – to argue. 'Dear Kate, allow me to do this, and don't argue. I have to go to Germany in less than two weeks and then it will all be put on hold until I can get back, if we haven't found the answers. I'd like it settled before then.'

Kate looked at him. It was a very long-suffering look. 'You just w...want to get it all done wh...ile you can keep an eye on m...me.'

'And your point is?'

'I a...am an adult, David.'

'Oh, yeah! And amen to that.' David threw her a wicked look and watched the blush, which had only just subsided, bloom again in her cheeks.

'You're in a very w…wicked m…mood.'

'And again, I ask what your point is?'

Kate found herself grinning; David had been like this since she'd told him about the baby. You'd think no one else had ever managed to get pregnant. She glanced across. He was gently humming to himself as he drove along. She watched his elegant hands turning the wheel and found herself blushing even more fiercely as she remembered the lovemaking early that morning.

David spared a look at his very quiet wife and burst out laughing.

'Shush, you'll wake th…em up.'

'Looks like I already have woken something up, love.'

'David.' She flapped her hands and had one of them caught by her husband's.

He continued to hold it, driving one-handed until he began to negotiate the traffic onto the housing estate. 'Now the Roman remains are along here, if I remember correctly. So if I've read the map right, Kate, the school should be down this street and left and … there … those big gates.' David pulled up the handbrake and switched off the engine.

He looked over his shoulder at his children. 'Double buggy or carry?'

'Buggy.'

The twins were transferred without opening their eyes and Kate stood gently rocking the pushchair as David slammed the tailgate and locked the car. He put an arm around his wife and they began to walk towards the school. 'It's typically Victorian, Kate. Red brick and lots of green lawn.' He stood with his wife as she peered through the gates, much as her brother had done a few days before.

'Do you th…think she liked working th…there, with disabled children?'

'I think you have to be pretty dedicated to work with disabled children, Kate. You have to want to teach, and be very patient; but the rewards are wonderful, I'm told.'

Kate nodded. 'She was patient w…with me, David.

Almost as p...patient as you are.' Kate very rarely spoke about her speech impediment and David squeezed the arm he was holding.

'She did love you, Kate. Almost as much as I do.' He turned her around and pointed up the street with his chin, 'The post office is just up the road. Brave enough to go?'

'Yes, David.'

They set off at a leisurely stroll along the pavement. David could feel the faint tremble going through his wife's body, but she would hang in there. However, that tremble made him all the more determined to find her twin and her mother before he left for Germany.

JUNE 2011

WHITBY

ANTONY GREY WAS TALKING about his mother to Amy. He wasn't looking at her but he was holding tightly to a hand as they sat on the settee.

'I went to the library on Saturday. I wanted to get some books for research, as I told you, but I was doing something else as well. I was trying to understand the threats in these poison pen letters, and I discovered something about my mother.'

'What kind of threats?' Amy observed the profile turned away from her. 'And what about your mum? I thought you'd been brought up in a home.'

'I have; I was.' Antony's lips quirked upwards for a second. 'I did have parents though; everyone does.'

'Hmm! So ... these letters?'

'They started arriving when I was in hospital. They're nasty threats and I don't want any harm to come to you or your family, Amy. The police seem to think that if they can keep me under observation for long enough then this person will slip up and they'll discover who it is.'

'What kind of threats?'

'To start with they were just general; the person seemed to be claiming they were behind the hit and run and, if I didn't leave town, well...' He glanced at her face and then away again, looking out of the front window. 'It all sounds so bloody dramatic, Amy: "Go, or next time I'll kill you". But I don't have a clue who I've upset that much.'

'Nor do I. You're too nice to hurt anyone deliberately, Antony.'

'No, I'm a man, Amy; and I'm living in your parent's house, and I'm growing attracted to you.' He felt the heat in his cheeks and kept his eyes on the scene outside.

'That's all right, Antony; I kinda like you, too: you're cute.'

'Cute!' Antony looked at her, first with astonishment writ large across his face until it dissolved into disgust. 'Cute is for dolls and babies.'

Amy grinned, 'Got your attention.' She turned pretty brown eyes up and observed his embarrassment, before she took pity on him. 'So these letters are death threats; so why did you go looking for information about your mum, then?'

'The last one called me a bastard. The detective asked if I was actually one in the legal sense.' He looked at the eyes watching him so seriously, then looked away. 'I said, "no". But it looks as if I might have been.'

Amy used her spare hand to flick blonde hair from her eyes. 'So what? My Joy is and I don't care. People don't care about that sort of thing these days.'

'Nooo. Perhaps not. Joy is a beautiful child. But ... you see … I thought I knew who I was and where I came from, but I don't, and it's suddenly become important to me.' He took a breath and looked at her. 'Because my circumstances have changed a bit.'

'Ah!' Amy went pink. It was perhaps fortunate that her parents chose that moment to return with a tray of mugs of tea.

Jack Watt came in and dumped the tray on the small coffee table and sank heavily into his chair. He looked across the room at his daughter sitting close to Antony on the settee and raised one eyebrow, but didn't pass any remarks.

Joyce seated herself near the empty fire grate and said, 'It seems I've been kept in the dark about these letters.' She watched Antony open his mouth and then said, 'Jack says you've had three or four since you were knocked over; that the police are watching the house and that we're all perfectly safe.' She sniffed and reached forward for her mug. 'I for one find it creepy that we've been watched by police and criminals alike and not known about it.' She took a sip of tea and hastily put it down – pushing it towards her husband and picking up a second mug – while exclaiming, 'Sugar!' She made a face. 'So, since we all know about it now, can you tell us what it's all about?'

Antony looked from one face to the other. There wasn't the reserve he'd seen all weekend, just concern. Before he could get his brain into gear Joyce spoke again. 'We care, lad. That's why we were so upset over the weekend. We care about our Amy and we're beginning to care about you.'

'Aye.' It was all Jack Watt said, but Antony warmed to the look on their faces. He took a breath and decided he'd break the habit of a lifetime and trust these people.

'I was telling Amy ... I don't know what I've done to incur the wrath of this person. They claim to have knocked me over and threaten to do worse if I don't leave town. This last one told me I was a bastard.' He cocked his head on one side and smiled wryly. 'It seems I might be.'

'Oh. What a nasty thing to say. As if anyone can help the situation they're born into. You didn't choose: your parents decided to have you, and they were the ones who decided whether they would be married or not.' Joyce was quite pink in the face with indignation.

Antony relaxed a tiny bit more. 'I found some newspaper reports at the library of the accident when my parents were killed. I'll go and fetch them; you might remember the event and be able to add something.' He stood up as Amy's parents nodded.

Amy nodded too, 'I'll just check on Joy, Mum; don't start without me.' She grinned at Antony and followed him out of the room.

2011

NEWCASTLE, ENGLAND

THE POST OFFICE STILL smelt of pipe tobacco and newspapers. David held the door open while Kate pushed the double buggy through and then bent over as a whimper came from young Rose. 'Hush, p...poppet; you'll wake your b...brother.' She flicked the clasp and hoisted the small girl up into her arms.

David turned at the small gasp coming from the elderly lady surveying them from behind the newspaper counter. He looked across the intervening distance, his eyes flicking from Kate – busy with her child – to the woman and back, his brows lowering slightly.

'How can I help you?' She came round the counter and stood looking at the small family.

David advanced, holding out his hand. 'My name is Professor David Walker. I spoke to a Mr Samuel Hamilton last night and he gave this as the last known address of Scarlett Hamilton. He was unsure if she was lodging here or if this was being used as a post office box. Would you know anything about that, Miss...' he looked up from reading the badge on her lapel and spoke as he observed the shrewd old eyes, 'Coote?'

'That depends on what you want to know, sir.' She ignored the outstretched hand and paused before saying, 'And why.'

David watched as her eyes were drawn magnet-like to his young daughter's face again. 'Yes; she's very like Kate would have been at that age, isn't she?'

'Pardon? I don't follow you, sir.' But the flush on her

217

cheeks said differently.

David shrugged. 'So, did Scarlett lodge with you or only use you as a postal address?'

'Why do you need to know? You're the second person asking about poor Scarlett: why can't you leave her alone?' The words were almost forced out of the old frame.

David looked around. Seeing the door to the back of the shop he stepped over to the main door and flicked the 'Closed' sign and the bolt and then came back, putting a hand under the frail arm. Kate watched him with astonishment. 'David, wh... at on earth are you d...doing?'

'It's lunchtime, Kate. Miss Coote has closed for lunch.'

'I never...' The old face looked at him in bewilderment, perhaps wondering if she should dial 999. Kate was thinking the same thing, only she was thinking more of psychiatric nurses than members of the law.

'I think we should all go into the back for a minute. Bring the babies, Kate. Miss Coote has just said something very interesting.' He gently led the mildly-resisting woman through the narrow door behind the counter. Kate, mystified, followed, pushing the buggy one-handed.

David was just sitting the old woman in what was obviously her chair. Next to it, and resting on an occasional table draped with a chenille cloth, was some gossamer-fine knitting. A cat, ignoring the humans, sprawled on the rag rug in front of a gas fire which hissed slightly. David smiled; it was a gentle smile, but Kate knew it of old. It meant he was going to have some answers.

Kate nursed her daughter, who had dozed again, and gently rocked the buggy as she looked from her husband to the bewildered old woman.

David stepped back. 'Sorry about the strong-arm tactics, Kate.' Kate noted he didn't apologise to Alice Coote as he turned back to her. 'My Kate was fostered by Scarlett, but you knew that. You recognised her in our daughter, didn't you?' He didn't wait for an answer but his voice gentled even more as he said, 'I'm sorry to tell you that Scarlett died last

November.' He watched the old eyes filling and pulled out a handkerchief, offering it.

The claw-like hands took it and the swimming eyes looked at him, before Alice blew vigorously on her nose. Two faded blue eyes looked up. 'She was a lovely woman.'

'Yes. But she's left her affairs in a bit of a mess.' David's lips twisted. 'Kate didn't know that Scarlett wasn't her real mother until after Scarlett died. Now she's trying to find her real parents.'

'I don't know who they were.'

'What can you tell us?'

Alice looked across at the silent Kate, then back at David. She drew in a deep breath – as if about to refuse to answer – and then shook her head. 'Dead?'

'Yes, I'm afraid so.'

'Ah, well.' Alice Coote paused again, then began to speak, addressing David but keeping her eyes on Kate. 'She worked at the school down the road. It closed and she came to live with me for a few months. She was always popping in with the little bairns from the school, teaching them how to go on, and we'd got friendly. So when the school closed and she had nowhere to go I said she could stay with me till she was settled.' Alice leaned back in the chair and David looked across at Kate, who had ceased rocking the pram and was looking at Alice in astonishment.

'The school closed in 1985, didn't it?'

'Yes.' Alice nodded, glancing briefly at David before the old eyes swung back to Kate again. 'She lived with me for about six months; like a daughter she was. Then she met that Jardin.' She looked at David for a second. 'He was a nasty piece of work if ever I saw one. But Scarlett, she couldn't see past his charm. He was all flowers and chocolate and she hadn't had much luck with men.' She sniffed and wiped her nose on the handkerchief she still clutched in her hand.

'Scarlett ... she couldn't have babies. There'd been a car accident when she was little, she told me, and they took away her womb; she'd been all messed up inside. The doctors hadn't had any choice; but it wasn't the physical scars, it was what it had done to her mind. She said no man would want her like that. So when he came calling – all over her – saying he didn't care and it didn't matter, she fell for it.' Alice looked at David. 'She loved him and he married her … '86, that was. She'd moved out by then. She was working over Jesmond Dene, in the primary school there. They set up house and then you appeared about eighteen months after that, I think it was.' She looked at Kate. 'You were such a quiet thing; but Scarlett, she was over the moon. Said she'd got a daughter, against the odds.'

'Did you know m…me th…en?'

Alice nodded. 'She came to visit; not often, but she didn't forget her friends and she showed you off.'

'So when did you lose touch?'

Alice swung her old head towards David. 'When he went to prison. He soon showed his colours, once they'd married; back to his old ways, thieving and cheating.' She looked at Kate, who was rocking the child in her arms again. 'She was that ashamed. He went to prison and she said she'd divorce him, only it turned out they wasn't married; he was married to a Carol somebody. She was terrified; thought the police would lock her up for bigamy and take you away.' Alice wiped her nose again. 'She hid. I don't know where she went. She never wrote; she said as how she wouldn't get me into trouble by making me tell lies.' She looked from one face to the other. 'I wouldn't have cared. What's the little girlie called?'

Kate had suddenly gone very pale and David – watching his wife carefully – walked swiftly over, taking his daughter from Kate's arms and nudging her onto a kitchen chair in front of a scrubbed pine table.

'Her name is Rose and my son is Paul.' He was still watching Kate, who had closed her eyes and lowered her head to her arms resting on the table top. 'Kate is pregnant.'

Alice stood up 'I'll put the kettle on; a nice sweet cuppa will help.' She bustled about until David was obliged to sit down at the table, too, to get out of her way. She lifted dainty china from a cupboard and set matching cups and saucers on the kitchen table, before picking up a wooden barrel by its silver handle and setting it down in front of Kate. 'Gingers: you'll feel more the thing if you nibble on one of those, dear.'

Kate lifted her head. 'Sorry, David.'

He shook his head. 'Have a biscuit, like Miss Coote says.'

'You call me Alice.' She poured water on the tea and brought the pot over, setting it on the table near her hand before sitting down. 'Where did she go?'

'Salisbury,' David answered, still keeping a wary eye on his wife. 'She went down there and started teaching. Bringing Kate up by herself.' He looked at Rose, who had woken up and was pulling gently at his beard. 'Can I give Rose a biscuit?'

The barrel was pushed towards him. 'I'm sorry we had to bring you bad news.'

'I'm pleased you came. I've kept quiet all this time; feared that the police would catch up with Scarlett and take your wife away from her.'

'You said someone else had been asking about Scarlett. When was that and what did they want? Can you tell us?' He held the biscuit out to his daughter and waited for the, 'Ta,' before handing over the treat.

Alice poured tea into china and looked at Kate. 'It was a young Catholic priest; said his name was Father O'Connor.' She smiled a bit grimly. 'He wasn't as persistent as you, Professor.'

'O'Connor.' Kate looked from David to Alice, who was nodding. 'Wh...en?'

'Last weekend.'

'Wh...at did he lo...ok li...ke? Wh...at did he ask? Wh... at did he t...tell you?'

'Drink your tea, Kate.' David nodded at the cup and then looked, with one eyebrow raised, at Alice Coote.

'Not a lot, to tell the truth. He just asked about Scarlett; did I know her? Or where she was.' Alice turned as Paul gave a little grunt and opened brown eyes on the world and started to wriggle. Alice looked at David, got a nod, then bent and unfastened him before lifting him onto her knee. 'Would you like a biscuit, like your sister?'

'Ta.'

'Good boy.' She held him snugly against her while she looked at his parents. 'He was just a priest: blond, brown eyes, nice smile.' She grinned, a trifle wickedly. 'Easily intimidated by wool.'

David cocked his head on one side, shifted his daughter and sipped tea. 'Tell.'

Alice told him about her friend, who'd come in for a ball of wool, and how she'd kept her talking until he went away. When she had finished describing the brief interview David smiled, then sighed. 'So you don't know where he came from or went to?'

Alice shook her head. 'I'm sorry. I didn't know what he wanted and I wasn't about to betray Scarlett.'

JUNE 2011

WHITBY

Amy was pushing Joy towards the shops with Antony walking at her side. Rain ran off the canopy of the pushchair and left long streaks as the wheels turned on the pavement, making a quiet shush shush sound. 'What do you want to buy, Amy?'

'I need nappies. I hadn't realised I was running short but Wednesday is early closing, so we'll have to be quick. I'll meet you at the library, shall I?'

'Yeah; that would be good.'

They parted at the end of the street, Amy pushing the pushchair along the busy main street and Antony going along a side road and round a corner to the library. He was making some headway with his research. The library had rung that morning to tell him a couple of books he'd ordered had arrived, if he'd like to come in and pick them up.

He pushed open the doors and the heat sprang out to meet him, so that he automatically began to undo the buttons on his coat as he advanced towards the desk. 'Ah, Antony. Here you are.' Two hefty tomes were laid on the counter. 'I found some more references to that accident in the old stacks as well, if you'd like them.'

Antony raised an eyebrow. 'That's very kind of you, Mrs Jones.'

Mrs Jones was rapidly approaching retirement and corseted; she creaked like a tea clipper in a south-westerly. She had known Antony since he had started coming into the library as a teenager, when she was a middle-aged librarian. She was also very inquisitive. 'I was wondering what relevance they had to the research.'

'Oh, this is a different project.'

'Oh, that's interesting; did the man do something important?'

Antony just looked at her. She had known him a long time: she wasn't dim; the accident involved a Mr Grey and his name was Grey. She must have put two and two together. He continued to look and she turned away – slightly shamed – saying, 'I'll … I'll just find those pages for you.'

Antony stood waiting patiently at the counter, the rain dripping slightly off his coat and running down his neck from his hair. Mrs Jones returned with a sheaf of photocopied pages. 'I hope they help.' She looked full at him and he caught not just the curiosity but the sympathy, at the back of her eyes.

'Thank you very much, I appreciate it.' He gathered the pages and the books and stuffed them into his rucksack, slinging it around one shoulder and going back out to wait on the pavement for Amy to reappear.

Half his mind was occupied reading the advert on the side of a bus across the road, the other half filled with curiosity as to what Mrs Jones had found for him, when the incident happened. It was as if the world was in slow motion. The car came along and pulled out, seemingly to overtake the parked bus, then – like a heat-seeking missile – appeared to head towards him on the pavement. The world snapped back into focus and Antony leapt backwards.

'Antony … oh, God! Oh, God! I thought you were going to be killed.' Amy, out of breath from her sprint with the buggy, was clutching his arm as they watched the car rev off into the distance.

'I'm OK, love.' Antony found himself clutching an armful of shaking woman – who was dropping tiny kisses on his face – and finding it very pleasant, despite the shock to his system. Indeed, his body was enjoying this second shock rather too much for his peace of mind. He eased her back and glanced down; Joy appeared to have slept through the incident.

'I got the make and number, young man, if you want to phone the police. These hooligans should be put in the stocks.' A moustache bristled at him, and a pair of gimlet eyes peered from behind thick black spectacles. The elderly gent was dressed in a black overcoat and carried a black umbrella. He had 'Services' stamped all over his posture.

'Thank you.' Antony smiled, watching as Amy pulled out a mobile, and aware that there was a uniform next to his elbow. He looked at the man in blue.

'I saw it. Name's Frank Smith; tell the coppers. I've got to shift me bus, but they can have a statement when I get off shift. Nasty bugger, too impatient to wait for me to pull out. They ought to take his licence away.' The bus driver headed back to his bus of gawking passengers and Antony looked at Amy as she talked into the phone.

'We've to go to the police station, Antony, and speak to a Detective Sergeant Tierney.'

'I shall come with you.' The moustache bristled some more and the gent walked at the side of them as they turned towards the city centre. 'It's terrible the way these people go on; he could have deprived this lovely child of her father with his carelessness.'

Amy opened her mouth and encountered a look from Antony. 'She is beautiful, isn't she?' Antony looked down at the sleeping child and then across at Amy again.

Their newfound friend escorted them to the police station – talking volubly about modern youth – with barely a pause for Antony to utter a 'Yes' or 'No' in agreement.

The police station was busy when they arrived; a youth was alternately crying for his mother and cursing as he stood in the grip of two sturdy minions of the law. Antony and his little band, however, were met by Detective Sergeant Tierney almost as soon as they entered. He looked at the natty suiting of their escort and raised an eyebrow at Antony.

'This gentleman was kind enough to come with us, Sergeant Tierney. He witnessed the incident.'

'Ah! If you'd be so good as to come into an interview

room, Mr…'

'Alfred Schott. These two young people were just going about their business and the driver was too impatient to wait for a bus to move.'

'This way, sir.' Tierney indicated with a hand a brilliantly lit passageway and a door at the end. They all trooped along after Mr Schott.

When everyone was seated and Tierney had a pen in his hand he started the questions. Alfred Schott was concise and clear. 'This young man was standing on the pavement outside the library. There was a parked bus depositing passengers on the opposite side of the road. A car, green – a souped-up Golf, I think – with the number plate ending 54L … I didn't get the first part, unfortunately. He shot out from behind the bus and deliberately mounted the pavement. It very nearly knocked this young man over.'

Tierney nodded, writing in longhand and drawing out extra details. 'Can you describe the driver?'

Schott frowned, 'Aged about thirty, I should say. Unwashed hair – as is the current fashion – a five o'clock shadow; not very clean; leather jacket.' He smiled. 'That's the best I can do I'm afraid. I think I'd recognise him again, however.'

After a few more minutes Tierney stood up. 'You've been most helpful, sir, and I'm sure Mr Grey is grateful.'

Antony too stood up and shook hands and Tierney, with a brief 'I'll only be a moment' left to escort Mr Schott out. He returned and shut the door of the office, coming around the desk and sitting down again. 'A very pleasant gent, and the description is good. I've asked the desk sergeant to put out an alert, but we know who owns that car.' He looked at Amy. 'Don't we?'

Amy nodded. 'That scumbag.'

'Which scumbag?' Antony looked from one face to the other, his own face reflecting his total perplexity.

'My ex: Stanley bloody Hunt. He hasn't been near me; oh no, he hasn't broken the law. But he's making bloody sure no one else gets near.'

'Eh? But...'

Amy looked at Tierney, then at Antony. 'I said you were too nice a bloke to have upset anyone.'

Tierney nodded. 'Yes, it looks very likely. I agree with you, Miss Watt.' He looked at the confusion on Antony's face. 'You were aware of the restraining order that Miss Watt has in place with regard to her ex-boyfriend?'

Antony nodded. 'But I didn't know his name; never thought to ask. Stan Hunt. Good grief.'

'The car that Mr Schott described is the same make and plate as a close friend of Hunt's. It would seem that Hunt still has a few issues, and we will be talking to him about them as soon as we find him. We have looked at him – of course – but there didn't seem any rhyme nor reason to connect him to you, sir, except that you had become part of the Watt household. You did claim to know him, but it still wasn't grounds for pulling him in.

'But that was after the first attempt; I don't see how he could have connected me to Amy before that.'

'No; we'd come to the same conclusion.' Tierney gave a tiny shrug. 'Which is why he was still on the streets and not answering questions here at the station. We aren't that slow, sir.'

Antony frowned, shrugged, and then said, 'So do you think he's behind the letters and that nasty gossip as well?' He cast a puzzled look at Amy. 'How could he possibly know about my parentage?'

'Parentage, sir?'

Antony smiled a bit sourly, 'It seems I am a bastard in the technical sense, after all, Sergeant.'

'Oh!' Tierney frowned. 'Well, we shall certainly ask him about that. Now, can you give me your version of this incident?'

Antony and Amy settled down to tell Tierney what they had been doing up to the moment when the car came around the bus and nearly squashed Antony against the library doors. Joy slept blissfully on as they talked, only waking as they left the warmth of the station for the cold mist of the rainy street.

Amy hugged an arm as Antony pushed the pram along. 'See, I said you were a nice bloke.'

Antony grunted acknowledgement of the comment, but in truth his mind wasn't on the attempt on his life but on the reaction from Amy at the time. 'Were you...? Did it...?' Antony looked down at the blonde hair surrounding the pretty face and stopped in the middle of the street, forcing the foot traffic to detour with sour looks and several tutting noises. 'Amy, I don't quite know how to put this ... but no one has ever cared before if I was there or not. Do you think you...?'

'Silly.' Amy looked at him with a gentle smile. 'Let's go home.'

JUNE 2011

GALWAY

BEN WAS ALREADY HOME but so much had changed that it no longer felt like the sanctuary of his childhood and youth. Whatever his grandfather wanted to tell him was still to be told. Ben had sat holding the old hand, waiting, but it seemed that – having got his grandson back – Eoin O'Conner could finally relax, and he had fallen into a deep sleep.

Bridget, coming back into the room ten minutes later with a mug of tea for her nephew-in-law, set the mug down and looked from the old face to the young. 'He's hardly slept for two days.' She whispered the words as she looked at Ben.

Ben nodded. 'And you need your rest too, *Aintin*. I'll sit with him.'

Bridget hesitated a minute before nodding her head. 'Aye. I'm tired and Micheál has the farm to run, and a man down.' She nodded her head again and Ben caught the faint scent of roses and washing powder as she moved away.

Ben moved so that he could still hold his grandfather's hand but relax into the chair slightly. He looked at the familiar face and let his mind drift. He had left the farmhouse in anger three weeks ago. Now he started to remember what it had been like to live here as a small child.

He remembered his sister's face, snatches of laughter and tears… Her tiny figure running into their bedroom, hiding under the bed from her grandmother's wrath… The pair of them giggling as they shared the big tin bath in front of the fire. Both standing on chairs at the sink – one washing and the other drying the dishes – with *mórai* standing behind them making sure they were safe, and did the job.

He'd gone in search of Kate, and she was here. Ben must have dozed for the next thing he became conscious of was his uncle coming in and touching him gently on the shoulder, speaking softly. 'Will you eat something, Ben?'

Ben looked around in surprise. The little alarm clock on the side table next to the bed said nearly one in the afternoon. His grandfather still slept.

Micheál – after a glance at his father – whispered, 'He's still fast; I'll stay while you have a bite.'

Ben stood, hearing his shoulders crack and feeling his back protest as he stretched. 'I'll not be long.' He left the room after a backward glance at the sleeping face. Bridget was downstairs putting soup into a brown tureen; the old table had a granny loaf on a bread board with a crock of butter next to it. He sat in his old place as Bridget set a bowl of soup in front of him as he sat down. 'Have you slept, *Aintin*?'

'Aye, I'll do. Eat up; the doctor will be here later. He can tell you what's happening with *Athair*.'

Ben nodded, the first stirrings of hunger making themselves felt as the smell of the soup wafted up to his face. 'All *Uncail* said on the phone was that it was his heart.'

'Aye.' Bridget served herself and sat down. 'He complained of a pain a couple of days ago; the doctor said it was the angina. He's to rest in bed; he refused when the doctor said he should be after going to the hospital.' She applied herself to her soup and both ate in silence for several minutes.

Bridget set down her spoon and sliced more bread, offering it to Ben before continuing with her meal. 'How has he been coping, *Aintin*?'

Bridget looked across her soup bowl at him and spoke sharply. ''Twould have been better if you'd stayed and listened, Ben.'

'Aye. I'm sorry, *Aintin*.'

'So am I, for I never held with the secret. I understood why Maeve would want to keep the shame of the suicide quiet.

But that she should deny you the knowledge of your sister, or indeed the splitting of you, was a wrong thing. But I could not gainsay her, for what was done was done and there was no turning back, lad.' Bridget shook her head. 'Have you had no word of Kate?'

'Hints. Aunt Lara has been busy for me, and some of the cousins. We've found a trail for Jardin's woman. She seems to have been a good person. I've heard about Kate over in Cumbria; indeed that was where I was when *Uncail* phoned.' Ben paused and finished the soup, laying down his spoon. 'I'll tell you what little more I've found when *Uncail* is here.'

'Aye. But she was safe? In Cumbria?'

'She was at the trial of Jardin's murderer.' Ben crossed himself. 'But, aye, she was safe then. Though who was supporting her through it I don't know.' He shook his head. 'We should have been there ... I should have been there for her.'

''Tis not a bit of good, reproaching yourself. You didn't know about her or the trial.'

'And whose fault is that? To forget my own sister.'

Bridget stretched out a hand, just touching the nearest arm. 'Hush, lad. Hush, Ben, *a chara;* it wasn't your fault.'

'I'm having a hard time forgiving myself, *Aintin.*'

'We all have things that need forgiveness. Don't take on those things not your fault.' She stood and went over to the stove, turning her back for a minute, but Ben had caught the glint of tears.

'I'm sorry. 'Tis not your fault, either.'

Bridget swung back with the teapot in her hand. 'You were a child. I could have said something, but I didn't. I just let Maeve have her way because it was easier.' She straightened her shoulders and walked back with the teapot. She kept her eyes down as she poured him tea before she spoke again. 'Take your tea and send Micheál down. He'll need to get back. We've a few sucky lambs to see to, out in the barn.'

Ben picked up the mug and came around the table. 'Thank you for my lunch, *Aintin.*' He dropped a kiss – soft as a whisper – on the down-bent head, and left the room.

Micheál was sitting at the window, looking out on the yard below. Ben offered a half smile. 'You've to take your lunch; apparently you have some lambs to feed afterwards.'

'Aye. Bridget has been with Da for the last two days and the wretched creatures are looking for their *mammi*.'

Ben gave a quiet chuckle at the pained look on his uncle's face. Then he went to sit by the bed and wait for his grandfather to awaken.

He was quietly telling his rosary when the old man opened his eyes. 'Thank God we haven't killed your faith, Ben *a chara*.'

'It's been touch and go there for a while, *Daideó*.'

'Aye. Help me up a bit, lad.' Ben looked at him doubtfully. 'I feel fine now.' It was said a shade testily.

'Here am I rushing to your death bed and it's all a big fraud, is it?' Ben's lips quirked as he slid an arm under his grandfather's shoulders and heaved him up onto the pillows.

His grandfather shook his head. 'I did want you, Beineon. But I'm not for dying just the now.'

'The doctor might tell a different story.'

'The boy is young; he's got learning yet to do.' Eoin, sighed 'I'm sorry, Ben.'

'Well, then so am I.' Ben sighed. 'Let us have done with sorry, *Daideó*. We all made mistakes.'

'Yes.' His grandfather reached out and took one of the hands lying quietly in Ben's lap. 'Have you found her?'

'No. The trail is rather cold.' He looked at the age-spotted hand holding his. 'I think I might be able to, given a little more time.'

'You'll bring her home?'

'I don't know, *Daideó*. I've had time to think. She may not want us; she may have a life of her own. We sent her away; why should she want to come here?' He shook his head as he saw the tremble on the hands, and sighed. 'I miss her so, *Daideó*.'

'Aye. I've missed her, and Maeve did. We've prayed for

her every night since she left, Ben. She wasn't forgotten. We searched, when we heard her father was is prison.'

Ben looked up into the old face. 'So I've discovered.'

'Tell me what you've found out, Ben.'

Ben began a reprise of the information he'd obtained so far, ending with, 'She was cared for, *Daideó*. This woman Scarlett – who Jardin was living with – seems to have kept her after he went into prison. She was on the list as living with Scarlett in Jesmond Dene up until the end of 1988, and going to the local infants' school. But after that I lose her until about three years ago. Jardin was murdered and Kate was at the trial.'

'Dear God.'

Ben looked anxiously at his grandfather as he uttered the words. 'I'm sorry; I shouldn't have told you.'

'Yes you should, Ben. What have I done to my little Kate?' It was almost groaned, and Ben began to look quite alarmed as he saw the colour leave the wrinkled cheeks. Thankfully at that minute a stranger pushed open the door, leading with a smile and an outstretched hand.

'Ah! Mr O'Connor, you're looking much better. And you'll be Ben. I'm Dr O'Neil.'

Ben stood up and went forward to shake the hand. His lips twitched. 'I hear you're young and have a bit to learn.' He glanced back at his grandfather, who was recovering his colour.

Dr O'Neil gave a chuckle. 'Yes, so I'm told.' He set his bag on the chair that Ben had been sitting on and cocked his head on one side. 'I'll listen to that chest of yours. I might learn something.'

'I'll just…'

'Stay, Ben.' Ben looked at his grandfather and nodded.

'OK.' He went over to the window and looked out, as his uncle had been doing, at the farmyard below. He tuned out the soft conversation going on at the bedside, not moving until the doctor cleared his throat and looked across the room.

'Your grandfather is much improved. Stress and tiredness.

Another couple of days in bed for now and then I'll have him to the surgery and take some bloods, run a few tests.' He glanced down at Eoin O'Connor. 'And if further procedures are necessary I hope you'll let me arrange them.' He shook hands and quietly left the room.

Ben came back over to the bed, one eyebrow raised. He'd heard the emphasis on you.

His grandfather shook his head. 'Maeve wouldn't let him help; I could have had her for a few more years if she'd listened to his advice and gone to the big hospital. She always thought she knew best.'

Ben took the old hands and held them gently, neither speaking for a while, until Eoin said, 'So tell me what else you found out?'

'Well, *Mórai* was right about one thing: my mother wasn't married to Jardin.'

JUNE 2011

WHITBY

ANTONY WAS FEEDING TOAST fingers and egg to Joy as she sat in her high chair at the kitchen table. Amy was pottering about, making the adults cheese on toast. 'Here you go, Mam.'

Joyce took the offered plate and moved her chair nearer to the table. She picked up a half slice but then just held it as Antony deftly captured an eggy finger of toast and popped it in while Joy wasn't watching. 'You do that like you've been feeding her all her life, Antony.'

Antony looked across and gave a half smile. 'As we got older at the children's home we had to help with the little ones.' He grimaced. 'I do like children.' Then he grinned suddenly. 'Where did you think I'd learned to change a nappy without throwing up?'

Amy brought her own and Antony's plates to the table and sat down. 'Here, give me the feeder.' She set it down in front of Joy. 'There you go, poppet.' She watched critically for a few seconds to see that her daughter had got the hang of it, then picked up her own slice of toast.

'Would you mind very much telling us about the home?' Joyce looked at him across the table. 'Not if it bothers you.'

Antony shrugged. 'It's not that it bothers me, exactly; it was just such a miserable time that I've done my best to forget it. In fact I did my best to forget my childhood. I didn't even enquire about the accident; I didn't want the unhappy memories.' He picked up his lunchtime mug of tea and leaned back. 'I can't remember much about my mum, just little bits.

She sang to me and I had a yellow teddy that my father used to pretend was dancing and talking when I was going to bed.' His lips twisted a bit. 'Only, according to the papers, he wasn't my father. He and my mother were living together, but he was married to someone else at the time and they didn't want "the other woman's child".' He put the words in finger brackets with a slight sneer in his voice to go with the bitter words.

Joyce looked at her daughter, who had uttered a small sound. It was apparently enough to stop Amy speaking.

Antony sipped tea for a minute and then looked at Joyce. 'Sorry.'

'Doesn't matter, lad.'

'No, I don't suppose it does at this stage in the game, but I would like to know who my father was.' He shrugged again. 'So after my mother was killed in the car accident I was placed on the list for adoption and put in a council children's home, then several other private foster homes. Some of them were nice, some ... we were little more than extra hands to look after the younger children. I didn't "take".' He grinned. 'I asked too many questions, and after a while I wouldn't mix. Self-defence mechanism, I suppose.'

'Jack and I were trying to remember the accident but it was Newcastle, not the local papers, so we can't recall much about it.' Joyce frowned. 'I do remember the accident because it was in the summer holidays and the town was thronged with shoppers. The accident closed the city centre that night.'

'Yeah, so the papers say.' Antony suddenly abandoned his mug and stood up, leaving the room abruptly. Amy looked alarmed and Joyce set down her mug and pushed back her chair.

'Antony!'

He came back into the kitchen with his rucksack. 'I'd forgotten, in all the fuss this morning. The librarian gave me some more information that she'd found in the newspaper stacks, she said. I haven't looked at it yet.'

'Well don't get them all over grease from the toast, and eat something, for heaven's sake.' Joyce took the rucksack out of his hand and pushed the rapidly cooling toast towards him.

Antony grinned at her, picking up the toast and sitting down. 'Open it up; I want to know what she found out. Now I find I want to know all about my parentage; I'm positively agog, for some reason.' He gave a chuckle as he watched the pink rise in Amy's cheeks and then bit into the toast as he watched Joyce undoing the buckle and pulling out the sheaf of papers.

Joyce looked over the first page and then looked up. 'Well, it's a bit more upmarket than the papers you showed us on Monday. It's the funeral of Mr Henry Grey ... that would be your ... dad.' Joyce hesitated as she looked at Antony; he nodded at her to continue. 'It's only a little piece: "*The officiating minister was Reverend Thomas Stokes. The mourners of Mr Henry Grey included his wife Deborah and teenage sons Allen and Robert, as well as his mother and father. Mr Grey will be deeply missed in Gateshead where he was, until recently, a member of the Neighbourhood Watch. No flowers, by request. All donations to go to the Prisoners' Benevolent Fund.*" It doesn't sound as if you were his child, Antony, not if he'd moved out "recently", does it?'

'As I said, I was the child of the "other woman". I don't think he fathered me. I think this Carol was just living with him as his wife. How she met him is something I'd like to ask the wife or sons, if I thought they'd tell me, but...'

'If they still lived in the area you could maybe find them on the electoral roll.' But Joyce sounded doubtful.

'I'm not sure it would be right to bring back such painful memories, Joyce.' Antony shook his head and removed the mug from the sticky hands of Joy. 'Do you want to get down, petal?'

'Here; I'll manage her.' Amy stood and went over to her daughter, using a cloth for her hands and lifting her out of the chair before giving her a kiss. She set her down and said to Antony, 'Do you think the Benevolent Fund people might be a clue? They did want donations to go there.'

Antony pursed his lips. 'It might have been the wife who

wanted the money to go there.'

'Oh! Come on, Antony; what have you got to lose?' Amy grinned at him and nodded at his half-eaten lunch. 'I'll make you a fresh cuppa if you'll phone them.' She swung around and lifted the telephone book from the top of the fridge where it had inexplicably come to rest, setting it down in front of him and swinging back to pick up the kettle.

'Amy?'

'He'll always be wondering if he doesn't do something, Mum. This is important to Antony. If he'll just shift himself and stop worrying about upsetting people.' She grinned cheekily at both her mother and Antony.

Antony nodded slowly. 'Yes, you're right.' He began to thumb through the directory. After a minute he said, 'Not in.'

'Try the Prison Service; they might be able to give you a number.' Joyce was getting almost as interested as her daughter, though maybe for more altruistic motives.

Antony applied himself to the pages again, sniffed and got up to dial on the landline. The others watched as he asked his questions. 'Thank you; you've been very helpful.' He turned to look at the two women. 'Well, I have another number. Shall we try again?'

'Get on with it.' Amy nodded at him.

Antony punched in yet another set of numbers and started explaining himself again. 'You can? That would be very helpful.' He set the phone down and dialled yet a third number. 'Reverend Stokes?' Amy exchanged a look with Joyce, then they both sat watching Antony – who had explained his needs – nodding like a Mandarin. 'Yes, I'm free this afternoon. I could come over. That would be great.' He set the receiver down.

'The Reverend Stokes was the minister who buried Mr Henry Grey, as we have just read. He's also a chaplain at the remand centre. He's willing to talk about my mother if I can come today.'

JUNE 2011

CUMBRIA

KATE WAS UNWILLING TO talk. David had tried discussing the events of the previous day with her but she'd just shaken her head at him. Now he'd had enough; he'd given her all of Wednesday to digest the information.

The children were abed and he was too impatient to wait any longer. He'd try shock tactics and see where that got him. 'What's distressing you most, my Kate? That we missed your brother by a whisker? That he's looking for you? Or that your father didn't appear to have been married to either Scarlett or your mother?'

'All of the a...a...above.' Kate had known that she wouldn't be able to evade her husband's questions for long. She'd feigned tiredness from the day out, and then sleep last night. Now she knew she would have to deal with it. 'I'm glad he's d...dead.'

'I assume you mean your father. Well as fathers-in-law go he was certainly an original.' David grinned a bit evilly. 'I have to say I'm rather glad he's not around myself, but not for my sake; for yours, Kate. However, being dead does pose certain problems: we can't exactly ask him what the hell he was playing at, can we?'

He stood up and went over to the computer. 'I did, however, have an idea at lunchtime. Come and sit next to me, darling.' He held out a hand and Kate moved reluctantly across the study and sat in the hard chair next to his at the desk. 'That's better.' David gave her a quick hug around her shoulders. 'We've looked for your mother's name, but so far we haven't looked for her name as Jardin.' He paused. 'Or the name Carol Jardin.'

'But…'

'But what, Kate? I see no reason to doubt Miss Coote or Scarlett, either. What would be the benefit to them? Let's look and see what we can find out.'

She watched silently as he booted up the machine and waited patiently for the internet connection to produce the three blue lights. 'OK, David.' She watched as he scanned the births, deaths and marriages for the eighties in the Newcastle area.

He was scrolling down yet another page as he spoke to her, apparently casually. 'You never hesitate over my name, or the children's, or Scarlett's. Yet you struggle with s, p, w and t, normally. Why do you think that is, Kate?' He kept his eyes on the screen as he asked the question.

Kate lifted her eyes from the contemplation of the words on the screen and looked at her husband with a puzzled frown on her face.

David stopped the cursor from moving and looked at her. 'I've listened to you for several years now, love. During normal day to day conversation, and while there's no pressure, you hesitate and struggle with the odd word.' He took her hands. 'But you never hesitate or stutter when we're making love.'

'David!'

He watched the blush rising like the sun coming up. He grinned, his emerald eyes lighting up. 'I know; I shouldn't be noticing things like that at a time like that.' His lips twitched. 'But I can't help it; it's in my make-up to observe, no matter what I'm doing.'

'I love you.' Kate smiled.

'Yes, you say those words prettily, too.' David leaned over and dropped a quick kiss on her lips. 'Not often enough to reassure me, but you don't hesitate over them.'

'David, you kn…ow I love you. Wh…y do you need rea…

reassurance?'

'Because contrary to popular opinion, my love, I'm as human as the next man ... and you are a very desirable woman.'

'I didn't th...ink you w...would ever feel like that.'

'Well start thinking along those lines, love. I'm sure part of your problem is insecurity and that insecurity stems right back to the time when Scarlett took over your care. But I ... hope ... you feel safe with me, which is why you don't struggle as much. The reason I say this is because I recognise the symptoms of insecurity; I suffer from them myself.'

David smiled softly as he looked at her serious face. 'I don't care about your stutter, Kate. I love you, but I do care that you might feel insecure. So long as you want me I'm yours, darling, and no one will part us; understand?' He smoothed back her hair. 'I don't care about your parentage; I just want you.' He turned back to the computer.

Kate sat, stunned. David had always appeared to be so very confident that she hadn't thought he could ever have the kind of fears and worries she seemed to suffer from all the time. 'I'm s...sorry, David. I do love you.'

'Good. Ah!' David held the cursor over a name. 'Do you think this could be it, Kate?'

Kate peered at the screen.

'Carol Bathurst married Philip Jardin in the register office at Newcastle upon Tyne on 21 January 1981.'

'It's the r...right p...place anyway, David.'

'I shall send for the marriage licence, Kate. It should give us an address.'

'Wh...at good w...will that do?'

David smiled. 'It gives us somewhere else to look. I rang Bob McInnis at lunchtime.' He smiled, taking his attention from the screen again. 'He's a good Roman Catholic, is Bob. I thought he might be able to tell me if there's some sort of register of Catholic priests which might give us a lead with regard to your brother ... always assuming that was him.' He smiled into his wife's serious brown eyes. 'I know that assuming makes "an ass of you and me" but we have to start somewhere, Kate.'

'Yes, you're r…right, David.'

'Of course I am.'

David swung back to the screen. 'Jardin's dead. I wonder if she is, too. You'd think she would have appeared at the trial, wouldn't you?' But David was talking to himself as he looked at the monitor and clicked the mouse. 'This could be her: July 1986. I'll get that one, too.' He typed busily for a minute, arranging for the certificates.

'He m…married my m…mother in September '83.'

'Yes, and he married Scarlett in March '86, making him a bigamist twice over, Kate. We could allow him the excuse of a broken childhood, but I am of the opinion that that is just a cop-out. You didn't exactly have an easy run of it, love, and you're not a crook. That nice young man who is doing my research over in Whitby was brought up in a children's home and he seems to have turned out OK.' David swung idly on the seat, letting his hands rest on the keyboard as he spoke, 'No, Kate. We make our own paths. You can learn from the nastiness, but you don't have to add to it.'

'I w…wonder how he's getting on. We h…haven't h… heard from him for a couple of w…weeks.'

'Who?' David looked startled.

'Antony Grey.'

David nodded. 'I'll give him a ring in the morning. There isn't any rush yet. Maybe go over next week.' He frowned. 'I fly to Germany a week on Saturday. I don't like leaving you with this unresolved, Kate.'

'It's b…been unresolved for years; a f…few more w… weeks won't make any difference, David.'

David scowled then shrugged, and then with a quick move had his wife on his lap. 'I've got to stock up on kisses before I go.' He proceeded to act out the statement to the detriment of Kate's hair and any further research.

JUNE 2011

GALWAY

NOT HAVING A WIFE to distract him, Ben was talking about his research to his relatives. His grandfather was tucked up comfortably in the big bed that he and Maeve had occupied all their married lives. The big patchwork quilt was made of cast-off clothes from both her children's and grandchildren's lives, and Ben found himself searching the material for signs of Kate.

The clock was a small cheap alarm that had been bought back in the late eighties when they had gone on holiday to the Isle of Man; it had a familiar and comforting one-legged tick. Ben had been told as a child that it was because the Isle of Man was famous for its extra leg. His lips tipped up at the thought. Everyone in the room could hear it lurching through the minutes as they recovered from Ben's latest bombshell.

'He was already marrit?'

'Aye. The papers from the police list a Caroline Bathurst as next of kin –when he was arrested in the eighties – but this Scarlett Hamilton in the nineties. No mention of my mother at all.' Ben poked the pile of paper lying at the foot of the bed where he had been laying them as he explained what he'd found.

Bridget stirred in her chair; she had been quiet, dividing her time between her father-in-law and Ben as he spoke. Now she said, 'So he was married. He got Theresa in the family way without meaning to, I've no doubt. She wouldn't have gone with him without, so he pretended to marry her. I wonder was it the shame of it she couldn't bear, and not the post-natal depression. What must his poor wife have thought about it if she knew of his goings on and her maybe with bairns of her own to care for?'

Ben drew in a shocked breath. Before he could speak his grandfather nodded, like Jove pronouncing judgement. 'Well … he missed out on all his babies and it serves him right, deceiving women like that.'

'But…'

'Aye, Ben; you might have more out there than our Kate.' Micheál nodded. 'And will you search for them, too?'

Ben shook his head in confusion.

'Leave him be, Mike; and hasn't he had enough shocks for the time being.' Bridget stood up on the words and shook down her skirt. 'I'll away and make us a drink and you can have your night time pills, *Athair* Eoin.' She bustled out of the room.

Micheál looked from father to nephew and offered a half smile. 'I'll away and settle the stock for the night.' He too left the room.

'What will you do now, Ben *a chara?*'

'I don't know, *Daideó*. I'll wait until I hear the results of these tests you're to have before I head back to England. I'll ring the Monseigneur tomorrow and tell him what I'm doing; I have leave of absence for as long as is needed.'

Eoin stirred in the bed. 'No, I've seen you now. You understand, lad, I had to see you; know you really did forgive me.' Ben opened his mouth and Eoin waved him to quiet. 'Sometimes the phone isn't enough. I had to see your face and feel your hand and take your blessing, *ghra*. To know you really did forgive.'

'Aye, *Daideó;* I know. I needed the same, though I didn't know it.'

'So you'll go again to find the little colleen for us?'

Ben offered a half smile. 'So now you want rid of me?' He shook his head. 'I'll stay another day or two; I have a grave or two to visit.'

'Take your ease then and you must, but not for too long, Ben, for I need Kate's forgiveness, too.'

JUNE 2011

WHITBY

ANTONY WAS TALKING ABOUT his afternoon with another minister of the cloth, this one of the Anglican persuasion but just as keen on people finding forgiveness in their hearts. He was seated in his old place at the pub and Amy was sitting opposite him, their twin reflections dancing on the window panes as they talked. Antony took a tentative sip of his shandy and smiled across the table. He had been greeted by Amy saying, 'Go and sit down. I'll take my break. I want to know what you found out.'

She'd plonked herself and the two shandies down within minutes and smiled across the table at him with a 'Tell, pretty please,' and a grin.

'This reverend was old, all silver grey hair and decorum. He had this huge study of books.' Antony had a slightly dreamy look on his face.

'Never mind the books. What did he tell you?'

Antony, brought back to the matter in hand, grinned himself. 'One day, Amy, I'm going to have a study full of books and the peace and leisure to read them.' His grin widened a bit at the long-suffering look that was crawling across her face. 'OK, OK. He was very nice. I told him I was searching for my birth parents; that I'd got as far as discovering that Henry Grey wasn't in fact my father and what could he tell me about the man and my mother?'

Amy wriggled a bit impatiently but held her tongue.

'He asked a lot of questions, Amy. Seemed to want

assurances that I wouldn't approach the widow – who is still alive and living in Gateshead, apparently. I told him I couldn't approach her even if I wanted to; I didn't know where she lived. He made me promise, said she'd been through quite enough.' Antony scratched absently at his hair as he looked at the eager face opposite.

'Anyway, after that he got down to details. Henry Grey had lived a respectable life. He was a tax collector, would you believe.'

'Yes, I would. Get on with it!'

Antony shook his head. 'He was the typical upstanding citizen: good job, nice home, wife in the suburbs, two boys – whom he went to football matches with – pillar of the community and church, involved with the families of prisoners. Then he met this Carol and that was it. Her husband was in jail and she was struggling to bring me up. He went to offer financial support and ended up moving out of his home and living with her.'

Amy nodded for him to continue.

'The Reverend Stokes said he'd known Henry for years. They'd worked together for nearly fifteen years for the Prisoner's Family Service. He said Henry just fell in love. His marriage had always seemed comfortable, his wife apparently supporting him. Then, wham! Henry just changed: it was the real thing.'

'Was your mum some sort of a femme fatale, then?'

Antony shook his head. 'No, that was the weird thing. He...' He stopped speaking as a hand grabbed his collar and he was lifted bodily from his seat, the table pushing roughly against Amy.

Amy screamed, 'Stan' ... and all hell apparently broke loose.

Antony, slightly stunned, dangled for a second or two before beginning to fight back. Amy was struggling to get out from behind the table; the bar clientele were for a second or two as stunned as Antony. Then several came to his assistance and several others decided to settle a few scores of their own in the mêlée.

The bartender, an old hand, ducked behind the counter and punched 999 into his mobile. He was joined behind the bar by the other two girls who acted as waitresses, all three ducking down as a body briefly spread over the bar in front of them and then disappeared again.

Antony was now showing that he might be a peaceable sort of bloke but that he knew exactly what his fists were for when push came to shove, and this was definitely a push and shove fight for the most part.

Amy backed into a corner, and held the tray she'd been using to serve the drinks in front of her like a shield. One passing patron who got too near her corner was thumped on his head in the approved fashion, with a resounding tympanic twang. He turned, grinning and shaking his head, winked at her and then returned to the fray.

She watched Antony with anxious eyes. He seemed to be holding his own well, delivering some nicely targeted hits at Stan's chin and once a blow to his ear that made her wince. Not that it was going all his way – Stan was getting in a few punches of his own.

Both had settled down to steadily slugging each other when the police arrived and pulled them apart. 'All right, all right; stop it. I said STOP IT!' Antony, brought to his senses by – literally – the long arm of the law grabbing hold of him, pulled back. Stan Hunt, however, didn't seem to get the message as quickly and was wrestled to the ground amid the cursing crowd of men who had mostly stopped fighting among themselves to form a circle around Antony and Stan.

'Quit while you're ahead.' The cuffs were snapped into place behind Stan's back and he was heaved upright.

Another policeman was looking over the crowd. 'Anyone need an ambulance?' He watched the shaking heads and noted the incipient bruising that was appearing on several faces, along with shamefaced looks. 'What started all this? You?' He pointed at the bartender with his chin while pulling out a notebook. The bartender, who had emerged from the protection of the bar along with the two girls, dusted a small amount of broken bottle off his shoulder and looked with disgust at the man in cuffs who was swearing the air blue around him.

'He started it.' He nodded at Hunt. 'Amy was just having a quiet drink with her boyfriend and THAT came in and dragged him out of his chair and started beating him up.'

Stan apparently wasn't happy with this statement. 'She's mine. I'll break his fucking neck if he thinks he's gonna fuck her.' He struggled to get to Antony, who wisely stepped back a few paces.

Amy strode from her corner and grabbed his jacket front with one hand, pushing her face up to his. 'I'm not yours. Don't you come the macho over me. You beat me up once – and that was plenty – and if I want to sleep with a gentleman I bloody well will, and it's nobody's business but mine.' She stepped back as a policeman put his hand on her arm. She didn't take her eyes off Stan Hunt as she carefully and very ostentatiously wiped the hand that had clutched the jacket on her serving cloth and dropped it on the floor.

A small patter of applause made her look around, and then she ignored them and went over to Antony.

'Do you wish to prefer charges, sir?'

Antony hesitated for a fraction of a second, then nodded.

'I'll fucking prefer charges. That wanker sat in the window, sniggering and laughing with my girl, I'll…'

'I respectfully suggest you shut up, sir.' The policeman tightened his hold, ably assisted by two others, and began to drag the struggling man – still cursing indiscriminately at everyone within sight – out to the waiting police van.

A remaining policeman looked the crowd over. 'I'm issuing a general warning. Any more of this and I'll fill the cells and charge you lot with affray.' He looked at Antony and glanced at the door.

'I'll come and make a statement, officer.' He walked outside as a sense of peace descended on the room behind him.

JUNE 2011

WISBECH

THE REST OF THE week passed quietly for Kate, if not peace-fully. She was trying to come to terms with so many different things that she didn't know where to start and had allowed her old coping mechanisms to swing back into place, retreating from everyone.

David was trying to get one job finished before starting another, while being aware that it was not just he who would suffer if he didn't. He was also terrified – an emotion he'd rarely experienced – that he'd pushed too hard, too fast and alternately blamed and cursed himself for his impatience. She was tossing and turning every night now with nightmares which held her rigid and had her sweating – the only outward sign of her distress.

He couldn't even reach her during their lovemaking and that was the scariest thing of all. He'd always been able to touch the core of her then but even that door had been shut quietly, and firmly, in his face.

When Friday night arrived he sighed with relief that at least he'd got the bulk of the paperwork out of the way. They had driven to his parents in almost total silence that afternoon. It wasn't a nasty condemning silence, just a desperately sad one. He climbed out onto his parents' driveway and slammed the car door as he watched Kate getting out the other side and opening the back door.

'Kate.' He spoke as he opened the other back door and began to undo Paul's seat, preparatory to lifting him out. She smiled at him but didn't speak or stop her own work of lifting out Rose in her baby seat. Both looked up as the security lights came on and his father spoke behind Kate.

'Here, let me do that.' He took over the task while he continued speaking, 'You aren't supposed to be lifting now.' He swung the small girl, still asleep in her seat, up into his arms and looked across at David. 'Ruth has killed the fatted calf; off you go.'

David, burdened with his son, nodded and followed the other two inside. Kate had gone into the kitchen and David nodded as his father said, 'Straight upstairs?'

'Yes; we fed them on the way down. Hopefully we can slide them into their beds without disturbing them too much.' He turned as both his mother and Kate came into the small nursery.

'That's it, David. Get them settled and then you can have something to eat.' David and his father gingerly unfastened belts and put the toddlers under covers. Kate turned on the night light and all the adults left the room with sighs of relief.

They had been served a lovely evening meal, but Kate had just pushed hers around the plate and David hadn't done a lot better. His parents exchanged a look. 'Is the morning sickness bothering you again, Kate?' Ruth gave her an excuse and a sympathetic look.

Kate shook her head. 'It's b...been a long j...journey. D... do you m...mind if I go up?'

'No of course not, darling. I'll be up myself very soon; it has been a long week, as you say.' David smiled at her and Kate felt guilt rising up in her as she stood from the table. These lovely people shouldn't have to put up with her; she seemed to be causing grief to everyone she loved.

She slowly went up the stairs and looked around the door at her children. They had been put into a single divan bed and curled together, sleeping peacefully. She went out and entered the bedroom that David and she had occupied from the first time he'd brought her to visit his parents. She trailed over to the bed and sat down, her shoulders slumping with despair.

Meanwhile David was being observed by his parents. Neither seemingly wished to pry, but he could tell they were worried by their silence. 'This whole situation is getting to Kate. Me too, if I'm honest.'

'Is there anything we can do to help?' His father looked at him across the napery and dishes.

David shook his head, 'If I knew what was going on in her head I might be able to handle it but she's shut me out, Pops.'

'Is it too late to abandon the search?'

'Way too late. She knows her brother is out there looking for her, too.'

'But surely…'

David shook his head at his mother as she stopped the question half formed. 'I thought knowing he wanted to find her would be a boost. But since she discovered that, well, she seems to have totally retreated and she won't talk to me about it. She tells me she loves me, but … oh, God! Mum, I don't know what to do for the best any more.' David stood up abruptly. 'I'll go up; I don't want her thinking I'm talking about her behind her back.' He offered a strained smile and left his parents exchanging unhappy looks.

WISBECH HAD A GREY look about it on Saturday morning. David had agreed that they should visit his parents as arranged, but now he wasn't all that sure. Maybe he should have kept his family in Cumbria. Maybe he could have persuaded Kate to open up to him if they hadn't an audience. He was thinking about it as they bought milk and papers and headed back to the car.

Kate's hand was icy and David pulled it into the pocket of his overcoat as they walked. He stopped as they arrived at the passenger door of the 4x4 and pulled it open and looked at his wife's face. 'OK?'

'A little queasy. I'll be all r…ight in a m….minute.' She offered a soft smile and a hand to his cheek before getting into the passenger seat and hunting for the seat belt.

David went around and climbed in, settling his frame and also fastening himself in. He started the car. Then turned the key off and sat still. 'Can you not tell me what's wrong, love?' He looked out of the windshield and watched the wipers: one, two, one, two. He counted them moving back and forth and then turned and looked at Kate. 'You were dreaming again, nightmares: do you remember them?'

Kate avoided his eye, shaking her head.

'I wish you could trust me, darling.'

An icy hand moved and rested on his, on the wheel. 'I do; I love you. It's j...just... Oh, God! I'm so tired, David.' She started to cry quietly, thereby alarming him even more.

David, undoing both seat belts in a hurry, pulled her close. 'I'm sorry, too. I'm pressuring you and I'm not being fair. It's just I love you so much, darling. Forgive me?' He proffered a tissue and Kate nodded as she rested against him.

'I w...will tell you, but it's all such a m...muddle in my h...head just now.' She looked up, offering a watery smile. 'And I f...feel so sick.'

'Yes, it's not the ideal time to offer a hostage to fortune is it, darling?'

'I'm s...'

'Don't.' David flicked the key without looking at her, and then he spoke more quietly. 'Just don't, Kate. Let's get you into the warm and settle that stomach of yours.' He set the car in motion and his eyes on the road as he negotiated the back streets of Wisbech, heading to his parents' home.

JUNE 2011

GALWAY

He sat quietly reading; it was another quote by Bacon, this time about misfortune, inscribed on the stone under his mother's name and the date: *Maria Theresa O'Connor, June 5th 1987*. The spring sunshine bounced off the white marble of the gravestone, except for one corner where it was mossed over and a little lichen covered, the tête-à-têtes nodding in the light zephyr as they snuggled up to the base and brushed against the words carved into the stone. He read them, as he had many times before. *Children sweeten labours, but they make misfortune more bitter.*

Ben was meeting his Nemesis, and his punishment for the hubris of thinking he knew better than both his mother and his grandmother was to accept that he had acted without forgiveness – and thereby without the justice they deserved.

His grandmother had had the words inscribed; he always thought the quote was because of how she felt about Theresa, that she'd felt her daughter's actions were a bitter pill to swallow. Now he wondered how much his grandmother had known, as well as suspected, of the real situation.

He looked at the fresh plot, the soil newly turned and weed free, humped up over the coffin. Then he put his head in his hands and wept quietly for both women and all that they had suffered in their minds.

Micheál – coming to find him – stood still at the gate of the churchyard, feeling the waves of sorrow on the air. His own heart sore, he turned his back and waited patiently under the lychgate, gazing out across the fields towards the horizon and the Atlantic he knew was a scant five miles away.

Ben, when he came up to him, put an arm around the shoulders of his uncle and squeezed briefly and gently, before turning out and setting his foot on the path homeward. 'I forget she was your sister as much as my mother.'

'Aye.'

'Can you tell me about the day?' He didn't elaborate, and Micheál nodded as they began to walk along the deserted road back to the farm.

Micheál kept his eyes on the distant horizon as he walked and talked. 'She was sad. She had been sad for a long time. She would try; I could see her trying for your sakes, to take an interest, to read to you and play with you. She loved you both, but then the black dog of depression would seize her again and she would sink. It was like watching someone drowning in quicksand. It didn't matter that we held out a hand to her; she couldn't free herself from it and eventually she stopped struggling and allowed herself to sink under.' He finally looked at Ben. 'She just couldn't take it any more.'

He looked away from the younger man. 'Kate had been careless that morning; she'd knocked over her milk. *Mamai* had spoken sharply, telling Tess to control her children and Kate to be more careful. It wasn't much; it had happened before. Tess got up and left the table and you babes to finish your breakfast. Kate finished and slipped away to find her mam.' Micheál offered a brief smile. 'She was always a little careless, Kate, forever knocking things over or spilling things. It used to annoy *Mamai*, but she didn't mean anything by her sharp tongue.

'Anyway,' Micheál stopped and leaned against a gatepost and looked over a field bright with early grass. 'Kate got down and went in search of Tess. The next thing we heard her screaming; Mam rushed upstairs and Kate was in the bathroom, all over blood, and so was Tess.'

He gulped in air and Ben reached out a hand. 'No; 'tis all right, *a ghra*.' He took another breath. 'Mam went into the bathroom and grabbed Kate, gave her to me and told Da to phone the ambulance. They came and took her to the hospital and Mam with her. I was left to look after the animals and watch over you two.'

He gave a short laugh. 'I was that befuddled I forgot about you until lunch. You were asleep in the hay by then, and thank God no harm come to you.' He turned and looked at Ben. 'You missed your mam, but Kate ... she kept looking for her. The house was a muddle; Mam was away to the hospital for the week until Tess died and then the funeral after ... by the time we had time for you and Kate ... she was ... damaged somehow. She cried, she wouldn't speak, and when she did she stuttered so badly we couldn't understand her. We didn't know what to do for the best.'

Ben nodded. 'I remember little snapshots, not much: perhaps I didn't want to remember, either.'

Micheál nodded. 'I wish to God I could forget.' He paused long enough to make Ben wish he'd not asked for this explanation. 'So ... we sent her to your dad. *Mamai* thought it best, but we didn't know what he was like. I swear to God we didn't. Tess hadn't told us the half, or we wouldn't have done it; we'd have managed somehow.'

He stood looking at his nephew. 'But, Ben, he didn't know about you; so we wronged him, too.'

'He didn't know...'

'He didn't ask for you. I don't think Tess had told him she'd had twins. He didn't ask and we didn't tell, because we couldn't bear to be parted from both of you and you the only link left to Tess. So we separated you and the guilt of that tears at me every day, for I agreed with your grandparents to that deception.'

Ben nodded. 'Thank you, *Uncail*, for speaking.' They turned and began to walk back to the farm in silence, each feeling some sort of peace.

JUNE 2011

WHITBY

IT WAS NOT PEACEFUL in the Watt household. Young Joy was not living up to her name or giving joy to anyone within hearing. She wanted Antony, and no one else would apparently do. Antony, coming in from a brisk walk around the harbour, was greeted with overwhelming relief by the female members of the family.

'Thank heavens you've come back.'

Antony, mystified, received a hiccuping child into his arms and stood gently patting her on the back as he looked from Joyce to Amy with astonishment. 'What?'

'Where have you been?' Amy sighed as she sat down at the table.

Antony raised an eyebrow. 'I went for a walk to organise the research I'd discovered for Professor Walker. I was going to type up a report this afternoon and needed a little thinking time.' He moved to a kitchen chair and sat down with the little girl on his knee. She – apparently happy now – stuck her thumb in her mouth, gripped his coat lapel and closed her eyes.

Antony continued to pat gently. 'What's wrong?'

'I'm sorry, Antony. Joy wanted you, and no one else would do.'

'Oh. She seems all right now.' He looked down at the sleeping toddler, gently rocking her. 'Shall I put her in her cot?'

Amy nodded. 'I'll make you a cuppa.'

Antony came back down a couple of minutes later to find just Amy in the bright kitchen. He'd shed his outdoor coat and put on a pair of trainers instead of the shoes he'd been out walking in. Now he settled at the table and took the mug of tea with a murmur of thanks. He watched Amy sit with another sigh and her own mug.

'Care to share?'

Amy set the mug down after a small sip. 'She was outside playing. She tripped and banged her knee and scraped her hand trying to master the sit-and-ride toy. Next thing I know she wants Antony and the more you weren't there the more she yelled for you.'

Antony cocked his head on one side. 'Full marks for succinctness: four out of ten for grammar.' He grinned across the table and then stood hurriedly and came around as Amy's face crumpled and she began to cry. 'Hey! I was just teasing.'

He handed a tissue from his trouser pocket as she sniffed and ran a fist under her eyes. 'I know, but ... but you won't always be here, and I didn't know what to do with her, and I don't want you to go, and I'm scared and you're clever.' The tears poured down her cheeks along with the words, and Antony stood totally confused and tried to make sense of the sentence.

He gave a shrug and pulled her up out of her chair and into his arms, patting her on the back in much the same way he'd comforted her daughter ten minutes before. He waited for the tears to subside somewhat before he spoke. 'Taking things in reverse order you're just as clever as me, if you'll give yourself a chance.' He wiped away a stray trickle and looked at the drowned blue eyes. 'You got an A for the last paper if I remember.' He smiled as she gave a little nod.

'You're allowed to be scared sometimes but if you tell me what about, maybe we can fix it. Is it the exam papers?'

'No.' It was a very watery no.

'OK. Is it Joy? You're doing a great job with her; she's a lovely little kid,' his lip twitched, 'most of the time.'

'No. Maybe yeah, a bit.'

'We're all here to help you with her.'

'Yeah, but you won't be.' Amy looked at him and ran a finger under her nose.

'Ah, yes; you don't want me to go. Well I wasn't planning on moving out at the moment.' He raised an eyebrow.

'But you will. You're clever and you want a house with books and a study and quiet.' Amy moved out of his arms and sat down again, pulling a tissue from her own jeans pocket and blowing her nose as she spoke and avoided his eyes. 'Joy and I, we don't fit into that.' It was a sentence muttered into her lap.

He looked at the down-bent head, then crouched down so that he was on eye level with her. He turned her head and forced her to meet his eyes. 'Let's get this straight; you think I haven't said anything because I'm going to go away, having found people who care about me, so that I can enjoy my quiet life of luxury.' He watched her give a tiny shake of the head.

'Dammit, Amy; I'm a bastard, but not that big a bastard.' His lips grimaced. 'And that's the problem. I am a bastard; I don't know who my parents are any more. I haven't got a home, a job or any money in the bank. Do you honestly think I'm going to make a move on you in those circumstances?'

He stood up and took a couple of steps to the window and looked out on the neat lawn outside and addressed the windowpane. 'And who says I don't want the quiet book-filled study and the noisy nursery full of our kids? But I can't have them.' He spun back. 'Not until I've got something better to offer than a fifty-pound bank balance and a pile of research papers.'

'If that's a proposal, lad, it's one of the worst A've ever heard. What's more, I only had twenty-five in the bank when I proposed to her mother.' Jack Watt walked through the door and across to the teapot, pouring himself a mug of tea before swinging round to the two silent people in the room.

He looked from his drooping daughter to the white faced man, and a small smile popped into his eyes. 'I don't hold much with this being in love lark, but you two ... well, it's like walking into an electric charge every time I get between you. Why do you think she all but argued my ears off to get you to come here that first day? Why do you think she chewed us out when the police came with their nasty insinuations?' He took a small sip of tea and looked at Antony.

'Why are you so upset about your parents? You didn't give a damn before; it matters because of her. For God's sake, you love each other. All the other stuff is detail.' Jack Watt took another sip of tea, nodded at them both and strolled out of the kitchen again as the stunned pair looked after him and then at each other.

JUNE 2011

GALWAY

SATURDAY NIGHT WAS A relief to several people. Ben, much as he loved his family, was almost pleased to be away from the family home. He had delayed his departure, stretching the 'just one more day', for nearly a week, so that he might be easy in his own mind about his grandfather's health.

He sat quietly in his own room at the seminary, a place he'd left nearly a month before. He leaned back against the headboard of the bed, hands behind his head and legs stretched out and crossed at the ankle. He let the peace of the place wash over him and relaxed for a few minutes.

He had driven away from the farm that afternoon knowing that his relationship with his grandfather and uncle was on a better footing. Now all he had to do was sort himself out with his God and find his sister. His lips twitched as he thought about that sentence, and then he smiled grimly.

Tomorrow – after he had spoken to Father Joseph – he intended to head back across to Cumbria, and Monday he would see if his cousin's introduction to the Cumbrian police would give him a lead to his sister's whereabouts. For now … he swung his legs off the bed and gathered his rosary and bible from the side table, preparing to go down to confession in the chapel.

JUNE 2011

WHITBY

ANTONY AND AMY WERE lying on a bed, too. Antony, much to the hidden amusement of the rest of the household, had insisted that the door to his bedroom be left open.

Amy's father was watching the football on the TV. Every so often the sound of cheers or boos would filter up through the floorboards. Joyce was in the kitchen washing up the supper things, so the odd clatter of dishes and pots could be heard as a counterpoint to the football.

The room was warm and smelt slightly of cooked meat. Antony wasn't conscious of that; all he could smell was the woman in his arms. She smelt of baby talc, and her favourite shampoo, and warmth. He shifted and inhaled and then gave both of them the pleasure of kissing some more.

'So, do I live up to expectations?'

'Mmm.'

'You'll have to do better than that if you want another A.'

Amy moved, smoothing back the red-blonde hair. 'Are you sure, Antony? It's Joy as well.'

'Very sure. I love you both. Nothing else seems very certain but hang onto that thought, love.'

Amy smiled. 'I love you, too.' She leaned back against his arm and looked at the ceiling. 'You never did finish telling me about what the Reverend Stokes said.'

'Well, between work and you hiding away from me for the last few days I've not had much chance.' He watched the colour mount her cheeks and felt her body grow hot as it lay tucked against his side.

She shifted away slightly. 'I'm sorry, Antony; I didn't mean to ... but it wasn't ... then I realised what I'd said in the pub ... and everyone heard me...'

'You're adorable and you did rather nail your colours to the mast, love. I've been living on that meagre statement for several days now.' He turned her head back and planted another kiss on the pouting lips. 'I don't know if I'd have said anything because nothing is sorted, but since my hand has been forced...' He sighed rather theatrically.

Amy hit him gently on the chin. 'The reverend?'

Antony grinned but then pulled her upright on the bed so that they sat against the head of it, he with an arm around her shoulders. 'I can't talk about vicars and kiss at the same time. It doesn't seem right.'

'Don't see why not. They have wives and children too.'

'True.' He shrugged. 'But...' He gave her a gentle hug. 'So where had I got to?'

'Henry Grey had fallen in love and run off with your mother.'

Antony nodded. 'Yeah. The odd thing was my mother was a plain woman.' He wriggled off the bed and went over to the desk, coming back with his briefcase and pulling out a sheaf of papers, before settling back on the side of the bed.

Amy crawled across and sat next to him as she said, 'What's that got to do with anything? You don't have to be a looker to get yourself a fella. If you did, half the female population would be left on the shelf.' She took the picture from his hand.

'That's a copy of a photo the reverend had.' He laid a gentle finger on one of the women. 'That's my mother. It was taken at a coffee morning; she'd raised some money for the fund.'

Amy looked at his face as Antony looked at the coloured newspaper photo that had been clipped out and copied. 'Haven't you seen a photo of your mother before?'

He looked up. 'I've got one that the home gave me. There was this box of effects that they handed over when I left: a few pieces of jewellery, a few books with her name in and the photo ... but it's just a snapshot. There wasn't a photo of Henry Grey; there weren't any certificates either, but I honestly didn't think about it. I didn't want to. I know it's odd, love, not to be curious, but...' He paused and looked away for a moment. 'It hurt too much. I don't think I quite forgave them for abandoning me.' He held up a hand. 'The adult me knows they didn't. They died, but it's always felt like they abandoned me to the system and I found it hard to forgive, so I wasn't going to take any interest in them either.' He offered a half smile. 'That was how my young self thought and ... and I ... I never bothered to grow up.'

Amy leaned over and placed a kiss on his lips. 'You've got a family now and we aren't gonna let you go, not for anything.'

Antony returned the kiss then looked at the paper still held in Amy's hand. 'It's a bit weird, actually. I keep looking at it and trying to see what I've inherited from her.'

'You've got her nose. But the hair must have come from your father; she's jet black.'

Antony sniffed. 'Genetically, black haired people often carry the red hair gene.' He raised his nose in the air.

Amy gave a quiet giggle. 'OK. I can't see what colour her eyes are.'

'The reverend said brown like mine.' Antony turned those eyes on her. 'He was a prisoner, my father. Theft and fraud. Another reason I didn't think I had any right to ... to ... to...' Antony looked away and carefully set the picture down.

'To what? Love me, kiss me? Let me ask you this, Antony; have you ever stolen anything? Defrauded anyone, hurt anyone on purpose?' Amy took his hands and gently smoothed them.

'No, of course not.'

'What makes you think you're going to start now, just because your father did?'

'Faced with that logic, what can I say?'

'You could say you loved me. And then you could give me a kiss.'

Antony nodded, kissing her until she was quite breathless. It was the briefcase falling on the floor that brought them back to their senses. Antony recovered first. 'Yes, well; this won't buy baby a new bonnet and you, young lady, have to keep me in a manner I'd like to become accustomed to until I make it big as a professor.'

Amy wrinkled her nose, then grinned. 'I might have known; a slave driver.' She slid off the bed and stood up, wriggling the legs of her tight jeans down her legs and straightening her red top. She looked up to find Antony watching her with a very male look on his face.

'What?'

'I like that top, but not when you're going to work in it.'

'Tough.'

'When's your day off?'

'Monday. Why?'

'How do you fancy a trip to Carlisle? You and Joy? I think I need to talk to Professor Walker about his research. I can borrow your dad's car, he said.'

Amy nodded. 'That would be great.' She blew him a kiss and went into her own bedroom to change for work. Antony smiled to himself as he walked over to the desk and set his briefcase down before going back to pick up the scattered notes and newspaper cuttings that had fallen to the floor, laying them in a heap on top of his research before going down to see his girl off to work.

JUNE 2011

CUMBRIA

DAVID AND KATE WERE sitting in his study. Both were supposedly working, but this Monday morning hadn't started well and was going from bad to worse as far as David was concerned. Kate had thrown up with a vengeance. She'd managed to make it to the toilet, but only just. David wanted her to go back to bed but she refused, saying she'd be fine in a bit.

Then the post had arrived. The certificates, ordered the previous week, were helpful. 'I'm fairly certain this is his first wife, Kate. Caroline Bathurst. Her details match, date and place of birth. They married over in Newcastle.' He peered at the second certificate. 'And she died there. Yes. I think she's the right one.' He laid down the certificates and looked at his wan-faced wife.

Kate nodded, but she couldn't seem to work up any real interest any more. So what if they had found her father's wife? They were both dead; nothing could change events. She sipped on the lemon water that Thea had given her. 'I don't s...see h...how it h...helps.'

David bit back impatience, then grabbed the phone as it rang. 'Hello.' He softened his tone after the first harsh word. 'Oh, hello, Antony. How can I help?'

Kate leaned back in her chair, watching as he buried his feelings and dealt courteously with the young man on the other end of the line. After a few minutes he set the receiver down. 'We are going to have visitors for lunch, Kate; Antony and his young lady and their child.' He looked at her rather apologetically. 'I didn't want to put him off. I'm away next week and he wants to discuss what he has so far, and which direction I want him to go in next. I can take them out to lunch in Carlisle.'

'No. It's all r...right, David. I'll g...go and sp...speak to Thea.' Kate stood up and dropped a light kiss on his head.

David watched her leave the room and sighed. He just didn't know what to do for the best. He busied himself with work for nearly an hour until Thea brought him coffee and told him Kate had gone to get some groceries. They exchanged a look. 'Leave it, Master David. She's hurting; give it time.'

'I've given it so much time, Thea, and I'm hurting too.'

'I know.' Thea nodded at his mug. 'Drink your coffee and take a break.'

His lips twitched under the beard and moustache, but he dutifully picked up the mug and took a sip or two. His eye fell on the certificates and he looked speculatively at the closed study door before swinging his chair and settling in front of the computer screen. He had just finished following up his search and printing out when he heard the little car Kate drove parking outside. He quietly shut down the site and picked up the printouts, sliding them under a sheet of his research on the desk.

JUNE 2011

GALWAY

'Do you think he'll find her, Micheál?'

Micheál leaned back so that the kitchen chair was resting on its back legs and the back was propped against the wall of the kitchen. He looked at his wife and shrugged, before drinking from the mug in his hands. 'Who knows? It's a long time. Even if he finds her, will she want to know us? We disposed of her like an unwanted parcel, Bridget. We sent her to a foreign land. I hadn't thought about it much, didn't want to, but she only knew the Gaelic. God knows how she managed.'

'Ben said we had to have done with "Sorry".'

'We all have more to be sorry about, *a run*, than Ben; he was a child in the hands of adults. Adults who made decisions he had no say in.'

'Aye; why should she forgive us?'

'Even the prisoner at the bar is entitled to his hearing.'

'And when she's heard, will it change things? Will it give her back the years of happiness, of family?' Micheál slammed back onto all four legs of the chair and set the mug down. 'Will she forgive and forget? I doubt it and I don't know how to live with it.' He stood up abruptly. 'I'll go and tend to the stock.'

He left and Bridget bit her lip and looked helplessly at her neatly folded hands. So many actions, and who to blame? Were she and Eoin both complicit because they'd looked the other way, seeking peace rather than standing up to Maeve?

She heard her own teenage boys upstairs and wondered how she would have felt if she'd been in Theresa's position. Desperate, angry and finally defeated by life. She sighed and stood up. The normal household chores didn't stop because people were heartsore.

JUNE 2011

CUMBRIA

Ben was standing at a desk in Carlisle Police Station. He was a very frustrated young man because he'd just been told the detective he wanted to speak with was in court and would be there all day. He might be available on Wednesday. But the policeman who spoke sounded very doubtful. Ben sighed and shook the young desk sergeant's hand. 'Thank you for your assistance. I'll come back in tomorrow.'

'Is it police business? Can we not help?'

Ben shook his head. 'No, it's personal. I'll come back.' He turned away and headed out, walking across to his car and driving off into town.

He headed to the public library; he was looking at the old newspapers for the area, most of them on film, some on the computer. He had found other reports of the trial of his father's murder. He tracked back through that, to accounts of the archaeological dig that the man had been stealing from when he was killed.

There was no mention of Kate except at the trial, as having been part of the dig. Then she was named as Kate Hamilton. She'd obviously taken Scarlett's name. But the fact that she was Jardin had leaked out, too. He kept digging as the morning turned to afternoon. Some reporter had tried to make mileage out of the fact that her name was Jardin, the same as the murdered man, but had apparently come up against a wall of silence from members of the dig he'd interviewed.

Ben shrugged in the silence of his little corner of the library;

he already knew she was living with Scarlett so it didn't strike him as new knowledge. He was even more frustrated as he left to go and get himself something to eat.

It wasn't until he had taken a bite of sandwich that he suddenly realised the significance of what he was thinking. He set the bread down slowly and stared into space. He'd been looking for a Kate Jardin or O'Connor, not a Kate Hamilton. He frowned at his coffee cup.

'Is everything all right, sir?'

He looked up into the worried eyes of the young woman who had served him. 'Yes, fine, thank you.'

'Only I can get you a fresh sandwich if it doesn't taste right or something.' She looked as though she was going to burst into tears. 'This is my first day.'

Ben shook his head. 'No, everything is fine; I've just had an idea.' He pushed back his chair and glanced at the man behind the counter. 'Thank you for your service. I've decided to take away, if that's possible.'

The young woman zipped across to the counter and brought back napkins and a paper bag, decanted his coffee into a Styrofoam mug and accepted his tip with a beaming smile. 'Thank you, sir.'

'Not at all.' Ben gave her the benefit of his charming smile and left. He would have blushed if he'd heard her saying it was such a waste of a fella!

He walked off clutching his lunch in one hand, and headed for the quiet of the cathedral close to have another think about his idea.

As BEN WAS SITTING down to the toasted sandwich from the coffee shop, Antony and Amy were drawing up in front of David and Kate's old farmhouse. 'Oh. Wow! Are you sure they don't mind me coming, Antony?'

'No. I told you. David said you were more than welcome.' He glanced back as Joy burbled at them. 'And you, pet.' He got out of his borrowed car and opened the back door, releasing the toddler from her seat and setting her down at the gate. Amy, coming around, took her hand as he locked up and picked up his old briefcase before turning to look at the panorama that was the Solway Firth.

'Wonderful, isn't it? I never tire of watching the tide come in and out.' David spoke from over the gate as he came to open it for them. 'In you come; Kate's looking forward to seeing you again, Amy.' He followed them up the path and into the welcoming warmth.

Two small children hurtled down the passage and grabbed a leg each. David bent and gathered up his clamouring daughter. 'Yes, Topsy. It's lunchtime.' He swung her around his hip and smiled at his guests. 'This is my daughter Rose and that,' he nodded at his son, who was eyeing Joy, 'is Paul, sometimes known as Turvey. If you'd like to put your briefcase on my desk, Antony, and come through into the kitchen. We're eating in there because it's easier with the children.'

Antony nodded and went through the door into the study as the rest trooped around the corner and into the kitchen. Amy smiled at Kate as they entered and said 'Hello' as David swung his daughter into her seat and fastened her in. He leaned over and picked up Paul, then frowned as Amy said, 'Antony's got lost. He's hopeless,' and grinned at her hosts.

David cast a look at Kate and she went out of the kitchen and down the hall. He had barely finished securing his son when there was a loud crash from the study. David glanced at Thea and shot out of the room. He entered the study to find a chair on its side and Kate clasped in the arms of Antony. She was struggling and white, as she was held firmly by him.

Antony's face was white, too, and his expression was unreadable; David's murderous. He advanced and took his wife from Antony, a trifle roughly. 'Kate.' David lifted her up and set her in one of the chairs. 'Dammit, girl, you're not well.'

'I'm OK.' Kate shook her head, and looked at Antony. David swung around. 'What happened?' His face said 'it had better be good, because she's my wife!'

Antony shrugged. 'I came in and put my case on the desk. I knocked your papers off and went to gather them up.' He grimaced. 'I wasn't prying. But the printout caught my eye. I was just wondering why you were checking up on me, Professor. Is that why you have a photo of my mother on your desk? Because if you don't trust me, I'll go.' Antony was no longer pale; instead he looked rather flushed as he controlled his temper.

David looked at Kate. She was regaining her colour. He looked across the room at Antony. 'Don't be a bloody fool.' He swung his eyes back to his wife. 'All right, my Kate?'

'Yes, David; I th...ink it's just lack of f...food. I lost my b...breakfast and my s...supper from last n...night.'

'So you did, love.' He took her hand in a warm clasp before looking back at the glowering young man. 'This picture of your mother' – he raised an eyebrow – 'show me it.'

'You...'

'Just show me it, son.'

Antony picked up the printout and held it out as if it was a poisonous spider.

'Ah.' David glanced at it, then looked at Kate. 'Did you ask Kate about it?' He swung his head and looked at Antony. Antony gave a brief nod. 'Ah! I always said you were bright, my Kate. How are you feeling now?'

'I'm al...right, David.' She looked from him to Antony in silence. But her eyes said an awful lot, most of it not repeatable in mixed company.

'That's good, love, because I think we should get all the shocks over with before lunch. Ready?'

Kate nodded. He gripped her hand. 'I'd like you to meet your half-brother, Antony.'

He watched the siblings both go pale again and wondered if he'd have to catch Antony before he hit the floor, too.

Antony stretched a hand back and gripped the side of the desk. He opened his mouth, shut it, then croaked 'Awk!' before closing it again.

'Before either of you ask ... yes, I'm sure and no, I'm not

273

going to explain any further just this second. I can hear the babies and they appear to be getting a bit fractious.'

Antony pulled himself together first, as Thea came through the door. 'David, where are your manners? That poor young woman has been left in a strange house...' She glanced at Kate, then David. 'Do you need the doctor?'

'No, Th...ea, I'm all r...ight, just a bit of a f...faint.' Kate stood up, hanging on to David's hand just in case. She left the room still holding his hand. Antony picked up the chair and set it straight before he followed them. Thea came up the rear, closing the study door with a slight snap and allowing the printout to flutter back onto the desk in the sudden silence.

JUNE 2011

WHITBY

'THE ONE TIME YOUR parents met he can't have had to struggle much. She must have made it easy for him. He must have been really sick about that, pig.' The policeman thus addressed, raised an eyebrow as he hauled Stan Hunt out of his cell and took him down to an interview room, ignoring the aspersions about his conception, parentage and the morals of his mother and father. He'd had worse aimed at his head, most of it by better educated people.

'Prisoner for you, sir.' He went and stood by the door, having thrust the unruly tough onto a chair. Hunt looked around, noted his solicitor and gazed insolently at the senior uniform behind the desk.

'Good afternoon.' The sergeant didn't smile. 'Unfortunately we have to let you go. We were enjoying your company so much, but...' He shrugged. 'We just have one or two questions beforehand.' He watched the sneer.

'You have been remanded in custody for the last forty-eight hours because you broke the terms of the restraining order set in place by the court last year, forbidding you to come within five hundred yards of Miss Amy Watt or her child. You have been charged with causing grievous bodily harm to Mr Anthony Grey on Friday night, starting an affray, public order offences towards the police and resisting arrest. Have you any comment?'

Hunt smirked. 'No comment.'

The sergeant had expected nothing more. 'We would like

a sample of your handwriting.' He pushed a warrant at the presiding solicitor and a sheet of paper at the thug, along with a pen.

Hunt ignored both, looking at his solicitor. He got a nod.

'What ya want it for?'

'We don't actually have to inform you of that, sir.'

'Then I ain't doing it.'

'A word with my client, officer.'

'Interview suspended.' The sergeant scraped back his chair and walked out of the door. It closed with a solid thunk.

Hunt leaned back. 'I don't have to if they won't tell me why.'

'Yes, you do; the warrant is quite clear.'

'And if I don't?'

The solicitor shrugged. 'Contempt, and you stay in the cells.'

Hunt frowned. The solicitor waited patiently. 'Oh, fuck, give me the pen.'

'I'll fetch the sergeant; you need to take off the cuffs.'

A few minutes later he had scrawled 'the quick brown fox jumped over the lazy dog' and was sitting back, waiting with that annoying smirk back in place.

'You are being released on police bail, sir. If you are seen or reported to be within a mile of Miss Watt's home or place of work or you attempt to speak to Mr Grey you will be rearrested.' He ended the interview and took the paper through to Detective Sergeant Tierney.

'Nasty customer, sir. I've got the writing. What's the idea?'

'Grey's been getting nasty letters, hand-printed address but cut-outs for the message. I think that piece of work might be behind them. If he is we might be able to pin attempted murder on him.'

The sergeant lifted an eyebrow and watched as Tierney pulled a file forward and compared the newly written sheet with the envelopes in their plastic casing. 'Don't look like it from here.'

'Could be, but … nah, they don't to me, either. I'll let

forensics have a go…' He shrugged. 'Pity. I wanted to get that
scum off the street.'

JUNE 2011

CUMBRIA

DAVID'S TWO TODDLERS HAD been put into their cots for a nap, Joy was currently falling asleep on her mother's shoulder and the four adults were standing in the study again. 'I'll just put her in the pushchair. Don't start without me.' Amy grinned at the others, disappearing out of the room.'

Antony looked sheepishly at David. 'I think I owe you one hell of an apology.'

'Oh, a lot can be forgiven among family.' David's lips twitched. 'Have you heard the one about the Finns and the Russians?'

He looked from one bemused face to the other. 'What do the Finns call the Russians? Family. You can choose your friends.' He gave a slight cough of laughter. 'Forgive me; I'm slightly lightheaded with current events.'

'Pardon?'

David waved the comment aside as Amy came back into the room. 'Thea says she'll keep an eye on Joy for me.' She came over and sat down next to Antony, who'd moved to a hard chair near the desk and lowered his weight rather heavily onto it. 'So what's the big mystery?'

David grinned. 'Since Antony tells me you two are to be married, I'd like to congratulate you.' He watched the blush, waited a moment and then said, 'And introduce you to Kate, who will be your sister-in-law.' He watched the stunned look on her face and then looked across at Antony, before glancing at his watch. 'We've got about an hour before ours wake.

Yours?'

'About the same.'

'OK. I'll tell you what I know if you'll tell me your side.' He nodded at Antony and took Kate's hand, towing her gently over the carpet and sitting in one of the squashy chairs in the window embrasure with her on his knee. 'Kate is pregnant so she needs a bit of cosseting just now and so do I.' David smiled at his wife who had perched, rather than relaxed, onto his knee. 'Relax, love.' He pulled her gently back and looked expectantly at Antony.

'I'm not quite sure where to start.'

'When we met in Whitby you said your parents had been killed and you'd been raised in a foster home. Start there.'

Antony nodded; he stretched out his hand without taking his eyes off David and felt Amy's warm one clasp his. 'Actually, I need to go back a bit further. You remember I was run over?' He waited for the nods. 'I started getting poison pen letters. One of them queried my parentage. I'd never bothered to check it out but...' Antony settled to the tale, talking about the Reverend Stokes and how he'd been given the photograph of his mother and told that she was a prisoner's wife. 'Only I hadn't got as far as discovering which prisoner.' He looked expectantly from Kate to David.

'Ah. You may not like the next bit of your history.' David gave Kate a careful hug. 'I believe your mother was married to Philip Jardin. In 1981. I'm assuming...' He paused. 'When were you born?'

'August '82.'

'Then I should think it's almost certain that he was your father.' David looked from Kate to Antony. 'I told Kate there was something about you that reminded me of someone. You have the same colour eyes as Kate and my children. I was very jealous of you.' He noted the amazement on both the faces of the younger couple. 'I sensed a connection and you're a young man, whereas I'm old and not so handsome.' He shrugged. 'We're all entitled to feel vulnerable. Kate is, and probably always will be, my weak spot.' He hugged Kate, who was looking at him with astonishment.

Amy had listened in silence. Now she suddenly grinned. 'Hey, you aren't a bastard, after all.'

Antony shook his head at her; he got a little further in his deductions.

'But they were married.'

'Yes, darling; but Kate's mother wasn't.'

'Oh!' Amy looked across the room. 'I'm sorry, I'm only thinking of Antony; he's been fretting about it.'

Kate shrugged. 'Don't w...worry, Amy; I've had t...time to get used t...to the idea.'

Antony nodded at Kate, then looked at David expectantly.

'Right. Jardin. Thief, fraudster and eventually murderer, before he was murdered in his turn.'

'D...avid!'

'What?' He looked at Kate. 'Antony isn't a child and it's no good pussyfooting about, Kate.' He looked across the room. Antony was a trifle pale but composed. Amy looked as though she'd been flattened by a steamroller.

'Our end goes something like this. Kate's foster-mother – and the third woman Jardin married in eight years – died last November. When we came to sort it all out we discovered the marriage to Scarlett wasn't legitimate. In fact up till then we didn't even realise that Scarlett wasn't Kate's birth mother; we just thought they'd been a bit late tying the knot.' His lips twisted a bit ironically. 'If only.'

'However, this all came as something of a shock to Kate, especially as we are about to be parents again. Kate is worried about the genetic history she might be carrying.' David looked down at his wife, hoping it really was that which was troubling her. 'I incline more to the nurture theory myself, but the jury's still out for Kate. I should imagine you've had similar thoughts, Antony?'

Antony nodded. 'I'm who I am, but falling for a girl can make a difference. You wonder just what you might be foisting onto the unsuspecting world.' He looked down at Amy. She was sitting clasping her hands tightly together and he wondered if his romance had come crashing to a halt already. He wasn't sure she'd want anything to do with a murderer's son.

Her next comment was vast reassurance, as David said, 'You must have been down this path already, Amy. You'll forgive me for bringing it up, but Joy obviously isn't Antony's child.' He spoke gently as he looked at her serious face.

'No, she's mine. I don't know the father.' It was said a shade defiantly.

David shrugged. 'Judging by her behaviour I'm still in favour of nurture; she's a lovely little thing.' Kate gave a soft squeeze to the hand holding hers.

'David loves me re...gardless, Amy.'

Amy nodded. Her hand moved and held Antony's again as she looked across the room at the other couple.

'But we digress.' David's lips twitched up and his emerald eyes twinkled for a minute. 'I often do; it's one of my many failings, as you'll find out. So,' he looked at Kate, then across the room. 'We discovered that Jardin had married your mother, then Kate's, then Scarlett, in quick succession, without benefit of divorce. From what you tell us he was in prison for much of your babyhood, and your mother found a man who cared about her.' He watched as Antony nodded. 'Going back to genetics for a minute she was obviously a good person, Antony, and you've got half her genes.'

Antony smiled a bit grimly, 'I've got half his, too.'

David nodded. He'd rather that comment unsaid for Kate's sake but it couldn't be helped, and his wife wasn't a fool. 'So has someone else.' He glanced at his wife. 'We said we were expecting. We have one lot of twins and we might be having another lot, and Kate is herself a twin.'

'Another sister?'

Kate shook her head. 'B...b...brother.'

'Oh, wow!' Amy spoke softly. 'That must be so hard. Did they split you at birth, then?'

'We don't know the circumstances, yet. But,' David smiled a bit grimly himself this time, 'we do know he is searching for

281

Kate. That much we have discovered.'

'When we started our search we went to Liverpool. That was the place Kate's birth was registered. A priest obligingly sent us the baptism record. It showed both their names on the same page; same date of birth and same name.'

'What's our brother's name?' Antony looked, not at David, but at Kate.

'Ben.'

'Ben.' Antony repeated the name and nodded at Kate. 'I'm having a little trouble processing all this.'

David looked from one sibling to the other, smiled then continued, 'Anyway – to coin the Johnny Cash song – we've been everywhere, man. We've been to Salisbury – where Kate was brought up – and in touch down in Southampton, where Scarlett's solicitor lives, and then to Benwell Dene where Scarlett taught at the Victoria School for the Blind. Tracking backwards; when we got up north we discovered Ben was on the same trail.'

David gave a faint chuckle. 'Apparently some things do run in families. You've got a DD; I never got around to asking you why.' He shook his head. 'Your brother, Ben, is a priest. Probably Roman Catholic, since his baptism was in that faith.'

'Good grief!'

The silence in the room could be felt, a soft dark cloud as they came to terms with the revelations. David stood up abruptly, heading for the desk. Antony leaned back, looking surprised as David began to shift papers about. 'Now where…? Ahh! Your father's missive, Kate. I think perhaps we'd better have a look at this. Can I open it, Kate?' He waited for a nod. 'Sure?' He thumbed open the flap. He was conscious of the siblings watching – both held stiffly upright – as he briefly scanned, then settled to read properly, the words on the sheet of cheap writing paper. He cleared his throat. 'I'll read it out, darling.

'Dear Kate, I always wanted a child, some-
one of my own, since I didn't have anyone who

282

really belonged to me; I was brought up in a home. I was so happy when your mother's relatives gave you to me. They wouldn't tell me what was wrong with Tess, your mum, and I didn't want to know because that meant I got you, but I did love her. Scarlett stole you from me and I really didn't much care any longer, I went back to doing what I'd always done.

But I'm older now and I know what Scarlett did was better for you. I'm sorry I spoiled things; I always seem to have spoiled them. But I want you to know you were the best thing I did, also you need to know you have a brother somewhere in Newcastle. My first wife said I wasn't a fit father, and she was right. I lost him too, but you should find him. His name is Antony. Then you'll have someone of your own too.

Love, Dad.'

David cleared his throat. 'Hmm! I think that will take some thinking about, Kate. He was a selfish bastard to the last. We can all be selfish, though.' David's lips twitched into a half smile. 'Especially when it comes to love. He was right about one thing, though: we all need someone of our own.'

A wail from above their heads had all four adults looking heavenwards as if expecting Henny Penny's sky to fall on them. They did all look a bit shell-shocked by this time. David sniffed. 'Out of time. I vote for tea and abandoning work for today, Antony. We can check out the research another time, unless there's something urgent?'

'Urgent or not I don't think I could concentrate on it today, David.'

David grinned, 'You've met them once, but come and meet your niece and nephew.'

Antony stood up. 'It seems I've got more relatives than I

can shake a stick at all of a sudden.' He walked over to Kate, who was standing next to David; she still looked to both men as if a barrage balloon was exploding overhead. Antony looked at David and offered a lopsided smile before saying, 'Hi, Sister. Care to give me a hug?'

Kate nodded and moved into the embrace. It was a brief hug before Antony stood back. 'We'll get acquainted in a bit, when your new niece has had something to eat. She takes after me that way; really crabby when not fed at regular intervals.'

BEN HAD EATEN. HE was a trifle absent-minded about his food most of the time but since the sandwich was in his hand he had eaten it, staring at the east window of the cathedral and thinking about the new ideas in his mind.

Not Jardin or O'Connor but Hamilton. Maybe that would explain why he hadn't found her on the electoral rolls of Newcastle. Should he go back over there, or was it more productive to stay where he was and keep searching around Carlisle? After all, that was where she was four years ago; she might still be in the district.

He shrugged, finishing the last bite and folding the paper bag neatly before stuffing it into the empty Styrofoam cup and standing up to place the squashed remains in the bin. He glanced once more at the cathedral and opted to walk along the grounds, through the archway, and down the street to the back entrance of Tullie House and its grounds and thence to the library. He would check out the name Hamilton instead.

The library was just as quiet as before. Ben pulled out a seat, set his briefcase on the table, and abstracted his note pad before going over to the desk and asking for permission to look through the stacks again.

He had been trawling for a good two hours when he hit gold. The wedding of Kate Jardin – known as Hamilton – to Professor David Walker of the Parish of Burgh by Sands, Cumbria, had taken place in Wisbech two and a half years ago; among the guests had been the bride's mother Scarlett

Hamilton and the groom's parents Paul and Ruth Walker. There was a bit about the professor's occupation and his recent dig near Carlisle Castle. The city was duly grateful for his work on their behalf in unearthing the city's hidden history.

If Ben had been given to punching the air this would have been the time. He too was unearthing hidden history. He grinned. He was closing in on his sister at last. He checked his watch and stuffed all his papers back into his briefcase. He would go back to the B and B for the night and tomorrow he would head to Wisbech.

JUNE 2011

WHITBY

THE PERPETRATOR OF THE letters was smirking to himself. Stan Hunt had meant to cause mischief for Antony Grey and by God he had. A quiet word to his girlfriend at the home had seen the police rounding Antony up. It was a pity Amy hadn't ditched him: she was a tasty piece and obviously free with her favours if that baby was anything to go by. But after one date she'd given him the bum's rush. She'd got that baby so she must have said 'Yes'. Chances were she meant 'Yes' no matter what she said.

He'd seen Antony and her in that pub with their heads together and lost his cool, using his mate's car and knocking him over and then he'd driven off. Served him right, in Stan's opinion, walking around with his nose in the air just because he had a degree.

Antony Grey with his insinuating ways, always hanging around the carers at the home. Getting himself a scholarship to university. Stan Hunt sneered. He could have gone there if he'd wanted to but why should he, when the social would pay for him to watch TV and go to the pub?

Stan had seen Antony and Amy getting into the old car of her dad's and driving away that morning. He'd watched the house for a good hour because he couldn't be sure her mother had gone out. Then, blast it, he'd seen her coming back with her shopping.

Now it was afternoon; he knew the place was empty. He nipped out of his mate's car and across the road with the letter in his hands. He would give the bastard another fright. He chuckled to himself as he crossed the street. Yeah, that was a good one. He remembered the gossip at the home, how this little brat had been in a car with some guy and his adulterous mother.

They'd been all over him, petting him and giving him cuddles just because his mother was dead. Stan's mother was dead too, but no one had hugged him. Oh, no; he'd just been shown his room and left to get on with things.

Stan flicked the gate open and walked up the path, the letter ready to shove through the letterbox, thinking dark thoughts.

'I think we'd like to see that, sir.'

Stan nearly had a heart attack on the spot. He swung around to find a police constable right behind him and another standing at the gate, who looked as though he was ready to give chase if necessary. He recovered fast. 'What's this? I was just dropping it in for a mate.' He tried to shove the letter through the convenient hole but was forestalled by the meaty paw of the copper.

'And who is this mate?'

'Just a mate. He asked me to give it to Antony 'cos I know him. I was going to stick it through the box. I've got to go; I'm busy.'

The constable raised an eyebrow and smiled. It wasn't a nice smile. 'Oh, I don't think you're that busy, sir. You've managed to sit over the road there in your car, for the past hour.'

The other policeman nodded. 'We could see you while we had our lunch.'

Stan nodded. 'I was hoping Antony would get back so I could give it to him personally, like. But I gotta go now.'

'He's got an answer for everything, John.' The first copper glanced very briefly at the second; not long enough for Stan to make a move, however. 'I think you need to come with us, sir.' He grinned mirthlessly. 'That isn't a request. We have a few more questions which need answering. Unless you can contact this mate right now and get him to speak to our

287

detective sergeant.'

'He's at work. That's why he lent me his car and asked me to deliver it.'

'Uh-huh.' The tone said, 'I believe in flying pigs, too. So you'd better cancel whatever you were going to be busy with, because you have to come with us.' He paused. 'Now.'

Stan looked from one tough man to the other and walked back down the path, still holding firmly to the letter. They hadn't taken it off him; if he could burn it or flush it they wouldn't have anything to go on. 'Well, if I've got to cooperate with the law, I'll cancel my plans.' He crossed the street, frantically scanning for a drain to ditch the evidence into.

'We'll have the letter.'

He had been manoeuvred so that he was next to the door of the squad car with no chance of running. 'Whatever. I don't know what his business with Antony is; I've posted a few letters for him.'

'Well, that's very obliging of you.' The nearest copper, John, whipped an evidence bag out of the front seat and slid the letter into it. 'In you get, sir.'

The dust had barely settled when Antony and Amy arrived back in their borrowed car and pulled up in the space recently occupied by the squad car.

JUNE 2011

CUMBRIA

DAVID AND KATE WERE outside. They were supposedly enjoying the setting sun outside their front door. It had, as David said, been a long and exciting day. Now they could relax. David wasn't looking at the sunset, however, or only in a peripheral way. He was watching his wife. Finally he broke the silence. 'I thought I'd figured it out, darling, but I was wrong, wasn't I?'

Kate turned her head and looked at him, adjusting her glasses and shading her face.

'I thought you were worried about the children. That you were bothered that your father's bad ways might have been inherited. But it isn't that. You looked at Antony and you didn't see any bad. So...' He sighed. 'Talk to me, Kate, because I can't go to Germany and leave things like this. You're hurting too much, love, and it's tearing me apart.'

'I'm s...'

'No, Kate, don't say you're sorry. You have nothing to apologise for. I love you. What hurts you will hurt me, and I wouldn't have it any other way.'

Kate nodded 'C...can we go f...for a st...roll? Thea's watching the babies.'

David stood up, holding out a hand. Kate took it and allowed herself to be pulled up and have her arm tucked through his. 'Slowly, Kate. There's no hurry, but I must know what's wrong.'

'Yes, David. It's j...just that...' Kate gripped his hand

tightly and they walked over the road and along the bank at the side of the Solway. They paced for a few minutes before she began to speak. 'Wh...en you brought me out h...here – to your h...house that f...first t...time – remember?'

David nodded.

'I loved you so m...much. I'd loved you f...for a long t...time. I was overjoyed wh...en I got a pl...ace on one of your digs. I'd heard you lecture and I f...fell in love, b...but I knew about you long bef...ore th...en. Scarlett had t...told me about you. She said we owed you. My f...father had wr...ecked one dig and you'd lost m...money. It was up to me to m...make s...sure he didn't wreck any more. But I've always kn...own I needed to...to...even the sc...ore.'

David stopped and swung her around. 'Kate, this is old history. What your father did was his responsibility, not yours. You were a schoolchild when he was jailed for manslaughter.

'Yes, but my...but Scarlett said it was our resp...onsibility. My resp...onsibility.' Kate looked at her husband and offered a half smile. 'S...someone had to be resp...onsible.' She shook her head. 'It s...seems I'm resp...onsible for Antony being in that ch...ildren's home, too. If my m...mother hadn't conceived us maybe my father would have st...ayed with his w...wife.'

'I doubt it, love.' David shook his head. 'And again, you weren't born. How could the blame lie with you?' But Kate didn't seem to be listening. She was caught up in recalling old fears, and new.

'I c...can remember – I was very s...small – I can remember an argument, I think. It was just before he w...went into p... prison, and we m...moved; Scarlett said it was my f...fault, that he'd started st...stealing again. I was t...terrified; she s... said she was going to leave me with him. S...she didn't, but I was always fr...frightened after that, that if I was naughty she w...would. And now I f...find she cut herself off from her f... family because of me. What else am I to th...ink? But I knew I was b...bad b...before that. I don't know wh...what I did, but I did s...something t...terrible. That I kn...know.'

'Kate.' David lifted her chin with two fingers and looked at her. 'Listen to me. Before you lived with Scarlett you would have been a baby. What could you have done that was so terrible? You wouldn't blame our two if they did anything to cause others harm; they're just tiny babes ... no more responsible than that child you're carrying.'

'I th...ought maybe I'd k...killed my tw...in. Maybe that was wh...y they sent me away.' Kate looked at David. 'But he's se...arching for me. I don't want him to f...find me, David. I'm sc...scared he'll want to pu...nish me. Wh...y is he looking for me now?'

'Maybe he didn't know about you any more than you knew about him until now.' In the face of her fears David tried reason, but Kate was beyond being reasoned with, caught up in a living nightmare compounded of dreams and dimly awakening memories.

'Wh...at if he was in a h...home, like Antony? I get to live with Scarlett and have a pr...oper home and he gets an inst... itution. I did something, David, and these angry faces and voices shout at me in a tongue I know, but I can't understand. I keep having night...mares about bl...ood on my hands, too.' She held them out in the manner of Lady Macbeth and David took both in his, looking at her tortured face.

'Ahh, I wish you'd told me, darling. We could have sorted it out sooner.'

Kate still wasn't listening. 'Ever s...since we started looking and I started th...inking about my p...past there's been blood on my hands. I'm so sc...ared.' Kate moved, burying her face in the warmth of David's jumper. He put his arms around her and held tight while she sobbed.

He allowed her a few minutes but then moved her and offered his handkerchief. 'Come on, Kate, you'll make yourself ill. I don't believe you have, or could, do anything to another human being to hurt them. You, my darling, put the entire world before yourself. Now if you really want this to stop now, then it shall. You have changed your name to mine; you are not going to be that easy to find.'

'But Antony deserves to find his b...brother; he was so p...pleased at the idea of having f...family.'

'He can have his brother; we don't have to have him, too. I shall speak to him, say you don't want to have any contact.'

'But wh...at about his w...work?'

'What about it? My colleagues don't have to mix with my wife.' David spoke a trifle arrogantly as he pulled her close. 'I shall keep you safe, Kate. No one is going to hurt you. Come along, you're getting cold; let's go home. But ... Kate, I won't have you persecuting yourself thinking you're evil incarnate, darling. And...' He smiled down at her. 'You have to stop hiding from me, my Kate. I can't help you if you don't. And it's tearing me apart, love. I love you, Kate.' He kissed the cheek near him and wiped away a stray tear. 'OK?'

'But...'

'No, Kate. No buts. I shall get angry in a minute.' David leaned over and dropped a kiss on her hair, then drew her hand through his arm and began to walk back towards their home. He thought about the research he had done that morning, but pushed the guilt away. He would find out the truth but this time he wouldn't insist on Kate being involved. He would put it all away until he came back from Germany and then do it when Kate was otherwise occupied.

JUNE 2011

WISBECH

BEN HAD BEEN DOING his own share of suffering, imagining his sister alone in the world. The pleasure he felt in discovering that she was married was mitigated by the stated age of the bridegroom. Had she just been looking for a protector and this Professor Walker taken advantage of a vulnerable young girl? If so, she had a family who were willing to care for her; she didn't need any sugar daddy.

Ben grinned to himself as he drove down the motorway looking for the turn-off to Wisbech. 'Sugar daddy'– what kind of a phrase was that? For the first time since his grandmother had died – and he'd discovered that he had a sister – he could feel his spirits lifting. He spotted the sign and signalled to move into the outside lane.

He finally felt he might be getting close to finding his sister. He would find her; it was a vow. He turned onto a quieter road and drove sedately along. He had been hurtling along the motorway, rushing past possible exits, but now he could start searching more closely. He flicked the switch and had a CD of Gregorian chants playing. He started to pray along with the monks, unaware that he'd taken a step back towards his God.

Wisbech was a small town, really. Ben, arriving at the town centre and having learnt a lot in the past few weeks, went first to the library to check out the Electoral Rolls. He couldn't find David Walker but he found several others, among them a Paul and Ruth and they had been named as parents of the groom. Ben noted down the address and then went to find a mug of coffee and plan what he intended to do next.

Unfortunately David Walker had already rung his parents that morning. He'd rung them while Kate was in the shower, filling them in briefly as to how Kate felt about the search for and by her brother.

'She doesn't want to be found, Pops. It's irrational, but she's easily overwrought at the moment and I won't have her distressed any more.'

'Then she won't be. We won't give anything away, David.'

Ben had spent five minutes debating between phoning and ringing the doorbell and had opted for going out to the house and trying to speak to Mr and Mrs Walker. He nipped to the loos in the café and checked that his hair was tidy and his collar straight and said a quick prayer that a priest on the doorstep might just gain him a few precious minutes to gain answers to his questions.

He parked neatly at the kerb and looked at the old house dreaming in the spring sunshine. These people had money; he could tell by the size and general care of the house. Maybe Kate had fallen in with good people. He got out and went to the door with his heart pounding as if he'd just run the marathon.

The white-haired man who opened the door to him didn't look too friendly. 'Yes?'

Ben smiled. 'I'm not sure if you are who I'm looking for. I'm trying to make contact with a Professor David Walker.'

'He doesn't live here.' Paul, reflecting that this was the exact truth, nevertheless felt a twinge of guilt. This young priest didn't look vengeful; Paul could see the joy draining out of his face.

'No. I know.' Ben frowned. 'I understood he was your son.'

Paul shifted slightly. 'Can I ask what business you have with my son, if he is indeed the person you are looking for?'

'I think his wife might be my sister.'

Paul raised an eyebrow. 'Don't you know?'

Ben frowned some more. 'No. But I'm desperately hoping

she is.'

Ruth Walker appeared behind her husband and looked over the strange man on the doorstep in a hostile manner. What she read in his face and what David had told them about Kate's brother being a priest had her nudging her husband aside. 'Why do you want to speak to my son's wife?'

It was a blunt question. It got a blunt answer. 'Because, God help us, we've lost her and I love her.'

'Oh.' Ruth stood back. 'Paul, go and put the kettle on. You'd better come in, young man. What's your name?'

Ben smiled. Ruth recognised the smile. It wasn't that he resembled Kate, it was more an expression, a way of turning his head, and Kate smiled that way too sometimes. 'Father Beineon Aiden O'Connor. Most call me Ben.'

'Step into the front room, Ben, and we'll have a little talk.' She nodded at Paul as he came back through and watched as his wife led the young priest into their comfortable sitting room. 'Did you put…?'

'Yes. But…'

'Let me ask some questions first, Paul.' She offered a lopsided smile. 'It's a mother thing.'

JUNE 2011

CUMBRIA

Stan Hunt was wishing he had a parent or two to help him out. The two uniforms who had taken him into custody had had a spurious air of believing him, which didn't mask the underlying atmosphere of disbelief in his every utterance. He hadn't been arrested. He was, in those famous words, 'helping the police with their enquiries'.

He had slipped the small cube of cannabis resin from his back pocket into the back seat of the squad car. He felt safe from that charge; he had no drugs on him. He slouched on the chair in the interview room, waiting for someone to come and speak to him. He wouldn't have been so laid-back if he could have seen through the wall where his two erstwhile chauffeurs where showing Detective Sergeant Tierney the small black lump they had removed from the back seat.

'The car was cleaned from the last prisoner. He's the only one who could have hidden it there, so we have reasonable cause to book him, sir.'

Tierney nodded. 'You might be able to stretch a point; there's a restraining order on him, too.' He gave a mirthless grin. 'And you say he was sitting there casing the joint for a good hour before he made his move?'

'The car that did the pass earlier today noted the number from this morning and reported it in. We were just having our break and thought we'd keep an eye on the house while we did. He sat there well over an hour. He didn't make a move until Mrs Watt left this afternoon. Then he approached. Tell the truth, Sarge, we thought he was planning a B and E. The letter was a hell of a bonus.'

Tierney nodded again, comparing the envelope with the previous ones. 'No address, but Grey's name is printed the same. We'll check for fingerprints and hopefully DNA from the envelope. That stuff takes time, though. Is there enough for dealing?' He poked a finger at the cannabis resin, pursing up his lips.

'Nah. Personal use, and he hasn't got form. Just the order. But...' The senior man, John, held up a long digit. 'One, we haven't searched him yet ... and two, he was loitering with intent. Might even get "going equipped" if we're lucky.'

'OK. You process that bit and I'll see what I can do this end.' The three men left the room with satisfaction writ large on their pleasant faces, as if they'd just discovered a minor win on the lotto.

JUNE 2011

WISBECH

BEN WAS SITTING NURSING tea in a thin china mug. He was telling his story to a woman the same age as his grandmother would have been, and feeling that he might be gaining a bit of sympathy. He wasn't getting the same reaction from the man. Armed neutrality was the best he seemed to warrant from that quarter.

He'd kept to the bare facts; he didn't feel it was right to tell Kate's story to others first and he wasn't that sure how close Kate was to these people, so he was walking a narrow line between hoping for help and keeping secrets.

'My mother died when we were little – nearly four – and Kate was devastated. My grandparents asked her father to care for her, not knowing the calibre of the man, and we lost our Kate. They didn't have the contacts to find out what had become of her and I was too small to remember her. We were isolated out on the farm, we didn't see other family members except for special occasions and *Maimeo* had sworn them to secrecy to try and protect me.' He took a sip of tea, 'I feel guilty, having forgotten Kate. I want her to be happy and I want to find her to tell her we love her.'

'And that is all you want to do?'

'Yes, of course. What else?' Ben looked totally puzzled as he looked at the expressive face in front of him.

'Why didn't you go with your father, too?' Paul Walker looked at the priest and raised an eyebrow. He hadn't, so far, touched his tea; he was not prepared to give an inch,

298

apparently.

'My father didn't know of my existence; *Maimeo* didn't tell him. I was no bother, apparently.' Ben folded his lips on the other words that would have spilled out.

The two older people exchanged a look. 'And Kate was a bother?'

'I don't know the ins and outs – I was a toddler myself – but Kate was very upset by her mother's death. She was grieving and they thought it best to send her away.' He shrugged.

'And how do your family feel now? Do they still think she will be a bother?' Paul almost spat the question.

'No. Oh God, no.' Ben shook his head. 'They want her back, to love.'

'I'm not sure we understand the kind of love that sends a toddler away from her home because she's a bother.' Ruth shook her grey locks and looked at the young man. 'I'm not sure about any of this. I'm certainly not comfortable about providing you with Kate's whereabouts.'

'Is she happy?'

The other two exchanged a look. 'Yes.' But it was a guarded yes, and Ben picked up the nuances of the word. He looked from man to wife.

'Does he – your son – does he love her?'

The 'Yes' this time was positive and final from both parents.

Ben set down his mug. 'I don't know what to do.' It was spoken softly, almost under his breath, as he looked at the elderly and determined faces.

Ruth exchanged another look with Paul. 'You can write a letter and we will see that it is delivered. If you give an address or phone number Kate can contact you if she wants to.' She hesitated, but this man deserved the truth if nothing else; he was apparently as much a victim as Kate. She sat thinking for a minute, looking at the closed face in front of her.

'You also have another brother.' She watched the blood drain and his skin turn waxy. 'His name is Antony Grey; Kate met him for the first time yesterday. She didn't know of his existence, either. If you wish we will see that he also receives this information.'

Ben sat staring at them for so long that Ruth started to speak again. 'Do you und…'

He nodded. 'Do you know how he fits in? Older? Younger?'

'I'm sorry, we don't have any more information than that.'

Ruth stood up. 'I'll fetch you some paper. Have another drink.'

She left the two men sitting facing each other.

'I love my son and my daughter-in-law. I won't have either of them hurt. If Kate doesn't want to know, will you give up this quest to find them? I can assure you that she loves David and they are happy together.'

Ben looked at the old man. 'I can't promise. My *daideó* is ill; he wants to make his peace with Kate.' He paused. 'And so do I but I need to find my twin sister too, for my own sake.'

'Well, that's honest, at least. Who is your *daideó*?'

Ben gave a quick smile. 'Grandfather. We speak the Gaelic in Galway.'

'Kate doesn't. Did she?'

A horrified expression crawled slowly across Ben's face. 'Oh, God! What did we do to you, *a ghra*?'

Paul raised an eyebrow but said no more. Ruth came back into the room with paper, envelopes and pen, and offered them to Ben before exchanging a look with Paul. 'Paul?'

'Nothing; I said nothing to him that he didn't know already.'

'Ben. Write your notes. We'll see that Kate and Antony receive them, we promise, but that's all we can promise. She has a life, and she has the right to keep herself private.'

'Yes, yes, you're right. I'm not sure we have any rights any more.'

Ben looked up and took the papers hovering in front of his face in the old hands. Ruth jerked her head at her husband and they left quietly as Ben bent his head, clicked the biro, and smoothed out the paper.

JUNE 2011

CUMBRIA

DAVID WAS WRITING IN his study that evening when the phone rang. He swept it up quickly at the first ring: 'Mum.' The pleasure swept through him and was gone; he was too worried about his wife. Kate had gone to bed at the twins' bedtime, saying she was tired. He had tried to bury his worries and fears in work but it hadn't really been working.

He held the receiver and used the other hand to save his work on the computer. Only giving his mother half his attention, it registered as she moved on to the next sentence. 'He's what? Say that again. Please.'

He nodded as his mother told him about their visitor of that afternoon. 'So I think it would be better if we came up there and spoke to both you and Kate, gave her the letter and let her decide.'

David frowned at the screen. 'I just don't know, Mum. What does Pops think?'

There was a hum on the line and his father spoke into his ear. 'I think he's sincere, but I don't know how Kate will feel, David. I thought – with your agreement – we might come and stay. Say you've said she's not well and we want to help with the babies. What do you think?'

David continued to frown at the screen until his father said rather impatiently, 'David?'

'I think it's a good plan.' David gave himself a quick shake. 'Yeah, a good plan. When?'

'Quicker the better. He wouldn't promise to call off the

search, but he did say he'd give us time to give Kate his letter.'

'Right. Tomorrow?'

'Tomorrow. See you then.' His father set the phone down and looked at his wife and nodded.

David was shutting down his computer. He would go and see his wife. He'd have to tell her that her in-laws were paying a surprise visit and his Kate had never been stupid. She would figure out something was in the wind. He was wondering what story to tell to put her off the scent until he'd spoken more fully to his parents.

Kate was sitting up in bed. She had her favourite new nightie on. Copper-coloured silk. David had seen it and thought his wife would look beautiful in it.

'I was right. That looks amazing on you.' He grinned at her as she looked up from her book and peered over her glasses at him.

'Have you f...finished?'

'I've done all I want to do. I want to be with my wife.' David crossed the room and offered a cup of hot chocolate.

'David, wh...at have you done now?'

'Nothing. Can't a man want to come to bed with his wife?'

Kate cocked her head on one side and looked at him as he radiated innocence. 'Not wh...en you look like th...at.'

David's lips twitched. 'OK, I admit I have an ulterior motive. Mum has just phoned; she says "would you like company while I'm away?"' He held up a hand. 'Not for the duration, just for a couple of weeks.' He leaned over, kissing her cheek simply because he couldn't resist. 'I said "Yes", because I'm worried about you.' His lip lifted in a half smile. 'I've confessed. Can I have absolution?'

Kate smiled. It was a genuine smile that went all the way to her eyes, and his heart jumped at the sight. 'Yes, f...forgiven, because I w...would have done the s...same if it was you.' She took the hot chocolate and set it on the side table. 'I love you.'

David looked at her curiously. Something had happened to his wife. He couldn't put his finger on it but he sensed a difference.

Kate looked at the hot chocolate and then at her husband as he perched on the side of the bed. She looked up at him, pushing the glasses back up the bridge of her nose. 'You d... do it all the t...time.' It was said almost accusingly.

'Eh?' David shook his head. In truth he'd been far away, thinking about the advent of his parents on the morrow and how he wouldn't have Kate to himself in the same way; he was wishing he hadn't agreed to their coming, now. That was plain selfish, he acknowledged – if only to himself – not putting her needs first.

'You h...hold me up and p...put up with me and I'm s... sorry, David.' She stretched out a finger and laid it against his lips, 'I know you don't w...want me to say that – but I haven't been h...honest, either.'

David gently laid her book aside and took both her hands in his. Looking down at her face, noting the freckles that had emerged with the sunshine of the past week and the curls clustered about her ears. 'I don't understand, love.'

'I've been th...inking, David, about w...what you said w...while we were away, and yesterday.'

'I said lots of things, love. Some of them better unsaid.'

'No, David. You're r...right, I "got it" last w...week; I just didn't w...want to. I am hi...ding from you and that's as much lying as anything my f...father and stepmother did. But I'm s...scared. I s...seem to have been s...scared all my life.' Kate offered a half smile. It didn't go up to her brown eyes this time; they continued to regard her husband seriously.

'You told me I didn't s...say the words. But if you d... don't, then people don't know, and they c...can't use it against you.'

'But, darling...'

'Hush, or I m...might lose my c...courage and I haven't got m...much.' Kate took a breath and spoke slowly, trying to prevent the dreaded stutter from overcoming her speech. 'I love you, David, madly and pass...ionately, too. I want you so m...much...' She took another breath. '...So much, emotionally, but ph...ysically as well. I need you, David, so m...much it hurts. If you w...want me, I'm yours.' Kate reached a hand to David's beard and stroked gently down it before stilling his lips against her finger again, and looking at the brilliant emerald eyes loving her. 'I know the person inside th...ough, and she's a c...coward and not very nice; she's demanding and jealous, t...too.' She felt his hands tighten around hers. 'If you w...want me then you have to take the w...whole deal and you might not w...want that because I've done something bad, David; I know I have.'

David bent his head and began to kiss her. It seemed that sometimes things happened when you least expected them. He loved her and finally it seemed she was allowing him behind the walls. Not just an open door, like last summer, but a complete demolition job of the whole building.

'Oh, God.' He moved, holding her tight, just breathing in the scent of her hair. 'I love you so much. I thought – before I met you – I thought love was meeting a physical need and finding comfortable companionship, Kate. But then I saw you, covered in mud and wielding a trowel, and I discovered how wrong I was. It's a savage possessive desire, love: half pain, half rapture. You don't know what you want, but it consumes you.' He gave a half grin, pulling back slightly. 'The Germans have a word, *sehnsucht*. It doesn't translate well, but ... half craving, half yearning for the unknowable. Only you can do that to me, darling.'

Kate had always known David loved her but now he let her see just how much he'd kept hidden, because of his fear of scaring her off. 'I love you, David.' Kate offered her lips again. 'I wish your p...parents weren't coming.' She offered a half chuckle, half sob.

David grinned. 'Yeah, me, too. Only I didn't like to say. You've me wound up and now I'm one big ache for you, only you, darling.'

'Oh, how nice!' Kate grinned.

David grinned too, and bent his head; finally he'd got her, and this time he was making sure she didn't build any more walls. Tomorrow would be soon enough to deal with all the other baggage. The kiss lasted a long time and left them both wanting much, much more.

DAVID'S PARENTS WERE DUE to arrive about three that afternoon. David had waited until after lunch and the children had been settled for their nap before he'd broached the subject – the reason for the sudden descent of Kate's in-laws. He hadn't wanted to dim the glow on his wife's face. But now he must; he had less than half an hour before they arrived.

He drew her into the study – always his favourite place in the house – and settled her onto his knee, sitting in one of the soft squashy chairs placed to look out over the Solway Firth and the roadway.

'I love you, Kate.' He laid a finger on her lips as she had done the night before. 'I have a confession to make and my store of courage is limited, too.' He smiled as she kissed the finger.

'Mum and Pops had a visit yesterday. From your brother Ben.' He felt her stiffen and took the hand away to hold her tight for a moment. 'They didn't tell him where to find you, Kate. But after Mum had asked a few questions, they suggested that he write to you and that they would give you the letter. Then the decision would be up to you.'

'Wh...at did he w...ant?'

'I don't know all of it; I wasn't there, Kate. Mum said he seemed desperate to contact you.' David paused to drop a kiss on the pale cheek. 'And that he said he loved you.'

Kate said nothing, her eyes going blank.

'No hiding, Kate.' David gave her a gentle shake.

'No.' She offered a very faint smile, like a pencil line of the real thing.

'If you don't want to discuss it, or even see the letter, I'll deal with it.'

'Do I seem th...at big a c...coward, David?'

'You're incredibly brave, my darling, but I see no reason

to suffer needlessly.'

'But he is too, my b...brother. My f...father seems to have caused s...suffering everywhere he went. You were r...right; I'm not res...ponsible for him, only my own f...faults.'

'That's my sensible girl. We'll read this letter together and see what he wants, and then move on from there. OK?'

'Yes, David.' She leaned back against him and he held her close, watching the incoming tide through the window and waiting for his parents to arrive and possibly swamp them with unwanted information.

Ten minutes later the wait was over. Kate slid off his knee and straightened her skirt as the old BMW drew up at the door and David's parents got out.

'OK, Kate?'

She offered him a smile. 'OK.' David leaned over and dropped a kiss on her lips and then took a hand to walk her out of the room and go and greet his parents.

Ruth walked through the gate and took Kate in her arms. 'I hope we've done right, Kate.'

Kate nodded. 'C...come in and Thea w...will make a pot of tea.'

Paul looked at David. David read the signs on his father's face and as the women went into the house said, 'What's up?'

'I love your Kate, David. What they did to her – it was disgusting.'

David watched the anger throttled back; his father was normally a phlegmatic man. 'I think you'd better talk to me before we speak to Kate.'

'No, he hadn't, David.' David turned at his wife's voice behind him. 'L...let's have it a...all out in the open, love.' She smiled at her husband. 'Remember, n...n...no hiding.'

David put an arm around her waist, nodded and walked her back into the house and study.

JUNE 2011

LIVERPOOL

BEN, FOR WANT OF another destination, had headed back to his aunt Lara in Liverpool. He'd rung and asked for a bed for a night or two.

Lara thought he'd sounded desperate on the phone and – looking at the young man on her doorstep – she thought he looked desperate, too. 'In you come, Ben.' She watched him walk slowly through to her kitchen and, as she shut the kitchen door, sink heavily onto a hard chair. 'What is it, lad. Can I help?' She stood looking at him. Then the fear leaping into her eyes said, 'Is she dead?'

'No. No, she's not dead, Aunt. But I don't know if we have the right to find her any more. Or if she'll want us to.' Lara walked over and put an arm around his shoulders.

'Tell me about it, Ben. Maybe talking will help to clear your mind.'

Ben leaned against her sturdy body for a moment before straightening and sighing. 'Yes. Will you make me a drink while I talk? I've not slept and I'm so tired, Aunt.'

Lara nodded, setting the kettle to boil and getting mugs from the cupboard. 'Will you take a bite?'

'No, I can't.' He tried to smile but it was a poor effort.

'All right, Ben. Wait now while I make the tea, and then you can start.' She busied herself getting the mugs ready and set his in front of him, giving his shoulder a gentle squeeze before sitting down herself.

He looked across the table. 'I hate secrets; they cause so

307

many ills, hurt so many people. I've had to keep revising my ideas these last few weeks.' Without elaborating further he picked the mug up and sat nursing it between his hands. Looking at the brew he started to speak. 'I found Kate's in-laws. They wouldn't tell me where she lived.'

'Well, can you blame them, Ben? They can't see your heart, lad. They will want to protect her, and to keep her whereabouts secret is understandable.'

'Thank God someone wants to protect her, for we haven't done much of a job of it.' Ben took a sip of tea. 'You speak the Gaelic, *Aintin*.'

'Badly, and not for many years.' She gave a half laugh as she looked across at him.

'Kate and I, we spoke nothing else. I learnt the English when I went to school.'

'Oh. Oh, I see.' Lara nodded slowly. 'She was young; she would pick up the English quickly, hearing nothing else.'

'Aye, but can you imagine how she coped until then. Taken from her family and not a soul understanding her.'

'It wasn't your fault, Ben.'

'No, but I grieve for her, Aunt, like it was me who suffered.'

Lara sipped her own tea, wondering how to comfort him.

'What else have you learned, Ben?'

Ben sipped again, 'My father was a bastard and so am I.' His lip curled a bit at the shock on his aunt's face. 'I mean that literally; he was brought up in a state-run home. He was already married when he married my mother.' He set the mug down with a slight thump. 'And somewhere along the line he sired another brother for me.'

'You mother wouldn't have slept with him without he married her, Ben. But we none of us guessed he already had a wife.'

'Apparently, she wasn't alone in that.' Ben settled to relating what he'd discovered about his sister up until the day before.

'So you wrote. Can you tell me what you said?'

'Aye, I said I loved her.'

Lara raised an eyebrow.

'What else could I say that had any meaning?' Ben sighed and picked up the mug of cooled tea, finishing it off before showing his aunt a miserable face.

JUNE 2011

CUMBRIA

'WHAT DOES IT SAY, Kate?' David was having a hard job keeping his hands still; he longed to snatch the letter from her hands. He looked at her face; she was a little pale but otherwise didn't look distressed.

Kate held it out.

David looked at her again and then down at the words on the page, reading them aloud, 'I love you. Your brother, Ben.'

He looked across the room at his parents, who were watching Kate as anxiously as he had been.

Kate looked at his father and smiled softly at him, her head on one side. 'Tell m...me about him, Pops.'

Paul sat forward in the chair. 'He has the same colour eyes, but he's blond and his face is a different shape. He's got the same...'

'Same smile,' Ruth interrupted and then smiled apologetically at her husband.

'Yeah, same smile.' Paul offered one of his own to his wife before continuing. 'He's a priest. He has a strong Irish brogue; he speaks Gaelic at home.' He heard his wife make a small noise but ignored it. 'You did, too – until they sent you away, Kate.'

'When? Why?'

David noted the lack of stutter and frowned in thought.

They sent you to your father after your mother died. You were three ... nearly four.'

'Wh...y not Ben, too?'

'Because – and I quote the young man – "he was no bother".' David watched his father grind his false teeth and reflected on the fact that they would all need new molars if this situation carried on much longer. Paul sniffed, 'And apparently your father didn't know of his existence.'

Kate nodded. 'Wh...at else did he s...say?'

'He said you had been distressed by your mother's death and they felt it better to send you to him. I'm sorry, Kate, but he didn't trust us.' Ruth looked at her husband and he reached out a hand for hers. 'But it was mutual. He gave us a mobile phone number for you to contact him if that was what you wanted. We agreed to pass on a letter to your other brother, too.'

Kate nodded again as David came over and sat on the arm of her chair. 'What do you want to do, Kate? Sleep on it?'

'I th...ink you should ring, Antony and te...ll him about the le...tter.'

'And you, darling?'

'I'm g...going to g...get Mum and Pops a dr...ink and th...ink a bit, David.'

'You won't...'

'No I won't sh...ut you out, darling.' She exchanged a look with him before looking at Ruth. 'Tea?'

'I thought you'd never ask, Kate.' She stood up and came over, putting a friendly arm around Kate's waist and leading her from the room.

'Why are you so angry, Pops?' David looked at his father curiously.

'She was a "bother", so they got rid of her. Like a pup that couldn't be trained. She's a beautiful woman, your Kate. And now they want her back. Well, I don't think they deserve her. But that young man, he's damaged as well. Hell, David, how could they split them up at that age? You should have seen his face when he realised she had been sent to the equivalent of strangers in a foreign country. Serve him right.' There was a degree of vengeful satisfaction in his father's voice.

David raised an eyebrow.

'He was blown away by this brother, too.'

'Antony's a pleasant young man.'

His father grinned at the neutral tones. 'Jealous, David?'

'You bet ya.' It was vulgar but it made his father smile some more.

'When we first met anyway.' David went on to talk about his new brother-in-law and watched his father cool down slightly from white-hot anger to gentle simmer.

JUNE 2011

WHITBY

ANTONY MUST HAVE FELT his ears burn; he was certainly experiencing warmth, anyway. His putative in-laws were listening to the joint story related by Antony, with interruptions by Amy and Joy, of their visit to David Walker the day before.

'But how incredible, Antony, to find you were working for the man.' Joyce Watt grinned as she nursed her granddaughter on her knee.

'Aye, life's like that; think on.' Jack Watt also had a grin on his face. 'So what happens now?'

Antony sniffed, running a finger under his nose and raising his eyebrows. 'We await events. The Prof is going to do a bit more digging for this other brother, when he gets back from Germany. I need to go over again sometime this week to sort out the research I didn't get done yesterday.' His lips twitched. 'For some reason I couldn't seem to keep my mind on ancient texts.'

'No, I don't suppose you could, lad.'

Silence fell for a minute while everyone thought about the story Antony had related. He shifted in his chair and then looked at Amy's parents, 'So I might now know who my parents are. I'm legitimate. But my situation is not greatly improved for all that ... son of a murderer isn't exactly better.' He waited, watching for the expected rejection.

'What's that to us? Our Amy isn't marrying your father, she's marrying you, and we like and trust you, Antony.' Jack shrugged. 'And before you start, Joyce, I don't want to hear how wonderful Joy will look as a flower girl. You sort it out and I'll foot the bill.' He exchanged a rueful smile with Antony. 'Quicker the better, lad, then they can't make too much of a meal of it and drive us crackers.'

His daughter's, 'Dad!' was almost drowned by his wife's exasperated, 'Jack!'

The laugh that broke the tension was itself broken by the raucous tones of the landline in the hall. 'I'll get it.' Amy moved and went out of the room.

'I suppose you want the banger again to go over to Cumberland.' Jack leaned back in his chair.

Antony nodded, 'It would be nice, but I can get a train.'

'Nah; call it a wedding present. I'll sort out the paperwork.'

While Antony still had his mouth open to protest, Amy came back into the room. 'It's the professor for you, Antony.'

Antony rose swiftly, looking puzzled. 'Did he say...'

'No.' Amy grinned at him and bent to take her daughter. 'I'll put her to bed, Mum. She's had a long day.'

She passed Antony, carrying the infant as he sat on the bottom step of the stairs and nodded at the phone. She caught a 'Yes, OK,' a 'Mmm!' and a, 'No, of course not,' before she went into her own room. He was still sitting at the bottom of the stairs when she came back down. The phone was back on its cradle.

'OK, love.'

'Yeah. My brother has made contact with David.'

'Oh. Wow. That's great. When will you get to see him?'

'I'm not sure; David will give me a ring in the morning after he and Kate have talked.'

'You don't seem very happy about it.'

'Truth to tell, Amy, I don't know what I feel. It's all coming at me a bit fast, love. I don't know how I'd cope if you weren't around to...'

'Thank you, Antony.' Amy stood on tiptoe and kissed him.

They were still locked in an embrace that threatened to get very personal when the phone rang again. They sprang apart as Jack walked into the hall. 'Hire a room, lad; it's more comfortable.' He edged passed them and picked up the phone, grinning at their red faces. 'Yes. Oh hello, Sergeant Tierney. For you, Antony.' He handed over the phone and went away whistling to himself.

Antony took the receiver; he accepted Amy's hand as she gripped his hand and looked anxious. 'Sergeant?'

'Ah, Mr Grey. Mr Stanley Hunt?'

'Yeah...' Antony looked mystified as he answered. 'We were at the children's home together. I saw him the other day, as a matter of fact.'

'We believe he is behind these letters of yours.'

'Stan? Why, in God's name?'

'Faced with a charge of "threatening to kill", he tells me it's because you were spoilt at that home and he thought you needed bringing down a peg.'

'Eh? But ... but that was years ago and I wouldn't say any of us were exactly spoilt.'

'Well that's his reason, sir. He was also behind the accusations of child molestation. His girlfriend reported you after he dropped several heavy hints. She wouldn't admit where she'd got the information. But she's worried about a charge of spreading malicious gossip and has dropped him in it now.'

'So what happens now, Detective Sergeant?'

'That's up to you. Do you want to lay charges against these people?'

Antony shook his head. 'Good God, no.'

'That's up to you, of course, sir. We will be speaking to him. He's already going to get an earful for possession, and breaking the restraining order with regard to Miss Watt, so he's a shaken man at the moment.'

'Do you want me to come to the station?'

'Not this evening. He's being detained. I'll get back to you, sir.'

'Thanks.' Antony shook his head as if to knock water out of his ear. 'And, Sergeant, thank you for all your help.'

'Not at all, sir; goodnight.'

JUNE 2011

CUMBRIA

IT WAS TWO IN the morning. Kate was sitting bolt upright in the bed, shivering all over. David had woken to find her thrashing about in the bed in the middle of a nightmare. He'd woken her up and held tight until she'd stopped shaking quite so violently. 'OK, darling? Do you want a drink of water?' He got out and came around to her side.

'No.' Kate leaned against him as he sat on the side of the bed.

'Can you tell me about it?'

'S…same old, s…same old.' She offered a sad smile. 'I sh…all never have p…peace until I sp…eak to him, David.'

'Probably not.' David tried to be pragmatic while his insides churned.

'Ph…one t…tomorrow for me. Set it up, pl…ease; but David, don't le…ave me.

'Couldn't if I wanted to, darling. I'm not even half a man without you in my life.'

'I m…meant when he comes.'

'That, too.' David offered a lopsided smile. 'I'm going to make a mug of hot milk for you and put a dash of whiskey in it. I know you aren't supposed to drink, love, but we both need to settle our nerves.'

'Even you?'

'Especially me. You scared seven shades of hell out of me, love.'

Kate climbed out of the bed. 'I'll co…me with you; I w…

ant the loo.'

'Prosaic but reassuring, my love.' David took her hand and they went down into the warm kitchen and set the milk to warm in the microwave.

JUNE 2011

LIVERPOOL

HER BROTHER WAS ALSO sitting in a kitchen. He hadn't been to bed. He had been having a one-sided conversation with God. He'd gone from arguing, to offering bribes, to pleading with the Almighty. Now he was just sitting. His aunt, coming down at six, looked at him with astonishment.

'Ben.'

He stirred in the hard chair. 'I've got damn all to offer, have I?'

His aunt looked at him curiously, walking over and filling the kettle while she absorbed his cryptic utterance. 'None of us have when it gets to the wire, lad. He's God and we're ... well,' she came over and laid a gentle hand on his shoulder, 'we're just his creation. Maeve ... she tried to bargain with God, too. It's a hard lesson to learn.'

Ben nodded. 'What'll I do?'

'Wait. It's all you can do. Keep busy; pray.' She went over and put tea bags in the pot.

They both jumped when his phone rang – exchanged a look – and then he pulled it out of his pocket with a shaking hand and glanced at the screen: 'Unknown caller'. He pressed for 'Receive' and spoke hesitantly into the mouthpiece. 'Hello.'

'Yes. Yes. Yes, I can be there in two hours. Thank you; you don't know how ... what this ... you ... all right.' He set the small machine down and looked at his aunt as she stood holding the teapot, her whole body one big question.

'That was Professor David Walker. Kate would like to

318

speak to me.' He gave a hiccup of laughter. 'But could I wait until after breakfast, please?'

'Right. Let's feed you and you can be on your way.'

'I can't.'

'You haven't eaten since you came into my house, Ben O'Connor. You will eat like a sensible child before you set foot in your car.' Lara nodded at him and lifted the frying pan out of the cupboard. 'Eggs and bacon.' She waved a finger at him. 'And a slice of toast. No arguments.' She glanced at the photo on the wall of her sister Maeve and she smiled softly before turning to the homely task of feeding her great-nephew.

JUNE 2011

CUMBRIA

ANTONY HAD ALSO RECEIVED a phone call from David at an unexpectedly early hour. David set the phone down again and looked at his wife. 'Done.'

Kate nodded. 'Mum s…says they'll take the ch…ildren out f…for us, David.'

'Good. I love my children but we need to concentrate on you today, darling.' He came across the room and took her hand. 'We shall go into the study after breakfast and sit and cuddle until people arrive.'

He had debated the merits of setting up the meeting on neutral ground, but Kate couldn't take much more stress and he thought it better to meet on home turf. He could always show this Ben the door if he upset her. He smiled and they went into the chaos of the kitchen to feed the twins.

At ten the coffee was brewing nicely, Kate was nursing a mug of fruit tea and Thea had disappeared into the kitchen to make bread with a vigour belying her age and expressing her anxiety.

David and Antony were talking quietly about the research, shifting papers about on the desk – not that either was managing to concentrate very well but watching Kate play with the mug wasn't very productive, either. David had filled Antony in on the meagre information he'd received from his parents the previous day. Now all they could do was wait. 'I shall come over when I get back from Germany, Antony. We can sort out the final details then.' He began to stack papers in neat piles.

The car, when it pulled up, caused all of them to sit straighter in their chairs. Kate refused to look out of the window. She looked at David a trifle desperately. 'Courage, Kate.' David went to answer the door.

He came back into the room with a very strange expression on his face and went straight across to Kate. He was followed by Ben. Kate's first impression was of nerves. It preceded Ben into the room, and she relaxed at this evidence of someone as terrified as she was.

They stared across the room at each other. Ben wanted desperately to grab hold and never let go, but simply didn't dare.

'Ben?'

'*A ghra. Dia Duit!* I thought I'd never find you.'

It seemed to the others watching that both leapt and were in each other's arms. Ben held tight, the tears streaming down his face. '*Ciamar a tha thu, Piuthar, a run.*'

David raised an eyebrow, opened his mouth and then stared at his wife.

'*Thu gu math, Brathair.*'

David looked at Antony and a half smile crossed each face, before he gave a slight cough. 'When you've done hugging my wife I'd like you to meet your half-brother, Antony Grey.'

Ben looked across the room. 'My apologies, *Brathair*, but...' He smiled over the top of Kate's head at David. 'It seems I have waited so long, and thought I should never find her.'

'Kate?'

'Yes, David.' Kate swung around in Ben's arms so that he held her shoulder and smiled down at her. She smiled through tears at her husband.

'Since when did you speak Gaelic, darling?' He grinned at her.

'I d...don't.'

'You just did, love, and without a hesitation.'

Her lips made a soundless 'Oh'. Ben let go and moved

across the room to shake hands with Antony. Antony shook, then pulled him into an embrace. 'Just this once I'd like a hug from you. It's sort of special.'

Ben nodded and hugged back, then gravitated back towards Kate, who was still standing looking surprised.

'I think we'd better sit down.' David rescued his wife and went to sit in the window embrasure, pushing her gently into a seat and sitting on the arm of her chair. He grinned at Antony. 'We'll tell you our side if you'll tell us yours. You first. Preferably in English.' He raised an eyebrow and smiled at Ben.

Ben sat opposite, just looking at Kate, until David gave another slight cough. He looked at the older man, watching as David gently kneaded the shoulder next to him. He could see how much this man loved his sister and while part of him rejoiced for her, another sighed. He might have found her, but she wasn't his any more.

He gave a sigh and smiled. 'Where to start? I had forgotten you, Kate. Or, rather, I didn't want to remember. It hurt too much.' Kate leaned over slightly and offered two hands, which Ben gripped hard as he started to talk.

'When *Maimeo* died and *Daideó* spoke of you, I was angry. With them – with God – with myself, for forgetting. And I wanted you, my Kate; I needed to know you were well and loved. And I see you are both.'

She looked up at David – offered a half smile – then said, 'Wh...y do I dream of bl...ood? Did I h...harm you, Ben? Is that wh...y they sent me away?'

Ben held the hands tightly. 'They sent you away because you found *Mammí*.' He glanced at David before looking back at Kate. 'Our *Mammí* had post-natal depression, Kate. She couldn't take the misery any more and...'

'She cut herself and I found her.'

But only Ben understood her, for Kate spoke in Gaelic and then leaned back against her husband. David felt the fine shiver and pulled her close. Ben nodded. 'Yes, *a ghra*.'

David focused his attention on Kate, ignoring everyone

else as she moved into his hold and started to cry soft, healing tears.

Ben looked at Antony. They stood and left the room, walking quietly outside and across the road, standing looking out over the Solway as the water crept ever closer to the shoreline. 'Tell me about yourself, brother.'

DAVID WAITED OUT THE tears until Kate calmed again. 'I find myself strangely jealous of a priest, my Kate. Not only do you embrace him but you speak a different language with him.' Kate offered a gentle smile as he mopped at her face with his handkerchief. 'Can you tell me?'

'I f...found her. It came back to me when Ben s...spoke, called her *Mammí*. I could see her p...poor face and her hands all bl...oody ... she had c...cut her wrists ... I f...found her in the ba...bathroom, David. I thought it was my f...fault that she was hurt. I c...called her and she didn't answer and then when I was s...sent away I was s...sure.'

David nodded; they would look at it some more when she could take it. He wasn't going to leave any splinters of fear to fester in his wife's soul – maybe go over to Ireland with her – but for now... He looked out of the window and saw that his parents were back and offloading the twins. 'I think I'd better speak to Thea and organise lunch, Kate, while you talk to your brothers.' His lips twitched. 'My parents will be delighted to look after Topsy and Turvey for a while longer.'

BEN HAD GONE. DAVID had offered him a bed for the night but he said 'no'. He'd prefer to come again tomorrow, with David's permission. David had looked at him. 'Could I keep you away?' Ben had laughed. Antony was back in Whitby. He and Ben had arranged to meet up over there so that Amy and Joy could meet him as well.

Kate had gone early to bed and David was sitting on the side of it holding her hand. 'I love you, my Kate.' He grinned.

'I've seen your brother's face before. I was sure I'd met him somewhere; I've finally placed him. It was about three weeks ago, in Liverpool Cathedral.'

'Did we?' Kate grinned. 'How strange.'

'This whole thing has been a bit bizarre, Kate.'

'I love you, David, I w...wouldn't have m...met you if I'd lived in Ireland.'

'Oh, yes you would, my Kate; you were always mine. We just had to meet; you are my other half, darling. Despite Ben and Antony.' He leaned forward and gave her a kiss. 'I love you.'

THELMA HANCOCK

Born in Carlisle in the footprints of the Romans, Thelma became fascinated by history at an early age. The past as well as the present has always enthralled her, particularly the inter-weaving of both together. The mixed motives that result in actions for good and harm mean she is always questioning, why? Why mankind does what it does?

Marrying a sailor meant a nomadic lifestyle; something she still embraces. Her occupation has ranged from teaching in Derbyshire, to a steam-engine fireman in Wales, to nursing gunshot wounds in New Zealand; South-West Scotland is her present home.

ALSO BY THE SAME AUTHOR

Relative Dating. (2008)
ISBN 978 184386 456 1

Tree Dimensional. (2009
ISBN 978 184386 512 4

Grave Doubts. (2009)
ISBN 978 184386 557 5

Diverse Distress. (2009)
ISBN 978 184386 558 2

Smokescreen. (2010)
ISBN 978 184386 649 7

Collide and Conquer. (2011)
ISBN 978 190349 048 8

In the Loop. (2011)
ISBN 978 184386 702 9

Timeline. (2011)
ISBN 978 184386 912 2

Enter Two Gravediggers. (2011)
ISBN 978 190349 066 2

Disreputable Truth. (2012)
ISBN 978 184386 829 3